4 Love Stories Are Quilted into Broken Lives

Mary Davis
Grace Hitchcock
Suzanne Norquist
Liz Tolsma

BARBOUR BOOKS
An Imprint of Barbour Publishing, Inc.

Print ISBN 978-1-64352-051-3

eBook Editions:
Adobe Digital Edition (.epub) 978-1-64352-053-7
Kindle and MobiPocket Edition (.prc) 978-1-64352-052-0

All scripture quotations are taken from the King James Version of the Bible.

This book is a work of fiction. Names, characters, places, and incidents are either products of the author's imagination or used fictitiously. Any similarity to actual people, organizations, and/or events is purely coincidental.

Cover Photograph: Ilina Simeonova / Trevillion Images

Published by Barbour Books, an imprint of Barbour Publishing, Inc., 1810 Barbour Drive, Uhrichsville, Ohio 44683, www.barbourbooks.com

Our mission is to inspire the world with the life-changing message of the Bible.

Printed in Canada.

Bygones

by Mary Davis

Dedication

Dedicated in loving memory to my dad, Art. I miss you, Dad.

Lord, how oft shall my brother sin against me, and I forgive him? till seven times? Jesus saith unto him, I say not unto thee, Until seven times: but, Until seventy times seven.

MATTHEW 18:21–22

Chapter 1

Texas

December 1884

Matilda Rockford knew life ebbed and flowed on an ever-changing current. But had enough changed in her absence?

She pressed her cheek against the cold glass of the train window. She had delighted in the green landscape of eastern Texas, awaiting her first glimpse of Dallas in four years. Her skin tingled all over. Ma and Pa would be waiting to take her home. She licked her dry lips. The train clacked along, gently rocking her back and forth.

When the train rounded the last bend, the first buildings of town came into view. She sighed.

Home.

Though she didn't live in Dallas, she would see Ma and Pa and welcome the two-hour wagon ride to their nearby town of Green Hollow.

When the station came into view, she gathered her belongings and clasped the waist-length cape around her neck. The train clattered and screeched to a stop, jerking her forward in her seat.

She pinned on her wide-brimmed hat, stood, and smoothed down her wrinkled green traveling suit. Carrying her reticule in one hand and a hatbox in the other, she made her way up the aisle. Her backside ached from days of travel, coming from the East Coast. She stepped off the train and onto the platform, searching for Pa and Ma. She sucked in the cool December air, crisper than she remembered.

Her gaze went from face to face in the crowd. Where were they? They knew her train and arrival time. They wouldn't have forgotten.

"Tilly!"

She froze at the familiar voice, and dread coiled around her spine. She hadn't been called Tilly in the four years since she'd left. Her aging great-aunt abhorred sobriquets, stating they broke etiquette, and never allowed their use. When the person shouted out the nickname from her youth again, she turned slowly.

In brown trousers and a tan canvas duster, Orion Dunbar strode toward her, more handsome than when she'd left. His wavy, coffee-colored hair touched his collar, and his shoulders seemed broader. He nearly took her breath away. Nearly. Too bad he didn't have a good disposition to go along with his looks. She forced herself not to wince and pulled her mouth into a congenial smile. "Good day, Mr. Dunbar."

He furrowed his brow. "Why so formal? It's just Orion."

Her great-aunt had drilled into her that a lady always addressed a man by his title, but Tilly wasn't in Baltimore anymore. She dipped her head. "Orion." When he smiled, something inside her melted. He'd always had a captivating smile. Ever since that first day fourteen years ago when he'd arrived in Green Hollow.

"You're looking as lovely as ever." His Texas drawl poured over her like warm molasses.

She had missed the easy way people spoke here. Unlike the tight, rushed speech back East. Everyone in a hurry to do nothing of importance.

How uncharacteristic of Orion to pay her a compliment. "Thank you."

"Where's your luggage?"

"My pa and ma should be here somewhere." She scanned the people, desperate to find her folks and have an excuse to part from his company.

"They sent me."

She snapped back around to him. Her folks wouldn't do that to her. Orion had tormented her and teased her when they were in school. And ruined her new dress. "Why would they do that?" No, they would *not* do this to her. They knew the pain and torture he'd caused her in their youth.

"Your pa hurt his leg, and neither he nor I felt it fitting for your ma to travel by herself. So I volunteered."

Neither her pa nor *him*? Since when had he become companionable with her folks? "What happened to Pa?"

"Nothing serious. Just a broken leg."

"Nothing serious!" People had lost limbs with less of an injury. "Has the doctor seen him?"

"Of course. He'll mend fine. He's not fit to travel just yet."

Concern laced her voice and gripped her throat. "I want to see him."

"I have a buggy over here. But let's get your baggage first."

She pointed to a trunk being set onto the platform and an oversize green-and-blue tapestry carpetbag. "Let the baggage handler help you with that."

He gave her a lopsided smile. "I can manage it."

That smile. She inwardly sighed.

Manage it? He hoisted it up as though it were her reticule. She grabbed hold of her carpetbag and had considerably more trouble with it than he had with the heavy, bulky trunk. She waddled along behind him with the carpetbag weighing her down on one side. Her hatbox didn't provide much of a counterbalance.

He heaved the trunk onto the back of the buggy. The burden caused the conveyance to dip and the frame to creak. He turned. "You should have let me get that." After relieving her of the carpetbag, he strapped the pair to the back of the buggy then slung her hatbox onto the floor in front of the seat. "Only one trunk?"

"I have several more that should arrive tomorrow."

"Why didn't they come with you?"

"Those trunks weren't ready for the train. I was anxious to be on my way home." Since her parents regularly came to Dallas to pick up orders for the store, she hadn't seen it as an inconvenience, but now she realized it would be.

Orion stood next to the buggy and held out his hand. "Let me help you up."

Who was this Orion who was being so cordial? When she'd left, he'd scowled at her as she rode out of town. And growing up, he had teased and tormented her then ignored her. She wasn't sure which had been worse—being teased or ignored.

Taking a deep breath, she placed a hand in his broad, strong one. Would he squeeze her hand until she cried like when she was a child?

No, he held it gently, helping her into the buggy. He laid a quilt across her lap to keep her warm on the ride.

Her breath caught as she recognized the covering. This wasn't just any quilt. This was hers—or rather the first she'd made as a girl. An appliqué tulip pattern. She'd been so proud of her yearlong work, practicing her sewing. Now she could see how the stitches were uneven and the seams crooked.

When Orion had arrived on the orphan train from the East and been adopted by the blacksmith, her mother encouraged her to give him something. She had chosen her prized work. No wonder Orion had taunted and persecuted her. She'd given him a quilt with big red flowers on it. A girl's quilt.

Now, soft from wear, it had a few holes clear through it. Did he remember from where this had come? She chanced a sideways glance at him as he climbed aboard and took the reins. When would this Orion vanish and the one from her youth return?

The bumpy ride did nothing to quell her concern for her pa and fueled the ache in her backside. "Why didn't Ma come with you?"

"She's looking after the store and your pa."

That made sense.

Orion cleared his throat. "I'm sorry about your aunt."

Her aunt passing away had released Tilly from her duty to care for her aging relative. "Thank you."

After that, neither spoke for the nearly two-hour ride. She didn't know what to say to him, and obviously he didn't know what to say to her either. What was there to say? So they rode with only the creaking of the buggy springs for conversation.

When the buggy crested a hill and her little hometown of Green Hollow came into view, excitement welled up in her.

Home.

Finally.

Orion guided the buggy through a very cold-looking puddle up to the front of her folks' general store. He wasn't going to park *in* the puddle, was he? But Orion set the brake, turned away from her, and jumped to the ground.

She pulled back the quilt and peered over her side of the buggy at the puddle too large for her to avoid. How did he expect her to get down? Splash into the muddy water? This was the Orion she remembered.

He appeared in front of her.

The muddy water surrounded Orion's boots, covering the lower laces so the frigid water had to be seeping in and soaking his feet. He held his hands out toward her waist. She glanced past his outstretched arms offering help but could only see the ten-year-old boy he'd been. A boy who wouldn't have hesitated to take advantage of such a sloppy puddle to push her down in.

Would he drop her in it now?

She wanted to believe that he had grown up enough to not dump her in the dirty water but was unable to make herself move, staring at him and then at the puddle.

Orion forced himself to hold his smile and bite his tongue. How long would Tilly make him stand in this cold water? Did she realize it was bleeding into his boots? Certainly she wasn't making him wait in order to return his cruelty from their youth. She had always been kind. He was trying to make up for his transgressions of the past. He would wait her out.

He wiggled his numbing toes. Or maybe he wouldn't wait. "Put your hands on my shoulders. I'll carry you to the boardwalk."

A worried expression crossed her face before she stretched out her arms. She didn't trust him. She couldn't seriously believe the little boy who had mistreated her in their youth would still find joy in her ending up in a puddle. He had much to atone for. Seeing her safely across the cold, muddy water would be one small reparation for the sins of his past.

Her hands settled tentatively on his shoulders, the weight of her now dependent upon him. One step back, and she would splash into the puddle. From her wide-eyed expression, she knew it as well.

He gripped her waist. "Don't worry. I've got you." Which was probably what concerned her. "Put your arms around my neck."

She obeyed and gave a little gasp when he lifted her off the buggy floor and settled her in his arms. Completely at his mercy.

And they both knew it.

He would surprise her by seeing her to safety. Show her she could trust him.

His heart sped up at having her so close. She smelled of lavender and vanilla. Her breaths came in short puffs. Her stiff hold around his neck caused her strawberry-blond curls to brush against his cheek.

When she'd left town four years ago, he'd been upset. He'd fancied himself in love with her. But over the years, he decided he'd just been enamored with a sweet girl as he had been in his youth. Even so, he would stop in often at her folks' store on the off chance they would mention any news of her. . .and consequently, he'd purchased things he hadn't needed.

Now with his heart thundering and her vulnerable to him, he knew he wanted more than anything for her to forgive him for all the wrongs he had done to her growing up.

He needed her forgiveness and wanted something more but would have to settle for amiable friends. Anything more would be too lofty an aspiration. Maybe once he made amends, he would find out where things could lead with her.

He sloshed out of the puddle and up the two steps of the boardwalk. He lowered her to her feet and waited for her to be steady before releasing her waist.

She quickly let go of him and stepped back. "Thank you."

The astonishment in her voice tore at him. He did indeed have much to atone for. Gaining her trust would be tougher than he'd thought. He swung back around and plodded through the cold water to retrieve her hatbox. As he handed it to her, the store door swung open, and Mrs. Rockford came out.

His moments alone with Tilly, gone. Likely the last he'd ever have. A hollowness gaped inside him. A place longing to be filled with her forgiveness and trust. The same place that had always hungered for her attention.

Tilly turned and threw her arms around her ma. None of the reluctance she'd had with him.

The two women started into a quick litany of catching up, neither finishing their sentences, neither needing to, apparently, to be understood. Back and forth on three or four topics at once. Too dizzying for any man to follow. The women slipped inside without notice of him.

He returned to the puddle and around to the back of the buggy where the pool of water didn't reach. It had been his good fortune that the puddle had been accommodating and the horse had stopped where he wished.

Unstrapping the luggage, he swung the carpetbag onto the boardwalk and hoisted the trunk. What did she have in this monstrosity?

He lugged it inside.

Mr. Rockford sat behind the counter with his casted leg propped up on a wooden stool.

Tilly dipped to hug her pa. "Are you all right? How are you feeling? Are you in pain? What did the doctor say? Should you be out of bed? When did this happen?"

Mr. Rockford chuckled, which quickly burgeoned into a full laugh. When he caught his breath again, he spoke. "I missed you too, little one." He shifted his gaze to Orion. "Thank you for bringing her home. I'll never have a moment's peace now." He chuckled again.

Orion smiled. "Where do you want this?"

Mr. Rockford pointed. "You can leave it there."

At the same time, Mrs. Rockford said, "Take it upstairs." Facing her husband, she planted her hands on her hips. "And how do you propose it gets upstairs? Fly? You are in no shape to take it. The doctor said you aren't to be doing anything this first week. He probably wouldn't even like you being downstairs. Tilly and I certainly don't have the strength to carry that thing across the floor let alone up the stairs." She turned back to Orion. "I would greatly appreciate it if you would take it upstairs. Tilly's door is on the right."

"Ma!" Tilly blushed.

Mrs. Rockford paid no heed to Tilly's objection and gave him a nod to continue.

Orion ignored Tilly's protest as well. "I'd be glad to, ma'am." He headed up. He'd only ever been upstairs to their living quarters once, a few days ago, when Mr. Rockford first broke his leg. He'd helped carry the older man up to his bed.

The landing opened up to a sitting area. He knew which room belonged to the older couple, so the closed door had to be Tilly's.

He didn't relish the idea of setting the trunk down and then having to pick it up again. He raised his leg and pressed his knee against the doorframe, resting the trunk on his thigh as he turned the knob.

The door swung open to reveal a very feminine room with pink on the bed and on the window curtains. He set the trunk at the foot of her bed and gazed around for only a moment. He didn't want to linger and be accused of snooping.

He savored the coolness of her room after his exertion with her trunk. But he allowed the door to remain open when he withdrew so the room could warm for her. When he returned downstairs, Tilly's friend Jessalynn had joined the trio. Jessalynn was Tilly's age and ran a café in town. He carried Tilly's carpetbag upstairs.

With hardly a notice from the foursome catching up, he stepped out the door. He wished he could stay to enjoy the camaraderie of a family. To belong. He'd lost his father in the War Between the States and his mother a few years after that. He'd been grateful the blacksmith had adopted him and loved the burly man. But now he was gone as well. He missed family.

He stepped off the boardwalk and into the puddle.

"Mr. Dunbar—I mean Orion."

He swiveled around at Tilly's lilting voice. The water sloshed with his motion. "Yes." The eagerness in his voice almost made him laugh.

"Thank you for giving me transportation and for seeing to my luggage." Her cheeks pinked.

"I was more than happy to oblige."

"Would you like to return later to eat with us?"

She was inviting him to supper?

"Ma said, with all you've done, it is the least we could do."

His elation dipped. Mrs. Rockford had invited him. "I'd never say no to a meal prepared by as fine a cook as your ma. I'll be back at six."

Though she wasn't the one inviting him, he wouldn't turn down an opportunity to be near her. Maybe one day, she would see he was no longer a mischievous ten-year-old bent on making her miserable to win her attention.

He would distinguish himself in her mind with kindness, as she had always done to him. An eye for an eye. A kindness for a kindness.

Chapter 2

Orion sat in one of the two chairs at the small table in the compact living space, a kitchen and cramped bedroom. His quarters resided inside his livery that housed his blacksmith shop. Pa hadn't had much when he'd adopted Orion but offered all he had to the scrawny orphan boy fourteen years ago.

He unlaced his boots and worked them off. He wiggled his toes. Good. They still had feeling. They had already been cold before wading in that puddle. But the discomfort had been well worth it to carry Tilly. After peeling off his soggy socks, he propped his feet up onto the second chair to warm them near the still-warm stove. Ah, heat.

He didn't have a lot of time to linger before he would need to wash up and dress for supper. But he did need to bring life back into his trotters.

"Hello? Smithy?"

Orion sighed. A customer. "That's all you get, feet." As he stood, he upended his wet boots on the warm stove to dry. The braided rug on his skin was scratchy, but not nearly as prickly as the straw-covered floor beyond it.

He stepped out of his living quarters into the main part of the stable to see Matt, a middle-aged man who ran one of the two saloons in town.

Matt inclined his head. "Ah, there you are." His gaze shifted to Orion's bare feet, back to his face, his feet, and finally settled on his face.

Orion opened his mouth to explain, then closed it, then opened it. What could he say? "How can I help you?"

"I'd like to rent your wagon tomorrow."

"Which one?" He had the buggy, the buckboard, and the freighter wagon.

"The big one."

"Can't do. I have a load to pick up in Dallas tomorrow. Will the buckboard suit your needs?"

Matt rubbed the back of his neck with one hand. "I's hopin' for the big one, but I guess I'll have to make do with the buck. Can you have it ready for me at sunup?"

"No problem." He shook Matt's hand, and the man left.

Now he ought to get himself ready for supper with Tilly. And her parents.

He'd bathed this morning before heading out to fetch Tilly, so he just needed to wash off today's road dust.

After cleaning up, he dressed in his Sunday suit. He never wore it but to church, so it rarely got soiled and had yet to wear out.

He wished for some meadow flowers he could pick for Tilly. Then he shook his head. She hadn't been the one to invite him to supper, even though she had done the speakin'. It was her ma's invite. Dressing clean would have to do.

Ma opened the oven and slid in an apple pie. "Tilly, go downstairs and wait for Orion."

That would make her seem anxious for his arrival. Her first supper back with her folks in four years, and it had to be spoiled with Orion Dunbar's company. "It's only a quarter of. He won't likely arrive until six."

Maybe he wouldn't come at all.

"It would be impolite to keep him waiting." Ma closed the oven. "Go."

Tilly took a deep breath and plunked slowly down the stairs to the store level. She glanced toward the door on her way to the stool behind the counter to wait. Orion was climbing the outside steps.

He was early.

She changed direction and pulled the bolt locks at the top and bottom to open the door. "Welcome. You're early."

He removed his hat and gave a slight bow. "I didn't want to be rude and keep you and your folks waiting."

Just about what Ma had said about manners. "Come in."

He stepped inside, and she moved to rebolt the door.

"Let me get that." Orion reached up with much more ease than she to lock the door.

She stared at his back as he did so. Who was this stranger? Was this really the boy of her youth? Or had she been gone so long, she had forgotten what he looked like, and this man was someone else entirely who also went by Orion?

At least the new Orion had shown up and not the hooligan of her youth. Maybe supper wouldn't be so unbearable after all.

After Orion greeted Ma and asked Pa how his leg was, they all sat at the table, but not before Orion insisted on helping Ma put out the supper dishes. That was Tilly's duty, but Orion wouldn't let her or her ma carry one dish.

Pa blessed the food and the hands that had prepared it.

Orion held out the chicken and dumplings pan on the folded towel to Tilly. "I'll hold this for you."

"That's not necessary."

"I've got it. It's hot, and it's heavy. Go ahead."

She dished herself up a portion. Why was he behaving this way? What was he up to? Luring her into a false sense of security?

He took a serving for himself, then set the pan in the middle of the table.

Tilly took a bite.

"Mr. Rockford," Orion said.

"Please. After all the help you have given us and most recently with my injury, you should call me Henry."

Orion's eyes widened. "Thank you. . .Henry. I'm honored." Not only was his surprise evident, but it seemed difficult for him to address her pa by his first name. Strange, at the very least.

Ma gave him a nod. "And you may call me Henrietta."

He looked as though he might choke, only he had no food in his mouth. "Thank you."

Pa held up his fork. "You were going to say something?"

Orion seemed to need a moment to think. Calling her folks by their first names had apparently thrown him. He took a deep breath and swallowed. "Yes. I am heading back to Dallas. Tilly said she had some trunks arriving. I would be more than happy to pick them up while I'm there."

So that was what he was up to. Tilly turned to him. "No need to bother yourself. We'll manage."

Pa pinned her with a stare to tell her this was not her decision, then turned back to Orion. "I would normally be going in a day or two anyway for the store, but being laid up, I obviously can't. We would be most grateful for your assistance. I'll pay you, of course."

"That won't be necessary."

"With my leg as it is, I would have to pay someone. I'd rather it be you."

"I can't take your money. I'm going anyway."

Pa gave a nod of acquiescence. "Tilly will accompany you. She can make sure all the trunks arrived."

Tilly's stomach knotted, and she jerked her gaze to Pa. He couldn't be serious, but she knew better than to express disapproval to Pa twice. It would do her no good, so she studied her plate instead.

Orion had been agreeable thus far, and certainly he wouldn't resort to the antics of his youth. But any more time spent traveling with him held no appeal. Being forced together today had already been awkward enough. She hoped tomorrow wouldn't be as well.

"I'll come by when the store opens to pick you up."

She shifted her gaze to him, and her retort caught in her throat at his pleasant, expectant expression. For a moment, she regretted her ill feelings toward him. Then she pictured him laughing with the other schoolboys after he'd ruined her new dress. The memory still stung, but she pushed it aside. He'd grown up. He wasn't that mean boy anymore. "That will be fine."

Ma turned to Tilly and broke the strained silence that followed. "I told Mr. Henderson that you would fill in for Miss Keech for a week or two until she returns."

Mr. Henderson had been the town mayor when she left. "I don't believe I know Miss Keech."

"That's right, you wouldn't. She came after you left. She's been our schoolmarm for three years now."

She wouldn't mind teaching for a week or two. She loved children. It would be a welcome challenge. "What happened to Miss Keech?"

"Her mother's ill. Miss Keech is taking care of her."

"When do I start?"

"Monday. We thought you'd like to get settled in here at home for a few days first."

That she would. With the other trunks arriving tomorrow, she would have three days to unpack what she could use now and store the remainder.

There wasn't much need for her to speak to Orion, and the rest of supper was affable. Afterward, Orion thanked them and left.

Later, as Tilly sat in front of her mirror, brushing out her hair for bed, Ma came into her bedroom. Taking the brush, she continued with Tilly's hair. Tilly had missed Ma doing this.

Ma stroked several times before she spoke. "I believe you owe Orion Dunbar an apology."

She owed him an apology? It should be the other way around. She gazed at her ma in the mirror. "What?"

"Your manners were a bit inconsiderate."

"I never said one rude word to Mr. Dunbar. I hardly spoke to him."

"Exactly. The man drove all the way to Dallas to bring you back when we couldn't. He has a business to run. You could have been more grateful. And when he volunteered to retrieve your trunks tomorrow, you shunned his offer. You need to be more pleasant to that young man."

Tilly turned on her stool. "Ma, he's the boy who pushed me down in the schoolyard, teased me, and called me names."

"He was an orphan who'd been displaced."

"He dipped my braids in his inkwell, ruining my new, pretty dress. I'd saved and saved my money for the taffeta and worked hard to sew it."

"For which his pa reimbursed us. And I made you another dress that you never so much as wore outside your bedroom."

"I was afraid he'd ruin it too. He has always been mean to me."

"He's not a child anymore, and neither are you. It is your Christian duty to seek reconciliation and forgive him for his past transgressions."

"I don't know if I can."

Ma took Tilly's shoulders in her hands. "An unforgiving heart hurts you more than the person you harbor resentment toward. Let bygones be bygones."

She knew Ma was right.

After Ma left, she tried to figure out how to forgive a person who'd hurt her so often as a child. It hadn't been just once, but dozens of times. The two of them would likely not even see each other after tomorrow unless their businesses required it.

Lord, how do I forgive? When I look at Orion, I see the boy who tormented me. I remember feeling sorry for him when he arrived in town. He had no parents and was alone. That's why I gave him my special quilt.

She turned in her Bible to Saint Matthew, chapter 18. *Lord, how oft shall my brother sin against me, and I forgive him? till seven times? Jesus saith unto him, I say not unto thee, Until seven times: but, Until seventy times seven.*

"I must forgive him, or I am as guilty as he is. Lord, I forgive Orion Dunbar for the many mean things he did to me as a child."

She paused, knowing she was holding back. She took a deep breath. "I even forgive him for ruining that new dress."

But no release came.

Chapter 3

Orion finished hitching the pair of draft horses to his large freight wagon. Not knowing how many trunks or how heavy each was, he'd chosen the drafts. They made a strong team, and the wagon was sturdy enough to carry whatever she had.

Today would be a fine day. The sun shone brightly, and he'd get to spend a good portion of the day with Tilly. Two hours traveling to Dallas, an hour or more there in town, taking time to enjoy lunch at a restaurant, and two more hours home. A right fine day.

She hadn't spoken much last night at supper, but she was probably tired from her trip. And she'd seemed a bit peeved at returning to Dallas. But today they'd be able to talk without her worrying about her pa. He would be able to make some favorable progress in getting Tilly to see he'd changed since his youth. That he was a man who didn't resort to such nonsense.

How foolish of him to think that teasing and pushing a girl into puddles so her dress got muddied had somehow been a fitting way to capture her attention. He'd captured her attention all right. But not in an agreeable way.

He drove up to the Rockfords' mercantile. A small, two-wheeled trap sat parked out front. A restless white thoroughbred stood hitched to it.

Orion set his brake, jumped down, and climbed the steps. The door opened. Tilly stepped out, a vision in a navy-striped walking suit under a red-plaid, full-length cape and a medium-brimmed hat with a wide blue ribbon and large bow. She was taking no chance of being cold today.

Then Conrad Tolen exited the store behind her and closed the door. Conrad ran the bank and lived in a large house. He had much to offer a young lady.

Conrad wrapped Tilly's hand around his arm and pinned Orion with a stare. "We were hoping you'd be here soon."

We? The mercantile didn't even open for another ten minutes.

Orion acknowledged Conrad with a nod but turned his attention to Tilly. "I have the wagon ready."

"Matilda will ride with me." Conrad pointed to the trap.

Matilda? Since when did she go by Matilda? "I'm taking *Tilly* into Dallas to retrieve her belongings." Orion gritted his teeth. "She can take a ride with you another day." But he hoped she never would.

"I know. Matilda will be more comfortable in my buggy. Top of the line with a padded seat."

Conrad planned to go to Dallas? "You don't have to trouble yourself."

"No trouble."

Orion didn't want Conrad taking *Tilly* anywhere. "Did you get that wheel fixed on your trap?" He doubted it, since Conrad hadn't brought it to Orion's livery.

"My buggy's wheel is just fine."

"Your trap may not be sturdy enough for the road to Dallas. It's rough in places."

Conrad narrowed his eyes. "You can follow along behind."

"There's no point in both of us going. Since I have the vehicle that can transport her trunks, I'll take her."

"I have the more comfortable conveyance. What kind of gentleman would I be if I allowed her to ride on a hard wooden seat?" Conrad escorted Tilly to his buggy.

Tilly glanced over her shoulder at him with what he hoped was an "I'm sorry" look before Conrad helped her in.

No denying the man had been right about his vehicle offering a more pleasant ride. Why hadn't Orion thought of Tilly's comfort?

Conrad rounded the rig. "We'll see you in Dallas."

Follow like some servant. Like he wasn't as valuable a person because he had calluses on his hands. Because he worked hard for every mouthful of food he ate. Because his clothes didn't cost as much as a pair of good horses.

The trap jerked into motion.

No longer a fine day.

He watched as the conveyance swayed down the street. It wouldn't make it halfway to Dallas. He rounded his draft horses and climbed into his driver's seat but didn't put his wagon into motion. Could he stand to ride behind the pair for two hours, wondering what Conrad was saying to her?

The trap reached the end of the street and turned out of sight. Orion best be going, and so he snapped his reins. Brutus and Socrates lumbered into motion. This would prove to be a very, very long day. And a miserable one.

Within five minutes, his team had caught up with the trap. Orion hadn't even been hurrying them. He'd hoped to stay far enough behind them to not think about Tilly sitting so close to another man. The rig wasn't fitting for this trip. The seat could barely fit the pair. And with only two wheels, the weight of the conveyance rested on the horse's back, a white thoroughbred ill-suited for pulling any conveyance—even one that small. The stallion fought the vehicle attached to him. His high-stepped prancing seemed more like he was trying to get away rather than trying to haul.

Orion's wagon lumbered along, minute after long minute. Mile after torturous mile. Why hadn't that wheel broken? It must be sturdier than it appeared.

Why had he volunteered? Because he thought he'd get to spend the day with Tilly. He could hear his own voice echoing in his head. *I'm going to Dallas anyway.* The only reason he was going to Dallas was to retrieve Tilly's trunks. To amend for another of his sins. That her pa had insisted that Tilly accompany him had been a boon. Something he had hoped for and gladly welcomed.

Now he wished Mr. Rockford hadn't even suggested it. Or that Orion had refused to have her go along. He would rather go alone than have Tilly seated next to another man. He needed something to distract him from the pair ahead, so he turned his attention to the brush off to the side of the road.

He focused on the elm, pecan, and mesquite trees. The long pods of the legumes. If he kept his attention on the vegetation, he wouldn't be thinking about Conrad whispering in Tilly's ear. The sway of the various grasses, Texas wintergrass, bluestem, switchgrass. He wouldn't think about Tilly laughing at something clever Conrad said. Buffalograss, sideoats grama, and some tall dropseed next to some hairy grama.

Soon his wagon stopped. Orion glanced up. His team had nearly run into the trap. Why did Conrad insist on driving so slow? He looked past the rig and noticed the thoroughbred favoring his rear right leg. Wasn't Conrad aware? If he didn't see to the cause, his horse could go lame. Didn't he care? It would serve him right if his horse couldn't pull his inadequate rig.

Orion kept his gaze on the horse. *Come on, Conrad, notice your horse.* But Conrad had his full attention on Tilly, talking. Did the man ever take a breath? He wouldn't likely notice his horse until the stallion injured itself. Well, Orion wouldn't wait until it was too late for the horse. He pulled his wagon around the trap and stopped in front. He jumped out. If not for the stallion facing the back of Orion's wagon and knowing to stop, preoccupied Conrad wouldn't have halted his rig.

Conrad stood. "What's going on?"

Orion glared at the man. "Your horse is favoring a leg. Didn't you notice?" He ran his hands down the leg in question but found no issues, so he bent it to raise the hoof off the ground. "He's picked up a rock."

Orion returned to his wagon and retrieved a leather tool holder. He laid it on the ground near the back of the horse, untied the fastening strips, and unrolled it. Using a hoof pick, he gently worked at the rock, careful not to injure the horse any further.

"Is he all right?" Tilly asked.

But Conrad didn't ask after his own horse.

"No permanent damage. It may be tender for a while." Orion also found a smaller rock in each front hoof. Then he checked his own horses but found none.

He pulled his wagon off to the side of the road and let Conrad return to the lead position. He wanted to be able to keep an eye on what took place. Make sure they didn't get left behind when the wheel finally gave way.

Unfortunately, the trap made it all the way to Dallas without a problem. Even though the trip took well over the two hours it should have. Orion couldn't blame the man. Conrad liked having Tilly all to himself and sitting so close to him. Hadn't that been what Orion had hoped for?

He drove his wagon up to the loading area of the train station. His gut tightened when Conrad gripped Tilly around the waist to help her down.

Inquiring at the office, Tilly identified all eight of her trunks and signed for them.

Orion glanced at Conrad, but the man appeared to have no intention of helping. So what use was he? Why did he bother to come? Orion hefted the largest trunk, wanting to load the biggest first. He'd been right to bring the freight wagon and large draft horses.

Tilly spoke in a congenial tone. "Maybe you could help him."

Conrad replied in a neutral timbre. "I think he can handle them."

Tilly's voice took on a lyrical quality. "But you could help."

Conrad's reply held distaste. "I'm not dressed for manual labor."

The popinjay had made sure of that. Orion waved a hand at the pair as he returned to heft another trunk. "I'm just fine." Just *fine* and *dandy*.

"Since you have everything in order here, we'll take lunch and see you back in Green Hollow."

Had he just been dismissed? Sent on his way? Return to Green Hollow without Tilly?

Tilly motioned toward her luggage. "I would like to stay until all my trunks are loaded."

Was Tilly being polite? Or did she not trust Orion to do an adequate job?

"Then we can *all* take lunch together." She indicated the three of them.

Neither dismissal nor distrust but inclusion.

Or perhaps, she hadn't wanted to be alone with Conrad. Orion would hope for that.

The two men had glared at each other all through lunch, but Tilly chose to ignore them and enjoy her food. Now she wandered through a department store with the two men skulking about, neither far from her. They were both being ridiculous. She purchased fine, rich chocolates for her parents and left the store.

Orion managed to maneuver himself in such a way as to be the one to assist her into the buggy.

She had no interest in either man, so they needn't try so hard. "Will you follow again or take the lead this time?"

"I have a few things to pick up before I leave town."

Right, he'd said he had business in Dallas anyway. "We can wait."

"No need. I won't be long. My team will catch up."

Before she could insist on both vehicles leaving together, Mr. Tolen snapped the reins and set the buggy into motion.

"It wouldn't hurt to wait for him."

Mr. Tolen shrugged. "You heard him. He said no need. Did I tell you about my trip to France?"

He had, but she let him tell her again. It had been an interesting story.

Not long into the trip, the traces of Orion's wagon jangled behind them. She breathed easier. She didn't like the idea of leaving him behind. Was that because of etiquette? She didn't think so. Her trunks lagging behind? No. Strangely, she trusted Orion to bring them. Or something else? She glanced back just to make sure it was Orion and not another wagon. He sat on his wagon seat in an easy manner, swaying with the rhythm of the vehicle. A smile pulled at her mouth.

He raised his hand in a wave.

She returned his gesture. When she turned back around, she noted the frown incised into Mr. Tolen's face.

He'd arrived in Green Hollow three months before Tilly's departure for Baltimore four years ago. He'd paid her unsolicited attention then. He'd obviously not found a wife in the interim. She wished he had.

His expression quickly turned to neutral then ebullient. "Let me tell you about the time I faced down a mama bear."

She had heard all about it on the way to Dallas. Didn't he remember? She supposed she would have to hear it again. After the bear story came the repeat of the time he spent in New York City and then another rendition of growing up in New England.

Right in the middle of his retelling of his visit to the White House, she heard a moaning creak close at hand. Before she could decide what had made the sound, a *snap*, and the buggy pitched to the left. Tilly fell against Mr. Tolen, who grappled at the side and the brake lever to keep himself on the now-tilted seat. Unsuccessful, he toppled to the ground onto the broken-off wheel.

Tilly grabbed her side of the buggy and jammed her foot against the small ledge on the edge of the floor. She didn't know how long she could hold on before tumbling out on top of the sprawled Mr. Tolen.

Suddenly, strong arms wrapped around her and pulled her up and out of the buggy on her side.

Orion set her safely on the ground. "Are you all right?"

She nodded. "Mr. Tolen?"

Orion took off around the back of the broken conveyance, and she followed.

Mr. Tolen stood, brushing off his expensive suit, cursing under his breath. "Well, that was. . ."

She waited to see what he might say. Distressful? Harrowing? Unexpected? Shocking? Maybe even interesting?

He straightened. ". . .embarrassing."

Embarrassing because he'd fallen? Or because Orion had been right? "But you're all right? You didn't get injured?"

"Only my pride." Mr. Tolen turned to Orion. "I'll bet you think you are so clever, predicting the wheel would break."

Orion shook his head and held out his hands. "I'm stumped. I thought the other wheel would break. This one had seemed fine."

Mr. Tolen narrowed his eyes. "How long will it take you to repair it?"

How insolent of him to assume Orion would just fix it, as though Orion was his servant.

Orion stiffened.

Oh no. He wasn't going to lash out as he'd done when he first arrived in Green Hollow?

But he only shrugged. "A few days."

"Days! We don't have days."

"I don't have the tools nor the materials to repair it out here. Everything's back in town." Orion walked up to the thoroughbred, stroked his neck, and spoke soothingly to him. His voice eased Tilly as well.

"Take a wheel from your wagon then."

Orion stared at Mr. Tolen, apparently in disbelief. Even Tilly knew that wouldn't likely work.

"Well?"

"The wheel would never fit." Orion unharnessed the stallion.

"What am I supposed to do? I can't make Matilda walk."

Tilly watched Orion's face go from tense to relaxed. "She can ride on the wagon seat with me."

Mr. Tolen scowled. "I'll take Matilda in your wagon. You can stay with my rig and see what you can do with it."

Mercy. Tilly studied Orion. How much longer would Orion put up with Mr. Tolen's arrogant attitude? She hoped the two men didn't start swinging at each other. What could she say or do to distract them?

But Orion kept his easy manner and stance. "No one but me is driving my wagon. My team won't tolerate a stranger handling them."

"What am I supposed to do?"

Orion pointed to the wagon. "You are welcome to ride in the back with the trunks."

"That is hardly an appropriate place for a gentleman to travel."

"Well, if you can ride bareback—"

"*I* am an accomplished horseman. *I* can ride bareback."

"Then I think you would be wise to head back to Dallas and hire their blacksmith to return with you and repair your rig." Orion held out the reins of Mr. Tolen's horse.

Mr. Tolen grabbed them with a jerk and turned to Tilly. "Matilda, I can set you on my horse and take you back to Dallas and rent another conveyance there."

Tilly's stomach tightened. She didn't want to go back—she wanted to continue toward home. She'd hardly been home long enough to eat and sleep. "I'm anxious to get back to Ma and Pa. I think I'll ride in the wagon."

Mr. Tolen took her by the arm and walked her away from Orion. "I don't think it's wise for you to be alone in the company of such a man. . .a laborer."

How derogatory! Orion would be a welcome relief from Mr. Tolen. "I appreciate your concern. I will be fine. Orion drove me from Dallas yesterday."

"It's not prudent to get familiar with a blacksmith."

He sounded like her aunt. Always needing to behave properly. But what was proper about treating one person as less important than another? "I will be fine." She returned to the wagon. "I'm ready to go."

Mr. Tolen jumped onto the back of the horse on his stomach then swung his leg over and into a sitting position. He turned his horse toward Green Hollow.

"Dallas is the other direction."

Mr. Tolen glared at Orion. "I know which way is which."

"What about your rig?"

"It's broken. I'll buy a new one." He turned to Tilly, smiled, then goaded his horse into a gallop.

Had he smiled at her to make sure she had heard that he could afford to purchase a new conveyance?

Shaking his head, Orion walked to the buggy.

Tilly followed. "What are you doing?"

"Surveying the damage." He picked up the wheel, which was mostly intact. He pointed to the inner ring that had been toward the buggy. "This is rotting here. That's why I didn't notice its weakness. It can be repaired."

"Maybe Mr. Tolen will return for it." But she doubted it, and the expression on Orion's face said he doubted it as well.

Orion reached into the buggy and pulled out her reticule. "You don't want to leave this behind."

She took it. "Thank you."

He walked her back to the wagon and helped her up. Climbing aboard, he took the reins and released the brake. They were on their way once again.

She drew in a deep breath and realized her relief. Where Mr. Tolen behaved like a fox stalking his prey, Orion was more like a stray dog hoping for a small bit of kindness.

Every so often Orion would say, "Giddy-up, Socrates," and snap the rein over the tan draft horse.

"Why do you keep saying that?"

"Socrates is lazy. He relaxes his gait just enough to make Brutus pull most of the weight."

She studied the black draft horse. With his head down, he seemed to be working hard. When Orion said "Giddy-up, Socrates" again, she could see Socrates pull his share. "Why doesn't Brutus do the same thing and let Socrates do the pulling?"

"Brutus is a really hard worker. He knows his job and isn't going to slack off."

Brutus and Orion seemed to be a lot alike.

"I'm sorry the wagon seat isn't as comfortable as the buggy."

"It's not so bad." The ride was actually much more pleasant. Quiet. Mr. Tolen had prattled more than a group of women at a quilting bee. His cadence like that of some of the uptight people in Baltimore. Now, all that filled the air were the jingling of the traces, the clomping of hooves, and the crunching of the wheels on the dirt road. She could relax.

Once back in Green Hollow, Orion unloaded one trunk after another. Tilly asked if she could give the horses a treat. With a carrot on the palm of each hand, she held them out to the two horses. She petted Brutus's nose and neck.

He wrapped his large head around to her back and pulled her toward him. She gasped.

Orion chuckled. "He likes to hug."

"Is that what he's doing?" She put her arm around his neck and hugged him back.

Brutus released her and bobbed his head.

She smiled at him and stepped in front of Socrates. "And what does he like?"

Socrates stretched out his neck toward her.

Orion grabbed Tilly from behind and pulled her backward. "He likes to eat hats."

Socrates wiggled his stretched-out lips toward what sat atop her head.

Tilly leaned back into Orion and gasped. She didn't normally get this close to a man. She felt Orion's laugh before she heard it.

"He has no manners at all."

Turning around, she gazed up at Orion Dunbar. Who was he? She could picture a young Orion laughing so hard he fell on the ground if a horse snatched her hat and ate it. He really had changed. Grown up. So male she couldn't breathe; even so, she forced air into her lungs. "I'm sure Ma would want to invite you for supper."

"I wish I could. I got work to tend to."

"Of course." She understood, since he'd been gone all yesterday to get her and then again today, but still a shadow of disappointment settled inside her. "Thank you for getting my trunks for me."

"My pleasure." He shifted from one foot to the other. "Tilly, I have something to say to you that is long overdue."

Her heart seemed to flutter. Was it his nearness? Or what he might say?

"When we were children, I teased you something fierce."

Yes, he had. Pleasure rippled through her that he realized it.

"Will you forgive me for calling you all those names?"

Some of them had cut deep, while others had merely been nuisances. "Of course I will." And so much more. She waited, wanting to tell him she forgave him for everything.

Socrates whinnied.

Orion chuckled, deep and genuine. "I best be getting these two back to the livery." He gripped Brutus's harness and led them away. In the back of the wagon sat a brown paper-wrapped parcel the size of a folded quilt. Was that all he'd gone to Dallas for?

Tilly gazed after Orion and the retreating wagon, waiting for more, but he kept walking. Traces jingling, hooves clomping, wheels crunching the dirt.

That was all he was going to ask forgiveness for? What about all the puddles he'd pushed her into? What about stealing her schoolbooks and hiding them from her? What about letting her schoolwork flutter out of his hand and land in the creek? *What about dipping her braids in his inkwell and ruining her new dress?* What about all those things? The name-calling had been the least of his offenses. Yet that was all he'd asked forgiveness for? Didn't he realize all the rest had hurt more?

Just when she'd thought maybe Orion Dunbar had changed, he hadn't. Just like Orion.

Later that night, before she dressed for bed, she peered out her window at the moonlit street. The air seemed to be clearer than normal. Likely an illusion and nothing more. The air was just the air.

A lone wagon swayed down the street. Orion sat in the driver's seat and drove to his livery.

And Orion was Orion.

Had she been a fool to think he'd changed? But he didn't seem to be the same heartless person he had been when he came to town fourteen years ago. He had changed. Could he not see how much he'd hurt her when they were young? She shook her head. Oh, why did she hold on to the past so tightly? She should just let it go. Let bygones be bygones, as Ma had said.

On the back of the wagon sat Mr. Tolen's broken buggy. Had Mr. Tolen hired Orion to retrieve it? Not likely. Mr. Tolen had discarded it as useless.

Orion worked hard, just like Brutus. That much had changed.

Her next thought came unbidden. Not even sure it was her own. *And you need to truly forgive him.*

But she had. Hadn't she?

Maybe not, if the past still bothered her. Not if she still held it against him.

But his past offenses didn't bother her as much as his lack of acknowledging them.

Chapter 4

On Monday morning, Orion put one more log into the potbelly stove and closed the door. Looking around the one-room school, he noted with satisfaction that everything seemed ready. The fire blazed hot and had begun to take the chill off the room, the lamp glowed on the teacher's desk, and the chalkboard waited, cleaned and ready. The only thing missing before the students arrived was a certain pretty teacher. And if he didn't leave soon, he might get caught by her. He grabbed his coat and strode for the back of the classroom. Movement outside the window captured his attention.

Tilly.

Pretty in her red-plaid cape, she strolled out of sight around the front of the building.

He stepped backward, not wanting to be seen. Turning in the

opposite direction from where she would enter, he headed for the other end of the room, which had an exit that led toward the outhouse. As he opened the rear door, the front one rasped. He slipped out without a sound.

One deep breath and then another.

He scooted around the corner to peer through the window.

Tilly scanned the classroom as though searching for someone. She had sensed his presence but not seen him.

Another sin atoned for. His actions weren't about her knowing about his penance—that was between him and God—it was about making amends for wrongdoings. He wasn't doing it to get recognition—that would defeat the purpose—only to put right his many wicked deeds.

Striding up the aisle, she made her way to the potbelly stove. She frowned and opened the stove's door. Closing it, she perused the room once again.

He ducked, waited a moment, and took another peek.

She pulled off her gloves and held her hands to the heat.

Someone entered through the back of the room.

Conrad Tolen.

No doubt he would take credit for providing the fire.

Orion wished now that he *had* been caught. Then at least she wouldn't give the wrong man credit. He could grab an armload of wood and go back in, surprised she had arrived.

God pricked his soul. No, it wasn't about her knowing and him getting appreciation. If he did, he would be no better than the hypocrites who prayed in public, who'd received their reward in recognition.

Tilly turned to Conrad.

And smiled.

Orion's insides twisted, and he slipped away. He just couldn't watch.

Tilly hoped her smile didn't appear as forced as it felt. "Mr. Tolen, what brings you to the schoolhouse?"

"Wishing you a fine first day. We all appreciate your filling in for Miss Keech."

"I am happy to do so." She hoped he wouldn't be garrulous today. She'd had enough of his prattling the other day and needed to prepare for the students' arrival.

He turned to the potbelly stove. "Ah. The fire is already warming the room."

Had he been the one to build it for her? "Yes. It's very nice. The children will appreciate it."

"Let me put another log on for you." He opened the door and fed the fire. Though it didn't really need it yet.

Why didn't he come right out and say he started it for her? Should she say something? Or just express her gratitude? "I am very thankful for the fire. The children will work better if they're not cold."

"You have a splendid day. I am just over at the bank if you should need anything."

"Thank you."

He took her hand in both of his. "The whole town is delighted at your return. No one more so than I." He bowed over her hand.

She resisted the urge to cringe.

He smiled, tipped his hat, and left.

Grateful to have a half an hour alone to prepare, she sat behind the desk and read through the lesson notes Miss Keech had left, then the children arrived. When she took roll, a few of the older students offered up false names, so she gave the whole class a surprise "test" that she would enter into the teacher's grade book as completed or not. The questions all pertained to the students. First their own name—the only way she could give them credit—then questions about family members, favorite color, favorite food, pets, and best friend's name. The answers would help her learn about them and which students were likely to team up with the troublemakers. After that, everyone cooperated for the most part.

At the end of the day, when she closed up the schoolhouse to leave, Mr. Tolen waited outside next to his buggy. He bowed. "I thought you might be tired and appreciate a ride home."

She should walk so she didn't encourage his attention toward her, but she *was* tired from standing in front of the classroom all day. The option of not having to walk took over, and her legs lost what little energy they'd had left. "Thank you. I see you have your buggy back."

"Yes. The blacksmith repaired it."

The blacksmith had a name.

He helped her in and climbed up next to her. "Thank you for taking me up on my offer for a ride."

"It is I who should thank you." But she already regretted her decision.

"I did have an ulterior motive."

Oh no.

"I wanted to apologize for my curt departure the other
road back from Dallas. I behaved rudely and disrespectf

very good company at all, I'm afraid. My buggy breaking down was one of many difficulties last week. I didn't handle things well. Forgive me?"

His behavior had been a minor infraction, and yet he apologized. "Of course." Maybe he wasn't as annoying as he'd seemed on the trip to Dallas?

Why couldn't Orion be as free with his apologies? Did he not realize the pain he'd caused her?

Then Mr. Tolen spoke of his day at work. She sighed internally. Was his apology worth putting up with his self-centered conversation?

As the buggy passed the livery, Tilly turned toward the clanging metal against metal. Orion glanced up from his hard work. She really wished she'd walked now. But why had that feeling intensified right now?

Mr. Tolen escorted her into the mercantile and took his leave.

Pa spoke. "Mr. Tolen?"

Tilly turned to Pa sitting behind the counter. "He gave me a ride from the schoolhouse."

"Today *and* the trip into Dallas."

"It was nothing, Pa." She didn't want him drawing the wrong conclusions.

Pa squinted one eye like he did when trying to discern the truth. "Nothing?"

"Nothing."

Pa struggled to his feet and propped his crutches under his arms. "Come with me. We need to talk." He lurched forward from foot to crutches, foot to crutches, heading toward the back storeroom. If not for the crutches, he would have probably headed upstairs for what would likely be a pressing talk.

She could think of nothing she'd done wrong. She wasn't a child any longer.

Pa sat on a barrel and motioned for her to sit on one as well. This must be serious if he wanted her to sit. Her stomach tightened as she eased down.

Pa stared at her a long moment before speaking. "Mr. Conrad Tolen paid me a visit today."

She let her shoulders relax. If this was about Mr. Tolen, then it didn't really concern her. Unless Pa owed money at the bank.

"He asked me if he could court you."

Her stomach balled up tight and fast, halting her breathing. "What did you tell him?"

"I said I would think about it. What would you like me to tell him?"

She knew Pa had the final say on who courted her, but he'd asked for her input. "I don't care for him in that way."

"So you would like it if I told him no?"

"Yes, please."

"Though I can see nothing wrong with the man, I can't picture you being happy with him. I'll tell him I'm not ready to give up my girl when I just got her back."

Tilly jumped off the barrel and hugged Pa. "Thank you." And she would not be accepting any further rides from the banker.

Tilly's good intentions didn't last a day. An afternoon storm rolled in on Tuesday, trapping her in the schoolhouse if not for Mr. Tolen waiting at the back of the room. "I have brought you a carriage to keep you nice and dry."

She put on her cape and walked to him. "Mr. Tolen, I appreciate your offer, but I fear you have expectations beyond what I can give."

He dipped his head in acknowledgment. "I spoke with your father. You may not have feelings for me now, but when you are ready to be courted, I hope to have won your affections."

Won? As though she were a prize? "I don't think it's fair to give you false hope when I don't even know my own heart."

"The rain is coming down like the Great Flood. Certainly you aren't going to walk."

It would be rude to turn down his offer. So she went with him. The next day brought mud deep enough to lose a shoe in, then wind, then bitter cold ushered in by the previous day's gales. And each morning, a fire in the potbelly stove greeted her, and each afternoon as she passed by, Orion glanced up from his work, causing her heart to cringe.

Then came blessed Saturday. No reason in the world to need a ride from Mr. Tolen. Or to see him, for that matter.

Tilly relaxed in that knowledge as she stood in the storeroom at a large shelf, dusting and organizing jars of canned goods. Ma joined her.

Ma took Tilly's rag. "You have a caller."

Tilly's mood sank. Couldn't Mr. Tolen leave her be for one day? "I have work to do."

"Don't keep him waiting."

"Who is it?" She could imagine no one but Mr. Tolen calling on her.

With the raise of her eyebrows and tilt of her head, Ma dismissed her.

Tilly took her time making her way to the front of the store. She halted. "Orion?"

He smiled and held out his hand. "I have something to show you."

Every time he'd said that to her in the past, she always wound up covered in mud while he laughed. He wouldn't do that now. He'd certainly outgrown such nonsense. "Let me get my wrap." She donned her long cape. Though the day was not as cold as the previous one, it still held a bit of a chill.

Orion led her kitty-corner across the street to his livery and left her near his blacksmith fire. "Wait here." He climbed the ladder to the hayloft above.

She held her hands out to the heat. She could hear him walking around above, swishing hay back and forth, and whispering. What was he up to?

He came down and searched behind crates, barrels, under burlap bags.

What was he searching for?

About the time he strode to the back and into a horse stall, a calico cat wandered up to her. She crouched down to pet it. The cat rose up, pushing its head into her hand. It had long, soft fur.

Orion strode back toward her. "There she is."

He had been seeking the cat? Tilly craned her neck to look up at him. "You have a cat?" He didn't seem like the type.

"She keeps down the mouse population. Did you see where she came from?"

Tilly pointed to a door cracked open about four inches.

Orion pushed it farther open and entered. The calico trotted after him.

Tilly stayed put but could see into the room where a small cookstove stood with a pot and kettle squished on top of it, and next to it sat a table and a chair with the red tulip quilt hanging over the back of it. This must be where Orion lived.

His voice drifted through the doorway. "Peaches! That's my Sunday suit."

She smiled. Peaches must have done something to his suit.

Orion soon appeared with his hands full of three mewing kittens. One all white, a black-and-white fluffy one, and a tricolored one that resembled a puff of cotton.

Tilly opened her mouth and hurried toward him. "Ooooooh. They're so adorable. Can I hold one?"

"You can hold them all if you like."

She took the tricolored one. Peaches meowed at her feet. She crouched. "See, she's all right."

Peaches put her paws on Tilly's legs, stretched out her neck, and took her kitten by the scruff of the neck, then ran back into Orion's living quarters.

Tilly stood and took the white kitten, which mewed. "How old are they?"

"I figure about four weeks now. It took me a while to find where she'd hidden them." He pointed toward the loft.

"But she moved them."

"To my room where it's warmer."

Peaches circled the two of them, looking up at her babies and meowing.

Tilly lowered the white kitten to his worried mother. "What did she do to your suit?"

Peaches took off with her second baby.

"Made a bed for the kittens. I'll have to give her something else. She likes it behind the stove. The cold we had yesterday must have caused her to seek out the warmth."

Tilly took the last kitten, the black-and-white fluffy one. He didn't mew but blinked his big yellow eyes. "Of course. She must have been thinking of her babies." She rubbed the kitten's soft fur against her cheek.

"They aren't old enough yet, but you can have whichever kitten you want."

Tilly smiled. "Really?"

"Do you know which one you want?"

She cuddled the one she held under her chin. "This one."

"You'll have to think of a name for him. But not Honey Bear."

She stared at him. "Honey Bear?"

"You had an orange-striped cat years ago named Honey Bear."

She tilted her head. "You remember him *and* his name?"

"Of course. He ran away a week after you turned fourteen." He reached down to pick up Peaches, who had returned for her last kitten. "Have you thought of a name yet?"

Peaches reached her paw across the gap between them and patted her kitten.

"Banjo." She set the kitten on the dirt floor.

Peaches jumped out of Orion's arms, snatched her baby, and trotted off. "You can visit him anytime until he's old enough to leave his mama."

"Thank you. I will. He's so adorable." She wished she could take him now. "How do you remember my cat?"

He shrugged. "I remember a good many things."

"You do?"

His expression turned melancholy. "I remember swiping your McGuffey reader and climbing a tree so you couldn't reach it."

She almost smiled at that memory. It seemed humorous now,

but at the time, she had been fraught with anger.

"Will you forgive me for swiping your books?"

So that was why he'd brought that up. "I will." She waited for him to ask for more. But he didn't. "Anything else?"

He studied her face for a moment before shaking his head. "I just wanted to show you the kittens."

He wasn't going to mention the dress he'd ruined? Why did it pain her so that he wouldn't ask for absolution for the one thing that had hurt her most? Disappointed, she lowered her gaze. "I should be going."

Orion watched Tilly cross the street and go into the mercantile. She had been surprised that he remembered her old cat. The poor cat had probably gotten eaten by another animal. Orion had searched weeks for Honey Bear. He'd wanted to return him to Tilly. To make her smile after ruining her dress.

He recollected everything concerning her. From the moment she gave him the quilt, to the day she left town to take care of her aging aunt. From the frown she flashed him when he'd done something mean, to the smile she shared with her friends. From the time she was a little girl of eight, to a grown woman of twenty-two. He tucked them all away in his heart.

But what he couldn't figure out was why each time he asked her forgiveness for his past sins, she seemed more upset than pleased. He was striving to make up for his wrongdoings. One good deed at a time. She had liked the kittens but not his apology.

What am I doing wrong, Lord?

Chapter 5

Tilly waited beside Ma outside the church after the service while Orion assisted Pa down the few steps. It was Pa's first time being able to attend church since he had broken his leg. Doctor's orders.

She couldn't figure out Orion being so helpful. She kept expecting. . .

Expecting what?

For him to push her in a puddle? She knew he wouldn't do that anymore. He had been so gentle with the baby kittens and had obviously gotten the cat hair off his Sunday suit. So what was she expecting from him? She just wasn't used to Orion behaving. . . nicely.

"You're frowning." Ma stood beside her. "You've been frowning all morning. In fact, since yesterday afternoon. Did you have a disagreement with Orion?"

"No." It had actually been a pleasant visit with the kittens. So why did Orion Dunbar nettle her so? "Ma, what do you do when someone does several things wrong but only asks forgiveness for one of them? And not even the worst one?"

"Are you having difficulty forgiving Orion for his unruly youth? He has grown into a fine young man."

"I thought I had forgiven him, truly, in my heart, but then I get upset that he asks forgiveness for some misdeeds but not the one I want him to." Tilly fisted her hands. "It's like I forgive then take it back. What's wrong with me?"

"Sometimes you have to forgive a person over and over until you are tired of taking it back. Forgiveness isn't always easy."

So true. "I am tired of it." She studied Orion, who steadied Pa as he spoke to the preacher. He had changed. Not the ornery boy of his youth. *Lord, I forgive Orion for everything he ever did.* Every *last thing. Help me to not take it back.*

"He still likes you, you know."

"Still? Orion Dunbar *never* fancied me. And I doubt he does now."

"He has been smitten with you since the day you gave him your quilt." Ma paused. "He came into the store every couple of days while you were away under the guise of purchasing some small item. He always managed to ask, in some roundabout way, about you. I looked forward to his visits and how he would move the conversation around to ask after you. Some days I would take pity on him and just tell him so he didn't have to work so hard for the information. I doubt he needed half the items he bought."

"Smitten? Hardly. He was mean to me as a child. Meaner

than to anyone else."

Ma gave a small laugh. "That's how little boys get the attention of the girl they like."

"By pushing her down and taking her books?"

"He had your attention, didn't he?"

"He didn't have to be mean to get it. There were better ways." He'd had her attention from the first day he'd arrived in town with his untamable wavy hair, dark eyes, and brooding temperament. She had suspected he hid a smile somewhere inside, and she'd wanted to find it. Until he'd pushed her too far and ruined her new dress. And laughed with the other boys.

"Boys aren't as sophisticated at showing their feelings as girls and aren't nearly as brave." Ma pointed to a blond-haired boy with a snake chasing one of the Cooper girls. "If a boy is mean to a girl, the girl dislikes him and the boy is safe, because the girl has a good reason to dislike him. If the boy is nice to a girl and she dislikes him, then he is crushed." Ma turned to her. "Women may be the ones to cry, but men are fragile emotionally too."

Orion fragile?

She pictured his well-muscled arms, honed from years of pounding metal. She remembered how easily he had hefted her trunks.

And her.

Twice.

Very manly.

Fragile? Not likely.

Walking home on Wednesday, her last day to teach because the regular teacher had returned, Tilly glanced toward the livery.

Orion stood at a saddle on a sawhorse. He pulled a thin leather strip threaded on a needle through the pieces of the saddle horn, stitching the leather back together. He didn't look up or notice her.

Her lips pulled up slightly. She felt no negative feelings toward him. Maybe she had finally, really forgiven him. Pleased, she went inside the mercantile and upstairs.

When she entered her bedroom, she noticed a parcel with her name written on it sat on her bed. She took it out to the kitchen where Ma peeled potatoes for supper. "Ma, is this a Christmas present?" Christmas was a week away.

"I don't know. It was sitting outside the front door when we opened for business."

"It wasn't there when I left for the schoolhouse. I wonder who it's from. Should I open it or wait?"

"That's up to you." Ma wiped her hands and smiled. "But if we can't know who it's from, I, for one, am dying to know what it is."

Tilly felt around on the package, causing it to crinkle. "It feels like yard goods. Do you remember selling someone this much fabric?"

"No. We tie packages with jute twine not a cotton string. Are you going to open it or just tease me with it?"

Tilly untied the cord and pulled back the paper. She stared at the pink-and-white wide-striped plaid taffeta with thin, green stripes. This fabric was unforgettable.

Ma leaned closer. "Isn't that. . .?"

"Yes. It is." The same fabric as the ink-ruined dress eight years ago. Her gaze shifted to the brown-paper wrapping. She knew who had sent this. The package looked like the same size and shape as the one that had been in the back of Orion's wagon. Certainly he hadn't traveled all the way into Dallas just for this? Then she realized he'd likely gone to Dallas that day just to retrieve her trunks. That he'd gotten the fabric had been an aside.

Ma fingered the material. "There's enough here to make two or three dresses. Who would buy so much?"

Someone trying to make up for the past. Should she tell Orion thank you? He'd obviously not wanted her to know he had left it. Should she keep his secret? "Ma, I want to start making a dress from this tonight."

"I'll pull out the pattern pieces after supper."

"Thank you. Do you mind if I run over to the café? I want to show Jessalynn."

"Tell her hello from your pa and me."

"I will." Tilly scooped up the fabric and dashed out.

As she exited the store, she glanced across the street, but Orion was no longer working on the saddle. His forge fire sat dark. Where had he gone? It mattered not at the moment. He would see soon enough that she had appreciated his gift when he saw her wearing the new dress she would make from it. If she worked quickly, she could have it done in time for the Christmas Eve service.

She hurried down the boardwalk to the Hollow Belly Café. So much had happened while Tilly sat idle in Baltimore, reading aloud in her aunt's parlor, sewing, or listening to the old woman snore. Jessalynn had written letters about losing her folks and opening her own café to support her brother and sister. So much had changed for her friend.

The place had sage-green paint on the bottom half of the walls with plaid wallpaper at the top and calico curtains on the windows. Jessalynn could easily seat and feed twenty-five people. And Tilly knew her friend could cook tasty meals for that many without any trouble. She'd always liked to cook.

Jessalynn waved her to a table near the kitchen as she pulled down two mugs and brought over a pot of coffee. She sat, poured the coffee, and reached out for the fabric on the table. "This is beautiful. Are you going to make a dress?"

"Yes."

"Where did you get it? I haven't seen that in your folks' store."

Tilly suppressed a smile. "It was a gift."

"I'll bet I know from who."

"Orion."

Jessalynn frowned. "Not a certain banker?"

"I doubt that."

"What will Mr. Tolen say about you receiving gifts from another man?"

Now Tilly frowned. "What does he have to do with it?"

"He's your beau."

Where had she gotten that ridiculous notion? "No, he's not."

"But he's courting you."

"No, he's not." Pa had told him no.

"But you were in his buggy every day last week, parading down the street."

Oh dear. That *would* make it seem as though he was courting her. "He only gave me rides home from the schoolhouse because of the erratic weather." Did half the town also assume he was courting her?

Did Orion?

Oh dear. That would never do.

Chapter 6

Orion swung his hammer down, striking the red-hot horseshoe on his anvil, sparks flying. After each swing, he glanced up at the mercantile where Tilly roamed somewhere inside. When she'd returned to town, he'd repositioned his anvil so that, with only a flick of his eyes, he could see when Tilly exited the store. Having the anvil in this direction made working a little awkward when he needed to put the iron back into his forge, but the inconvenience was worth the trouble for every glimpse of Tilly he could get.

He swung again and glanced up. The door opened, and Tilly stepped out in her short gray cape over a blue-checkered dress. Where was she off to? So as not to be caught staring, he jammed the horseshoe into the fire then pumped the bellows. When he thought she must be sufficiently down the street, he stole another peek.

His breath caught. She was headed straight for him—or rather his livery. Tilly would never come to see him. Not after the way he'd treated her growing up. She must be coming to visit her kitten. That had been why he'd given it to her after all.

He turned his focus back to the forge and shifted the horseshoe in the coals. Should he pretend not to see her until she reached him and then act surprised? Or should he notice her and step forward to greet her? Yes, greet her. So he reached up for the bellows handle, "noticed" her, and smiled.

Wiping his brow with his kerchief, he stepped forward, his heart pumping hard and fast. "Hello, Tilly."

She smiled back, and he felt as though he'd won first prize in a very long race.

"Hello. I hope I'm not disturbing you."

"Not at all." Tilly could never be a disturbance. "What can I do for you?"

"I wanted to visit my kitten. But if this isn't a good time, I can come back later."

"Now is great. It's time I took a break. And Peaches has gone off hunting." He pulled the horseshoe out of the fire so it didn't get too hot. "Wait here."

He entered his quarters. He knew it wouldn't be fitting to invite her to come in here. That would tarnish her reputation. She needed to stay in full view of anyone passing by. Especially Conrad. No sense having him cause trouble for her.

The kittens lay huddled in a furry ball on a blanket behind the stove. He picked up the black-and-white one. "You have a visitor, Banjo." He tucked Banjo in the crook of his arm and grabbed a chair on his way out.

He handed Tilly the kitten.

"Oh. He's so cute."

He set the chair in the open near the forge but not too close. "I brought you a place to sit."

"Thank you." She sat and snuggled the kitten under her chin. "He's so soft."

Orion took a dipper of water from his drinking bucket and drained the ladle before returning it to the bucket. Should he offer Tilly a drink? No. She wouldn't want to drink off his ladle. And she probably had plenty back at the store. He retrieved his other chair and set it across from Tilly away from the fire to catch any breeze that happened by. He was hot enough from working.

He watched as Tilly held the kitten up, petted him, hugged him, kissed his head, and played with him. He wished he could garner half that much attention from her. Banjo almost slid off her lap, but she caught him and held him safe.

Just like she'd caught Orion's heart.

When the kitten curled up in Tilly's lap to go to sleep, Orion thought she would leave, and his time with her would be over.

But she looked at him and tilted her head. "What happened to your parents? The ones before you came to Green Hollow. You don't have to tell me if you don't want to. It's really none of my business. I was just curious."

She almost sounded nervous. What did she have to be nervous about? "My real pa died in the War Between the States when I was five."

"I'm so sorry."

He believed she meant it. He didn't deserve her sympathy. "I don't remember much about him. I was only three when he left for the war. We had some rough years, but my ma got hired on as a housekeeper for a family of moderate means. They couldn't pay Ma much. They had five children and didn't mind me being with them. Ma took sick with pneumonia and died when I was nine, almost ten. An orphan train was heading west, so they dumped me on it."

"And no one wanted to adopt you before you reached Green Hollow?"

"I wasn't real adoptable."

"I don't see why not."

She was just trying to be nice. She was always nice.

Dare he risk opening up his soul to her? If she treated him poorly because of what he said, it would only be because he deserved it. "I was angry at Ma for dying and angry at the world. I didn't want anyone to adopt me. And I made sure no one wanted to. I wanted to cry but couldn't."

"But Mr. Dunbar took you in."

Orion's mouth pulled into a smile. "Pa said I could stay or go, it mattered not to him. But if I stayed, I'd have a warm, dry place to sleep and three meals a day, which was more than I'd get if I took off on my own."

"And you decided to stay."

He shook his head. "I ran away three times that first week. I would come straggling back when I got hungry. When Pa figured I had returned for good, he started teaching me blacksmithing."

Peaches strolled by with a mouse dangling from her mouth and darted into his quarters. She came back out, looked around, then snatched sleeping Banjo from Tilly's lap.

Tilly would leave now.

She watched Peaches trot off with Banjo swinging from his

mother's mouth. "Are you happy being a blacksmith?"

He shrugged one shoulder. "It's good work."

She was staying?

"Did you always want to be a blacksmith?"

"Never really thought about smithing before I arrived here."

"What did you want to be when you were a little boy?"

"Be?"

"Did you dream of being a sailor or cowboy when you grew up? Maybe even president of the United States?"

He couldn't believe Tilly chose to remain and wanted to know about him. "I wanted to be so rich that I never went hungry again."

"Instead you ended up here, being a blacksmith."

She made that sound like a bad thing. "I've never had an empty belly since coming here—except when I ran away—so I'd say I'm pretty rich." And having Tilly spend time with him made him all the richer.

Tilly studied Orion Dunbar in awe. He saw himself as a rich man. Mr. Tolen certainly wouldn't see him that way. As she took in the easy way he sat in the chair, his arms taut with muscles, she saw him as the boy who arrived in town fourteen years ago to the month. Not the boy who'd pulled her hair and made her life miserable, but the boy who'd stepped off the train, alone and scared. The boy with coffee-colored hair. The boy with despair in his rich brown eyes. The boy who'd tugged at her young heart. The boy she'd given her special quilt to.

Since Peaches had taken Banjo, Tilly supposed she didn't have a reason to stay. The kitten sleeping on her lap had been her excuse.

She didn't want to leave, but she should let Orion get back to his work. She uncrossed her ankles to stand.

"So what did *you* want to be?"

She stared at Orion a moment. He was giving her a reason to stay? She shifted her feet and cupped her hands in her lap. "Well, at some point, every little girl wants to be a princess who lives in a castle."

"And after that?"

Her dreams seemed so frivolous compared to his. "I wanted to be a famous singer onstage."

He quirked up one eyebrow.

"I know. To be a famous singer, I'd need to be able to carry a tune. So I gave up on that and settled for being Pa's princess and singing softly in church to the Lord."

After a moment, he said, "I think you sing just fine."

That lift of his eyebrow had questioned her singing ability. "Then you must be tone deaf."

Orion chuckled.

She smiled. This had been what she'd wanted all those years ago. To be his friend. "That was kind of you to repair Mr. Tolen's buggy. Did he hire you to do it?"

He shook his head. "I figured either he'd pay me for the repairs, or if he didn't want the trap, I could sell it."

"Retrieving it was very thoughtful."

"Naw. Just business."

Should she stay? Or go? Her reluctance to leave surprised her. "I never asked Mr. Tolen to give me rides home from teaching. He saw the inclement weather and showed up. I don't know what I did to garner his attention. He even lit the fire in the schoolhouse for me every day so I arrived to a warming room."

"Did he now?"

She had thought so, but now she suspected not. If Mr. Tolen built a fire for her each morning, why didn't he take credit for it? He didn't seem to be the kind of man to keep that to himself. And why only offer her a ride home if he had been at the school to start the fire? But if not Mr. Tolen, then who?

Orion? Would he have done it? He hadn't been at his forge any of the mornings when she'd left for the schoolhouse, so he could have. The old Orion never would have helped her. But would this new Orion? Why would he do it? And if it was him, why not say something? Why keep it a secret? So many questions concerning him.

He'd turned into a perplexing man.

"I'm not interested in Mr. Tolen in that way—or any man. I'm just enjoying being home." She had begun to babble, so she stood to cut herself off and felt something shift in her skirt's pocket. The carrots she'd put in there earlier. Digging them out, she held up the orange sticks, pleased. "I brought these for Brutus and Socrates."

He smiled. "They're in one of the back paddocks. This way."

She followed as he led her through the livery and slid open one of the back doors.

Brutus's head popped up, and he trotted over to the fence. Before she could hold out the carrot, he draped his head over her shoulder and "hugged" her. She patted his neck, then held out a carrot. Socrates strolled over, stretching out his neck toward the top of her head. She waved the carrot in front of him and successfully distracted him from her hat.

Movement in the large field caught her attention. A

black-and-white speckled horse stood two-thirds of the way through a fenced-in field with trees at the back. It bobbed its head. "Whose horse is that?"

"Mine. There are six of them. Wild Palouse horses. I rounded them up last week. I'm getting them used to living near people. That one's the leader. The others stay in the trees most of the time. Do you want to see if they will come to us?"

"Do you think they will?"

Orion pointed to tin bins attached to the rails of the next corral. "This is the only place I give them oats." He strode inside, returned with a bucket, and poured oats into the three bins.

The black-and-white turned toward them. Orion whistled. The horse walked slowly at first, then galloped toward them. Three more horses came out of the trees, trotting. The leader stopped a few feet away from the feed and sniffed the air.

Orion whispered, "Stand real still. He doesn't know you."

Tilly did as instructed.

The other horses stopped a little farther back still. The lead horse nickered and walked up to the closest bin. The others came to the bins as well. The remaining two walked at a leisurely pace.

Orion gripped her arm, and stepping forward, he pulled her with him. Once in front of the lead Palouse, he slid his large, strong hand down to hers.

Her heart quickened at his touch.

He talked quietly to the horse and put her hand on the soft black nose. When the Palouse didn't shy away, Orion let go of her, leaving his warmth behind.

She drew in a breath to steady herself from his contact and petted the horse's nose. "Why did you capture them?"

"I'm going to train and breed them."

He may be a blacksmith, but he had other ambitions as well. He would make a fine horse breeder. He would also make a great—

The alarm bell in the town square clanged, and a voice rang through the street. "FIRE! FIRE!"

The horses nickered, their ears twitched around, and they bolted for the far trees.

Orion's eyes widened. "I have to go."

"I know—"

Before she could tell him she was coming too, he spun and took off running through his livery.

Tilly raced after him and joined other townspeople in the street, all heading for the smoke. She struggled to see which building had caught fire. She stopped with a jolt in the middle of the street.

Smoke and flames poured out of the front windows of the Hollow Belly Café.

Jessalynn!

Orion and another man barked orders to get the bucket brigade going.

Most of the people scurrying to the commotion carried a bucket or two. Orion had two in each hand. He must have grabbed them on his way through the livery.

Why hadn't Tilly thought to do the same?

Jessalynn emerged from the smoky doorway with her ten-year-old brother, Drew, in tow.

Tilly rushed to her side. "Where's Penny?" Jessalynn's fifteen-year-old sister.

Jessalynn coughed. "Right behind me."

But she wasn't.

One bucket of water after another hissed onto the fire.

No sign of the girl in the crowd or anywhere.

"She must still be inside. Was she in the kitchen?"

Jessalynn's eyes widened. She coughed and took a step toward the burning building. "I have to go back for her." She coughed again.

Tilly held her back. "I'll go. You stay with Drew." She turned to the boy. "Keep her here."

He nodded and gripped his sister's arm.

Orion stood at the front of the bucket brigade closest to the heat. Keeping his eyes on the blaze, he swung his arms back with the newly emptied bucket, which got plucked from his hands, and a full one replaced it. He and the men near him had fallen into a good rhythm. He could keep this up until the fire wagon arrived.

When the next bucket in the relay failed to land in his hands, he turned. A second brigade line had formed, so he would be receiving every other bucket. That was good. They could get more water on the fire and in a larger area. What wasn't good was Tilly pulling her cape out of a watering trough. What was she up to? She swung the dripping cape around herself and headed for the front door of the café that billowed with smoke.

A bucket landed in his hands, and he automatically tossed it on the fire, then he handed it off and charged toward Tilly. He caught hold of her before she entered the building. "What are you doing? Get back!"

"Penny's still in there! I have to get her!"

Someone was still inside? He thought everyone had gotten out. He swiped her soggy cape and put it over his head. "Stay out here.

I'll get her. Do you know where she was?"

"Probably the kitchen."

Where the worst of the fire blazed. He yanked his neckerchief up over his mouth, grabbed a full bucket of water coming up the line that he dumped down the front of himself, ducked his head, and darted inside. "Penny!"

He couldn't see more than a few inches in front of his face. Good thing he patronized the café often and knew his way around. He navigated toward the kitchen and kicked a toppled chair on his route to the doorway.

The fire blazed mostly toward the front of the building. The majority of the room seemed to only be filled with smoke. Thick, light-snuffing smoke.

"Penny!"

"Over here. I'm trapped. The shelf fell over."

"Get as low to the floor as you can and keep talking so I can find you."

"I'm in the back corner by the pantry room."

Orion followed her voice and bumped into something hard and solid. The shelf she spoke of. He felt around and determined it leaned against a counter or the stove. There should be plenty of space under it. "Crawl under it. Follow my voice."

After a moment, she coughed. "I can't. There's too much stuff."

He knelt and shoved things from under it out of the way. "Push it aside. I'm working from this end." He coughed as well.

"I can't. Something big is jammed. I can't move it."

This wasn't working. He needed to get this girl out of the smoke. He wedged his shoulders under the shelving unit and heaved upward.

A barely distinguishable outline of a person showed through the smoke. He thrust out his arm. "Take my hand."

A tentative hand came through the smoke and touched his fingers. He gripped her wrist and yanked her to himself. He pivoted out from under the shelves, bringing the girl with him. The shelf crashed back into place.

The fire popped and cracked, sending a spark through the air and onto Penny's skirt. The fabric caught at once.

Penny screamed. "I'm on fire!" She tried to flee, which would only make it worse.

Orion intercepted her, swung the wet cape off his shoulders, and wrapped it around her skirt, putting out the flame. He draped the cape over the girl's head, scooped her up into his arms, and turned for the door. But which way was that? He'd gotten himself turned around.

"Orion!"

Tilly's sweet voice.

"Keep calling out!"

"This way! Follow my voice!"

He did. Even if his life wasn't in danger, he'd follow her voice. He reached the doorway and saw her standing there.

She gripped his arm and led him off the boardwalk. He staggered down the steps, coughing.

For the second time in his life, she'd saved him.

Tilly wouldn't let go of his arm. "Are you all right? I was worried about you. I was afraid you wouldn't come out."

"I'm fine." He lowered Penny's feet and lifted the cape off the girl's head.

Jessalynn rushed over and hugged her sister. "Are you all right?"

Coughing, Penny nodded. "Thanks to Mr. Dunbar."

Jessalynn turned to Orion. "Thank you so much." She led Penny away.

Orion held out Tilly's cape. "I think I ruined your cape. It's a little singed, and I got soot on it. I'll replace it."

"Nonsense. It would have had a lot more damage if I had been the one to go inside a burning building. And I'm sure it will all wash out." Tilly moved Orion across the street and pointed to the boardwalk. "You sit. You've done enough."

He studied the tangle of people battling the blaze. "I need to get back to the bucket brigade."

"The fire wagon is here. They'll do more than you can at the moment. Now sit."

"I could help with the hand pump."

"There are plenty of men to take care of that. You breathed in a lot of smoke." She pressed down on his shoulder. Not enough to make him sit, but he did anyway.

He gazed up at her. A deep worry line creased between her eyebrows. She was right, and he liked having her fuss over him. If it wasn't for Tilly fretting over him, he would be back at the front of the line. He drank in her attention.

Had she truly been worried for him? Could she possibly care enough? He would have thought she would be pleased if she could be rid of him. Evidently not. He definitely liked her fussing.

He coughed again, repeatedly this time.

She patted him on the back. "See, I was right. You're staying put right here, and I'm going to make sure you do."

She was rather endearing with all her demands. He would gladly stay anywhere near her. And since the others had the situation well in hand, he wouldn't feel guilty about it.

Her eyebrows pulled down. "Why are you smiling?"

"Am I?" *Because you're so enchanting, standing over me all protective.*

"You could have been killed in there."

"I guess I'm glad to be alive." *And to be with you.* He patted the wood flooring next to him. "Sit."

She folded her arms. "So you can run back into danger once my guard is down?"

He chuckled. "No. So I don't have to get back on my feet because a lady is standing." He patted the floor again. "Please. Don't make me get up."

She heaved a sigh and sat. Not as close as he would have liked, but close enough.

The surge of energy coursing through his body from fighting the fire and then pulling the girl out of the building picked up its pace with Tilly so near.

She could fuss over him anytime.

Chapter 7

The next day, Tilly peered out the mercantile window to Orion's blacksmith shop across the street. A smiling Penny Fairmont, Jessalynn's fifteen-year-old sister, stood with him in the large open doorway. Penny's arms moved around energetically as she spoke.

Orion seemed to be listening intently with what appeared to be his pre-smile curve of his lips.

What was he doing with a girl far too young for him? Tilly needed to find out the particulars of their exchange. Not for herself, of course, but to let her friend know if anything concerning was going on between the pair that Jessalynn should know about.

"I'll be back in a minute, Pa." Grabbing her shawl, she headed for the door. The bell jingled overhead on her way out. A strange feeling coiled around inside of her she didn't understand. It felt like. . .like—*Oh dear*—like jealousy. No, she must be mistaken, confusing her budding friendship for something more. Besides, Orion couldn't possibly be interested in Penny, could he? No. That didn't sit right with Tilly.

She stepped off the boardwalk and hesitated while a wagon rolled by with a jangle of the traces. She skirted around the back of the conveyance and hustled across the dusty street.

Penny's hands continued to flutter about. "I can't believe you came in after me, and you moved that big heavy shelf. You must be really strong."

Oh my. Penny was flirting with Orion. Why was he letting her?

"It wasn't that heavy. Just a few boards."

Was he flirting back? That strange feeling inside Tilly coiled tighter.

"I need to get back to work. Thank your sister for the muffins."

"Oh, I made those."

Orion nodded stiffly. "Thank you." He shifted his gaze to Tilly. His smile bloomed to a full one, lighting his face and sending her insides flitting about like a happy hummingbird. "Good afternoon, Tilly." He took two steps toward her. "What can I do for you?"

Tilly hadn't realized she'd already walked all the way across the street and stood a few feet from the pair. "I don't want to interrupt. I can wait until the two of you are through."

Orion turned back to Penny and shifted about. "Tell Jessalynn I'll be by later to take a look at her stove and reinstall the stovepipe to it. Have her make a list of anything else she needs help with."

Penny frowned. "I'll come back later for the bowl and napkin." She pointed to the items.

"Oh, I hate to trouble you." He pulled a clean, pressed handkerchief out of his back pocket and spread it out on his work surface. He folded back the corners of the blue-checkered napkin and placed the four muffins within on the white cloth. He handed the bowl with the napkin to Penny. "There you go. Thank you. I'll eat them later."

Though Orion looked genuinely pleased to have spared the girl some trouble, Penny seemed distraught at no longer having an excuse to return. She clutched the bowl to her stomach. "You're welcome." Her gaze darted between the handsome blacksmith and Tilly as if she was trying to figure out a plausible reason to stay. "I. . .I'll see you later." She spun around and hurried off.

Tilly shifted her gaze from the retreating girl to Orion. "That was nice of you to offer to help Jessalynn get her café fixed up. Closing because of the fire will really hurt her business."

"That's what neighbors are for." A mischievous twinkle danced in his coffee-brown eyes. "I do have an ulterior motive."

Oh dear. Tilly's insides tightened again. Please don't let him be interested in Penny after all. He seemed completely unaware of the girl's attraction to him. If he had noticed, he would have made more of an effort to flirt back. Then could Jessalynn have piqued his interest? Did he have his cap set for Tilly's best friend?

He rubbed a hand across his chin and strong jawline. "I'll miss the meals. I eat there several times a week."

Food was his motivation? Typical man. Tilly's insides uncoiled. "We can't have our town's only blacksmith growing weak from lack of nourishment. Would you like to come to supper at our place? I'm sure my folks wouldn't mind."

His face brightened. "I'd like that a lot."

She stood there silent, gazing back at him. What should she do? Should she say something else? "Penny's sweet on you."

His expression changed from dreamy to horrified in an instant. "No. No. She isn't. The muffins were just a thank-you for helping them. They didn't mean anything."

How naive. "They might not have meant anything to you, but I can assure you, they meant a lot to her."

His gaze darted back and forth, then he flashed her his smile. "I'm sure you misinterpreted it. I'm too old for her."

Tilly noticed he hadn't said that she was too young for him. Interesting. "Nine years isn't so much. Many a young girl has daydreamed about older men. Boys her own age behave like. . .well, like boys her age. They lack the maturity an older man has. Besides, you rescued her from certain death. That planted the seed of romance, watered it, and made it grow into a full-size tree overnight."

He shook his head. "That's not possible from one little event. You have quite the imagination. Her life wasn't even in any real danger. The smoke made it hard to see, and a shelf had blocked her escape. I didn't do all that much."

Tilly tried not to laugh at his discomfort. Jessalynn had nothing to worry about. This attraction was clearly one-sided. "Whether her life was in danger or not, *she* believed it to be *and* believes you saved her. The big, strong blacksmith moved the heavy, enormous shelves."

He shook his head. "Now you're teasing me."

But she wasn't, not really. That's exactly how Penny viewed the events.

He picked up his handkerchief, careful not to drop any of the baked treats. "Muffin?"

She smiled and shook her head. "Your adoring admirer made those for her hero who plucked her from death's door." She wiggled her fingers in a wave. "See you for supper." She headed off across the street.

Orion couldn't see what was right in front of his face. She almost felt sorry for him when he would next encounter Penny. Almost.

Orion hoisted his open toolbox and headed for Jessalynn's café. He hated that Tilly thought there might be something between him and Penny. Though sweet, the girl couldn't under any circumstance have feelings for him. Could Tilly possibly be jealous? He smiled at that thought.

The front wall of the kitchen of the Hollow Belly Café had more or less been burned out altogether. The volunteer firefighters who'd brought the fire wagon had determined that the fire had likely been started when someone tossed out a lit cigarette that caught the curtains in the open window on fire. No way to know who had been careless. Though not Jessalynn's fault, she suffered the consequences and lost business.

He turned the knob on the front door. Locked. He strode to the burned portion and stepped through an opening. "The front door's locked."

Jessalynn turned and gave him an appreciative smile. "Sorry. Habit. I'm on my way out. I need to talk to Mr. Tolen at the bank about having only a partial payment."

Conrad. "If he gives you any trouble, let me know."

"I'm sure he's a reasonable man."

Orion was sure he wasn't. "Do you want me to come back later?"

Penny, whom he hadn't noticed standing off to the side, spoke up. "I'll be here. I can help him." She scooted closer to Orion.

Jessalynn swung her shawl around her shoulders. "Don't get in his way."

"What do you need me to look at first?"

"The stovepipe is bent and has a leak that's letting smoke into the room. As though I don't have enough smoke smell in this place from the fire."

He glanced at the stovepipe with three separate cloths tied around it in different places. That would never work. And what if they caught fire?

"When I plugged up one hole, the smoke found someplace else to escape from. We were trying to cook on the stove, but I fear it's hopeless."

"But I did bake the muffins in it." Penny beamed.

Orion studied the girl a moment, then shifted his gaze back to Jessalynn. "I'll fix it."

"Thank you so much. I really appreciate this. You will have free meals here for life."

"I can't do that. I'm glad to help." He would help her anyway, but knew this could earn him some forgiveness from Tilly by helping her best friend.

"When I open back up, you will be receiving at least some free meals. At the very least free desserts." Jessalynn exited the kitchen, went through the dining room, and out the front door. Then she shrugged and gave him a smile as she passed by the burned opening she could have easily left through.

Penny held up a steaming pie. "I made you an apple pie." She gazed at him in the way he hoped Tilly would look at him.

His former pleasant thought of Tilly's potential jealousy evaporated in a flash. She had been right about Penny and also right to have warned him.

"Do you want me to cut you a piece?"

Suddenly feeling like a trapped animal, he swallowed hard. "I'm not hungry. I have work to do. You don't have to stay." He crossed to the hot stove. He couldn't work on heated metal. "Do you have a cinder pail?"

"See, you do need me." Penny reached behind the stove and handed him the black bucket.

The girl stood nearby, seeming to have no plans to leave his side. He couldn't work with her here. Alone. It wasn't prudent. What kind of errand could he send her on? A better idea popped into his head, and he rifled through his toolbox. "I need to go back to my blacksmith shop for a tool. Would you scoop out the coals from the stove while I'm gone so it can start cooling?"

"I'd love to." Penny's smile widened, and she crouched in front of the open stove door to get to work.

Tilly had been so right. "I'll be back in a few minutes." His voice sounded strained to himself. He hurried out through the burned wall, the quickest exit.

Hoofing it as fast as he could, he reached the mercantile and went inside. Mr. Rockford sat on a stool behind the counter with his broken leg propped up on a chair. "Is Tilly here?"

"Good afternoon to you too, Orion." Mr. Rockford smiled broadly.

"Pardon my ill manners. Good afternoon. I kind of have a problem that I need Tilly's help with."

"You do look quite perplexed. You'll find her in the storage room."

"Thank you." Orion rounded the counter and headed to the back.

Tilly stood on a small A-frame ladder, reaching toward the top shelf. Just the sight of her calmed him. She would fix this trouble with Penny.

Even though he took a slow breath first, the sharp tone in his voice betrayed his desperation. "I need your help."

Tilly squealed in surprise and tottered on the ladder. One foot lifted into the air, and her hands flailed about. "Ahhhhhh."

Orion rushed over and caught her in his arms, holding her against his chest. "I didn't mean to scare you."

"Oh, you didn't. I just wasn't expecting anyone."

"And therefore I scared you."

"I guess so, but you didn't mean to."

No, he hadn't. Just like he hadn't meant to ruin her dress all those years ago, but the result had still been bad. Hopefully, preventing her from falling and getting injured would wipe out his scaring her.

He lowered her feet to the floor but kept an arm around her for stability.

His own.

Grateful for his strong arm keeping her upright, Tilly gazed at Orion a moment. "You needed help with something?"

He gazed back. "You seemed to be the one who needed help. What were you reaching for? I'll get it."

She pointed. "The pair of oil lamps."

Releasing her, he stepped up onto the lowest ladder rung.

She felt the absence of his nearness. She would have thought she would be glad he moved away.

He handed down the items.

"Thank you."

"You're welcome." He stepped off the ladder. "Do you need me to reach anything else?"

She thought hard for something to keep him here. "No. That's all I was after. Oh, wait. You came for some reason besides to help me."

His eyes widened as though he remembered his mission, then he frowned, and the words tumbled out. "That's right. I need your help. I think you were right about Penny. I need you to talk to her and make her stop being sweet on me." His frown deepened. "You have to know I'm not interested in her. She's a sweet girl, but I'm not interested. She's at the café. Come back with me and talk to her."

"I'm sure it will pass." Crushes usually did. "In time, someone else will capture her interest."

"Please, you have to come. Jessalynn went to the bank. She made me a pie. In a broken stove."

"Jessalynn?"

"No, Penny. No one else is at the café. I told her I needed to get a tool, and I just left. Walked right through the burned-out wall."

Getting a little taste of the discomfort he'd caused others? If she wasn't painfully aware of all the turmoil he'd caused her over the years, she might feel sorry for him. He was almost adorable.

Almost.

"All right. I'll go to the café." She left the back room carrying one of the lamps and set it on the counter. "Here are the lamps."

Orion set the other one next to it.

Pa reached for one. "Thank you. I'll get them dusted off and ready for Mrs. Hawkins."

Tilly settled her shawl on her shoulders. "I'm going out for a few minutes. I'll be back soon." She stepped outside with Orion on her heels. She stopped and faced him. "What are you doing?"

"Taking you to the café."

"Where's the tool?"

"What tool?"

"The one you told Penny you left to retrieve."

"I didn't really need a tool. I already have everything I need there."

"You can't arrive with me or else she'll know you came to get me, and that will embarrass her."

"Should I wait until you come back?"

"I'll go to the café. You go to your blacksmith shop and get a tool, any tool, and then return to the café. That way, she won't know you came to get me."

"That makes a lot of sense. I'll see you there." He strode off across the street.

Tilly gazed after him. Adorable. Seeing him flustered like this tickled her heart. Simply adorable. *Stop thinking about him. Especially that way. You have a mission.* She pulled her shawl tighter and headed for the café. She entered through the front door. "Jessalynn?" The lingering smell of smoke from yesterday's fire hung in the air, and a thin layer of soot no doubt covered everything.

"In here." Not Jessalynn's voice but Penny's, as to be expected.

Tilly headed for the kitchen. "Good afternoon, Penny. Is your sister here?"

Penny sat on the floor in front of the open stove, shoveling coals and ashes out through the open door. "Jess is at the bank."

"Thank you. I'll head over there and see if she's done."

The damage to the place didn't seem as bad as she'd thought it would be.

She could step through the wall, as that exit would be slightly closer to her destination, but that seemed wrong, so she left the way she'd come.

The building next door had been constructed of brick, so it hadn't caught fire. The whole town was fortunate the blaze had been contained so quickly. But there would be no cooking in this kitchen for a while.

At the bank, she waited outside, having no desire to run into Mr. Tolen. She didn't have to stand there long.

Her friend came out.

"Jessalynn."

Jessalynn smiled. "Tilly, what are you doing here?"

"I need to talk to you." Tilly pointed to the bank. "Did it go well?"

Jessalynn nodded. "Mr. Tolen gave me an extension on my mortgage payment and is considering an additional loan for the café repairs. Can you talk to me while we walk?"

"Of course. It's about Penny."

"Is she all right? Did she get hurt?" Jessalynn picked up her pace.

"No, she's fine." Tilly touched her friend's arm to slow her down. "But she does seem to be infatuated with Orion since he rescued her yesterday."

"What do you mean?"

"She visited his blacksmith shop earlier." That strange coiling feeling returned in the middle of her chest. "She'd made him muffins. In a broken stove."

"Oh no. What should I do?"

"Whatever you do, don't tell her I talked to you about this. I think it will blow over, but it has Orion flustered. And don't tell her that either. Maybe keep her too busy to pay any attention to Orion or something."

"I can do that. There's plenty that needs to be done. I promise she won't bother you and Orion again."

"Me and Orion? What's that supposed to mean?"

"You came here to speak on his behalf, and I saw the way you fussed over him at the fire."

"I didn't fuss over him. Plenty of people were seeing to the fire, and he was coughing from all the smoke he inhaled. I wasn't fussing."

"Right. Not fussing."

"I wasn't."

"Does Orion know that? Because he seemed to be enjoying your attention. A lot."

That couldn't be true. Tilly opened her mouth several times, but no words came out, only an occasional sound.

Chapter 8

Orion squinted his eyes as he approached the mercantile, trying to see if he could catch a glimpse of Tilly inside.

She sat at the small desk in the corner. The bell over the door jingled with his entry. Tilly brightened at his presence. Or was that just his wishful dreaming?

She stood and crossed over to him. “Good day. Can I help you with anything?”

Orion could feel his mouth trying to pull into a smile at the sight of her, but he didn’t want to seem too eager. “I’m sure you can.”

He rattled off a list of items. Though he could locate them all himself, he drank in the attention from her. He had intended the list to help him ease into his question, but nothing made a good transition to his inquiry.

Once everything sat on the counter, she wrote down the prices, taking her time.

Drawing in several controlled breaths failed to help him figure out how to ask. Almost finished here, he would have to leave. If he didn't speak up now, he would need to arrange another meeting. Maybe Sunday at church. Yes, Sunday might be a better time.

From the corner of his eye, movement outside caught his attention. Another customer approached the door. Too late for much of a conversation now. But then he noticed who was closing in.

Conrad Tolen.

Orion's mouth opened, spilling out words. "Did you know there's a social at church after the Christmas Eve service next week?"

She gazed up at him. "Ma told me."

Conrad opened the door with a jingle.

When Tilly smiled at the man, Orion's invitation to the social lodged in his throat.

"Good day, Mr. Tolen. Let me know if you need anything." Tilly returned to her meticulous figuring of the numbers for Orion's purchase.

Conrad sidled up to the counter. "There is something only you can help me with."

Tilly's congenial expression dipped, and she set down her pencil. Then she shifted her gaze to Orion. "You don't mind waiting, do you? I'm sure this will only take a moment."

"Don't mind at all." He had feared she would hurry up his order, and he'd be forced to depart, leaving Conrad alone with Tilly.

Tilly turned an amiable smile on Conrad, but Orion thought it appeared a bit forced. "How may I help you?"

"I don't want to interrupt what you're doing."

Orion waved a hand over the counter. "I'm in no hurry." He would take every minute he could get with Tilly.

Tilly rested her hands on the counter. "What do you need, Mr. Tolen?"

Conrad took one of Tilly's hands. "I need you to accompany me to the Christmas Eve social."

No! That was what Orion had planned to do. *And let go of her hand.* How dare he take such liberties.

Tilly freed her hand. "I'm sorry. Orion just asked me about the social."

Orion turned his gaze from her unfettered hand to her face. He *had* asked *about* the social but hadn't gotten around to asking her to go *to* the social with him.

Conrad's smile fell. "You're going with *him*?"

Orion didn't care for Tolen's implication of his not being good enough.

"He did ask about the social first."

Why did Tilly make it sound as though he'd asked her to attend with him?

"Is there anything else I can help you with?"

Conrad glanced at each of them in turn, shook his head, and left.

Orion stared after his rival, then turned back to Tilly.

Shyness played on her face. "I'm sorry about that."

She was sorry? He wasn't. He leaned on the counter. "You can make it up to me."

"I can?"

"Let me escort you to the social." His chest tightened. He'd done it now.

Her smile filled her eyes before spreading to her lips. "That would be most agreeable."

His chest relaxed. Agreeable? Really? He breathed in and out several times, quickly. "So, that's a yes?"

"Yes."

Tilly's tight insides loosened as she watched Orion cross the street to his livery. Why had she said yes? She hadn't meant to. Surprise rolled over her as she realized she wanted to go with Orion, and she wanted the night to be a good one. She would wear her new dress. But first she had to tell Jessalynn.

Tilly stepped into the back room. "Ma, I'm going to the café to talk to Jessalynn."

Ma stopped counting spools of thread. "Will you be long?"

"I shouldn't be."

"Tell Jessalynn hello from me."

Tilly put on her cape and hurried out the door.

Orion had disappeared into his livery.

She still couldn't believe she'd said yes.

At the café, she entered and went straight to the kitchen.

Jessalynn, along with her younger sister and brother, was cleaning soot from the walls and surfaces.

Tilly pointed to the burned wall. "You got it boarded up."

"After repairing my stove, which doesn't leak a bit, Orion returned later in the day with some old lumber he had lying around and made my second entrance disappear."

"That was nice of him." Tilly would have to remember to thank him.

Penny narrowed her eyes at Tilly, dropped her rag in the dirty water, and disappeared through the swinging doors to the dining room.

Jessalynn waved a hand in her sister's direction. "Don't mind her. Drew, you can take a break too, but don't go far." After her brother left, Jessalynn gave Tilly her full attention. "So?"

"Soooo. . .what?"

"You have that look. You came with news."

Jessalynn knew her so well. She'd missed having her close friend to talk to while she had been away.

The words bubbled from her. "Orion is escorting me to the Christmas Eve service and social."

"I'm happy for you."

Tilly told her friend how it came about.

"So you coerced the poor man into taking you."

"No." Had she?

Jessalynn tilted her head and put her hands on her hips.

What if Orion had asked her only out of obligation because she had implied it? She couldn't have very well turned him down after her insinuation. And in turn, maybe he'd felt as though he *had* to invite her.

No. He could have simply told her that he would see her there and walked out.

Still, her jubilance withered.

Tilly stewed for two days over Orion's invitation. One part of her argued that if he hadn't really wanted to escort her, he shouldn't have asked, and he would just have to live with it. But then another part ached to know if he truly *wanted* to be her escort.

So here she stood next to his cold forge. Where was he? "Orion?"

No answer.

"Orion?"

Peaches came out from Orion's quarters and rubbed against her. Tilly squatted and petted the calico. "Where's your master?" She straightened, then walked through the livery and out the back door.

Orion stood in one of the corrals with the black-and-white Palouse horse. He had a blanket on the horse's back and lowered a saddle into place.

She could see the powerful muscles in Orion's arms and back flexing under his blue shirt. She stood perfectly still a few feet away from the enclosure, not wanting to spook the horse.

The Palouse turned his head to Orion and neighed a warning.

Orion spoke calmly to the horse. "Easy, boy. You know you can trust me." He reached under the horse and buckled the belly strap.

The Palouse momentarily lifted his front hooves off the ground a foot in protest but didn't rear completely. Instead, he pawed the dirt.

Orion patted the horse's neck. "See. That's not so bad."

The horse trotted around the corral and stopped at the fence closest to Tilly.

Orion saw her then and smiled. "Howdy."

Since he'd smiled, that must mean he was at least a little pleased to see her. Maybe that was enough to assume he didn't regret inviting her. She raised her hand to shade her eyes as she walked up to the fence. "Hello. I see you're making progress with the Palouse."

"We've come to an understanding. He's not happy with the saddle, but he's tolerating it." Orion bent and stepped through the fence rails. "What brings you my way? Come to visit Banjo?"

"Not today." She didn't want to make assumptions with him. She wanted to know for sure. She took a deep breath. Just get it over with. "It has come to my attention..." He didn't need to know it was two days ago "...that you—I mean that I...Well, I might have..."

He shifted, leaning one hip against the fence post, patiently watching her as she struggled to explain herself.

She started again. "I made a grievous breach in etiquette to insinuate that you had asked to take me to the Christmas Eve social. I do hope you didn't feel pressured into being my escort. That was not my intent at all, and I don't want you to feel obligated in any way. I hadn't expected to go with anyone but my parents. Then Mr. Tolen came in and you were standing there. He asked, then you asked. So if you would rather not escort me—I mean, you could have had some other girl in mind to ask. It's not like you couldn't. I've been away. You could have a sweetheart." That thought troubled her. And she had resorted to babbling again. She seemed to be doing that a lot with him. "So if you would like to take it back, I will understand. No hard feelings."

His mouth hitched up on one side, and he had that mischievous glint in his eyes like in his youth. "Now why would I want to take it back when I'll have the prettiest girl in town on my arm?"

She weakened under his intense gaze. She squared her shoulders to steady herself. "So you don't have a girl who has captured your attention?"

He pushed away from the fence post. "Oh, there is a girl." He swallowed hard, as though nervous. "And she is standing in front of me."

"Me?"

He nodded.

Ma had been right. "Then why push me down and act mean toward me? My ma said that was because you wanted my attention."

"Sounds about right."

"You know there were better ways."

"I do now." He took a step toward her.

"Is that why you gave me Banjo?"

Another step. "I figured a kitten might be worth a visit or two from you. I wanted you to see I'm not the same ruffian I was as a boy. I have better ideas of how to capture a pretty girl's attention."

He stood toe to toe with her.

She tilted her head back.

The muscles in his neck and jaw flexed.

A strand of hair blew across her face.

Orion pushed it away, brushing her cheek with his finger.

She licked her lips.

He leaned down.

She tingled all over.

Just as his lips touched hers, someone called out from inside the livery.

"Orion?"

Orion swallowed hard and stepped back. He moved toward the open door. "I'm back here, Brent." Once Tilly had arrived, he'd forgotten all about Brent coming to help him work with the horses this afternoon.

He raked a hand through his hair. What had he just done? Kissed Tilly Rockford. She had been so cute and irresistible. He hadn't thought about what he was doing. Just focused on her rosy lips that seemed to beckon him forward.

Good thing Brent had shown up when he did, or Orion could have been on the receiving end of a good, solid slap. He still might be, at a later time.

Brent walked through the open doorway. Brent had been his friend since he'd arrived in town fourteen years ago. He and Brent had gotten into plenty of mischief.

"Brent, you know Tilly."

Brent doffed his hat and bowed. "Tilly. I heard you were back in town."

Tilly aimed her wide, giddy smile at Brent. "Hello, Brent. You're looking well."

Orion's insides contracted as though he'd eaten rotten fruit. He would've rather received the slap than watch Tilly smiling at Brent. Or any man.

"You're looking quite fine yourself. I hope I'm not interrupting anything."

He had, but Orion said, "Just showing Tilly the horses."

Brent turned to Tilly and flashed his beguiling smile. "That's what I came to see Orion about. Horses. And to interrupt anything he might be doing."

"I'll leave you two men to your business."

Brent put his hand on his chest. "You don't have to leave on my account. I did interrupt something, didn't I?"

Tilly's cheeks highlighted a pretty shade of pink. "I should be getting back to the store."

"I'll walk you out," Orion said.

"That's not necessary. I've taken enough of your time."

She hadn't taken nearly enough of his time, and now she was dismissing him. He watched her disappear inside the dark interior of the livery, and his chest tightened.

Brent chuckled. "You still have it bad for her."

He swung around to face his friend. "Don't start."

"I haven't even begun." Brent smiled again, wide and wily. "Does she know you've been pining for her all these years?"

Tilly had no idea about his long-held feelings for her. "I'm escorting her to the Christmas Eve social."

"*You* asked her?"

"I did."

"And *she* accepted?"

"She did."

"Tilly?"

"Yes."

Brent shook his head. "Now how did that come about?"

Orion rubbed the back of his neck. "Well, she sort of backed herself into a corner to get out of going with someone else."

"And you took advantage of her misfortune." Brent clamped a hand on Orion's shoulder. "I'm proud of you."

"I didn't take advantage of her. I–I. . ." What had he done? Her rambling about her forcing him into asking her might have actually been her attempt to get out of the arrangement. He sighed. He *had* taken advantage of her. Or at least the situation. He didn't care. Tilly had agreed to go with him. It would give him another chance to show her he had changed. Show her she could trust him.

"You took advantage of her. That's all right. She's a pretty little filly. I would have done the same thing if I would have been the one to find her backed in a corner."

He wished Brent didn't have that knowing smirk on his lips. This would prove to be a long afternoon.

Chapter 9

Tilly hurried straight to the café. She waved to Penny, who stood on a chair scrubbing the walls. The girl didn't wave back. She needed time to get over Orion. Tilly understood Penny's attraction to him and let her be. Tilly bounded into the kitchen.

Jessalynn wiped her wooden cutting surface with a soot-stained rag. "All I seem to be doing is moving the grime around." She tossed the cloth into her bucket of cloudy water. "By the grin on your face, you have something fun and interesting to tell me. I'll get us some coffee, and we can sit in the other room."

Tilly grabbed a couple of white ceramic mugs and held them out.

Her friend poured the dark hot brew and returned the pot to the stove. "Thanks to Orion, my stove is in perfect working order." She lowered her voice. "I saw how Penny was acting toward him and had a little talk with her. She wasn't happy, but I think she understands." She led the way into the other room and to the far side with less smoke damage.

Penny climbed off her perch and went into the kitchen.

Jessalynn leaned forward. "Give her time."

Tilly knew the yearnings of a youngster's heart. No amount of logic could convince it not to long for that certain someone special. The problem was that the girl's someone special was also Tilly's.

"Tell me the good news that has put that smile on your face."

The kiss Tilly had shared with Orion leaped to the forefront of her mind. "I just came from the livery."

Jessalynn nodded. "That explains your grin."

"I felt bad about coercing him—as you said—into taking me to the social. So I told him he didn't have to take me if he didn't want to."

"I can guess what he said."

"That he wanted to take me. . ."

"Of course."

". . .then. . .he kissed me."

Jessalynn's eyes widened. "He kissed you?"

She nodded. "Sort of."

"Sort of? Either he kissed you or he didn't."

"His lips just touched mine when someone came into the livery." She hadn't even gotten to fully enjoy the kiss. Just the hint of what could have been. And what could have been would have been wonderful.

Jessalynn squealed. "I'm so happy for you. I hope to find love one day too."

"Love? I've just returned. I'm not in love with him." Too soon to be calling the confusion inside her *love*.

Jessalynn narrowed her eyes. "Say his name."

"What?"

"Just say his name."

Tilly's mouth stretched wide. "Orion."

"There it is. That smile. You're in love."

Tilly thought a moment about how happy she felt when she was near him and how he occupied most of her thoughts. Was she in love? She believed she could be. She giggled. "It feels wonderful." Amazing how her feelings for Orion could change in so short a time. "I wonder if he feels the same. He's been so nice since I returned."

"That's because he's trying to make up for being so mean to you. He's always been in love with you."

Ma had said that as well. "I don't think so. He's been nice to my folks." Tilly rushed on so Jessalynn couldn't say that was because of her. "And I'm sure other folks in town as well."

"His kindness has been focused on you. He's trying to make up for the past."

She had sensed that as well.

"Remember when you left, I asked you if you would be leaving your heart with any special fellow here?"

She nodded. "I said no." Which had been true.

Jessalynn waved a hand in the direction of the livery. "I fed that man chocolate cake, blueberry pie, peach cobbler, cookies, and an array of other goodies to gain his attention. All I received in return were inquiries about you. Asking if you had a beau in Baltimore. Did I know when you might return? Were you coming for a visit?"

Ma had said he'd done the same thing with her.

"That man pined for you the whole time you were away."

Then why hadn't he written? "You eventually gave up on him?" She didn't want to steal her best friend's fellow.

"My folks passed, and I couldn't think about flirting with a man in love with someone else anymore. I had to support Penny and Drew."

Love? Her friend thought Orion was in love with her? Doubtful, but she liked the thought that he could be.

Tilly stayed and helped Jessalynn scour a layer of soot from the kitchen counters. When she finally left, Orion stood outside on the boardwalk, leaning against the support post. Her mouth pulled up, and her heart fluttered at the sight of him. Jessalynn had been right about her feelings for Orion. Love felt nice.

She indicated the front of the café. "That was nice of you to board up the opening for Jessalynn."

"I was glad to do it." He doffed his hat. "Tilly, I need to speak with you."

"What is it?"

He turned his hat in his hands.

Was he nervous?

Oh dear. Her elation sank. "You changed your mind about the social after all, didn't you?" She held her breath.

"Of course not. I may have grown up since I was a kid, but I still know when the advantage is in my favor. And I intend to keep it."

She released her breath. "Then what?"

"I'm sorry for kissing you."

Her mood sank deeper. "What do you mean you're sorry?" She didn't want him to regret his action.

"I'm just sorry."

Did he not want to kiss her? Or almost kiss her? "You're sorry you kissed me?"

"That's what I said." He pulled his eyebrows together in confusion.

"So you didn't *want* to kiss me?"

"No. I very much wanted to kiss you. I've wanted to for a long time. I just didn't think it appropriate. I thought maybe you were mad at me for it. That you thought I had taken advantage of you and been too forward. If we weren't standing on the boardwalk and I didn't think you might slap me for it, I'd kiss you again. A real kiss this time."

Her earlier elation spiraled up inside her again, and she struggled to keep a smile at bay. "It is too bad we are standing out here. Because you would find out that I would not slap you for your efforts." She couldn't believe her own boldness. She had just flirted with Orion Dunbar. Unbelievable.

His eyebrows rose slowly. "So you *wanted* me to kiss you?"

Wanted? She hadn't known she had until he did it, but she couldn't tell him she looked forward to the next time. She'd been bold enough for one afternoon. "Let's just say I wasn't opposed to it." Her insides swirled at her audacity to admit that. Her aunt would have been appalled.

He gazed at her as though contemplating something. After a long moment, he smashed on his hat, took two steps away from her, and turned back. "Can I walk you home?"

Though the mercantile wasn't more than a few doors down the boardwalk, she hooked her hand around his offered elbow. "Thank you." How thrilling. She'd never felt like this with a gentleman caller before, and her great-aunt had sent many her way.

Something had just changed between her and Orion. They had told each other they were attracted to the other without actually saying so. The discord between them gone.

Once at the general store, Orion stopped. "Is there anything I can help you with? Any chores you need done?"

"I don't think so, but thank you for offering."

"Do you mind if I ask your pa?"

"I'm sure we can manage. You have your livery to run."

He stared at her, his coffee eyes beseeching her to let him help.

"If you want to ask him, I won't stop you."

Orion opened the door for her.

Pa sat behind the counter, casted leg propped up. "Howdy, Orion."

"Howdy, Mr. Rockford."

"It's Henry to you."

"Henry." Orion removed his hat. "Is there anything I can do for you?"

"As a matter of fact, there is. The stagecoach line delivered two crates. Left them on the front boardwalk. If you could take them into the storeroom, I'd be most obliged." Pa turned to her. "Tilly, would you show him where to put them?"

How had she missed seeing them a moment ago? Distracted by a handsome blacksmith was how.

Orion retrieved the first crate, and Tilly directed him. She waited in the storeroom while he fetched the second one, then addressed him when he hauled it in.

"I know what you're doing, Orion Dunbar."

Orion stacked the crate on top of another one and lifted his brown gaze to her. "What? Helping out?"

"Your motive behind helping. You're trying to earn forgiveness by doing good deeds."

"I have a lot to amend for."

"It doesn't work that way. You can't earn forgiveness. If you *earn* it, then it's not really forgiveness."

"I don't deserve forgiveness."

"None of us do. But the Lord freely gives His forgiveness to us."

"You deserve it. You have always been kind."

She took a deep breath. "Not on the inside." She knew just how uncharitable she could be. She'd been impatient with her aging great-aunt who complained about every little thing. And like Mr. Tolen, she thought herself better than Orion. Not because of money like the banker, but because of the goodness Orion spoke of. "Will you forgive me for my insolence toward you?"

"You have never done one bad thing to me."

"I have had disparaging thoughts. I'm sure in my youth I said an unkind word or two about you to others. 'All have sinned, and come short of the glory of God.'"

"I more so than others."

He couldn't see that he was as deserving of forgiveness as the next person. He didn't believe she could forgive him and therefore couldn't forgive himself. But he was the only one holding a grudge now.

Against himself.

Maybe when he saw the dress she was making with the fabric he'd bought, he would stop dwelling on the past. Then he could look to the future with hope.

"Outside the café, you made a bold declaration about what you would do if we weren't standing on the boardwalk."

His mouth hitched up on one side. "That I did." He moved closer. "And I'm a man of my word." He cupped her face with his warm hands and lowered his head.

Tilly rose up on her toes and met his lips.

Chapter 10

The day of Christmas Eve, Tilly stood with Orion in the mercantile by the far window. Pa sat behind the counter at the opposite end of the store.

Orion shifted uneasily. “I considered what you said about forgiveness. Though I still don’t feel deserving, please forgive me for getting all those dresses of yours muddied.”

She’d thought he had finished asking forgiveness for things of the past. “Of course.”

“Thank you.” He peeked over his shoulder at Pa occupied with a customer. He turned back with a lopsided smile, kissed her quickly on the mouth, and walked away. The customer left, so Orion stopped at the counter.

She stared at his back and realized something. He’d been careful to only apologize for the muddied dresses and not the one ruined with ink. The important one. The one that mattered. Why?

Why?

Why did he purposely avoid that one event?

She shook her head. Why did she insist upon flopping like a fish on dry land? One moment her attraction for Orion held strong, as though he'd never done one mean thing to her in his life. The next, the past reared up, biting her in the backside, reminding her of all the pain he'd caused her.

But he didn't behave like that any longer. Truthfully, the dress being wrecked didn't even upset her anymore. His refusal to acknowledge the event distressed her most.

Let it go. Just let bygones be bygones.

But she couldn't figure out how.

The bell over the door jingled, and Orion stepped outside. She marched after him. "Orion."

He stopped two paces into the street and turned. He smiled and hopped back up onto the boardwalk.

"I don't understand, Orion. You've asked forgiveness for every terrible thing you ever did to me. Except the one that really mattered. Why do you avoid the dress you ruined with ink? I know you remember it. You gave me the fabric."

His smile vanished. "I can never ask forgiveness for that."

That wounded. "Why not?"

"I don't deserve to be forgiven for that."

"Which of us do?" Hadn't he been listening to her the other day?

He raked a hand through his dark hair. "What I saw in your eyes that day was brokenness. Your anger, frustration, and disappointment because of all the other mean things I did to you were nothing compared to that day. I knew I had broken you. I had gone too far. I could never figure out why a spoiled dress would cause you such hurt, but I knew it did. A hurt I could never repair. I thought if I found your cat, Honey Bear, you could forgive me, but I couldn't."

"So you're never going to ask forgiveness for it?"

He shook his head.

But he had with the fabric, and the only apology she needed. "You're right. It was just a silly dress. My pride and vanity put far too much value on that dress. I forgive you." Now that she had said it to his face, the weight of her bitterness lifted. She'd actually forgiven him this time.

"You are too good to me. You always have been." Orion's lips curved gently. His gaze shifted to her mouth.

She wished he would hold her and kiss her again, but Pa and the whole town could see them.

He stepped off the boardwalk and turned back to her. "I'll come for you and your folks at four thirty to take you to the church. We should arrive there early, to get your pa settled in before the rest of the town arrives."

She wasn't as disappointed as she thought she'd be at his departure, because she would have him at her side all evening with the prospect of ending up under the mistletoe. And she would be in her new dress. The dress that would heal both of their pasts.

Later, ready for church and the social, Tilly sat at the small desk in the store, figuring numbers, waiting for Ma and Pa to be ready.

The bell over the door jingled, and she turned in the chair.

Orion stood inside the doorway, dapper in his Sunday suit. His gaze flickered over her as he crossed the room to her. "You look beautiful."

She placed the pen in the holder. She wanted to show him her dress. As she lifted her hand, Orion reached for it. The cuff of his coat sleeve caught on the lip of the inkwell. Sucking in a breath, she grabbed for it, but it tipped over. Ink rolled down the desktop. She shoved her chair backward, but not fast enough. The ink streamed off and onto her skirt.

Tilly stood. "Oh no."

"Not again." Orion pushed his hands into his hair and held his head. "I'm so sorry." He took several steps backward. "I can't do anything right." He fled out the door.

"Orion!" Tilly reached for a rag and wiped at the wet ink soaking through her skirt and into her petticoats. "Orion!"

But he was gone.

Ma hurried halfway down the steps. "What's wrong?"

"It's terrible."

Ma gasped and came the rest of the way down. "Your dress!"

"No, it's worse." The dress didn't matter. It honestly didn't matter.

"What happened?"

"Orion."

"Again?"

"It was an accident. And now he's run off."

Ma took the rag and tossed it in the dustbin. "You aren't doing any good with that."

Pa called down, "Is everything all right?"

"She's fine." Ma put her hands on Tilly's upper arms. "What happened?"

"It was an accident." Tears filled her eyes. "He reached for my hand, and his coat cuff caught on the edge of the inkwell. I tried to grab it in time but couldn't. It was an *accident*."

Ma put her arm around Tilly's shoulders. "Let's get you into a clean dress, and then you can go talk to him."

Tilly wiped her eyes with the back of her hands. "No, I have to go now." She swung her long cape around her shoulders.

"But your dress?"

"I'll change it after I talk to him." She opened the door. "I'll be back soon." She hurried out.

The cold afternoon air slapped her, squelching any further tears.

She maneuvered around the back of the buggy Orion had parked out front. Lifting the front of her stained skirt, she dashed across the street in an unladylike fashion.

The forge sat cold and dark. A patch of dim light splayed out on the hard-packed dirt outside Orion's quarters.

She stepped to the doorway, and his name caught in her throat.

Hunched in a chair, he had the tulip quilt wrapped around him and something small held between his fingers.

Peaches lay in front of the stove, the kittens nursing.

Tilly drew in a breath of hay-scented air. "It was an accident."

Orion startled, turned, and stood all at once. The object in his fingers tumbled out and rolled toward her.

With her ink-stained hand, Tilly picked up the solitaire emerald ring.

"I saw you looking at that in the jeweler case at the department store when we fetched your trunks from Dallas."

She could remember the display but not the ring, not paying particular attention to anything that day except for the two men trying to best each other. "And you went back and bought it?" For her? He couldn't have been that serious about her already.

She held out the ring between her blackened fingers. Her nerves prickled holding it.

He stared at it a moment before taking it. His fingers brushed hers. "It reminded me of your eyes."

Her heart fluttered at his touch.

He grimaced at her skirt. "I can't do anything right."

"Please don't feel bad. You know, someone gave me plenty of this fabric. I can replace the damaged section or make a whole new dress." She hoped to lighten his mood, but he wouldn't meet her gaze. "Orion, it's just a dress."

"But I ruined the same dress twice."

"Which is rather ironic. If you think about it, it's kind of humorous."

"You find it funny?"

Surprisingly, she did. "What are the chances that dresses made out of the same fabric would both be ruined with ink on their first outing?"

He finally lifted his gaze to her. "You aren't mad?"

"All those years ago, I don't think you realized your actions would ruin that first dress. And this one was an accident. You have to believe that."

"Then you'll still let me escort you to the social?"

"Of course."

He stood silent for several seconds. "Will you. . ."

She held her breath. Was she ready for this question?

He swallowed hard. "Will you forgive me for ruining your dress? Both this one and the other one?"

With a touch of disappointment, she released her breath and let her shoulders drop. "I already have." She pointed to the quilt he still wore. "You know I'm the one who made that quilt."

"I know. It saved my life."

"How could a quilt save your life?"

"I'd found where Pa kept his earnings. I was going to run away for the fourth time. With money, I knew I wouldn't be coming back, no matter what. You gave me this quilt, and I couldn't leave. Tulips were my ma's favorite flower. She loved the red ones best."

Tears pooled in Tilly's eyes. She'd had no idea it had meant anything at all to him.

"If. . .if it's all right with you, I'd like to. . .like to ask your pa to. . .to court you."

"I'd like that."

His eyebrows rose. "Truly?"

"I've always cared for you. That first day I saw you, I believe the Lord put you in my heart. That's why it hurt so much when you were mean. I didn't know what to think."

"I don't deserve someone like you." He put his hands on her shoulders and bent forward.

She tilted her head up.

His warm lips pressed down on hers.

Joy coursed through her, causing her skin to tingle all over. She slipped her hands around his waist. He put his arms around her back, wrapping them both in the tulip quilt. This was right where she belonged.

Orion pulled back. "I'm nervous about asking your pa to court you."

"He'll say yes." She tried to turn, but he held her in place. "Pa's at the store."

He kissed her again. "In case he says no to courting you."

"He has already as much as said yes."

"Not to me."

"Yes, to you."

"When?"

"When he invited you to call him by his first name."

He squinted.

She stepped back from him. "Trust me."

He put the quilt on the chair, took her hand, and walked her across the street.

When Orion opened the door to the store, Pa was scurrying on his crutches like a mouse about to be caught. Ma studied the counter, picking at some imaginary spot.

Had they been peering out the window at her and Orion? She turned toward the window. The shaft of light from Orion's living quarters was easily visible. They had seen him kiss her. She felt her cheeks warm.

Ma wiggled her fingers. "Come on, Tilly. Let's get you into a clean dress." Ma took her by the arm and led her up the stairs. "I think that hunter-green velvet dress you brought back from Baltimore will be lovely. It will complement your eyes."

A glorious dress, but not nearly as special as the one made from the fabric Orion had given her.

Orion swallowed hard. His chance to talk to Mr. Rockford alone had come. What if Tilly had been wrong and her pa said no? He had to ask. He had to know. "Mr. Rockford?"

"It's Henry." Henry's eyes gleamed bright and eager.

"Yes, of course, Henry." Orion hoped being invited to use her pa's first name meant what Tilly said it did. He shoved a hand through his hair.

Henry smiled. "Something on your mind, son?"

Orion took a deep breath. "May I court your daughter?"

Henry's expression dipped. "I thought that's what you were already doing."

"I never asked to court her."

"You implied it."

"I did?"

The older man nodded. "You have something else to ask me?"

Orion took a deep breath and shook his head.

"If you didn't think you were courting my daughter, just what are your intentions?"

"Mr.—Henry, I care a great deal for Tilly." He more than cared for her.

Henry narrowed his eyes slightly. "Care a great deal? Is that all?"

Orion shifted his feet. "Actually, I love her." He always had.

"Really." Henry raised his eyebrows. "Your intentions then?"

Orion fingered the ring in his pocket and cleared his throat. "I would very much like to marry Tilly someday. With your permission, of course."

"For a minute, I thought you weren't going to ask."

Orion held his breath. Though seemingly pleased, the older man hadn't answered him.

Henry clapped him on the shoulder. "Yes, son. You can marry my daughter. Now breathe."

Orion let his breath escape.

At the conclusion of the Christmas Eve service, pews had been moved to the edges of the room for the social portion of the evening. Tilly stood with Orion near the refreshment table. "I told you Pa would give his blessing to courting."

"He thought we were already courting. Is that what you thought?"

"Not formally, but I hoped we might be heading there."

"How—what—why would you ever hope *I* would court you? I was never nice to you. I hurt you repeatedly when we were children."

True.

"It's hard to explain. Ever since the day you arrived in town, I felt a special bond with you. I can only attribute it to God. He knew you needed people to connect to you. And because I knew there was something special about you, your misdeeds toward me hurt more. If one of the other boys had done any of the things you did, it would have only made me mad."

"But I *hurt* you, inside."

She nodded. "I know now that wasn't your intent. You just wanted my attention."

"Which I got in a bad way. I'm so sorry."

"You were young and hurting yourself. You didn't understand how to relate to people."

His mouth pulled up on one side. "How to relate to a pretty girl."

His compliment made her smile as well.

Whoops went around the room as another couple kissed under the roving mistletoe. Mr. and Mrs. Jensen this time. The older couple kissed and picked off one of the white berries. The pair of nine-year-old boys wielding the flora snickered.

The mistletoe had been hung from the ceiling, and Tilly had counted no fewer than a dozen couples kiss under it. Most "accidental" encounters had been gerrymandered by the gentleman. Then a group of five teenaged boys had taken the mistletoe down and fastened it to the end of a stick so as to steal kisses from young ladies. When they were done, the two younger boys took up the toy, seeing whom they could get to kiss each other.

Once all the berries had been plucked, the power of the mistletoe would be rendered inert, and any further acceptable kissing in public would be over. Only a couple of the white berries remained.

Tilly pointed to the boys across the room. "How come you haven't tried to maneuver me under the mistletoe?" They had kissed before, so he knew she wouldn't slap him or anything.

"I figured I'd caused you enough undue attention in public that you'd rather I didn't cause you any more."

Mr. Tolen strolled by and held out his hand to Orion.

Orion hesitated before shaking it.

"I believe the better man won." Mr. Tolen gave Tilly a nod and walked away.

That had been surprising, but Tilly sensed that the man harbored insecurities like most everyone else. He boasted to hide his vulnerability. That had been a gallant gesture of him to shake Orion's hand. Now if Penny would only stop shooting daggers with her glares at Tilly.

Jessalynn, standing next to her sister, leaned over to whisper in one of the mistletoe-wielding boy's ears, and pointed. Then she gave Tilly a sly smile.

The boys darted around people, heading straight for Tilly and Orion, and dangled the mistletoe over their heads.

Orion's mouth cocked up on one side. "I can't be blamed for this."

"You won't be." Tilly rose up on her tiptoes and touched his lips with hers.

His strong arms clamped around her for a more hearty kiss than she'd intended, but oh so wonderful.

He broke off the kiss but kept her close. "Courting you wasn't all your pa gave his blessing for." Orion pulled the emerald ring out of his pocket and lowered to one knee. "Tilly, will you—"

"Yes!" The word shot out of her mouth before she had time to think, but undoubtedly the right answer.

". . .be my wife?" He slid the ring onto her finger.

The room erupted into cheers, causing her cheeks to warm.

She angled her hand back and forth to get a better view of the green gemstone.

Orion tilted her head up with a finger under her chin. "I love you, Matilda Rockford."

"I love you too, Orion Dunbar."

He kissed her again, fully. His lips warm and gentle.

She wrapped her arms around his waist and settled in his embrace where she belonged. When she had returned home a few short weeks ago, she'd never expected a reconciliation such as this, but she was so very pleased with all the pleasant changes.

Elated that bygones were bygones.

Mary Davis is a bestselling, award-winning author of over two dozen novels in both historical and contemporary themes, eight novellas, two compilations, three short stories, and has been included in ten collections. She has two brand-new novels releasing in 2019. She is a member of American Christian Fiction Writers. She has led and participated in critique groups for over two decades.

Mary lives in the Pacific Northwest with her husband of over thirty-four years and two cats. She has three adult children and two grandchildren. She enjoys board and card games, rain, and cats. She would enjoy gardening if she didn't have a black thumb. Her hobbies include quilting, porcelain doll making, sewing, crafting, crocheting, and knitting. Visit her online at http://marydavisbooks.com or https://www.facebook.com/mary.davis.73932, and join her FB readers group, Mary Davis READERS Group at https://www.facebook.com/groups/132969074007619/?source=create_flow.

The Bridal Shop

by Grace Hitchcock

Dedication

To Liam, my treasure.

Acknowledgments

To my Dakota, for his encouragement, enthusiasm, and patience to discuss every bit of the plot; to my beta and critique partners for their sage advice; to Debby Lee for her invitation to be a part of this collection; to Tamela Hancock Murray for her guidance and support; and to the Lord for His grace.

He healeth the broken in heart,
and bindeth up their wounds.
PSALM 147:3

Chapter 1

Charleston, South Carolina
Summer 1886

Alice Turner rolled the silver thimble between her fingers and thumb as she stepped aside, watching the bride twirl before the bedroom's gilded looking glass.

The bridesmaid's eyes adopted a hungry expression, gazing at Alice's latest masterpiece of ivory satin and tulle. "I've never seen anything quite as beautiful as this wedding gown. What do you think, Constance? Would your mother have approved?"

The bride's skirts stilled as she picked at the cuff of the gown, causing Alice to stiffen. If Miss Constance Clayton did not approve and word circulated. . . Alice took a tentative step forward, her jaw tensing as she clasped her hands in front of her cream skirts.

"The lacework is unrivaled. I believe Mother would've been pleased." Constance sent Alice an approving nod. "It was a risk engaging a local seamstress for my wedding gown, even someone recommended by such a trusted friend as Mrs. Martin and her daughter, when I could have sent for it from Paris. But my early engagement was not expected, and since my fiancé and I wanted a double wedding with William and Meg, I dared not hope the gown would arrive on time."

Alice nodded at the not-so-subtle reminder that she was only hired because her best friend, Meg, was marrying Constance's brother, William Clayton. She would not squander this chance to break into the elite set, which was why she personally attended to this bride's fitting instead of her assistant.

"Eustace is going to be so pleased." Constance sighed as she ran her hands over the pearl beadwork on the bodice and preened in the looking glass.

Eustace. Alice's heart dipped at the name of her former fiancé. Surely the groom couldn't be *her* Eustace. *Could he?* She despised herself for asking, but she had to know. "Eustace, what a genteel name. He must be from a good family." She paused, waiting for the bride to fill in the surname, but Constance merely nodded, distracted with the demure puffed sleeves, so Alice pressed, "What is his family name? Perhaps I could stitch your initials together on the interior hem to add a touch of sentiment. I would, of course, stitch them with blue thread for your 'something blue' to wear."

"What a lovely idea." Constance turned her back to Alice, motioning for her to unfasten the row of satin covered buttons. "His name is Eustace Merrick."

Not my Eustace. The relief in her shoulders was short-lived, for she didn't know why she was *still* concerned if he had married or not. It had been five years. Five *long* years since he had broken her heart on those courthouse steps. Her fingers fumbled on the last button.

"It will only take me a moment," she whispered and lowered the gown for the bride to step out. Whisking the dress into the corner of the room where she had her sewing supplies stacked beside a Queen Anne chair, she set to work on embroidering the initials in neat, tiny stitches in Eustace's favorite color and wondered if it was still his favorite. *Stop it,* she scolded herself.

Since that horrid day nearly five years ago, she had attempted to put him out of her mind for good, but memories of him were spread across Charleston. The park where they had shared their first kiss beneath the swaying Spanish moss of an oak was on her way to Miss Clayton's, the fountain where he had proposed was only a few blocks from her shop on King Street. . .and the courthouse steps where he had broken her heart was a route she avoided altogether.

Forcing herself to set aside the painful memories, she snipped the ends of the thread with her scissors, shook the gown free from any loose threads, and draped it over her arm to display her handiwork to the bride, causing a squeal and an impromptu hug from the generally rigid Constance Clayton.

Miss Hyacinth Castle, the bridesmaid, ran her finger over the neat stiches as she slowly smiled. "What a clever touch. I'm sure your work will draw the attention of many at the wedding. Now, if you'll excuse us, my friend and I need to ready for the bridal luncheon."

"Of course. And if you have need of anything, day or night,

just send word to this address, and I'll be there." Alice handed them each her business card, dipped into a curtsy, and gathered her things, making her way back to her bridal shop.

Giles Clayton had to get out of the office. After dealing with an excessively demanding customer, he needed a breath of fresh air. Taking a stroll down King Street, he breathed deeply, enjoying the warm, humid breeze as it brought him to life even if it was tinged with the scent of the hired carriages' horses. Anything was favorable to sitting with that client for another minute. He stretched his shoulders, wincing at the stiffness that had set in from hours of sitting at his desk. After the thrill of playing in Wimbledon and years of instructing tennis abroad, banking felt positively suffocating. He missed the excitement of the courts, but with his father's impending retirement, he knew it was time for him to step up and become the man his family needed him to be, a tennis champion turned banker.

At the cheer of some boys in one of the alleyways, he paused to find a ratty baseball landing on the sidewalk in front of him and rolling out toward the busy street. Giles squatted down to catch it and keep it from entering the street, and a resounding rip and a cool breeze greeted him.

Oh no. He jerked to standing and pulled his jacket low to cover what he could of his exposed undergarment as he kicked the ball to the boys and turned his back to the alley wall, trying to gather himself. There were far too many ladies shopping on King Street for him to simply waltz back into his office for his tennis trousers, and if word got out at work, he would be a laughingstock. He might even be arrested for public indecency before he reached home. He scratched his chin. *And to hail a cab would mean to lift my arm. That can't happen with all these people about. Blast.*

Holding his jacket low, he shuffled out toward King Street again, but spying a gaggle of women coming his way, Giles ducked back into the shadow of the building and waited until they had passed before peeking out again onto the street. Squinting in the glare of the sun, he caught sight of a wooden sign depicting a thimble and a spool of thread. THIMBLES AND THREADS BRIDAL SHOP. Giles lifted his face heavenward and groaned. *A bridal shop, Lord? Not to sound ungrateful, but You couldn't have made it a tailor shop? And not some place full of women?* Seeing as he had no other choice, he waddled as quickly as he could to the bridal shop and let himself in, sending the copper bell above the door jingling and announcing his presence. Giles took a quick gander and sighed with relief. No women in sight.

From the back of the shop, a lilting voice greeted him from behind the curtain divider. "Welcome to Thimbles and Threads! Please take a seat. I'll be with you in a minute."

Sinking onto the tufted lavender settee, Giles ran his fingers around the brim of his stiff hat and studied the shop that was painted in a soft mint green and French cream trim. The front windows on either side of the door displayed a massive wedding dress in each along with an array of items to draw customers in from the street to view the well-stocked shelves of lace, gloves, veils, and all sorts of wedding paraphernalia that he had no idea existed until now. *Definitely a place for the ladies,* he surmised as he heard the click of heeled shoes on the wood floor and spied a tall, willowy young woman with full lips, fiery curls, and piercing indigo eyes pushing aside a curtain separating the workroom from the shop. And for a moment, Giles forgot why he was sitting in a bridal shop.

Alice set the gloves she was mending aside on the shop counter and smiled at the towering, athletic-looking gentleman who was sitting stiffly on her settee, blinking at her with his mouth slightly ajar. She gave him a tentative nod, unsure if he was quite well or if he was merely one of the many fiancés sent on an errand, overwhelmed by all the bobbles of a bridal shop. "Good afternoon, I'm Miss Turner. Can I assist you with something? Are you here to pick up an order for someone?"

"Uh, yes." He rose, gave her a small bow, and instantly returned to the seat, raking his fingers through his thick, wavy coal-black hair and turning his tidy pompadour into a riotous mess. "I'm here for uh. . .well, it's rather hard to explain."

Used to the peculiar responses of males in her shop, Alice simply folded her hands in front of her day gown and studied the striking man in front of her, waiting patiently.

His throat bobbed as he swallowed before giving a cough, as if his words were difficult to release. "I am in need of your assistance. You wouldn't happen to have any ready-made pants in the back, would you? I seem to have had a bit of a mishap."

She glanced at his pant legs, but seeing no tear or rip, she tapped her lip and motioned with her finger for him to rise, but he stayed firmly planted in place on the settee. "I haven't dealt with men's trousers in quite some time, but my father taught me everything he knew and since his, uh, retirement, I have turned his tailor shop into a bridal shop. What exactly needs mending? I don't see anything marring your clothing, Mister. . .?"

"Giles. Just Giles." He cleared his throat, crossed his legs at the knee, and drummed his fingers on his thigh. "I'm not sure how to put this delicately, so I'm just going to say it. I used to be quite active until recent months and now, in my present line of work, I do a lot of sitting, and I haven't had a new suit in quite a while." He laughed, revealing a charming small gap between his front teeth as he ran a hand over his strong jawline. "I should have listened to my sister and ordered a new wardrobe, but it's too late now. Today, the sitting finally caught up with me when I bent down to pick up a baseball for a group of boys and, well, my pants have perished, and that is why I am in your bridal shop and at your mercy, sitting in your presence, which is against what society dictates I should do, while I beg for your assistance."

Understanding made her chest swell with a need to burst into laughter, but as she was a professional woman, she swallowed her amusement and motioned for him to move into one of the two dressing rooms lining the right side of her shop. "Please step behind the curtain and remove your trousers so I can set to work on them." She felt the heat rise in her neck as he slowly rose with an embarrassed tint of his own. Alice whipped her back to him to afford him some privacy as he slipped behind the thick powder-blue curtain.

"Miss Turner, do you have anything for me to wear while you mend?" Mr. Giles asked, his voice muffled by the curtain between them.

She bit her lip, thinking of the small trunk of her parents' things in the attic that she hadn't touched in years. She had vowed she would never open it again, but thinking of the man's predicament, she relented. "I do believe I have some old trousers of my father's that you can borrow, but I can tell you right now that they will not fit your frame. My father was quite stout and short, but they will get the job done while you wait."

He poked his head through the curtains, clutching the fabric beneath his chin. "Anything would be most appreciated, my lady."

At the sight of his tousled hair and helpless tone, she couldn't help but shake her head and laugh to herself. "I will fetch them, sir."

Not stopping to dwell on what she was about to do, she ascended the stairs to the third-floor landing and into the stifling attic, sweat beading her forehead almost at once. Her body gravitated to where she knew the trunk would be. It was covered in a thick layer of dust and grime created by the humidity, so she used her handkerchief to flick open the latch. With a resounding creak, the lid cracked open, the scent of sandalwood flooding her. An unexpected ache formed in her heart at the sight of a perfectly folded, unfinished quilt atop her father's things.

She lifted the quilt out of the trunk and stroked the neat stitches, once again stung with her father's choices. Five years ago, she had been sewing the quilt from sentimental scraps from old gowns of her mother's as a Christmas gift to him, but when the scandal had broken and destroyed their happiness, she had tucked away her father's things along with the unfinished quilt and had intentionally forgotten about it. Now the torrent of memories the quilt held threatened to overwhelm her. Alice dropped the quilt onto the dusty floor and rummaged through the trunk, found the pants, stuffed the quilt back inside, and slammed the lid, wishing she could just as easily banish her feelings and her heart. Trousers in hand, she darted down the stairs, and standing outside the curtain, cleared her throat to alert the gentleman of her presence. "Mr. Giles?"

"Thank goodness. I was hoping you did not abandon me," he replied through the curtain, a forced laugh following. "And it's just Giles, if you please."

"Of course I didn't abandon you. Now, if you please, the pants, Giles." Trading trousers, she nearly laughed again as she examined the rip, grabbed her basket of scrap materials, and sank onto the settee to mend the seam by hand. *Professional. Be professional.* She was rummaging through the scraps to find some cloth similar in color when she heard the curtain rings scrape against the rod and her customer stepped out in her father's pants. This time, there was no escaping her laughter at the sight of him with his suspenders holding up the ample waistline of the pants and the hem cinched up to his calves, which thankfully were still covered by his navy hosiery, saving them both from further discomfiture.

He whistled through his teeth, his gaze on the large patch in her hand. "Can't you save them?"

She pinned the patch into place. "I'm afraid not, but the patch should be hidden enough under your coat for you to hail a carriage for home without fear of being arrested." She grinned at his reddening cheeks and lowered her gaze, stitching away. "So, tell me what sort of work you did prior to all this sitting?"

He joined her on the settee, watching her work. "I was a tennis instructor at the All England Lawn Tennis Club."

This brought her head up. "What, in London? What an exciting occupation! I've always enjoyed reading about tennis matches and have longed to learn, but—" She lifted his pants. "I'm afraid seamstresses don't make enough for the club fees, much less enough for an instructor. Did you play in the Gentlemen's Championship in Wimbledon?"

He grinned. "You've heard of Wimbledon? You really do enjoy the sport. Yes, I've played there the last three years. I placed well, but didn't win, a fact that my father does not fail to remind me."

"What an honor!" She checked her enthusiasm and returned to the pants, making quick work of the remaining stitches. "Here you go, Giles." She handed them to him. "I suggest you buy a new wardrobe as soon as you are able. I'm afraid that if the rest of your pants have this much wear, they won't last long, and you'll be in here again." She grinned. *Though it wouldn't be the worst thing in the world if you were to return.*

Chapter 2

A shimmering sapphire gown and fiery curls drew Giles's gaze to the threshold of the family drawing room, his heart hammering at the sight of her. *What is she doing here?* He swallowed. Despite his mortification at seeing the pretty seamstress who had saved him at his brother's engagement dinner, a thrill traveled through him. Taller than most women, but willowy and graceful, Miss Turner cut an impressive figure in the room of Charleston's socialites.

Clapping his younger brother, William, on the shoulder and nodding to Meg, he excused himself from the enamored couple and crossed the room, weaving through and around clusters of guests, his gaze never leaving her as she moved toward his brother's bride-to-be.

She began to pass him without seeing him, so he boldly reached out to her only to brush his fingertips on the short sleeves of her evening gown. "Miss Turner?"

Her indigo eyes widened and a dimple appeared in her left cheek as she smiled. "Giles? *Just* Giles," she teased. "Whatever are you doing here?"

"I was going to ask you the same. Are you here for. . ." He left off the end of his sentence, fearing it would be rude to assume that she was here only to work when she was dressed as one of the party.

"For taking the bridal party's measurements?" She laughed, shaking her head, dispelling any awkwardness he felt in his lingering question with her brilliant, full smile. "Not at the moment. I'm here as a bridesmaid to one of the brides-to-be. Meg and I have been friends since childhood. Her family's fortune wasn't made until she was nearly sixteen. But as I haven't met you until you visited my shop"—she looked up to him with those bewitching eyes—"I presume you are acquainted with the groom."

"Well, I wasn't his friend by choice, but over the years, we have come to endure one another's company at home and the workplace."

"Ah." She smiled and nodded. "You are the brother of the groom. A fact I should have pieced together, given you two look so much alike."

"Do you have any siblings of your own who help you at the shop?" Giles asked, eager to learn more about her. While he had been at her mercy in the shop, he had refrained from much small talk other than tennis, uncomfortable with his vulnerable appearance.

"I'm afraid that I was the first and last child, as my mother died in childbirth. Though my father was only five and twenty at the time, he never remarried, so I am the sole owner of the shop."

"I'm surprised your father retired so early in life. One would think a tailor of his age would only now be reaching the height of his popularity."

"It was an unexpected choice." She dipped her head, fiddling with the trim on her matching fan. He began to wonder what she wasn't revealing about her father, but before he could inquire further, she nodded to the corner of the room where Meg and William stood arm in arm. "If you'll excuse me, the bride is motioning for me."

He watched her retreating back, intrigued with the woman. He would have to arrange to sit next to her at dinner, even if it meant crossing his sister by switching Miss Turner's place with Miss Castle's. He motioned the butler over and whispered his instructions.

"But Miss Constance specifically—"

He clapped the butler on the shoulder. "I'll take care of my sister. Any wrath I ensue is worth it to sit next to such a captivating dinner partner."

How did he manage to find out bits of my life so easily? Alice shook her head to free herself from the fog of his presence. Giles could never be anything more to her than a customer, and she would not tell him her life's story. But it was rather pleasant to find the handsome gentleman from her shop, whom she had found herself thinking of throughout her week, at the party she had been dreading. She flicked open her silk fan, with its dainty floral-and-gold design catching in the candlelight, and gave a cursory glance over her shoulder. She smothered a smile when she caught Giles staring at her yet. *Stop thinking of his fine eyes and focus.*

Surveying the room for potential customers, she sauntered past a group of mothers on her way to Meg, showing off her stylish dress fashioned freshly from the *Harper's Bazaar* delivered only two days ago. In anticipation of tonight's group of potential clients, she had her seamstress help her finish it last night to capture the attention of all future brides.

Alice pretended not to hear the other women's whispers behind their silk fans as she took a seat on the settee next to the mother of the bride. Mrs. Martin, who gave Alice's hand a friendly pat, returned to her conversation with the other young ladies of marriageable age, speaking, of course, of Meg's wedding. At a break in the conversation, one of the girls commented on the delightful design of Alice's gown. Not wanting to boast of her own work, Alice graciously dipped her head in thanks as Meg and Constance joined them.

"It's Alice's latest piece. Isn't it a wonder what she can create? I'm thrilled that both Constance and I will be wearing an Alice Turner original gown for our double wedding along with our bridesmaids," Meg announced. Her unabashed admiration caused all the ladies to turn their attention toward Alice.

"I've been wanting to ask if you studied in France?" Miss Hyacinth asked, her gaze scrutinizing every tuck and fold of Alice's handiwork.

"Unfortunately, no. However, my father worked in Paris until he married and moved here to open his own shop, so my styles are French influenced."

At this, Miss Hyacinth's stiff gaze softened to that of a smirk. "Ah, now I know where I've heard the name of Turner. Wasn't your shop originally Turner's Fine Tailor previous to—what's the name again?"

"Thimbles and Threads Bridal Shop," Alice answered, her cheeks burning.

"That's quite the mouthful, but I can't quite place the reason why it changed over to you." She tapped her fan to her chin, lifting her gaze to the ceiling as if trying to recall the scandal that had almost ruined Alice.

Meg placed her arm around Alice's waist in a gentle reminder to remain calm. "I'm sorry to speak out of turn, and I know we weren't really planning on dancing, but William needs far more practice than a week can give." She turned to Constance. "Since your Eustace is out of town until the wedding, would you mind playing the piano so we can practice the quadrille? No one is quite as accomplished as you."

Constance gave her a pretty smile. "You are too kind to me. I wish Eustace were here, but since he is not, I will sacrifice any chance at dancing this evening and play for you."

Alice sent Meg a small smile, thanking her for her thoughtfulness. Meg had been like a sister to her since childhood, and even though wealth created a barrier between most people, Alice knew it would never separate them. Hearing the men's voices, she turned her gaze to the double doors to find Hyacinth smiling brilliantly on the arm of Giles as they glided into place to form the sides of the quadrille. Meg smiled back at Alice, took the head position with her fiancé, and nodded to Constance to begin.

Alice clasped her hands behind her back and watched the dancers as they moved in nearly perfect time with the lively music until William lost count of the steps and ran into the back of Miss Hyacinth. But Meg just laughed away the mishap and sent him encouraging smiles throughout the complicated dance. Seeing her friend's adoration for William, Alice felt the hardness of time soften a bit. If Meg could find such joy after going from suitor to suitor in search of a man with character, maybe there was hope for Alice. She supposed that deep down, there was a part of her that longed for the warm embrace of a husband, someone to protect her from the harshness of life. . .or at least be there to share life's burdens with one another. She sighed. She had long since surrendered that dream, and it would be for the best that she not take it up again.

With the quadrille in its final steps, Alice turned away, intent on finding a quiet corner for a moment of peace to gather her thoughts before sharing dinner with a stranger for a partner. She wasn't used to socializing with the people whom she was trying to secure as her clients, and it was exhausting to be so aware at all moments of potentially saying the wrong thing. When she measured ladies or hemmed gowns, she could remain mostly silent, intent on her work, but here, at a party she was expected to— She jumped at the hand at her elbow.

"May I have the honor of this next dance? Meg has requested a waltz." Giles bowed to her, offering her his hand even as she spied Miss Hyacinth in the corner glaring at her. Not quite sure how to refuse without insulting a client's brother, she nodded, placing her hand in his massive one, feeling petite for the first time in her life.

Constance jammed her fingers on the keys, sounding an introductory chord, garnering the attention of all as she stood and announced, "We don't want our impromptu dancing to ruin the chef's menu."

Meg and William moaned, protesting in unison, "Just one more dance!"

Constance barely disguised the scowl forming over her brow

and with a forced smile, returned to her seat. "As you wish it, but this is the *last* dance before dinner, my dear brother and future sister."

Alice could have laughed at how threatened Constance seemed to be. Did she honestly think her brother could be interested in pursuing a seamstress? He was only being kind as he had in her shop when he told her about the tennis championships. But as Giles began to whirl her about the room in a looping, dipping waltz, she felt herself grow a bit light-headed, and she had to admit to herself that she was quite enjoying the athletic feel of her handsome partner's thick arms. *You will not be caught up in the romance of one evening and one dance,* she scolded herself. But, for that one moment, nothing else existed.

She could hardly recall the music ending when Giles bowed to her and the couples breathlessly applauded Constance as the butler appeared in the doorway. She noticed the butler's gaze fall directly on her partner and give him the smallest nod, motioning the underbutlers to open the double doors and announcing dinner.

Giles bowed to her, obviously not seeing Miss Hyacinth expectantly craning her neck in their direction. "Shall I escort you to your seat?"

"O-of course," she stammered under the glares of Miss Hyacinth and Miss Constance. The moment her hand was tucked in the crook of his arm, she thought for certain Miss Hyacinth would faint. Miss Constance rustled over to them so quickly, Alice thought her bustle was in danger of flying off.

"Giles, don't you think you should escort your dinner partner?" Miss Constance nodded to Miss Hyacinth in the corner, who was desperately fanning her cheeks.

"Miss Turner *is* my dinner partner." Giles gave her a wide-eyed stare. "I made certain to check the table arrangement as you told me to, and that's what the dinner cards decreed."

"What?" She gave Alice a smile that could only be described as a grimace. "I'm so sorry, Miss Turner, but there has been some mistake and I must insist—"

"No need to apologize." Giles steered Alice toward the dining room with a smile and nod to Miss Hyacinth as an elderly gentleman hefted himself out of the armchair by the dormant fireplace and made his way toward Giles's rejected partner. "I shall see to our dear Miss Turner. I know our great-uncle will take great care of Miss Hyacinth as her escort."

Alice found herself standing in front of the elaborate dinner table set with the family's finest china with a short, wide arrangement of white lilies, gardenias, and roses framed by a silver candelabra on either side. She swallowed as Giles held the back of her mahogany chair and every eye turned to them once again. She sank onto the cushioned seat and ran her fingers around the length of her ivory napkin, draping it over her sapphire skirts. She wasn't prepared to chat with a groomsman, much less Giles! *Why didn't Meg warn me?*

"So, you mentioned you longed to learn tennis." Giles went on as if all were normal.

"Y-yes," she stuttered as a gold-rimmed china bowl of turtle soup was placed in front of her.

"Well, my home is only about three miles or so from your shop, and I happen to have a tennis court set up on my lawn." He lifted his soup spoon after his sister, the hostess and second bride-to-be, had taken her first sip.

"Oh, so you *still* play?"

He chuckled and broke off a piece of his sweet-potato roll. “That hard to tell, huh? I guess when one splits his pants from sitting too much it doesn’t lead you to assume that said pants-splitter still attempts to exercise.”

She diverted her attention to taking a sip of her lukewarm thick soup, unused to teasing and not knowing how to respond. “When did you return to Charleston?”

“After I lost a tournament in the spring. With my father’s approaching retirement, I knew it was time to quit my pursuit and join the family business.”

Her heart clenched. She knew what it was like to have to surrender to the responsibilities of life. She had once dreamed of becoming a wife and mother, but life had other plans for her. “I’m sorry.”

He shrugged as if it had not been a sacrifice. “I loved playing and teaching, but banking also holds my interest. And what of you? How did you come to fancy the sport?”

“As children, Meg and I enjoyed playing badminton together in the park, but when she became a lady, her mother encouraged her to give up the sport.” She wiped her mouth with her napkin. “But, as I can’t afford to join a club, I watch from a distance or read about matches whenever I am able.”

“Well, how about you and I have a match? I promise to go easy on you.”

Alice blinked. *He knows I’m just a seamstress, so surely he isn’t insinuating that he actually wishes me to play him. . .?* “I’m afraid you have overestimated my badminton skills, and I have never actually had the chance to play tennis.”

“Then I’ll give you lessons! It has been rather difficult on me giving up instructing since leaving London, and I think we could help each other out. I can teach, you can learn, and we can play, keeping me in better shape."

Better shape? Is that even possible? Alice could feel her cheeks grow warm from secret admiration. She knew she should decline, but her stomach fluttered at the prospect of learning to play the sport. "I don't know what to say."

"Say yes. I can have a carriage drive you to and from your shop so you won't miss your appointments with your clients, and you'd be helping me out by keeping me from going mad shut up in an office all day every day, shuffling paperwork." He lifted his hand. "Not that I dislike my work, but a fellow needs to have a sport to keep active, else risk developing a banker's paunch."

She pressed her napkin to the corner of her mouth again, considering his proposal. The man really did sound quite miserable, and it would be wonderful to take some time for herself. She hadn't really had much of a break since she started her bridal business. She lifted her gaze to see if anyone had overheard his gallant offer to teach her, but besides the pursed lips of Miss Constance from the opposite end of the table, everyone else was busy speaking with one another. "What should I expect to pay per lesson?"

Leaning forward, he said in a conspiratorial whisper, "Would the pleasure of your company over a glass of lemonade after each match on my family's riverboat be too much to ask?"

She choked on her drink and coughed, holding her hand over her mouth. "A riverboat? You jest."

He shrugged. "It's not as grand as it sounds. It's secondhand and quite old, but it gets the family to and from the plantation to visit others."

Rich people. She nearly rolled her eyes, but the thought of finally learning to play tennis was too tempting to pass up. "I will, on one condition." She nodded toward Constance. "We must keep it a secret. I don't want your sister to catch wind of our lessons and think there is anything more to them than getting us both outside for a few hours. Just the hint of gossip could ruin my business and every hope I have of breaking into the elite set of society."

"Of course. And you know we won't ever really be alone. The servants will be there, but I'll make sure they won't say a word."

She extended her hand to him. "Very well, sir. You have yourself a deal. When do we start?"

"My sister makes her morning calls every Monday. So how does that sound?" He waited for her answer as the footman removed their soup dishes.

"I say it will give me just the right amount of time to whip up a tennis gown."

Chapter 3

Alice stepped down from the carriage, gripping the tennis racket that Giles had sent to her shop that morning with a friendly note reminding her of their appointment. She held on to the brim of her hat as she craned her neck back to take in the two-story plantation. With its veranda that wrapped around both floors and massive white columns, it was quite impressive. She swallowed. *Could a man who comes from all this wealth really wish to spend time with me?* Making her way down the gravel path around the big house of the plantation and to the back lawn to where Giles had said to meet him, she couldn't help but take a quick glance up to the long windows to see if she could spy his family inside.

Her breath caught at the wide lawn that stretched from the

house to the winding Ashley River, where a riverboat was docked beside the cypress trees that lined the river. And even from that distance, she could tell it was far grander than the small, secondhand paddleboat Giles had described. This steamer could easily carry a hundred passengers, if not more.

She pulled at her lace-trimmed collar. It was going to be another blazing day. *Thank goodness Giles had the wherewithal to schedule a morning lesson.* As Giles was nowhere to be seen, she sank in the manicured grass beneath an oak cloaked in Spanish moss in sight of the lawn tennis court and arranged the skirts of her tennis costume over her ankles, secretly admiring the gown that she had altered from her simplest walking gown. Having adjusted a few of the intricate tucks, she'd arranged the folds of her skirt in a manner that would allow her limbs a little more room to lunge for tennis balls. She stroked the navy-and-white striped gown, loving the way her skirt fell and how free she felt without the layers upon layers of constricting clothing. *Well, even if I can't hit the ball over the net, I'll at least look splendid while attempting it.*

Nervous that she had arrived too early and was in danger of running into Giles's family, she checked her small watch pin again, absentmindedly rubbing her finger over the engraved pair of silver lovebirds. She was so deep in possible scenarios explaining Giles's absence that at the touch to her elbow, she jumped and inadvertently whacked the man at her side with her racket. At his cry, she looked up into the hazel eyes of her victim.

"Giles! I mean, Mr. Clayton."

"Quite a backhand you have there, Miss Turner," he chuckled, rubbing his elbow. "I didn't think you'd be this cross with my being five minutes late. I couldn't find my shoes. My valet had decided they were far too dirty and had taken them away last night to clean them without telling me."

Her cheeks reddened. "I'm so sorry. I didn't hear you come up behind me."

"Well, I certainly hope that was the case. Otherwise, it would appear that you don't like me very much." He sent her a wink, stilling the rising guilt in her heart. "Just a good thing you didn't knock me in the head, or else I might never recover." He spun his racket in his right hand's loose grip. "If you are ready, let's get started with the basic strokes."

He demonstrated a forehand grip, which she mimicked easily, so he moved on to the backhand, which she did not copy quite as well.

"You almost had it. Return to the forehand position, bring the racket across your body, and *then* add your second hand to the handle."

She scrunched her mouth and attempted it.

"Perfect. Now, turn your shoulders along with your body in a single, fluid motion, like this." He hammered the ball over the net.

After a few false starts, she managed at least to get the ball over the net, and they moved on to service strokes. She watched closely as he tossed the ball up with one hand and came down on it with his racket at a precise angle, sending the ball bouncing to the correct opposite box.

Alice threw the ball up into the air, swung, and missed, the ball hitting her atop her head. She rubbed the spot, scowling, and tried again and again, to no avail.

He rubbed his hand over his chin. "Hmm, why don't we

try to simply volley back and forth to get you used to hitting the ball first, and practice switching your grip from forehand to backhand?"

"That might be for the best. Serving is a lot harder than it looks." She laughed, wiping her forehead with the cuff of her sleeve. *Blast this sun.* She really did not enjoy being so sweaty in front of such a handsome instructor.

He trotted to the other side of the net and took his position. "Okay, I'm going to send the ball your way. Let it bounce once and then hit it back to me." He executed a perfect forehand, sending the ball flying over the net.

She waited for the bounce and tried to swing, but the pesky ball was coming straight toward her. With a squeal, she held the racket up to block her face. "I thought you were going to go easy on me," she protested, feeling her face redden but not from the heat of the sun.

He chuckled. "I was. You forgot to move to the side of the ball and were taking it straight on." He moved his stance from side to side in a quick stride-hop motion that had her scratching her head.

"Easy enough," she called in a false bravado and took her stance again, ready this time.

The ball came over the net and bounced once. She moved to the side and whipped her racket, expecting a *whack* and was met with a *whoosh.* She had missed. "Again!"

Not wanting her to become discouraged, Giles waved the tennis ball over his head, staying her swing before she could miss and send another ball flying backward into the Ashley River or smacking into the net. It was a miracle she hadn't lobbed a ball through one of the long windows of the house. "You've done wonderfully for your first lesson, but let's say we call it a day?"

"Oh, I thought we'd have an actual match?"

"I'm glad you still want to play after, uh—" He stopped short of saying "a disastrous lesson" and instead, grinned and said, "An intense first lesson, but we may be a lesson or two away from playing a set. Shall we take our refreshment now?" He offered her his arm, thankful that he hadn't perspired much. "I'm pretty sure it is lawn tennis rules that the instructor must give his student lemonade or risk dishonor."

She checked her watch again and appeared to be weighing his offer before she nodded and dropped the watch pin against her bodice. "I did promise you one glass, but then I must hurry back to the shop to change and meet with my new clients. I have a bride who is getting married in three days, and this is her final fitting. I want her to be as calm as possible, and my being late would not only upset her but also potentially lose me a future client in her sister."

"But why limit yourself to wedding dresses"—he gestured at her creative tennis ensemble, which he knew his sister would buy in an instant—"when you are obviously gifted in all styles?"

"Because I want to be known for my wedding dresses someday and not just be that seamstress who makes stylish dresses. I want the Turner name to stand for something beautiful, something pure, and not. . ." She drifted off as they stepped onto the plank of the riverboat. He led her up a flight of stairs to a deck with a wide promenade overlooking the water with a decorative railing painted in a pretty soft white. Her smile widened at a pair of wicker chairs on the deck, facing the river, with a glass pitcher of lemonade and two cups on a small table. "Well, this is lovely."

He gestured for her to take a seat. "Thank you. We could use the main cabin where my family usually dines while on the river, but I figured we didn't want to be inside when we had the chance to enjoy a bit of a breeze from the river." Giles lifted a pitcher and poured them each a tall glass of iced lemonade. He handed one to her, fascinated with learning more about her and loving the sprinkle of freckles appearing on her nose after a morning in the sunshine.

"Returning to what you were saying, I think I understand. I wanted my name to stand for more than just a family-owned bank, but life had other plans." He ran his finger over the rim of his glass. "I know that one day tennis won't be seen just as a pastime, but it amazes me how many people consider my time in London playing as merely the hobby of a young man who wasn't ready to accept life's responsibilities. It's different over there. If people here knew how much training it takes to play in Wimbledon. . .they wouldn't be so condescending." He laughed and raked his fingers through his hair. "I apologize for being so morose. I had rather a ridiculous encounter at the office as I was leaving to come for our lesson, and it rubbed me the wrong way."

"No need to apologize." She reached out and brushed her fingertips over his knuckles, but before he could even look up at her, she pulled her hand away and dipped her head as if suddenly aware of her impropriety. "I know what it's like not to be taken seriously. When my father left and I took over, the other shops on King Street thought I'd be closing within a month. They considered me a little girl playing at being a tailor." She lifted her glass. "And yet, I'm still here and my shop is still running, so they've begun to give me more respect as the years go by and as I get older. I hope for you that it is only a matter of time as well."

"Thank you." He smiled softly, dazed at her opening up to him. "Well, I am thankful that one of us is respected in our profession." And he meant every word. The more glimpses he got into this young lady's life, the more he admired her for persevering.

Shifting in her seat, seeming uncomfortable with the turn the conversation had taken, she downed her lemonade in three gulps and set it aside, rising. "I really must be going. I didn't realize how late the hour had become. I don't want to risk running into your family and raising an alarm when it is not warranted. Thank you for the refreshment."

He swallowed back his grin at her unladylike, albeit endearing, action as he rose to follow her to the carriage, not willing to part from her quite yet. "May I drive you home? I took the liberty of asking the stable boy beforehand to ready the buggy instead of the carriage."

"Well, as it is *your* buggy that is bringing me back, I can't rightly say no." She sent him a wry smile, but he could tell from her tone that she was pleased at his request—at least, he hoped that is what he heard in her voice. "But we best make haste. I need to take care of Cat prior to my next appointment." She gathered her beaded reticule and racket, fairly racing down the steps and descending the plank to the dock.

"Cat? You mean, you have a cat, or is that your pet's name?" he asked as he strode down the path after her.

"Cat is his name." She glanced over her shoulder at him as if it were the most natural name in the world.

He rubbed his hand over his mouth, fearing laughter would not endear him to her. Giles waved off the groomsman and assisted Alice into the buggy himself. After taking up the reins and giving them a little snap, he cleared his throat. "So, Cat. Why did you settle upon that name?"

She lifted her hand, shielding her eyes from the sun. "I didn't want to get too attached to him."

"He's a new pet to you?"

"I've had him for four years." She smiled as if quite aware of how confusing her words were. "But that doesn't mean he's getting another name. I don't trust he will stay."

He laughed as he turned the horse onto the road. "I'd say he's staying, but that's just my humble opinion."

The drive to King Street passed so quickly, Giles considered "accidentally" taking her around the block again, but knowing she had a client, he saw her to her shop door. Before she stepped inside, he grasped her by the elbow, turning her to him. "May I call on you?" He watched her lips twist with what appeared to be trepidation, and he began to think his chances were slim if not next to none.

"I'm going to be quite busy for the next month with all the summer weddings, and I'm already stretching my schedule by taking two hours every Monday to practice tennis with you, but once this month is over, and if you still feel the same, maybe you could ask me again?" She glanced up at him, an enchanting glint in her indigo eyes.

Giles lifted a finger. "One month?"

"One month."

He grinned and extended his hand. "It's a deal."

Chapter 4

In the week following their first lesson, Alice half-expected Giles to cancel. After all, she was only a seamstress, and he was a partner at a successful bank, so why was he interested in spending time with her? But true to his word, his carriage showed up at the exact time every week and continued to show up in the weeks following, gently reminding Alice of her promise to step out with him, cracking the wall in her heart with every sweet smile he sent her way. And as she grew more capable with a racket, she found herself enjoying his companionship even more.

It was nice to have someone to talk to besides Meg. With her wedding and her sister's debut coming up, Meg was often too busy to even have a cup of tea, leaving Alice with no one to converse with but Giles. To her surprise, he had proven himself to be a good listener as she talked about lace and ruffles and unhappy clients. And in turn, Giles confided in her about his time in London and of his disappointment over losing his last tournament, along with his struggles with becoming a banker and accepting the responsibilities that were laid upon him. Over their weekly pitcher of lemonade after their lesson, they formed a friendship that was sweet and treasured by both. Now with only a few days in the agreed-upon month until Giles asked her to dinner again, Alice was surprised to find that she was going to release all her inhibitions and accept. Their lessons had become the highlight of her week, and she ached to see him in the days between.

She was thankful that today, Meg's wedding day, she would spend the entire morning and afternoon with him and not just a few stolen minutes after a tennis lesson. When the clock on the mantel chimed eight times, she finished buttoning the back of her powder-blue bridesmaid gown and, yelling a good morning and goodbye to Cat, she gripped her satchel of sewing supplies and darted down the sidewalk toward Meg's home, breathing heavily as she rounded the corner and let herself in through the side gate. Taking the servant's entrance that was always open, Alice raced up the buzzing staircase to Meg's room on the second floor. Slipping off the light shawl she wore to keep the dust of the streets at bay, she stepped into the bustling room as the two brides and Miss Hyacinth, the other bridesmaid, made last-minute touches to their ensembles.

"Thank goodness you are here." Mrs. Martin grasped her arm and pulled her to Meg's side. "My daughter has been so nervous, she's been overeating, and well, we burst three of the buttons on her gown before we managed to tighten her corset and close the back."

"I'm so sorry. I thought we were helping her dress at half past eight."

"I wanted to start early because I knew something was going to go wrong." Meg's voice cracked as she waved her hands, fanning her face to keep her tears at bay. "People have been inserting their opinions all week regarding my choice of timing the first dance *after* our breakfast feast, the actual dance I've chosen, and even going so far as to question *why* we are dancing at all. And to top it all off, nearly every other woman I've encountered this week has inquired why I have broken from tradition and didn't ask my sister to be my bridesmaid." She hiccupped, her tears beyond control. "Does no one understand that it is *my* wedding day, and I'm doing what makes me happy? And now my dress won't be perfect."

Alice gently rubbed Meg's shoulder and pulled her into a hug. "Never you mind what people say. And as for your dress, it is a simple fix." She removed her sewing kit from her satchel, bent behind her friend, and proceeded to sew the silk-covered buttons back into place. "There. No harm done."

"Except that now I can't breathe from the tightness of my corset strings!" Meg pressed a hand to her waist. "Oh, why did I eat that last roll at breakfast?"

"Because sometimes even the most disciplined of us can't resist cinnamon rolls dripping in vanilla icing, but on occasions when one has to fit into a dress, it is best if you refrain from indulging your every craving day in and day out." Constance patted her perfectly coiled and pinned raven locks as she slowly spun in front of the looking glass, admiring her wedding gown. "I hope Eustace recognizes the great pains I have taken to embody the pet name he has given me."

"Oh?" Meg asked. "And what would that be?" She twisted her mouth toward Alice and whispered, "Miss Constantly Prissy, perhaps?"

Alice snorted into her hands, choking on her suppressed laughter.

"Angel, of course." Constance rolled her eyes.

Alice stiffened. Angel had been *her* Eustace's pet name for her. What were the odds that Constance was marrying another man named Eustace who used that pet name with his fiancée? *Don't be paranoid. It is a common enough term of endearment. You should be over this nonsense of even caring,* she chided herself. She checked her hair for any strands out of place as the clock chimed the ninth hour. "One more hour, Meg," Alice sang out, grasping her friend's hands and spinning her about the room.

"You'll wrinkle her!" Miss Hyacinth protested but was ignored amid the giggling.

"I've asked Giles to act as your escort for the wedding. I hope you don't mind?" Meg's eyes sparkled as if she already knew long ago that Alice was secretly attracted to Giles. She leaned in and whispered, "Between you and me, even though Giles is standing with my William, I was hard pressed to convince Constance that he should be your escort and not Miss Hyacinth's knight in shining armor, because apparently Constance believes that they are *destined* to wed."

Even though Alice was miffed at the heat crawling up her neck, she could not bring herself to protest, which she was certain betrayed her feelings upon the matter as she normally would've objected to any such arrangement. She tilted her head, pursed her lips, and lifted her brows at Meg. *Of course she knows I like Giles.* In the few moments she and Meg had spent together all month, all Alice had been able to talk about was her diverting tennis lessons with said groomsman. "I suppose you want me to say thank you?"

Meg kissed her on the cheek. "Yes, but not until you are safely engaged to your Giles."

"Meg!" she gasped, pulling her away from the others. "He is *not* my Giles, and you best not let anyone hear you saying such things."

Meg giggled. "I overheard him speaking to *my* William in the study, and I can tell you that he is quite smitten with you."

Alice dared not allow her heart believe those words and recounted to herself again the reasons why she and Giles could never be anything other than friends. *I am a seamstress. He is a successful banker, rapidly climbing society's rungs and getting even further out of my reach, which is most likely the reason why he is so comfortable around me. I'm not even on his mind as a potential bride.* She dropped her hands. "If anyone should think I am a flirt, my business will suffer."

Meg's brows raised. "Oh, and speaking of your business, I also wanted to let you know that your gowns are a colossal success. I have overheard Constance comment on the workmanship to multiple guests throughout the week."

"High praise indeed," she whispered to Meg, giggling as they pulled on their white kid gloves.

"The carriages are here! Girls, gather around for your instructions." Meg's mother clapped her hands together, gathering everyone to her with the flutter of her silk fan above her head. With her slim figure, Mrs. Martin looked like she could be one of the girls herself if not for streaks of dove gray appearing in her blond curls. "The brides will be escorted to the church by the parents.

Miss Castle, you will be escorted by Eustace's groomsman, and, of course, that leaves Miss Turner to Mr. Clayton's care. Now, as this is a double wedding, there will be a large number in attendance, so Miss Turner and Miss Castle, you two will need to attend Meg and Constance unceasingly to keep guests from lingering too long at their tables. The brides must be allowed to eat. Go to your escort downstairs and stay with them for the duration of the wedding and reception *beside* your bride. Your groomsman will act as your partner as well as your butler so that you don't leave your bride unless it is for attending their errand. Now, enough talk." She waved her fan again. "We have a wedding to attend!"

The girls tittered among themselves, hiding their giggles behind their silk fans.

Alice gave Meg's fingers a squeeze and whispered, "You are a vision."

Meg dipped her head. "I fear all these ruffles and laces are the true beauty."

Alice adjusted the bow at Meg's hip. "I wasn't referring to the gown. A bride's radiance brings life to my gowns, not the other way around, my friend."

Meg gave her a peck on the cheek. "This morning, I wed my Prince Charming and one day soon, I hope you will wed yours as well. Give Giles a chance and say yes to dinner."

Only a few weeks ago, Alice would've declared that she would never meet a man who would cause her to dream again, but that was before Giles appeared in her shop. "Maybe I already decided I will," she admitted softly. *Even if I can never call him mine.*

"Alice Turner!" Meg giggled. "Will miracles never cease? You had best go find Mr. Giles Clayton and get better acquainted before you change your mind. If he is *not* your Prince Charming, then at least be friends, for he is my brother now. . . Well, in an hour he will be."

Alice stepped into the main foyer to find Giles waiting beyond the front door threshold on the top step, his thumbs looped in the pockets of his silk waistcoat as he tilted his black top hat to block the morning light.

"Good morning, *Mr. Clayton*." Alice smiled up at him, enjoying the fact that he was one of the few men she had encountered who was tall enough for her to look up to.

His brows rose at her formality. "I thought we were past that, *Miss Turner*." He sent her a wink.

She inclined her head toward the carriage, whispering, "Except when we might be overheard by your sister or any guest who will report to your sister. You know as well as I do that it would cause an unnecessary stir." She placed her hand in the crook of his arm for him to lead her out to the carriage where Miss Hyacinth and her escort were already settling inside.

Alice and Giles took their seats opposite the couple, and Alice arranged her skirts about her so they wouldn't crumple. She glanced up to find Miss Hyacinth's dark-brown eyes piercing into her, shifting to Giles and alighting with a smile.

"Giles." She drew his name out, brazenly using his Christian name. "I had hoped to spend some more time with you after your call this week."

Alice's heart hammered in her chest, and she endeavored not to glance at Giles. *He called on her? After all his bravado of asking me out, he was merely teasing.* She felt her throat close with suppressed disappointment. She knew she shouldn't be surprised, but Giles had seemed so sincere in his attentions to her.

"Well, uh. . ." He appeared to be glancing at Alice, but as she refused to look at him, she couldn't be certain. "I enjoyed our discussion as well, but I was sorry that your father had to cancel our appointment after my arrival. Your father had some investment opportunities he wished to discuss, so I might try to catch him at the reception if there's a moment."

Miss Hyacinth gave a lilting laugh, pressing her hand to her ruffled chest. "Just like Papa. Always working." She leaned forward, adding, "It reveals a depth of character that is quite attractive to a woman."

Alice bit back a gasp at the girl's scandalous flirting. She averted her gaze to the window. Flirting was a luxury of the wealthy. If she dared say such a thing, she would be labeled as a—well, she would never flirt.

"I believe we are in the presence of another hard worker. Miss Turner, I heard you designed the brides' and maids' gowns, did you not?" Giles turned to her, but Alice knew full well he was aware that she had.

She dared not meet his gaze, not with Miss Hyacinth there, but where else was she to look, her lap again? She swallowed and lifted her head. "Yes. Do you like them?"

His gaze flowed over her light-blue gown with its cream trimmings of lace and ribbon, not in a way that would make her cringe, but rather as someone regarding a piece of art with admiration and respect. "I cannot imagine how you come up with such intricate designs."

Miss Hyacinth's lips pursed and she cleared her throat. "I must admit that I wished to have the gowns sent from Paris, but apparently Miss Turner has sunk her hooks into the family and is riding on their coattails to success."

Alice whipped her head to Miss Hyacinth, no longer caring if she was a potential client or not. "I've worked for *everything* I own. It was kind of Meg's family to use me as their seamstress, yes, but I earned the right to garner their interest on my own merit."

Miss Hyacinth gasped and beat her fan, causing a windstorm as she turned to the escort she had been ignoring for the entirety of the trip to Clayton Plantation. Miss Hyacinth made no effort to conceal her haste in exiting the carriage when it rolled to a halt.

Alice, a bit breathless from her altercation, was thankful Giles did not say anything further on the subject and accepted his assistance stepping down from the carriage and up the stairs to the main level of the plantation where the transformed ballroom awaited them. They took their place behind Miss Hyacinth and her escort, waiting for the music and procession to begin. Holding her shoulders back, she tried not to think of all in attendance turning to her before resting their gazes on the brides. *I'm essentially a decoration, a background for the brides, and nothing more. There is no reason to be nervous. I can do this.* She gritted her teeth as the underbutlers drew open the double doors, her pulse quickening at the sight of the crowded plantation ballroom. *At least I can take comfort in the beauty of my gowns and the manliness of my groom—groomsman!* Her palms grew sweaty from her ridiculous thoughts.

When Miss Hyacinth reached the middle of the aisle, Alice began her promenade, smiling and discreetly nodding to anyone she recognized. When she caught sight of Constance's groom for the first time, she stumbled. Giles gripped her arm, righting her at once and keeping his smile firmly in place as she felt heat flood her cheeks. *How can this be?* Giles's sister was marrying a man by the name of Eustace Merrick. . .*not* Eustace Burke, but there was no doubt that her former fiancé stood at the end of the aisle. Her stumble had drawn his attention, and their eyes locked. The groom paled and averted his gaze before anyone could notice what had transpired between them.

He must have changed his name, but does Constance know? She wondered if she should warn Giles's sister, but she wasn't sure if her warning at the altar would come out of a place of malice or kindness, so she remained silent and watched the man she once loved pledge his troth to another.

Chapter 5

Alice was uncharacteristically mute as Giles escorted her to their place at the breakfast feast, only returning his questions with stilted replies. He glanced up in the direction where her eyes kept drifting. *Merrick. She knows him, but from where?* He had mentioned Eustace's surname at least a dozen times in her presence, and yet she had not given any reaction. Something was not right. When the minister spoke Eustace's name, he had watched her face turn ashen, and he feared she would topple over before the ceremony ended. Holding the back of her chair, Giles caught sight of her trembling hands. "Miss Turner, are you quite well?"

She shook her head as if awakening from a daze. "Water, please."

Giles waved one of the underbutlers over and motioned to her glass. "Water and a couple of dinner rolls if you please."

The young man appeared distressed at the prospect of breaking tradition, but with one glare from Giles, he did as he was told. Giles took his seat beside Alice, and when she had downed her glass of water and discreetly devoured her dinner rolls, he whispered, "Feel any better?"

She nodded. "Thank you. I was in such a rush this morning that I didn't even have time for a bite." She pressed a hand to her corset. "I was afraid my stomach's dissatisfaction was audible in the ceremony."

He wished he could believe that was the only reason for her stricken facial expressions during the ceremony. "I saw you looking at Merrick as if you know him. But in all the times I've ever mentioned him, you never once said you recognized his name."

"I didn't recall the name until I saw his face," she answered, her finger rubbing the gold edge of her china plate as she craned her neck toward the head of the table. "I really should see if Meg needs me."

"Fainting will not help Meg. Besides, if she needs anything, she can beckon you for further assistance." Giles hated to press her, but concern for his sister urged him forward. He cleared his throat. "So, were you well acquainted with Mr. Merrick?"

She shrugged. "A long time ago, but I haven't seen him in years and years." She gave him a smile as if begging to be released from his questioning. "The cake is a masterpiece. Have you seen it?" She gestured to the corner of the room where a massive, four-tiered cake was displayed on its own linen-covered table.

He pretended to admire it, but his mind raced as she continued to point out the decor of the room in an attempt to distract him from Merrick. In his heart, he knew that she must be very well acquainted with the groom, else she would not have had such an adverse reaction to his sister's now husband. His gaze rested on Constance's beaming face as she leaned on Eustace's arm while the first course was brought out.

He had inquired about Mr. Eustace Merrick's character when his sister had first introduced him as a suitor in the spring. However, there wasn't much known about Merrick besides the fact that he was a wealthy owner of a highly successful tailor shop, who claimed that his grandparents were from Scotland. Giles could not locate anyone who knew Merrick more than five years ago, but Merrick had claimed the reason was because he was studying in Paris. Giles was beginning to think that Merrick's success, which seemed to have grown overnight, lent him more credit than Father probably should have given him. Having had no negative responses from their inquiries, they assumed that Eustace told the truth, and Father allowed him to court Constance. Father would never prevent a man who worked himself up from poverty to wealth from proposing to Constance. After all, Father's paternal grandfather had worked himself up from nothing.

But there was something more to this fellow that Alice was not telling him, and his pulse quickened at the thought that his sister had married a stranger.

Alice fled the breakfast room, desperate for a breath of fresh air. Descending the stairs as quickly as her silk slippers would allow, she made her way down the side path and sank down into the curve of a giant oak tree's low branch that rested on the ground. Leaning against the soft bark, Alice sighed. She had done it. She had survived her former fiancé's wedding. On a day that should have been about her best friend, she hated to be distracted with *him*. . .if only Meg hadn't been abroad those two years that Eustace had worked with Father, she might have recognized him. Alice brushed her curls from her face and straightened her shoulders. She had to get control of herself before Meg saw through her facade to her aching heart. It was too late to warn Constance anyway, so she would let the secret lie. Why would she *want* to tell anyone that he was once her own? If word ever—

At the growing laughter and the clink of glasses, Alice twisted around to find the guests had meandered out onto the veranda, chatting as they most likely waited for the ballroom to finish being cleared from the ceremony in preparation for the wedding dance. Alice may have survived the wedding, but she couldn't face Eustace. Not now. She needed a few more moments to compose her thoughts. Continuing down the dirt path that wound through the giant oak trees and was lined with azaleas sprinkled with magenta blossoms, she followed it to where she knew she would find the Ashley River. The path led her to a steep drop to the river, and she was faced with a choice, take a right toward the riverboat, where the servants were preparing it to take the two couples downriver, or take a left toward the swamp path that curled around the river by the old rice fields that were no longer in use. She knew she was neglecting her duties as a bridesmaid, but she also knew Meg would understand if she needed to take a quarter of an hour to herself. Alice picked up her pace when she heard footsteps behind her.

"Alice? Is it you?" His deep voice ripped her from the present to the brutal past.

Slowly, hesitantly, Alice turned around to find *him*. She had not allowed herself to study him during the wedding, but she could see that Eustace was unaltered, with his youthful glow still about him. His jaunty smile and even his wavy light-brown hair held the same brilliance. She had thought that after all this time, her memories had been corrupted and she had glorified his true beauty, but now. . . She could see that he was far more handsome than she had remembered. She flicked open her fan, gently cooling her cheeks, and hoped that she appeared the picture of imperturbable tranquility. "Hello, Mr. *Burke*."

His face darkened. "It's Merrick now, as you've very well heard." He joined her under the shade of the tree without waiting to be invited. "What are you doing here, Alice?"

His impertinent question raised her hackles. How dare he address her by her Christian name? She glanced over her shoulder, waiting for another guest to appear and save her from conversing with him.

"I go without seeing you for five years, and on the morning of my wedding you magically appear as a *bridesmaid*." He fairly spat the words. "Are you attempting to ruin me, since your father didn't finish the job?"

Her jaw dropped, and the temper she had tried so hard to control threatened to overtake her. She drew a deep breath to slow her racing heart, knowing that if her anger grew too far out of control, she would divulge her true emotions. She would not give him the satisfaction of seeing how much he had hurt her. Even though her motives weren't pure, she sought to keep her soul at peace as best she could. *Help me, Lord. Fill me with Your peace and guard my heart and my mind. You and I both know that I would rather slap him than turn the other cheek.* She eased her fist to lie flat on her skirts as her thundering pulse slowed. "No, Mr. Burke—I mean, Mr. *Merrick*. I am not attempting to ruin you. If you had any memory of our time together, you would recall that Meg is my dearest friend."

"Oh." He shifted his stance and changed tactics as he gave her that coy smile that had once captivated her. "So, tell me, Alice, how are you? I haven't seen you since. . ." His voice drifted off.

"Since you cowardly left me behind to deal with the shards of my father's business after the scandal broke the papers?" She couldn't help but stab.

"I see you are still bitter about that. Good." He laughed. "If you weren't, then you were not as much in love with me as I was with you."

You certainly had a strange way of showing your devotion. Not deeming him worthy of a reply, she strode away in the direction of the house.

"Well, aren't you going to ask me about how I am doing?" His long strides brought him beside her.

She inwardly cringed at his self-obsession and began to wonder what she had ever seen in him. She had been only a girl when they had begun courting. . .and a girl when he had jilted her. But that day she had become a woman. She didn't wish to know about his life, and she did not have to wait for him to tell her. Alice picked up her pace, eager to distance herself from him.

She may have made her peace with her lot in life, but she was only now beginning to realize the depth of the hurt that she had shoved aside in order to survive. She stopped short, whirled to him, and forced out the words. "Congratulations on your wedding." She added stiffly, "Constance is quite the beauty."

"Yes, she is a picture. Petite, hair the color of the night, with a porcelain complexion and—" He gave her a rueful grin. "Blessed."

Her cheeks flamed at his poor deportment. He would speak so vulgarly of the woman he was supposed to love with his former fiancée? Did Eustace wish her to be jealous of his lady fair's stature? He knew that Alice's height had been a sore spot. Was he attempting to wound her yet? Well, she would not take the bait. She was stronger now and did not need the opinion of a man to validate her beauty. She knew her fiery hair and freckled nose may not be everyone's ideal of beauty, but she fully embraced them as they reminded her daily of her mother, who she had been told had possessed an ethereal beauty. Eustace had pitiable taste to suggest her looks that had once so enchanted him were wanting. She only wished she had seen this side of him years ago so that she had not wasted another breath pining over a man that the Lord had spared her from marrying. "I'm sure Constance will make you the perfect wife." *You best treat her with respect, else Giles will set you straight, if Constance doesn't first.*

He shrugged. "Don't see how she couldn't. She's a banker's daughter and quite wealthy and is very sweet to me. Imagine me climbing the ranks so far as to marry a—"

"Eustace?" Giles appeared at her elbow, drinks in hand. "What are you doing all the way out here with Alice? The opening quadrille is about to begin, and Constance is inquiring after your presence."

Giles's tone exuded displeasure, causing her to barely cover her smile. For once, she didn't mind a man coming to her aid. She enjoyed seeing the jealousy light in Eustace's expression at the mention of her name.

"Giles? You know Alice?"

Giles ignored his question. "It appears that you do, so it begs the question as to why she bears such a disquieted expression?" He turned to her, concern etched over his brow. "Did he say something to upset you, Alice?"

"Of course not." Eustace lifted his brows as if daring her to say otherwise. "I knew her father quite well, and he inspired my first suits. And now, after years of learning the craft in Paris, I own the most sought-after men's fine apparel tailor shop in Charleston."

Because my father taught you everything he knows about menswear. She grasped the lemonade and downed it as she felt the strain in her lungs growing. She couldn't release her true thoughts, not in front of Giles.

"Giles, will you take me to Meg? She must be wondering where I am." She boldly grasped Giles's hand and retreated toward the big house, breathing easier with every step she took away from that horrid man.

Miss Hyacinth met them at the foot of the path, her gaze falling on Alice's hand wrapped around Giles's own. Her pink lips pursed as she glared at Alice. "Giles, I saw you come down here with two drinks and thought I'd follow. Thank you for confirming that our dear seamstress really is what I've been thinking." She turned on her heel.

"Miss Castle, it's not—" He called after her retreating figure. "Miss Castle!"

But Miss Hyacinth ignored him, confirming the future demise of Alice's bridal shop with the social elite if she did not remedy this situation at once.

Alice dropped her hold on his hand, sighing. "I'm sorry. I wasn't thinking. I just had to get away from him."

He grasped her elbow, gently turning her to him. "What did Eustace say to you?"

She regarded him, weariness seeming to press her very bones. "I think it might be for the best if we skip Monday's lesson. It's my busy season after all."

"Alice."

"Trust me." It was too late to warn anyone of Eustace's lie, and if she spoke now. . .would he despise her once he knew the truth about why Eustace left her? She bit her lip and fled to the house before she divulged the secret she had been bearing for far too long.

Chapter 6

Alice had kept clear of Giles for the rest of the wedding celebration, and when she sent back the carriage on Monday, refusing their lesson, he decided he needed to at least try to convince her to trust him enough to confide in him what she knew of Eustace. Despite his worries, Giles took a small measure of comfort knowing that if she thought Eustace a danger to Constance, she would have spoken up prior to the ceremony. So he was fairly certain Eustace wasn't a criminal, only someone Alice did not particularly like.

The jog to her shop cooled his fevered thoughts. Pausing to wipe away his perspiration, a flash of burgundy caught his attention and he discovered Alice, in a striking gown, working in the display window with her back to him. Giles lingered to watch as she arranged a long veil in the display of what he supposed to be her creations and latest shipment from Paris. She was so engrossed in arranging a fold in the veil in just the right manner that he finally tapped on the windowpane, chuckling as she jumped and nearly dropped the veil.

She turned a scowl to the window, but her agitation evaporated into pleasure when their gaze met before she smoothed her expression. She rolled her eyes and lifted up the veil. "Have you need of this veil?" she called through the wavy glass, motioning him inside and turning to hop out of the display window.

He hurried inside and caught her hands, assisting her descent. "I'll have you know that I didn't even take the time to conjure an excuse to see you." Her hands felt so right in his. *Will she ever allow me the chance to win them?*

"I apologize for sending your carriage home, but I thought I was clear about canceling today's lesson." Alice dropped her gaze and pulled her hands from his.

"I had hoped you would reconsider, but as you are still opposed, would you be willing to take a short stroll with me instead? I promise I won't ask any prying questions." He stuffed his hands into his tennis trouser pockets and gave her a half smile to assure her of his innocent intentions. "I only thought if you were too busy at the shop for a lesson, you could surely use a short break."

She sighed and seemed to be weighing her options. "I could use a bit of fresh air, I suppose. Let me fetch my chapeau and parasol."

Silently strolling down King Street, Giles wove Alice around the bustling shoppers and errand boys and diverted her toward the park, where the din of the city lessened to a hum and a lone bird chirped in the dogwood and magnolia trees, calling, Giles imagined, for his love. He cleared his throat at the nonsensical thought.

Whatever was the matter with him? "Well, I was disappointed you were, uh, detained this morning as I wanted to tell you that I think you are ready to play a tennis match with me."

She halted her promenade down the gravel path, her parasol rolling on her shoulder. "Well, I wouldn't have canceled on you if I had known that!"

"I wanted to surprise you." Giles laughed, feeling the awkwardness of their last interaction melting away in the heat of the day. He had wished to ask her to dinner after their morning lesson, but after her mysterious behavior at the wedding, he feared doing so would scare her away for good. Instead he suggested, "If you find that today wasn't as busy as you thought, why don't you come now? My father will be out on business most of the day, and well, Constance is gone for the week on her wedding trip, so you don't have to worry about running into anyone. It'll just be me and you and the twenty tennis balls that we will have nearby in case you decide to keep sending them flying into the river."

She rolled her eyes, bringing his gaze to her lovely auburn lashes. "That happened once. If I leave my assistant in charge, you promise we will finally get to play a *full* set and not just hit the ball back and forth without keeping score?"

He grinned. "I'll even let you win a match."

And with that, he found himself fairly trotting to keep up with her as she hurried to her shop, making quick work of changing, placing her assistant in charge, and joining him in the hired carriage.

Giles couldn't help but grin at her eagerness to finally play. *I should've told her she was ready at the wedding, and I might have avoided this whole almost skipping practice.* He glanced at her from the corner of his eye as she bounced her racket against her knee.

"I'm glad you came for me." She broke the silence as the carriage wheels crunched the gravel on his driveway. "I can become quite the recluse when I get caught up in my own thoughts." She viewed the scenery, swaying with the turn of the carriage wheels. "And sometimes, I can't even remember how to escape my thoughts on my own, so thank you." She sent him a tentative smile that made his heart ache.

What happened that hurt you? he was tempted to ask, but merely returned her smile and risked giving her hand a quick squeeze. "Anytime."

As the carriage rolled to a stop, her look of consternation vanished as she hopped out of the carriage without waiting for assistance. "Enough of that. It's *finally* time to play!"

Alice grunted. She would not give him this next point. She bent her knees and readied her racket as Giles positioned himself to toss the ball into the air, calling, "Fifteen love!"

His declaration caused her to stumble and miss her chance to dive for the ball. "What did you just call me?"

His brow creased. "Call you? I was calling the score. Fifteen to love—it's tennis slang for zero."

"Oh." The breath went out of her. "Of course. I know that from all the matches I've read about." *But it is surprisingly disappointing. Even though it would be ridiculous for him to say he loves me after only knowing me for—* The ball came hurtling over the net directly toward her, but her feet would not move as fast as her brain wanted them to and she tripped, the ball slamming her in the back of her head and sending her sprawling face-first.

"Alice!" Giles vaulted over the net and knelt beside her. "Why didn't you move to the side of the ball like I showed you?"

She twisted her mouth and sputtered out bits of grass. "I was trying to do just that, but you *hurled* the ball at me. And I am pretty certain you said you'd let me win."

"I'm trying to, but I'm afraid you are making it difficult," Giles teased as he helped her to her feet. "Now, are we quite clear on the scoring system?"

Resigned that Giles would win the set, she set her sights on attempting to win the next two. *Whack.* She imagined Eustace's face on the tennis ball as she smacked it with a grunt. Giles's jaw dropped as her passionate strike sent the tennis ball sailing into the river.

By the end of the third set, she was certain she no longer looked as fetching as she had when they first started. Her pretty coiled braid had come loose and tumbled to her waist, but she paid it no mind and brushed away at the perspiration beading on her forehead.

With his racket tucked under his distractingly muscular tan arm, Giles tossed the ball from hand to hand, calling, "I think we should stop for the day. It's gotten really hot out."

"I'm fine, so don't you worry about me," Alice returned, giving a weak laugh. Her loose skirts, which had felt so light earlier, now encumbered her every step. Dots lined her vision as she blinked against the glare. *So. . .hot.* She dropped her gaze to find, oddly enough, the lawn rising up to meet her. The cool grass crashed against her blazing cheek, and she sighed as the oppressive heat vanished from her thoughts.

Feeling something entirely different than the soft lawn, Alice became very aware of a linen fabric against her cheek that was *moving*. With a cry, she opened her eyes to find herself in Giles's arms and being carried toward the big house. "I'm so sorry," she murmured, pushing against his thick shoulder.

"No, I should be the one apologizing. I should have listened to my better judgment and stopped us when it grew too hot, but I wished to please you," he replied, misery exuding from his every word.

His kindness made her throat swell with suppressed emotion. How long had it been since a man tried to do something sweet just to please her? She dared to lay a hand on his broad chest, staying him for a moment as his brilliant eyes met her own, and she couldn't bring herself to ask him to set her down. "Thank you, but I'm quite well now. Would you mind taking me home?"

"As long as you allow me to send the doctor to attend to you there if you won't have him here," Giles countered.

"I promise you, I am fine." She felt his tense shoulders relax.

"Very well, but I am seeing you into your shop, and if your assistant is present, up to your second-floor landing, no matter how much you protest."

She laid her cheek against his chest once more. "Deal."

Chapter 7

Alice's shoulders sagged as she packed away her sewing supplies while Constance rushed down to host her first dinner party as a married woman, a fact that she mentioned at least three times in the space of a half hour. She rubbed her hand over her face, exhausted from being called out for a fitting emergency just when she was sitting down to her hot dinner. She wrapped her light shawl about her shoulders and took the servant's exit as disappointment filled her over not seeing Giles.

Ever since their match five days ago that ended without a dinner invitation, she'd been thinking about him constantly and had been trying to think of a way to see him again without coming across as desperate. So when the freshly returned Mrs. Eustace Merrick sent a servant with a message regarding a too-tight bodice, she had eagerly complied for a chance to see Giles, only to be crushed to learn from Constance that he worked late most nights.

Stepping out into the heavy evening air, she was surprised to see it had grown so dark. Alice squinted to read her watch pin. She must've been in the mansion longer than she thought. She bit her lip, craning her neck toward the stables, hoping to see a carriage ready to bring her home, but there had been no mention of the Claytons' buggy taking her home and there wasn't a groomsman waiting for her.

Alice checked her valise and grimaced. In her haste to possibly see Giles, she had forgotten her purse along with her coin for a hired carriage, but even if she had remembered, money was too dear to waste on a three-mile carriage ride home when she could just as easily walk. She clutched her bag, straightened her shoulders, and strode down the sidewalk as quickly as she could, praying that the coarse sailors who daily swarmed to Charleston's port would not be bothering her tonight. Once on King Street and in the glow of the gas streetlights, she picked up her pace, eager for her now-cold dinner, a pot of tea, and her magazine.

Her pulse quickened when two sailors from across the street at a public house caught sight of her, one pointing in her direction. Keeping her chin lifted in a confident manner, she strode onward, passing the pub and its cacophony of bawdy music. She had just as much a right to be out on the street as any man. She was dressed as a lady, and if these roguish-looking men did not treat her as one, they would soon find out that she was no damsel. Reaching into her valise, her fingers wrapped around her steel scissors and, gripping the handle like a knife, she held them at the ready as she strode home. Footsteps sounded behind her, and at first she pretended to ignore them, praying they did not belong to the two staring men. *Almost there.*

But when their rakish laughter and crude comments reached her ears, she twirled around, pursed her lips, and narrowed her eyes. In a firm voice, she commanded, "I suggest you step away from me and mind your tongue. You come near me, and you'll be sorry you ever approached me." She withdrew her scissors from her bag, the freshly sharpened blades catching in the gaslights. She glared at the sailors. She had worked twelve hours and would put up with nothing. The men did not even blink at her scissors. They laughed even louder and continued to approach her. Alice began to reconsider her stance of holding her ground and stumbled backward a few paces, her arm still poised, ready to stab if necessary. "Back off now."

"Looks like we have a fighter." The red-bearded man elbowed his taller companion.

"Good. I like a bit of a challenge. Come on, girly. You wouldn't have walked by here unless you wanted us to buy you a drink."

She hated that she could not keep the tremor out of her voice. "I've warned you. I *will* hurt you."

The men grinned, and the red-bearded sailor lunged for her, knocking her bag to the ground, scattering her precious silk threads and silver engraved thimble. In a single, swift motion, she shrieked and jammed the point of her scissors into the shoulder of her assailant. He cried out as she twisted the scissors and jerked them out and gave the tall sailor a swift kick to the shin, picking up her skirts to make a run for it. But the tall man caught her by her full sleeve, ripping it and baring her shoulder. *Dear Lord, help me.* She shoved her elbow into his nose and screamed, "Help!" His filthy fingers grasped at her waist as she tripped and cried out for help again, scrambling to her feet.

A gentleman in formal attire thrust himself between them and rammed his fist into the tall man's jaw, sending the thug staggering backward. "Did they hurt you, Alice?"

"Giles," she gasped, nearly in tears at the sight of him. Retrieving her scissors from the ground, she turned to find the red-bearded man rallying as the tall sailor snatched a log from a pile of firewood beside the bakery.

With his attention on the red-bearded man, Giles didn't see the other draw up the log like a club, his gaze on Giles's head. Alice screamed a warning, and Giles dodged, directly into the second man's fist. Giles went sprawling as Alice shoved the red-bearded man back to ground, taking care to hit his arm where she had wounded him and making him howl in pain.

Giles wiped his forehead with the back of his hand and, seeing blood, laughed, rising to his feet and pushing his sleeves up. He lifted his fists, the veins in his athletic forearms cording with power. "That was a mistake."

The tall man gripped the jacket collar of his injured friend and hoisted him up, scrambling away. "Come on before someone sends for the police. No skirt is worth a beating."

Before she knew what she was about, Alice dropped her scissors and flung herself into Giles's strong arms, ducking her head into his chest, the tears clogging her throat as she whimpered his name over and over.

Giles's heart stumbled at the closeness of her. He wrapped his arms about her and laid his chin atop her hair that held the faint scent of gardenias, ignoring the throbbing pain in his jaw and relishing the tender moment until he heard a sniff. He pulled back, his hands on her arms, reluctant to release her for even a moment. "Are you hurt?"

She shook her head, using her lace cuff to dab at her cheeks. He retrieved a cotton handkerchief from his pocket and pressed it into her hand.

Alice turned her back to him, affording herself a bit of privacy. "Thank you. I don't know what I would've done if you hadn't shown up. I'm so thankful you happened to be near."

"And I. Though, I have to say you were doing quite well without any assistance." Giles swiped at his chin with the sleeve of his jacket, not caring that his sister would raise a fuss over the state of his clothes. He would have words with Constance for sending Alice out in the darkness without even a thought of how she would return home. When he had discovered at dinner that Alice had come and gone into the night, he had left the party without a word, jogging down the streets looking for her when he heard a scream that struck him to the core.

He reached out, daring to gently stroke her cheek with the back of his hand at the memory. Giles shuddered to think what could have happened, and he was thankful that Alice had the presence of mind to withdraw her scissors from her bag to defend herself. Thinking of her scissors, he bent down and scooped them off the ground and wiped them against his black pant leg. She protested. "Don't! You'll ruin—"

But he had already smeared a dark stain across his pant leg. "Looks like you winged one of them pretty good."

"I wish I'd winged both of them." She straightened her hat, the poor decorative bird atop looking like it had seen better days, and examined her ripped sleeve. "Thankfully, I can fix this, but I can't say the same for my new hat." She looked up to his forehead, concern etched in her eyes. "Giles, you could have been seriously injured. . . and I couldn't forgive myself if something happened to you on my account."

His brows rose. "So, you finally admit it. You *do* care for me."

She gave him that dimpled smile that sent his heart skipping. "Why else would I be staying after our lessons for half an hour for the past month during busy season?"

He grinned, unable to contain his joy. "I've been thinking about you all week."

"Oh? Have you now?"

He tucked a strand of fiery hair behind her ear. "Yes. I've been thinking of the perfect excuse to come see you all week."

She lifted her brow and sheepishly returned his grin. "My excuse was to come running the second your family beckoned even though it was dinnertime and I had bought a delicious-smelling meat pie from the bakery across the street." She spoke so quietly he barely heard her as they walked toward her shop, but her confession gave him the courage to admit his own plans.

"Well, I thought about breaking my pocket watch to visit the clock shop next door and magically run into you, or losing Constance's favorite set of gloves prior to the dinner party, but those excuses all seemed too fabricated." *And I wanted our next meeting to be a little bit more romantic.* He paused at her doorway and leaned against the frame, waiting there while she opened the shop, entered, and lit a lamp. "Alice, it's been a month and I still haven't changed my mind," he said when she rejoined him at the door.

She lifted her lamp and gasped. "Giles! Your face is bleeding yet. Come in, and I'll dress it."

He regarded the empty, dark room and thought of her reputation. "I'm not sure if that is the best idea."

"We will stay downstairs by the window with the lamp glowing for all the world to see, so we won't truly be alone. I'm more worried about you passing out in the street from blood loss than my own reputation at the moment."

"I will on one condition." He gave her a half grin.

"What's that?"

"You allow me to take you to dinner tomorrow night. It's the least I can do since Constance spoiled your meat pie," he added with a wink.

She rolled her eyes and waved him inside. "You are incorrigible. Fine. Now, let me attend to your wound." She pulled him inside and set him on a stool in front of the shop window before ducking into the back and returning, balancing a basin of water that sloshed onto her skirt, another lamp, and a basket of what appeared to be medical supplies. "My assistant isn't as experienced with using the Singer sewing machine as I am and, well, running the needle over one's fingers can leave quite the mess." She pressed a clean, plain white handkerchief to the mouth of the amber bottle and flipped it over, allowing the liquid to seep into the cloth.

He inhaled sharply as she pressed the cloth to his forehead. His racing pulse from the fight must have distracted him from the cut on his forehead. . .until now.

"Does it hurt?"

"Not as badly as sewing my finger, I'd imagine."

"I'm sorry. I wish I could be gentler, but I can't keep the witch hazel from stinging." She lightly patted the wound with the handkerchief, dipped it into the water, and dabbed his head again. "Thank you for rescuing me. And just so you know, I would have said yes without the bribe."

"And that is the best medicine a man could ever want." He caught her slender hand in his, tempted to press a kiss on her fingertips. Giles wanted to state his intentions to marry her then and there, but he didn't think his declaration would be well received just yet, given her uncertainty with even meeting with him after that disastrous encounter with Eustace. And despite his best efforts, Giles couldn't stanch his lingering desire to know why she was so hostile to Eustace. Her past didn't matter to him, but he felt like it would help him better understand her. "Do you mind terribly if I ask what happened the day of my sister's wedding? Why did Merrick look as if he had seen a ghost?"

Alice sucked in her cheeks as she wrapped the gauze around his head, and he grew afraid that he might have asked something from which there was no return. But as she pinned the bandage into place, her indigo eyes met his, and he could read a sadness behind them.

"I suppose it is only fair for you to understand what a risk you are taking by even being seen with me." She leaned against the counter and crossed her arms as she kicked at a bit of ivory thread on the hardwood floor. "I knew Eustace Merrick by another name, a name he abandoned after— But, I am getting ahead of myself. Eustace *Burke* was an apprentice in my father's shop for two years. When he started, I was merely an overgrown girl of sixteen, gangly, and irrevocably in love with him. He, of course, did not notice me until my eighteenth birthday, when I grew into my limbs."

He swallowed at her bluntness, watching an alluring blush creep into her cheeks as she admitted this. *How could Eustace not have noticed such a beauty in all those years? I would have noticed you long before for your sweet spirit.*

"Our romance was forbidden by Father, and that made it all the more desirable for Eustace, I believe. When Father discovered us stealing a kiss inside the workshop when Eustace was supposed to be working, my father realized that prohibiting our love had done nothing to keep us apart. Reluctantly, he gave us his blessing, and Eustace and I were engaged and planned to wed shortly after my nineteenth birthday once the rush of the season was over and my dearest friend, Meg, had returned from her finishing school abroad."

She gave a short, bitter laugh. "To thank Father for his blessing, I designed a lovely, intricate quilt made from the material of a few of my mother's gowns, an old vest that he used to wear for special occasions, and a childhood dress or two of mine. I wanted to show Father that even though I was getting married—" She pressed her hand to her mouth and shook her head. "But, of course, that never happened. I almost burned it, but the memories it held were so dear that I just packed it away."

"And that's how Meg never knew Merrick was actually your"—Giles had never hated the words more—"*former* fiancé. He had ended things before she returned home."

She nodded. "Exactly."

Giles didn't want to think of Eustace stealing Alice's kisses or breaking her heart, but he had to know. "What stopped the two of you from marrying?"

"The thing that keeps most marriages from occurring. Even though Eustace said he loved me and I imagined myself in love with him and we had the most blissful courtship, it wasn't strong enough to withstand—" She dipped her head and wiped her eyes, laughing. "I don't know why I'm crying. It's been years since the scandal."

His heart stopped. The circumstances must have been truly horrible for a man to breach his promise and not worry about repercussions. But Giles remained silent and waited for her to speak.

"Days after our engagement, it was discovered that Father had been stealing from one of his clients. Or, rather, he had been caught by only one. He later confided to me that he had taken from a couple other clients, but had done so in ways that they did not notice or suspect him. A little here and a little there. But then we had an exceptionally poor month in the shop, and Father risked stealing a valuable antique vase." She swallowed. "He hoped for leniency from the judge and told me not to worry. However, it turned out that the worth of the vase he had stolen was far greater than he had originally told me. The court investigated, and I was shocked to discover the extent of my father's theft, which, as you can guess, went beyond the few clients that he had confessed to me."

"Oh Alice." He ran his hand over the back of his neck. *No wonder she is so enigmatic and untrusting. She's ashamed of her father's actions and lies.*

"Apparently, he had been lining his pockets with bills or items from people's houses with little consequence to himself for *years*. Multiple servants appeared in court, proclaiming they had been released from their positions without references on the accusation of theft brought on by Father's actions." Her voice cracked. "Many of the servants had families who depended on them, and the judge did not look kindly on Father profiting from his wealthy clients at the expense of modest servants. The judge condemned my father to twenty years' hard labor." She looked up at Giles, her fists clenched. "And he deserved every year he received."

Giles reached for her hand, his fingers encasing hers for only a moment before she stepped back from him and set to work putting away her supplies. "But you managed to keep the shop," he ventured, hoping to pull her from her dark memories to something he knew she loved.

"Yes. Only just. The judge was kind to me. Instead of seizing all my father's assets and turning me into a homeless pauper, he said I could keep a small percentage of whatever I sold from the shop and apply the rest to debts until they were paid in full."

"But I'm assuming Eustace was not as understanding?" Giles watched her carefully.

She gave a short laugh and set the basket under the counter, her hands trembling as she flattened them against the front of her skirt. "Eustace said my father's scandal would be the death of his career if word circulated that he was somehow connected with Turner's Fine Tailor, and he certainly could not be connected to it through a marriage with the thieving scoundrel's daughter. I begged Eustace not to leave me, but after the ruling, he abandoned me on the courthouse steps with almost nothing to my name but a failed shop and no one to share my burden. He had promised to love and protect me, but when it came right down to it, Eustace would only love and protect himself. He left me and evidently changed his name. I changed the tailor shop's name to Thimbles and Threads Bridal Shop and never looked back. It took me five years of backbreaking toil to work myself out of Father's debts and to build a name for myself. This past year was the first time I was able to hire an assistant and finally earn some high-society patrons." She straightened her shoulders. "And, my friend, that brings us to the wedding last month."

Giles clenched his jaw, ignoring the pain and wishing he could wring Eustace's neck for abandoning Alice all those years ago. No wonder she had been so reluctant to allow him into her life. Every man she had ever trusted had let her down in a colossal way. His throat tightened as he realized that she had been so crushed by men that she didn't even bother to name her cat anything other than "Cat" for fear that he would one day leave her too. Giles rose, taking her shoulders in his hands. "But I am not like them." *I would never abandon you.*

She gave him a stiff smile and a laugh that cracked with suppressed emotion. "You say that now, but your family would never accept me, and if they didn't—"

"You seem to forget that my father is only a banker because my grandfather married well and worked his way up to buy the bank." He gave her a sad smile. "And we already have a tailor in the family through Constance's marriage. It's not a stretch for us to court. Alice, you *know* me. . .possibly better than anyone ever has. You know I would never do that to you."

She rested her fingers on his, stroking his tan knuckles. "I know you wouldn't," she whispered, her long lashes fairly brushing her rosy freckled cheeks. "You are too kind to ever hurt a woman like that." She lifted her hands from his. "You are a good friend, Giles."

"For being so clever, how could you not realize by now how much I care for you *beyond* friendship?" He cupped her cheek in his hand and tilted her face up to his. "How could you not know that I think of you from the moment I open my eyes to the moment I close them to dream of you? Since I've met you, every beat of my heart is for you, my Alice. Won't you take the chance to fall in love with me? Let me court you. Allow me the chance to gain your trust and your heart." His eyes settled on her lips and, as she said nothing, he leaned forward, his lips a breath away from hers when she pulled back, nearly tripping over her skirts.

"The hour is quite late. You'd best be on your way, else your family will think something happened."

Giles prayed he had not been too forward, but then she rose on her tiptoes and lightly kissed him on the cheek.

"I'll think on it, but until then, be content with dinner tomorrow night."

Chapter 8

Alice dropped another gardenia that was meant for her hair. Her fingers could not stop trembling. She had expected to feel relieved after having shared her burden with someone after so many years. She drew a ragged breath as her stomach twisted. *How could I have allowed myself to be caught up in the emotion of the moment and risk my shop's reputation?* One word from Giles could remind her clients of her shop's less than desirable beginnings. She gripped the corners of her vanity, her head sagging, and gathered her rising panic. She knew he would never purposely harm her or her business. And yet, his sister was an influential client. If he inadvertently let it slip to someone who'd never approve of their relationship, Alice would be ruined. She shook her head to banish her train of thought that would only end catastrophically. She knew him. Giles was not like Eustace. He was not like Father. She straightened her shoulders and finished dressing her hair. She would not allow her past to mar the present.

She stared into the looking glass and saw in front of her a stylish woman in a silk russet skirt with so many tucks in the bustle, it caught on every piece of light, making it glisten. She adjusted the lace on her soft, pearl-white sleeves, satisfied that in every visible sense of the word, she appeared to be a lady of refinement. She turned, admiring the tucks and twists of her gown, and sighed. If only forging a new heritage was as easy as assembling a new wardrobe. Giles's family would never approve of her scandalous past, and the little money she had finally set aside was hardly enough to lure a fine gentleman into overlooking said past. *Stop it.* She kicked at the soiled blossom on the floor and plucked another gardenia from the vase, tucking it into place and enjoying the sweet perfume the white flower offered her ensemble.

Glancing at her watch pin atop her dresser, Alice grabbed her footed crystal hand lamp and decided she had just enough time to finish the last bit of embroidery on the bodice of a bridesmaid gown she had been working on earlier. She settled downstairs at her station, hoping to lose herself in her work, but with every stitch, she thought of him. *Be honest, Alice. The real reason you are so torn over tonight's dinner is because you allowed yourself to grow close to him and are deathly afraid of something happening to him or having to live through another heartbreak.*

She snapped off the ends of the blush-colored thread as if it were her relationship with Giles, doomed to be cut short. She shook the dress free of threads and, satisfied that she had finished the hardest parts, set it on the back of her assistant's chair as the clock shop next door sounded the time, chiming a cheerful six o'clock. As if on cue, Giles's buggy for two rolled to a halt in front of her shop. She watched Giles hop down from the buggy in a plain navy suit, and she ran her hand over her bodice, thankful he had told her to wear a visiting gown in place of a dinner dress. Even though it seemed odd, it lent an air of mystery to their outing that she quite fancied. She wrapped her embroidered silk shawl about her shoulders and stepped outside, locking the shop and dropping the key into her beaded reticule.

"Good evening, my lady." Giles bowed, pressing his stiff hat over his heart. "Are you up for an evening drive?"

"Certainly. It will be nice to spend more than a few minutes of my day outside," she replied as the lavender and russet sunset cast a glow about them. She placed her hand in his and allowed him to whisk her away into the unknown of the evening. "You seem to be healing quickly."

"Well, when my family saw my cuts, they sent for the doctor at once." He laughed. "You would think I'd never taken a blow before. They should have seen me in London when I attempted to teach this one young lord. He smashed my face with the racket at just the perfect angle to break my nose. The beautiful creature you see in front of you today is nothing short of a miracle. If there hadn't been a doctor at the courts when it happened, I'm sure my nose would've been ruined for life."

She laughed at his bravado and dared to admire his strong jawline and profile as he pointed out each bit of scenery in passing as if she were a tourist. She enjoyed playing along and trusting him with the evening's events. They turned onto East Battery, and the wind picked up as it flowed over the waves, drawing her attention to the harbor and the island of Fort Sumter in the middle. A gust slammed into her, sending her perfect coiffure into a riotous mess.

Giles sent her an apologetic smile. "Sorry about the wind, but I thought you'd enjoy the harbor view for a moment. I know how much you like being near water."

She blushed at his thoughtfulness, stunned that he remembered that tiny detail from one of their first conversations together. She laughed to distract him from noticing her heightened color and gripped the side of the buggy, the gardenias in her hair perilously loose. "While I do, I think perhaps the river might be our best hope for a water view since it is so windy tonight?"

"I'm glad you suggested that." Giles grinned as if he knew something she didn't and turned them down a street, headed in the opposite direction of the harbor. For the next quarter of an hour, they conversed on every topic *but* her confession of last night, and when they turned into his drive, her heart nearly pounded out of her chest.

"You can't be taking me to dinner at your house with your family?" she squeaked. Her hands flew to her hair, which she knew was a tangled mess. "And I'm not dressed for a formal dinner! You specifically said in your note—"

"Oh no, I wouldn't do that to you. We won't even be going in the house," he reassured her. "Besides, Father, Constance and, uh, her husband are all away this evening having dinner at William and Meg's new townhouse." He directed the gig off the main road and onto what appeared to be a wide walking path, jostling their shoulders together with each turn of the wheel.

"No need to avoid mentioning Eustace's name on my account," she replied, holding up her hand. "I have long since moved past him and feel no hurt at the mention of his name." *Though the sight of him turns my stomach.*

"Good. Though I'm afraid it may take me a bit longer to get over his treatment of you."

Turning the corner, Alice gasped at the sight of the riverboat on the Ashley River, bedecked with what seemed to be nearly a hundred candles surrounding a small table set for two on the promenade deck.

"I thought you might enjoy a peaceful evening on the river and possibly a river cruise after dinner?" He hopped down and reached up for her. "That's why I suggested a visiting gown, so you'd have sleeves to keep the mosquitos at bay."

"I wondered." She giggled, feeling lighter than she had in years. As it was too far for her to jump, she surrendered to him, allowing him to wrap his hands about her waist and gently lift her from the buggy to the ground. He didn't set her down but instead cradled her in his arms.

"Giles!" She gave a nervous laugh, glancing back to the house.

"The ground is still soggy from that heavy rain this morning," he explained, taking the pathway lit with lanterns to the riverboat where a couple of servants awaited them and a handful of men that she assumed were the pilot and crew, judging from their attire.

Her cheeks burned at being seen in such a manner, but she gave them a nod and attempted to smile with dignity as she said through gritted teeth, "Okay, you can set me down now."

Giles laughed, the small charming space in his front teeth making him even more endearing. "Your wish is my command."

With her feet set firmly on the worn floorboards of the riverboat, she gathered her skirts and followed him up the riverboat's stairs to the promenade deck. In the flickering candlelight against the last rays of the sunset, Alice was taken with the beauty of the swamp surrounding her, the croaking of the frogs, the gray moss fluttering in the light breeze as the boat swayed ever so slightly in the current of the lazy Ashley River. She peered over the edge of the rail to spy five turtles scuttle off a fallen log and plop into the green film resting atop the dark waters. She grinned as the smallest finally managed to wriggle off its resting place to join its family. Lulled by the splendor, she lifted her gaze to Giles, her breath catching at the expression on his face, captured in the light of a hundred candles.

Giles was taken with her exquisiteness, her delight with small creatures. His sister never took the time to stare over the railing once she had her sights set on higher things, like a husband with a fortune. He joined her by the rail and observed the river through Alice's eyes. He had long since taken the riverboat for granted as an extension of his home, but he had to admit that it was quite a luxury. He was struck by the thought that, unlike him, she had worked for everything that she owned. Admiration for her passion turned his gaze to her. Surrendering any pretense of being discreet, he openly studied the curve of her lips. His gaze finally rested on her wide eyes, and he knew he would never take her for granted should she ever trust her hand to him. "Alice, I've enjoyed our time together and—"

"Me too." She cut him off as if afraid of what he might say.

"While we've only been acquainted for almost two months, I want you to know my intent—"

"Oh, is that dinner I smell? I'm starving." She grabbed his arm, steering him toward the table as dinner was indeed being served. She nodded to the butler and, without waiting for Giles to assist her, she slipped into her chair and opened her napkin with a snap. She then lifted a crystal glass of water to her lips, her gaze drifting toward the stars.

Giles wished to press the topic, but from the way she fairly jumped into the river to shy away from him, he knew it was too soon. Yet part of him felt that if he did not declare his intentions, he was being as dishonorable as Eustace Merrick.

Alice directed their conversation to a humorous encounter with a client, tennis, and even spoke of her childhood as if to distract him from the topic on his heart. They were nearing the end of their meal when a few lamps bobbing in the distance seemed to be approaching the river along the path coming from—*the house*! He groaned and looked to Alice, who was finishing off her chocolate cake with such enthusiasm that he would have laughed if not for the impending doom of their dinner.

"I saw the riverboat from the house and I wondered what possibly could be happening. What on earth are you doing with all those lamps and candles? Are you trying to set the swamp ablaze?" Constance stepped from the dock and up the gangplank, waving away the servant escorting her with two lamps.

Giles pressed his lips into a thin line, certain that the servants informed his sister that he was entertaining a young lady, and she couldn't keep herself from marching down to find out who it was. He had purposefully not told anyone who his guest was so as not to draw attention to Alice. He knew how she detested being in the spotlight. His gaze darted to Alice, and he saw that her hands were busy twisting her napkin in her lap.

"Giles," she whispered through her smile as Constance's footsteps sounded on the stairs leading up to the decks. "You said they were gone!"

"Did he?" Constance's brow quirked, and her gaze settled on Alice as her mouth formed a disapproving line, all politeness banished from her eyes. "No wonder you were so secretive. You wanted to have your dalliance with our seamstress without interference."

Giles frowned as he rose with Alice. "Constance! You forget yourself."

Alice slowly wiped her lips free of any trace of chocolate. "Well, that was a delicious meal, and I thank you, Giles, but I'm afraid that the hour is quite late and I must be on my way."

"I quite agree with you." Constance's raven manufactured curls bobbed as she gave Alice a pert nod.

"Alice, it is hardly eight o'clock. We were supposed to go on a river cruise."

Her gaze darted to his sister. "Not tonight, I'm afraid. I remembered that I have some work to see to that cannot wait."

"Nonsense. You promised me an evening in payment of my near-death experience." He half-heartedly teased, but Constance had ruined any chance he had of telling Alice his intentions.

She backed away, sending her chair tumbling to its side.

"I'm sorry. This was a mistake." She moved for the stairs, nodding to his sister. "Miss Constance, I hope you won't change your mind about using me in the future."

"You can bet your bustle that I will no longer use your services, and I will be sure to spread the word among your clients that you *flirt* with your employers in an attempt to ensnare a rich husband."

"Constance, be quiet. You have no idea what you are talking

about." Giles stepped forward, wishing he could place a protective arm about Alice but knowing it would not be welcome.

Constance pursed her lips. "I am quite decided that Miss Turner will *never* work for any other decent bride in the future."

"But Mrs. Merrick, I—" Alice's voice cracked as his sister waved her along.

"I will not be moved. Imagine a *seamstress* going after one of my brothers." She shook her head, lip curling in disgust.

"You seem to forget, Constance, about our own heritage." Giles had expected a little resistance, but to have his sister be so blatantly rude to Alice was not to be borne. "And not to mention the obvious, but you happened to be *married* to a tailor."

She sniffed and lifted her chin. "Eustace is *successful* and wants to further himself. He dreams of becoming far more than his simple tailor beginnings, as you can see from his business growth. The difference between Eustace and this sad excuse for a designer is night and day."

"Constance." He clenched his fists. "Apologize to Miss Turner at once."

"I will not. Eustace told me everything about her past. She is nothing more than the girl who stopped at nothing to trap Eustace into an engagement, so you best rid yourself of this seductress!"

Alice picked up her skirts and fled down the stairs and toward the gangplank. Giles sent his sister a glare and trotted after Alice. He would have words with Constance later.

"Wait! Alice!" He hurried down the path, reaching for her elbow. "You can't just go running off into the dark. This is a swamp. Do you want to be eaten? There are alligators just waiting for a chocolate-filled treat to come along the path."

She swatted at her neck. "Too late. The mosquitos seem to have found me at last."

"Are you that eager to be away from me that you would risk swamp fever and life and limb?"

"You don't understand." Her voice cracked, and he could see her tears pooling. "I have worked for *years* to build my reputation, and in a single night, it is all gone."

"I'll take care of Constance. I'll explain that you didn't want to come. That I bribed you."

She jerked her elbow out of his hand and wiped at her cheeks, her gaze hardening. It was as if he could see the walls that had taken him weeks to dismantle go up again and rise even higher. "I need to go."

"I'll take you home," he replied, seeing that there was no way they could speak while she was so angry. "I'm so sorry for what Constance said to you. There is no excuse for her to treat you as she did, and I will let her know."

She drew a deep breath and smoothed her russet skirt. "She may have been rude, but she reminded me of why dinner with you was a mistake. Can you have one of your staff take me home?"

Her request throbbed more than taking a racket to the face. "If you wish."

"I do."

Chapter 9

Alice inhaled sharply through her teeth and jerked her hand away from the offending needle. She wrapped her finger in a handkerchief and set to work again on the intricate embroidery on the collar of a wedding dress, minding her needle this time. She could not afford to stain the cloth by her carelessness.

"Giles is here to see you, *again*," Meg called from around the thick curtain separating the workroom from the front of the shop.

"I'm busy."

"You've said that every day for six days. My new brother-in-law is in misery. It is obvious he is not just some dandy trying to—"

Alice sent her a glare. "I thought you came for a visit not a lecture."

"Fine." Meg lifted her hands in surrender and spoke softly to

Giles before the front door slammed, sending the copper bell jingling in protest.

She hardened her spirit. She could not risk being seen with Giles. So far, business continued as usual. Constance hadn't exposed the secret dinner rendezvous, but that didn't mean she wouldn't if she felt that Alice was trying to steal her brother's affections. But Alice had long since buried that dream of becoming a bride when Eustace had left her. And she had worked too long and too hard to have it taken from her by a spoiled, overgrown girl.

"When are you going to speak to him?" Meg reclined on the ratty settee that Alice only kept to take naps on if she needed to work late and was too tired to venture up the stairs. Meg selected an oatmeal cookie from the china plate and dabbed her forehead with the corner of her handkerchief. "You skipped your tennis lesson and you *never* do that, not even after what happened at my wedding. I've never seen you as happy as you have been since meeting that wonderful brother-in-law of mine."

"It is as hot as a frying pan this week. You can't expect me to play in this heat." She ducked her head before the real reason could tumble out.

Meg traced the edge of her cookie, causing some of the oats to shed into her lap as she brooded. "It hurts me to think you were in so much pain that day and I didn't even know."

"I wasn't about to ruin your day with my bit of nonsense from the past." She dropped her sewing into her lap and looked to her most trusted friend. "What would you have me do, Meg? If I don't cut Giles out of my life, I risk losing everything. . .for potentially nothing. How can I trust him with my heart after everything I've been through?"

Meg lowered her treat and reached out for Alice's hand. "But think of all you stand to gain if you let down your guard. You know I was afraid to surrender my independence to a man, but when I met William. . ." Meg gave her a half smile and shrugged. "I didn't give it a second thought, because he proved himself to be a true man of the Lord. You have spent enough time with Giles to know where his heart dwells. And I think you know where yours belongs."

The copper bell clanged again and, peering around the curtain to spy the back of a gentleman as he entered and examined the window display, Alice stepped out from her workshop. "Welcome to Thimbles and Threads Bridal Shop. How can I help you, sir?"

The customer turned to her, sending her heart stammering. "You can help me by keeping away from Giles Clayton. He is intended to marry Miss Castle, and you best guard yourself before he takes advantage of you in your vulnerable state. I heard from Miss Castle herself that they will be engaged by Christmas."

She gripped the counter at Eustace's announcement, but gathering herself, she pointed him to the door, her finger steady. "You have no right to bid me do anything. I suggest you leave."

He stepped toward her, lust flickering in his eyes. "I always did like it when you pretended to stand up to me."

"I'm warning you, Eustace. I'm not a weak little girl anymore, ready to crumple under your will. Get out of my shop or I'll have the police throw you in prison for trespassing."

"And who would the police believe? A successful married gentleman or a spinster seamstress desperate to save her shop after her father stole thousands?"

"The spinster." Meg appeared, her eyes narrowing at Eustace. "If you wish to continue living at Clayton Plantation with our father-in-law, I suggest you take your leave. I'm certain he would not look kindly on the man who broke his only daughter's heart when news of a scandalous tête-à-tête begins circulating Charleston, which is what will happen should you falsely accuse Alice of anything, *brother*."

Taken aback, Eustace's bravado wavered, and in that moment, Alice brushed past him and threw open the shop door, banging it against the wall. "Don't *ever* come back."

Giles hammered ball after ball over the net in the last bit of light, desperate for a distraction from his thoughts. He had sent notes, bouquets, chocolates, and come in person countless times to her shop, but everything returned to him untouched. He could pursue Alice all he wanted, but if she didn't even open the door for him. . . He squeezed the grip of the racket, grunting as his tennis ball bounced into the gardens, yards from where he had been aiming.

Lord, please let me not have pushed her away. I would never do to her what Eustace and her father did. Help me to understand the depth of her hurt. He tossed another ball up and slammed it with his racket. *But how am I supposed to apologize to her or get her to trust me if she won't even speak to me? I should have stood up for her more than just a light scolding to my sister. I should've—*

"So, I heard from Constance that you were having quite the clandestine meeting with my Alice." Eustace Merrick stumbled down the veranda steps, his hair askew.

Giles scowled at the man who had ruined his chance with Alice. "Drink some coffee, Merrick."

"Don't have to. The ladies will be gone for the rest of the

evening. Some nonsense about dinner on the riverboat with their lady friends. No husbands."

"Don't you have a business to run?"

Merrick laughed. "When you are as successful as I am, you have people who run the business for you and you just reap the profits." He reached the net and leaned against the pole. "So, tell me, has Alice become less of a prude with age?"

Giles clenched his racket and sucked in a breath, hoping to suppress his rage, but Merrick uttered an unforgivable assumption and snorted.

"You will retract your statement, else I will forget that you are married to my sister."

Merrick picked up a racket, a gleam in his eyes as he ran a finger over the frame. "You keep away from Alice, and I might consider it."

Giles scowled. "I repeat, *sir*, you are *married* to my sister. I do not think it is appropriate for you to forbid me to see any woman, especially not one you abandoned five years ago."

"So that little minx told you? Well, since we are brothers, as you keep reminding me, I don't think a brother should court another man's previous fiancée."

"I don't know what my sister ever saw in you."

"The same thing Alice did." He grinned. "Now, I'll ask nicely one more time."

Alice couldn't bring herself to go to bed quite yet. She decided to treat herself to a pot of herbal tea and the last of the oatmeal cookies from the bakery over a *Harper's Bazaar*. Not bothering to undress, she unfastened and kicked off her shoes, pushed back the mosquito netting of her small four-poster bed, and nestled atop her lace bedspread, tucking her feet under herself. She held the magazine up to the lamplight, but the latest fashion designs did not stir her creativity as they usually did. Her mind kept drifting to Giles and Meg's assessment of her behavior. *Lord, am I mistaken in wanting to protect myself from being hurt again?*

Cat arched his back and darted across the room, upsetting the porcelain basin and nearly knocking it to the floor. "Cat!" Alice scrambled off the bed and flung open her bedroom door, shooing Cat down the stairs. A pounding at the front door of the shop made her heart jump. Her gaze flew to the clock on the mantel. *Half past nine? Who on earth would be calling at this late hour?* She bit her lower lip until she spied something that could be used as a weapon leaning against the armoire. Her fingers wrapped about her racket and, lifting it like a mace in one hand and the footed lamp in the other, she drew a ragged breath and descended the stairs, her stockinged feet silent on the wood floors. She squinted, unable to see who was at her shop door through the voile over the door's window. Setting her lamp on the front counter, she shouted, "Who is there?"

"It's me, Alice. You have to talk with me."

Even as her shoulders sagged with relief at the sound of Giles's voice, her stomach knotted. *I can't see him now.* Her hands flew to her hair only to remember she had already pulled the pins from her coiffure, allowing her curls to spill loosely to her waist. She leaned against the door, thankful for the sheer voile lending her a bit of privacy to gather herself. "Giles, I—"

"I promise I will leave the instant you've told me that you feel nothing for me."

I can't do the same thing that Eustace did to me. There one day and gone the next. . .not without telling him why. She grunted, unfastened the bolt, and cracked the door open enough to see his face, a bloodied mess.

"What on earth!" She jerked it open and pulled him inside. Her hands fluttered to her mouth as she took in his state. "Giles, what happened to you?"

He shrugged. "It's nothing."

"Nothing?" She scowled, shaking her head. She pushed his shoulder down, forcing him to take a seat. "You call this nothing? For a man who sits behind a desk every day, you sure do find the time to get into brawls every chance you can get."

"We all have our faults. Mine happens to be my temper when someone insults people I love."

Is he implying I am one of those people? She swallowed back the lump in her throat. "Who did this to you?"

He clenched his fists and looked to the ceiling. "With the ladies out for the night, Merrick took the opportunity to imbibe and come down to the lawn court to discuss—well—you."

"You fought with Eustace?" She pressed her hand to her lips, sick that Eustace may have ruined her life a second time.

Giles touched his head gingerly. "Merrick cracked a racket over my head before I knew we were fighting. Apparently, he's been stewing over my friendship with you and was jealous. I didn't want to retaliate, but the fool kept challenging me. When he charged at me again, I knocked him out in one punch that hopefully won't leave anything more than a bruised eye and pride."

Her jaw dropped. "Oh Giles. . ."

"I know you think that your family had problems, but seems like my family is just as imperfect, and that our mutual friend, Eustace, wants only what he cannot have." He shoved his hands into his pockets as she dripped water from the crystal pitcher she kept for guests onto her handkerchief and lifted it to his forehead. He tilted his head back. "There's not witch hazel on that cotton, is there? I'm already in enough pain." The crack in his lip turned his smile into a wince.

"Just water." She dabbed at his wound. Had it really only been a week since the last time she had bandaged his wounds? "You can't stay long. If someone walks by the shop and sees you in here *again*. . . There will be no benefit of the doubt given this time."

"I have to speak with you. Light the lamps like last time and turn up all the wicks to show that we are doing nothing wrong. We are chaperoned by every passerby."

She dropped her hand and stepped away from him, acutely aware for the first time that she was without shoes. "I'm afraid that I am causing too much of a stir in your family's lives. Please tell your sister to take her business to Miss Cole. She is quite the proficient seamstress."

"Alice. If you no longer wish to see me, please tell me, and I will leave you be, but you can't just ignore me and expect me to retreat without an explanation."

"What makes you think I'm cutting you out of my life?" She turned away from him and grabbed the broom, setting to cleaning the spotless showroom floor.

"Maybe because you can't even look at me. Or perhaps the dozens of returned messages."

She propped the broom against the counter, slowly turning to him. "You say you want to court me. You say that you would *never* hurt me, but how can you not hurt me if you do not plan on marrying me?" Her voice cracked.

"What?" He blinked, rising from his chair so quickly that he swayed.

She threw her arms around his waist, fearing he would pass out and further injure himself. He leaned into her arms, his breath on her hair.

"Why in the world would you think that?" he asked at last.

His question jarred her into thinking properly, and she reluctantly slipped her arms from his side and stepped back. "Eustace came by today and told me that Miss Castle has implied you two are courting and are expected to wed soon."

"That is utter nonsense. My sister has been pushing me toward Miss Castle for years because they are best friends." He grasped her hand in his. "You have to believe me."

"I-I do," she whispered. "But that doesn't mean I can still see you. I'm too broken." She pressed a hand to her chest. "My heart was shattered the day my father left me, and I'm only now getting the pieces back. You deserve a heart that is whole and perfect."

He pressed a kiss onto each of her hands with a pain in his eyes that wrenched her apart. "My sweet Alice. Don't you know that we are *all* imperfect beings? We are all broken. If you are searching for healing in your own strength, you will never find it. You've been running from men and your hurt for so long, you seem to have forgotten from whom you are running. Mankind is broken. You know in your heart the only One who can make you whole again. Just stop your running and ask Jesus for healing." He stroked her cheek with his thumb. "He will bind your wounds and heal your heart if you only ask."

His words brought her to a halt. Had she really been leaning on herself for healing this entire time? *Dear Lord, forgive me.* Years of anger, fear, and bitterness began to crumble as his words burrowed into her heart. Tears filled her eyes and she dropped her gaze, convicted. Alice felt her body begin to shake, and she thought she was about to faint when the pictures began tumbling off the walls. She whirled around to see the old brick chimney pull away from the wall and Giles in its direct path.

Chapter 10

"Giles, it's an earthquake!" Alice shrieked and shoved him out of the way of the collapsing chimney. He wrapped his arms around her and, falling, rolling, they evaded the bricks slamming into the floorboards.

"We've got to get out of here before we're buried alive!" Giles pulled her up and they bolted for the door, but the upstairs floor began to crack and the floorboards rained down around them. With a yell, Giles pushed her against a wall that hadn't broken apart and formed a human cage around her, hunching his shoulders over her head to ensure that she would not be struck by the falling debris. "I've got you."

She looked up into his eyes that held protection and adoration. Knowing that this may be their last moments on earth together, she wrapped her arms around his neck and pressed her lips to his again and again, wincing against the debris hitting her hands. "I'm so sorry, Giles." Tears streamed down her face. *How could I have been so foolish to waste our precious time together because of my fears, my doubts. . . It doesn't matter now. All that matters is that I tell him before we die.* "I love you with all my heart."

For his answer, his lips sought hers again, but a board crashed into his shoulder, knocking him down into her. His startling look of peace calmed her as he answered, "My heart belonged to you the moment we met and forevermore, Alice Turner."

The walls trembled. *God help us,* she prayed as a bookcase filled with bridal accessories groaned and toppled toward them. She felt Giles's strong arms wrap around her again as he dove for the floor, appearing to be aiming for between the bookcase and the space between the counter and the floor. He tucked her head into his chest and let his shoulders take the brunt of the items tumbling out of the bookcase. The case slammed into the both of them but landed on the chimney rubble, saving them from being pinned to the floor. And with every violent tremor, Alice couldn't help but scream, clutching him.

Giles pressed a kiss atop her head. "If we get out of this alive, I'm going to ask you to marry me."

"If we get out of this alive, I'll say yes." She kissed his rough cheek. The house groaned again, and she screamed as something shattered on the bookcase and ash swirled about them.

The thoughts of Alice being his wife bolstered him even in the face of death. "It's all right. It's holding." Giles attempted to calm her, even though he had no assurance that they would be well or live to see another day. *Lord, You've brought us together. Please don't let our time together end so quickly.* "Lord, please, protect us and our families. Stretch out Your mighty hand and make the earth grow still." He prayed aloud, cradling her as the tremors began to subside. He exhaled. *Thank You, Lord.* The quake had been the longest minute he'd ever experienced.

"Is it over?" she whispered, looking up to him, her face covered in ashes and dirt.

He loosened his grip on her and twisted to peek out from under the bookcase. "Hope so, but we better move before the aftershocks begin." He moved to position his shoulders under the bookcase and grunted as he stood, lifting it enough for them to slip out. "Go, Alice!"

She crawled out, and in a single motion, Giles shoved the bookcase off his shoulders and rolled out from under it, allowing it to crash on the rubble, splintering the already damaged wood, when the room began to shake again. Alice cried out and threw her arms around him as the aftershocks overtook the house and the things that had already shifted loose came tumbling down about them. Giles wrapped his arm around her waist and darted for the gaping hole in the wall, desperate to escape as a beam came crashing down, missing them by a hairbreadth.

Diving out onto the sidewalk, he held Alice against him. They lay panting on the ground, staring at the shop as flames began to lick the corner of her building. She pressed her hand to her mouth, staring in shock as the flames grew. Giles helped her to her feet and led her away from the shop and stood, along with the other merchants on King Street, in the middle of the road, watching the destruction as the hot, humid air hovered over them like a cloud. Giles laid his head atop her hair and held her close as screams escalated behind them and the darkness took on an amber color. They turned to find the bakery across the street ablaze and the merchants next door to the bakery running in and out of the front door, trying to save merchandise as their wives in their dressing robes huddled with children in nightgowns at a safe distance.

Shaking, Alice rested her head on his chest. He felt her tears seep into his shirt as people began calling for their loved ones while others mourned the loss of their homes.

Thank You, Lord, that the women are on the river. Please let my family in Charleston be safe. He drew Alice's chin up to meet his starved gaze. "I mean it, Alice. If you'll have me, I want you to be my wife." He waited for her to raise questions, but instead, she offered him a tear-streaked smile.

"Everything you've done has proven you to be a man of your word. I know you do not ask me lightly or out of pity for my reduced circumstances." She laughed and gestured to her life's work in a heap. "You have waited for me to trust you, and I know I can. While every man in my life has left me, you are not every man. You are your own man, and you have my love."

His heart soared. "I half-feared it was the terror of the moment that led you to confess your love."

She placed her hands in his. "Giles Clayton, I want to be your wife more than anything I've ever longed for in my entire life."

He gently cupped her face between his hands and kissed her. "Then be mine."

"Forever," she whispered, stepping into his embrace. Just then a guttural hiss sounded from the corner of her fallen home. They turned to find Cat, arching his back atop a small trunk on a heap at the sie of her building that hadn't been eaten by the flames. "Cat! Oh Cat, you made it." She scooped up her black pet and buried her nose in its neck before looking down at the trunk. "I can't believe it. How did my parents' trunk survive?"

Giles dragged the trunk away from the building, and Alice, still dazed, stooped and opened the lid and withdrew a half-finished quilt to reveal what appeared to be a wedding gown beneath. She stroked the quilt and looked up at Giles. "Life and love are too precious to squander over bitterness of past hurts. If you are willing, let's marry as soon as possible. Then I will work on this quilt, and when it is finished, I will deliver it to my father in person."

He knelt beside her, brushing his fingertips on her cheek. "Are you certain that this is what you want?"

She laughed. "My shop is in ruins and the world is in chaos around us, but my heart has never been more at peace."

"We will rebuild again." He squeezed her hand. "Together."

Seeing that the merchants and their families about her were unharmed save for a few cuts, bruises, and the baker's broken leg, Giles held Cat in one arm, and with the trunk carried between them, they left her shop behind to find their family and friends to help in any way they could.

Epilogue

The days following the earthquake were filled with labor as everyone, rich and poor, attempted to piece their lives back together. Alice found that her assistant, Meg's family, and the Charleston jail had survived along with her father. Giles had word from his family that they were all alive and well. The number of fatalities overestimated in the newspapers lessened, but any number was still a tragedy felt by all survivors. Alice knew it would be a long time before their lives were mended and stitched back together, but with Giles by her side, she also knew for the first time in years that her burdens would be shared and her life would be full of love.

When Saturday arrived, Alice dressed in the only gown that survived the fire, her mother's wedding gown that spoke of blissful times gone by. In a simple ceremony, witnessed only by the preacher and his wife and Meg and William, Alice and Giles were married. And with their vows fresh on her lips, she stepped from the chapel with her husband at her side and her friends behind.

Husband. She sighed and rose on her tiptoes, pressing a kiss to his lips as their friends tossed handfuls of crimson rose petals into the air above them, calling out their congratulations.

"Giles! What on earth are you two about, kissing in the street?"

Alice felt her face turn crimson as she turned to find Giles's sister standing below them, mouth agape.

Constance's gaze fell to the gold band on Alice's finger and beyond to Meg and William. "Y-you didn't just get married, did you? I saw your note to Father and was coming to stop you. You couldn't have possibly gotten married without your entire family present."

"Dear sister, allow me to introduce you to my beautiful wife, Alice."

Her lips pursed. "Miss Turner, you took advantage of my brother during an emotional time. Despicable. And you, William, why didn't you talk some sense into him?"

Giles squeezed Alice's arm, silently reassuring her that *he* would fight this battle for them. "Constance, you know I love you, but it is not your place to say what is on my heart. Alice *is* my heart, and I won't stand by and allow you to disparage her. You cut her with your words and you in turn cut me. Please don't ask me to choose between you."

She turned her fiery gaze from Giles to Alice and back before sighing. "I suppose there is no turning back now that you are married."

Giles reached for Alice's hand, wrapping it in a strong, firm grip. "No turning back. Not now, not ever."

Constance's shoulders slumped as she threw up her hands. "Fine. But you'll have to give me some time to adjust to the idea of all this and not expect me to be all flowers and sunshine this morning."

"You? Not flowers and sunshine, my sister?" William chortled. "How uncharacteristic."

She cracked a smile and added, "But as I've always adored *you*, Giles, I'm sure I'll come around eventually for your sake, if for nothing else."

"Of course," Alice replied, understanding far more about the journey of forgiveness than her new sister-in-law knew.

"I suppose you'll be moving into the plantation too, with Father, Eustace, and me?"

"Actually, if you had read my message to Father through to the end, you would know of my plans for our living quarters. But I won't say what my plans are yet." He turned and grinned at Alice. "Because I wanted to surprise you. If you'll excuse us, Constance," he said, escorting Alice to his waiting buggy. And with a wave to their family, they wove down the streets toward the Ashley River, evading heaps of rubble and construction.

Spying the riverboat docked, she whirled to him. "We will be living on the riverboat?" she fairly squealed.

"Well, any of the vacant apartments that were still standing were snatched up after the earthquake, and we have such good memories of being on the river, I thought it would be fun." He looked to her.

"Did I make a mistake?"

She threw her arms around his neck. "It's wonderful! You're wonderful!"

He grinned. "Thank goodness. I was afraid you might not like the idea. I thought perhaps you could set up your business on the first deck until we can rebuild your shop. And on the top deck, we can practice tennis." He chuckled. "But I fear the river will eat most of your hits."

She rolled her eyes, ignoring his teasing. Alice looped her arm through his and, leaning her head on his shoulder, said, "Have I told you today that you are the most wonderful husband?"

"Compliments from my wife are always welcome. Now, are you ready to see your new home?" At her kiss of approval, he scooped her up and took her aboard.

With their few personal belongings in place, the first item she sat down to stitch was the quilt. She shed many tears as she worked on it, remembering all the happy times she had spent with her father. For the final square, she used the material from the skirt she had been wearing the day of the quake. She had washed it multiple times, but the ashes from the chimney wouldn't come away. She didn't like adding such a stained square to the quilt, but she knew that, like life, this quilt would not be as picturesque as she had intended when she had begun to stitch it all those years ago. In the corner, she embroidered *"He healeth the broken in heart, and bindeth up their wounds. Psalm 147:3."*

Snipping off the end of the thread, she stroked the quilt and looked up at her husband, studying his strong jawline as he read over his work notes, and smiled. "Mr. Clayton, are you ready to go to prison with me?"

Giles crossed the room and swept her into an embrace, bolstering her in strength and courage. "I'll go anywhere, as long as I'm with you."

Grace Hitchcock is the author of *The White City* and *The Gray Chamber* from Barbour Publishing. She has written multiple novellas in *The Second Chance Brides*, *The Southern Belle Brides*, and the *Thimbles and Threads* collections with Barbour Publishing. She holds a master's in creative writing and a bachelor of arts in English with a minor in history. Grace lives in southern Louisiana with her husband, Dakota, and their son. Visit Grace online at GraceHitchcock.com.

Mending Sarah's Heart

by Suzanne Norquist

Chapter 1

Rockledge, Colorado
1884

Sarah Anderson stepped from the boardwalk into her seamstress shop, newspaper in hand. As the only fine dressmaker in this Colorado mining town, competition from Emporium of Fashion shouldn't threaten her. But it did.

She breathed in the fresh linen scent from the bolts of fabric filling the shelves. The familiar sights and smells soothed her. Fine dresses covered wire forms in the display window, showing off her handiwork. Her younger sister, Rose, hummed a familiar tune as she selected a length of fabric from a table along one wall.

"It's like Emporium of Fashion is trying to drive me out of business. Their advertisement is bigger than my hand." She glared at the paper. "Why would anyone wear ready-made dresses?"

"I wouldn't." Rose spread a length of muslin over the measuring table. She cast a saucy grin in Sarah's direction. "Did you see Mrs. Whitaker's dress on Sunday? It bunched in all the wrong places. Poor woman looked as though a flash flood caught her on the way to church."

Sarah smoothed the crumpled newspaper on the table. Her patrons would want to read the other news while they waited for fittings. "Such outrageous claims. 'Dresses and hats. All sizes and colors in the latest styles. Lowest prices anywhere.' Impossible."

"I'm sure it's an exaggeration. No one could stock *all* sizes and colors." Rose measured a length of fabric and pinned the edge.

Sarah reached for a pair of scissors but thought better of it—no need to damage good scissors. She ripped out the section containing her competitor's name and crushed it into a ball. She opened the potbelly stove and tossed the wad on top of the hot coals. Its outsides blackened and puffed up before bursting into flames.

If only she could rid herself of competition with such ease. After the paper withered in a pile of ash, she shut the stove door.

Rose pulled another pin from a cushion and slid it through the fabric on the table. "William says it happens in every mining town. Gold will bring all kinds of new stores to Rockledge. Pretty soon, he expects a rail line to come straight from Denver."

Sarah didn't expect their brother to understand the operation of a dress shop. "He's not competing with poor-quality, cheap ready-made goods. His newspaper benefits from growth."

She appreciated his help with her young sons. But when it came to business, she managed the shop on her own. No matter that she was a widow. But how would she compete with garments shipped in from the east?

"Soon Rockledge will be a real city." Of course, Rose would benefit. As a singer at the opera house, she would see more patrons at each performance.

Meanwhile, Sarah faced the harsh realities of raising two sons on her own. Even God had let her down.

If Theodore were alive, she wouldn't have to earn a living. She wouldn't care about the Emporium and its impact on sales. Or, perhaps she would. Her husband's penchant for bad investments rendered him an unreliable provider.

Sarah stepped to the sitting area, a corner of the store furnished like a fine parlor. She laid the remains of the paper next to the latest copy of *Godey's Lady's Book*. "Three of my best customers have abandoned me."

Rose cut along the edge of the pinned fabric. "We'll see them again. No one wants to look like a puckered, ill-fitting mess when they wear their Sunday best."

Sarah shook her head. "Some women seem unaware of how unkempt a poor-fitting dress makes them look." She checked her reflection as she passed the looking glass. Her dress showed some wear. She could freshen it up with a new collar and matching cuffs. She dressed to draw customers, wearing something a little nicer than most of the women in town. A walking advertisement.

The front door creaked, and the bell overhead announced

a visitor. Before turning to greet her customer, she pasted on a professional smile.

A man pulled the door shut and stood in the entry. Men seldom patronized Sarah's shop. Her brothers frequented the establishment but not as customers. On occasion, a husband accompanied his wife. A lone man might purchase a gift, a rare occurrence.

Dressed like a banker or undertaker, this fellow would have caught Sarah's attention if she'd seen him before. He wore a tailored suit with a top hat, but his tie hung askew as if loosened with a tug. Although clean shaven, the stranger let his wavy brown hair fall past his collar. A mountain man trying to appear refined? Younger than the grizzled old-timers. About her age. Not more than thirty.

His angular jaw and confident demeanor caused her pulse to quicken. She stole another glance in the mirror. Her chignon appeared fresh and her skirt smooth. Good. Not that it mattered.

Her sister watched while pretending to work. She grinned like a child with a peppermint stick. Sarah would have chastised her if it weren't for the stranger.

He removed his hat and remained near the entry studying the shop. He perused each wall. One side, then the other.

Sarah followed his gaze.

Finally, he focused on her.

She cleared her throat to find her voice. "Are you meeting your wife here?"

He flashed her a smile. More of a roguish grin, one powerful enough to draw naive young ladies to his side. Not her. In another lifetime, she'd have longed for a fairy-tale hero like him. Not now.

Responsibilities ruled her world. Her boys. Her shop.

She hoped he had a wife but sensed he didn't even before he spoke. No respectable husband would study her the way he did.

"No." He shook his head, but the intensity of his gaze never wavered. "No wife. I'm here to see—"

A loud thump sounded outside, and the front wall of Sarah's shop shook as if something had hit it hard. The man would have to wait. She stepped toward her worktable where her shotgun hid.

The stranger flattened his back against the wall. Then he scooted toward the large display window. Remaining hidden, he leaned to peer out. "I can't see anything from here."

Rose continued to work. "A fight from one of the saloons must have made its way down the street."

As Rockledge grew, so did the number of skirmishes on the main street. Trouble usually stayed near the saloons. But not always.

"I wish Sheriff Bradford would keep the ruffians under control." Sarah released a latch to reveal a hidden compartment on the front of her worktable. Her hand shook as she retrieved her double-barreled shotgun from its hiding place. Although dreading a confrontation, she could hold her own. She'd faced threats before. She steadied her voice. "A warning shot should send them away."

The stranger cocked an eyebrow. "I'll handle this."

Another thud shook the wall. A shout sounded, but Sarah couldn't make out the words. Her boys would arrive home from school any minute. She needed to end this skirmish before they wandered into the middle of it.

More thumping.

More shouting.

Pulling his head away from the window, the stranger put a hand to his hip like a cowboy reaching for a pistol. He scowled and unbuttoned his suit coat. He pushed it back to reveal a Colt revolver and fingered its handle.

Sarah willed her heart to slow and wiped her brow. She cracked the barrel of her shotgun and checked for shells.

Loaded.

Good.

She slammed it shut.

Rose gave her a nod but stayed put.

Sarah tucked the stock under her arm, the barrel pointed toward the floor. After giving her sister a reassuring nod, she strode toward the door, head held high, showing confidence she didn't feel.

The stranger stepped away from the window toward her. "Stay inside."

She swept past him and pulled the door open in a quick motion. With both hands, she raised the shotgun and stepped outside to face the threat.

A circle of boys crowded near the front of Sarah's shop, half on and half off the boardwalk. Several of them bumped against her wall. In the middle, one boy lay on the dirt street, and another knelt over him, punching. Dust swirled around the group, causing her to squint and blurring her vision.

Boys. Not men.

She lowered the shotgun.

The stranger stepped up next to her and holstered his revolver.

The lad on top wore suspenders and a blue shirt, like the one she sewed for Teddy's birthday. No. He couldn't—

The boy on the ground pushed up to a sitting position and dodged a punch.

The crowd shouted encouragement to both fighters. Someone called out her son's name.

The boy in the blue shirt turned her direction, and she couldn't deny the truth.

"Teddy."

Her ten-year-old son engaged in fisticuffs? The other child must have provoked him. She pushed her way into the circle and marched to the middle, shotgun tucked under one arm.

The crowd quieted.

Teddy's jaw dropped, and his face went white as he froze.

She grabbed a handful of his collar and yanked hard.

He shifted his stance to keep from falling and grabbed his shirt with one hand.

She stood taller than her growing boy. What would she do when he matched her in size? She pulled Teddy toward the edge of the circle. She wanted to scream, but not in front of the crowd. What possessed her son to pummel another boy? There was some trouble last week, but she'd talked with him about it.

Where was William? She had asked her brother to walk the boys home to prevent this kind of thing. Couldn't she trust anyone to keep their word?

Teddy followed half sideways and made an exaggerated gagging sound as she pulled on his collar. He wiped the sweat from his face with one hand.

The stranger helped the other boy to his feet and dispersed the crowd.

Once inside, she let go of her son and handed the shotgun to

Rose, who returned it to its hiding place.

Sarah put her hands on her hips. "What is wrong with you? Beating up another child."

Teddy crossed his arms and jutted out his chin. "I'm not a child. And he started it."

Sarah's younger son, Kenny, trotted in, carrying his lunch pail and Teddy's.

The stranger followed, top hat in hand. What did he want? Why hadn't he left?

"I was defending myself." Teddy held his chin firm.

The stranger spoke before Sarah could. "In that case, son, you should have quit when he went down."

Son? What gave the man the right to speak to her boy in such a familiar manner? She moved closer to Teddy.

The stranger continued. "A man doesn't beat someone who is already on the ground. A real man does everything he can to avoid a fight."

"You been in a lot of fights, mister?" Teddy tilted his head to see around Sarah, and his gaze went to the holster on the man's hip.

The stranger pulled his suit coat closed and buttoned it. "A few, but a smart man stays out of trouble's way. Once, in the goldfields, a claim jumper tried to steal my horse at gunpoint."

Teddy's eyes went wide. "What'd ya do?"

"Enough." Sarah put her hands on her son's shoulders and faced him away from the stranger. No telling what kind of tall tales he would tell her son.

"I let him have the horse."

Teddy's shoulders slumped, and his head drooped. "Oh."

Sarah released a breath.

"Then I tracked him until he stopped for water and retrieved my horse."

Sarah glowered at the man.

He had the nerve to wink. "Acquired a new rifle in the process."

Chapter 2

Jack waited as the proprietress presumably scolded her son behind the closed door. How many times had his mother done the same to him? He would thank her if she were still alive. His gut tightened with guilt. If he'd been there that night, she might not have died.

He shook his arms and shoulders to loosen the tension.

The younger woman stared at him from behind a sewing table. She bit her lip before speaking. "Do you need something?"

Jack gave her his most reassuring smile. "I've come to speak with Mrs. Anderson. I have business with her."

"My sister is—indisposed—at the moment." She walked toward the rear of the shop. "I'll tell her you're waiting for her, Mr. . . ?"

"Taylor." He gave a little bow. "Jack Taylor."

"Mr. Taylor. I'll tell her you're waiting." She slipped through the door.

Jack studied the inventory while he waited, sizing up Mrs. Anderson's financial situation. Although tidy, the shop appeared understocked. Not that Jack frequented dress shops. But he figured a prosperous shop would have more bolts of fabric on hand. More garments ready for sale. More of everything.

After a few minutes, the proprietress emerged. Her red face and eyes didn't detract from the woman's natural beauty. A jeweled comb held her hair up in a style he saw on society women in Denver. Layers of fabric couldn't hide a fine figure.

The younger woman followed her. After giving Jack a little grin, she took a seat behind a worktable and cupped her face in her hands and watched.

The older sister halted a few feet from him. Would she smell of rose water if he neared? Or lilac?

"I'm Mrs. Anderson." She looked him in the eye, as if ready for a confrontation. "My sister tells me you wish to speak with me."

"My name is Jack Taylor. I partnered with your husband in the Griffin mining project." Jack twisted the brim of his hat. He could address men in all walks of life, but the handsome widow unnerved him. He needed her to accept his offer. "You know of it?"

Mrs. Anderson's expression clouded. "My husband passed away. Any dealings you had with him concluded at his death. Please speak to my lawyer. He resides in the office next to the newspaper."

"I heard of Theodore's passing, and you have my sympathies, ma'am." He stepped closer, thinking to touch her shoulder, but changed his mind. "Please, accept my condolences."

"If you knew my husband, then you know how many men

already came by claiming he owed them money. My attorney handles all such matters." She stepped behind the worktable, creating a barrier between them. "Good day, sir."

"Wait." His heart pounded as he lifted an arm toward her. "You don't understand. I sold the Griffin for a tidy profit. I haven't come to ask for anything."

She stilled, but her features didn't soften. "Doesn't matter. I have no interest in his investments, and I don't trust his partners."

Jack hadn't expected a warm welcome, but wouldn't the woman even hear him out? "I've come to give you his share of the proceeds."

At first, he'd planned to keep everything for himself. But guilt plagued him in the year since the sale of the mine.

He slowed his breathing to squelch his desperation. Payment to Mrs. Anderson could rid him of one of the shadows chasing him. A small measure of peace. He indicated the shelves with a wave of his hand. "You could use it to build your inventory."

The widow faced him, eyes red. A strand of hair dangled along the side of her face, giving her a frazzled appearance.

Her sister spoke up. "Sales *have* taken a downturn ever since the Whitfield brothers opened the Emporium of Fashion."

"Not now, Rose," Mrs. Anderson snapped. "This man doesn't need to hear about our affairs."

The younger woman picked up a piece of fabric but didn't actually do anything with it.

Head high, the widow's face tightened. Tears gave her eyes a glossy look but didn't spill over. "I don't know you or what you're about. No one offers money without expecting something in return. My shop is not your concern."

"Your husband invested in a legitimate business. As his wife, his share goes to you. Nothing more." He wanted to brush the hair from her face and reassure her.

Her bottom lip quivered, but she held her body rigid.

He knew the look. Hiding her fear under a professional facade. He should drop the money and run. Or seek out her attorney. He couldn't convince his feet to move. A whiff of floral scent drifted past. Lilac.

"Do you have papers showing his interest in this project?"

"You know prospecting deals. We seldom put pen to paper." The informality of his ventures benefited him. When Theodore died, Jack assumed full ownership without hesitation. The old Jack didn't concern himself with next-of-kin. "Trust me, we were partners."

She regarded him as if he were a child. "How long ago did you sell the mine?"

His face warmed. "About a year ago. The conglomerate that purchased it had the capital to develop the resource."

"You say my husband was a partner, yet you never consulted me about the sale, and you waited a year to seek me out." She put her hands on her hips, like a schoolmarm from his youth. "Why now? You could have kept the money. I never would have known."

He took a deep breath. "I had a change of heart."

"I see." She lifted a hand from her hip as if to gesture, but a tremble belied her confident demeanor. She pressed the hand against her skirt. "So, I should take you at your word? Like all the other men my husband associated with?"

He wanted to comfort her. Protect her from men like himself.

She straightened her shoulders. To show bravado to him or herself?

"If a stranger rode into town and offered your sister a large sum of money with a weak story like yours, would you encourage her to take it?"

What did he know about sisters and putting things to rights? He'd made a mess of his meeting with Mrs. Anderson. Life was easier when he didn't care about anyone but himself. He didn't know what to say.

"Exactly." Mrs. Anderson scooted behind a tidy desk. She sat and lifted a pen, turning her attention to a ledger, dismissing Jack. "Good day, Mr. Taylor."

He watched her for a moment as she opened a ledger filled with tidy rows of numbers. He strode to the door. "I will find a way to make things right."

After Mr. Taylor left, Sarah relaxed and sucked in a long, slow breath. "Oh my."

Rose dashed to the window and peered out. "How exciting. I can't wait to tell the family."

Sarah cringed. The family included four brothers and Rose's husband. Her parents had moved to a lower elevation last year with their youngest sister. Rose would make sure they all heard about the stranger. Everyone would subject Sarah to an unsolicited opinion. . . again.

David, the enforcer, would want to rough the fellow up.

William, the newspaperman, would want to research him.

And who knew what the others would suggest?

No thanks.

"Let's keep this our secret." Sarah rose and stepped to the

window near her sister. "He'll leave soon enough. No need to set tongues wagging."

Across the street, Mr. Taylor lingered near a couple of old-timers who played checkers in front of a tobacco shop. His roguish grin attracted her, but after Theodore, she knew better. She didn't need another unreliable wanderer.

"So handsome." Rose sighed. "Do you think he really has money?"

His fashionable clothes spoke of wealth. The crooked tie and the way he searched for his holster under the jacket indicated new money. "Probably. It's not my concern."

"His offer solves your problem with the Emporium. You could stock newer fabrics in a wider variety of prints." Rose waved an arm to point out the sparse shelves. "Take out a newspaper ad bigger than theirs."

"I don't trust him."

Mr. Taylor crossed his arms and lifted his head toward Sarah and her sister.

Sarah jumped away from the window, out of his line of sight. Her pulse raced.

Rose smiled in his direction and waved.

Sarah grabbed her sister's arm and pulled her away from the window. "Don't encourage him."

Rose floated toward her worktable with theatrical flair. "I wish a stranger would walk in and offer me money."

"Like the soiled doves down the street?" Sarah hovered near the window, peeking out from the side. Rose's fanciful whimsy grated on her nerves. Her sister lived in a dream world. "Besides, you're married."

"Yes, I am." As a newlywed, Rose perked up when anyone mentioned her husband, Patrick.

Sarah envied Rose and Patrick's perfect romance. The only thing that ever made her sister melancholy was her wish for a child. One that would come along eventually.

"So stop eyeing Mr. Taylor."

"I'm only thinking of you, dear sister." Rose put her hands on her hips. "Theodore invested in a profitable mine. You should take the money. It's yours."

"I don't know if Theodore invested with this man or not."

Rose shook her head. "What makes you so skeptical? You used to give people the benefit of the doubt."

"This happened." Sarah held her hands out. "I need to earn a living and raise two boys without a father. I don't have the energy for anything else." Weary, she dropped into a chair in the sitting area.

The kitchen door creaked, and Teddy peeked out.

Sarah gestured him over. "Come on out, Teddy." In the face of Mr. Taylor's offer, she'd set aside her concerns about the fight.

Teddy stepped into the shop, followed by his uncle William. As a professional newspaperman, he kept his hair cropped short and wore a simple mustache but no beard. Women found him handsome, but she didn't care about his romantic prospects at the moment.

He'd promised to walk the boys home from school. If he had been there, he could've prevented the fight before it started.

William stood beside Teddy and put up his hands in mock surrender. "Before you say anything, it wasn't my fault."

Teddy shoved his hands in his pockets and stared at a spot

on the wood floor.

A headache throbbed above Sarah's left eyebrow. If only she could relax in a quiet room sipping a cup of hot, sweet coffee. Instead, she gathered the energy to force herself to stand. Sitting made her feel small and weak. She needed an air of authority. "You agreed to see the boys home after school."

"I couldn't help it. I hounded the mayor's secretary all week about an interview. He granted me one this afternoon." Her brother wore the same contrite face as when Mother scolded him. "I couldn't turn it down."

Sarah focused on her son. "Did he tell you what happened?"

William's stance relaxed. "Sounds like he held his ground."

Teddy stole a glance in her direction.

So much for help from her brother.

"He pummeled another child." Her head pounded at the memory. "I won't have my son beating other children. I rely on you to teach him to behave—the kind of things a father would teach him."

William put a hand on the boy's shoulder. "From what Teddy said, the boy deserved it. A man needs to defend himself."

"Defend?" Sarah shuddered. "I arrived to see him holding a boy on the ground and punching him repeatedly. The others stood around egging him on."

"Is that true?" William addressed her son. "Did you keep punching him after he was down?"

Teddy lifted his head toward his uncle. "Yes, sir." Then he studied the floorboards again.

"Not very sportsmanlike." William touched the boy's chin and lifted his face. "It's important to know when to stop the fight or, better yet, how to avoid it altogether."

The boy broke into a big grin. "That's what Jack—I mean Mr. Taylor—said."

Sarah studied her son's face. He was in their living quarters behind the store when Mr. Taylor introduced himself. How much did he hear? She pressed her hands against her skirt to keep them steady. This business with Mr. Taylor could get out of hand.

Her brother pinned her with a stare. "Who's Jack? And why is he giving my nephew advice?"

Now her brother cared about Teddy's well-being. Not when she needed him.

She let Teddy tell his uncle about the exciting stranger and glared at Rose, who clearly wanted to add the part about the money. Thankfully, Rose kept quiet.

Sarah didn't need her brothers confronting Mr. Taylor. What a circus that would create. She prayed for the man to leave town quickly—and quietly.

Chapter 3

Jack leaned against a post on the boardwalk and crossed his arms, watching a couple of old-timers play checkers. No better way to learn about Rockledge, Colorado, and Sarah Anderson.

Buck and Slim prospected for gold in their younger years. His kind of people. Long white beards covered most of their leathery faces. Only two fingers remained on Buck's left hand, and Slim's large belly rolled across his lap.

Buck slid a red checker to a new square and spit a glob of tobacco toward the street. "How do ya think the guys up in Crawdad Gulch are farin' with their claims?"

Slim lifted a black checker and jumped it over a red one. "Couple o' city boys. They'll never find anything." He placed the red one in a growing stack. "They'll likely starve to death or freeze."

"Ya never know. Some dandies found gold while taking a couple o' ladies on a picnic." Buck scrunched his face as he studied the board. He put his finger on a red checker to slide it. "So I heard, anyways."

Jack gave a slight shake of his head.

The old-timer eyed Jack. He paused and lifted his hand to rub his beard. After studying the board, he touched another checker and glanced at Jack.

Again, Jack shook his head. Buck didn't know much about checkers.

Buck held his finger over a third checker and waited for Jack's reaction.

Jack gave the slightest nod, holding his face expressionless. A move he'd perfected.

Buck lifted the black checker and jumped a red one. He paused and then jumped another. And another. In a grandiose gesture, he lifted the three captured checkers. "King me." Crossing his arms, he reclined in his chair.

"You cheated." Slim scooted in Jack's direction, scraping his chair on the boardwalk. "The city fella helped you cheat."

"I don't need help from a dandy." Buck crossed his arms and waited for Slim to make a move. "You got a name, stranger?"

Jack touched the brim of his hat. "Jack Taylor. I put in my time poking through the hills and panning the streams."

A team of horses rattled down the street, kicking up a cloud of dust big enough to choke an entire herd.

Jack coughed. He reached for the handkerchief in his breast pocket, then thought better of it. The clean white cotton would alienate these men. "Did pretty well for myself."

A smile played on Slim's lips, what Jack could see of them beneath the beard. "Gold?"

"Of course." Jack's energy surged as he transformed the strangers into allies. One of the skills he'd honed in the goldfields. "Griffin Mine. I'm sure you've heard of it."

"Some big company took over the operation." Buck pulled a small pouch from his pocket. He removed a pinch of tobacco and tucked it in the corner of his mouth before pocketing the pouch.

"Bought out, gentlemen. Bought out." Jack held his arms up to show off his fine suit. "I like to take my money early."

Slim tipped his head toward Sarah's shop. "Has all that money got you buying women's frippery?"

"Can't blame a fella for wandering in. Have you seen the proprietress?" Jack's attention wandered toward the shop. "Gal carries herself like someone from a fancy ladies' magazine."

Buck nodded. "A pretty sight, but you'll have to go through four brothers and a brother-in-law if you're interested."

"Keeps to herself since Theodore died." Slim took two black checkers from the board and slid his red one in place for a king. "Family set her up in a shop for women's clothes. The way she holes herself up in there, you'd think she was under siege."

The woman didn't strike him as timid. More like fierce and protective. The old men's comments fueled his curiosity.

"Used to be a fun-lovin' gal." Slim cleared his throat. "Very proper, of course. Liked to dance at the socials and always helpin' folks at the church."

Jack nodded, not wanting to interrupt the stream of information. Had her husband's death changed her so much? Could

Jack have made a difference had he come forward with the money sooner?

"Theodore used to act like a big man. Played cards before he married. Once the wife banned him from the saloons, he 'invested.' More respectable than card games." Slim took a long drink from a tin cup.

Jack had never considered the families of the other prospectors. The lifestyle drew single men with a wanderlust. He couldn't imagine leaving a woman like Sarah behind while he poked through the hills. If she were his wife— He weighed Buck's words.

"Almost struck it rich myself." Buck pushed a checker. "Turns out the claim next to mine had gold. A narrow vein."

"Goes that way sometimes." Jack considered Mrs. Anderson as the old-timer rattled on. The more he learned about her, the more he wanted to protect her. At least make things right by giving her Theodore's share of the profits.

He bid good day to the old-timers and wandered down the boardwalk toward his hotel, passing the Emporium of Fashion. Her competitor.

If she wouldn't accept money, he could help her business. He studied the ready-made dresses and trousers through the window.

He stepped inside. Twice the size of Sarah's place and packed with merchandise. Women's clothes filled shelves on one side of the store while shelves of men's clothes filled the other. Dresses hung on the walls. A sharp contrast to the sparse stock in Mrs. Anderson's shop.

He fingered a tag pinned to a pair of men's trousers. If Mrs. Anderson charged prices this low, she would starve. Had he foreseen the success of ready-made clothing, he would have opened a store himself.

Mrs. Anderson needed his help, whether she wanted it or not.

A couple of days later, Sarah listened for her boys to return home from school. She didn't want a repeat of the fight from the other day. She smiled as she remembered Mr. Taylor's attempts to protect her. Rumor was he hadn't left town, yet neither had he returned to see her.

The bell above the door rang, and William came into the shop followed by Teddy and Kenny.

Rose sorted through several spools of thread, testing each against a blue dress and setting it down again. "Boys, I brought some cookies I baked this morning. I left them on the kitchen table."

"Cookies? Good thing I came by." William rubbed his hands together and licked his lips.

Rose tossed a spool of blue thread at him. "You're not a boy."

He caught the thread before it hit him in the face. "I could be if cookies are involved." He handed the spool to Sarah. "No trouble today."

"Because you're with them." Sarah mussed Kenny's hair.

"We're not babies." Teddy stormed toward the kitchen behind the shop. "Stop treating us like we are."

Sarah opened her mouth. What could she say? Yes, they were babies.

Kenny strolled after his brother, lunch pail dangling from the end of one arm. "Bye, Uncle Will."

"See you tomorrow." Her brother waited for the door to shut

behind the boy. "Tell me about Mr. Taylor. Word is he offered you money."

Sarah shot Rose a hard look. She'd hoped to avoid this conversation. How could she talk about the man without sorting through her own feelings first? She shrugged. "What's to say?"

William crossed his arms and gave her a big-brother stare. Although three years her junior, he acted like an older brother, and others accepted his authority. "I can't help you if I don't know the facts."

"You don't have to play newspaperman with me." She crossed her arms and stared back. "I sent him away. Nothing to tell."

"He's been asking about you around town. He's not going anywhere." William steepled his fingers. "Tell me."

He might as well hear it from her. The man knew a story when he smelled one. She recounted Mr. Taylor's visit, leaving out her attraction to the stranger.

When she finished, he rubbed his clean-shaven chin. "If Theodore earned the money, it belongs to you." He glanced at the empty dress forms behind the worktable. "You could use the funds."

True, she could purchase more supplies. "We don't know where his money came from. Could be ill-gotten gains."

He gave her a wary glance. "What did Theodore invest in?"

"I'm not sure. He would disappear for days. Sometimes he would come home with money. Other times he lost it all. Until the one time he didn't come back." She pushed the memory aside. "Mr. Taylor doesn't have any proof he and Theodore were partners. He could take advantage of a widow."

"By giving you money?" William shook his head. "I don't think so."

"I don't trust him." She wanted to trust him but didn't need the distraction. "He'll move on to his next target."

Her brother stood to leave. "I'll check into his background. You'll see him again. Mark my words."

Could she find the strength to send him and his money away again?

Chapter 4

Jack sat at a round table in the hotel dining room —his makeshift office until lunchtime. Stacks of papers covered half of the surface. An inkwell and pen sat to the side. Sunlight streamed through a window and reflected off the dust motes dancing in the air.

A bacon scent lingered, and pans clattered in the kitchen as Matilda cleaned up from the breakfast crowd. The Rockledge Hotel seemed more like home than his grand house in Denver.

He would return to his family home if he could. But after his mother passed, his sister sold the farm and bought a house in town, removing everything familiar.

If only he had stayed home, he could have fought off the attackers who killed his mother.

If only. . .so many "if onlys."

If only he'd contacted Theodore's widow immediately.

She struggled to make a living, if the sparse contents of her shop gave any indication. She acted tough, but a gruff exterior wouldn't put food on the table. She needed someone responsible. Someone stable. Someone who would stick around.

All areas where he'd tried and failed.

He rummaged through the disarray of papers littering the tabletop. How had this become his life?

Everyone wanted him to invest in their harebrained schemes. Partnership propositions, calling cards, and even a handful of marriage opportunities from desperate fathers. Not to mention prospecting hopefuls looking for a grubstake, start-ups who heard he was in town, and an inventor who had the ridiculous notion men could fly.

If he had known a gold strike would saddle him with investment decisions, he'd have waited to reveal its value until he grew too old for adventure. A businessman he was not.

One entrepreneur wanted to sell ready-made clothes, like the Emporium of Fashion. A profitable opportunity—for another town. Factories in the east produced clothing much more cheaply than a seamstress making one dress or shirt at a time. Mrs. Anderson didn't need more competition in Rockledge.

He should send the requests to his accountant in Denver. Roy Sanders, who kept track of his finances, lived for numbers. He spent his whole life in town with no interest in leaving.

The prospectors' requests interested Jack most. They didn't submit written proposals. More often a whisper from the alley, promising a rich mineral deposit but giving no detail. Too much danger of claim jumping.

His pulse quickened at the thought of finding another rich ore body. From Rockledge, he could visit the sites and judge for himself. A high-risk venture, but the thrill of finding a new claim called to him.

He didn't care about the cost. He already possessed more than he could spend in a lifetime. But money couldn't make up for his past sins.

A cool breeze rustled his papers as the front door opened. A skinny man in worn trousers and a shirt that hinted at once being white stepped into the dining room. He pulled the cowboy hat from his head and crossed to Jack's table. His recently cut hair contrasted with his scruffy beard. Had he left the barbershop in a hurry? "Jack, you old dog. Heard you hit the big one."

"Sid." Jack rose to shake his friend's hand. "What brings you to town in the summer? I figured you'd be holed up in the hills until the weather turns cold."

Sid dropped into a chair across the table from Jack and hunched forward. He peered around the room and lowered his voice. "I found it. The vein that feeds the placers in Black Bear Creek."

Goose bumps formed on Jack's arms for the first time since he sold the Griffin Mine. He kept his voice low. "Where? How?"

"Can't say. You know." Sid held a smug grin. "Unless you were to invest."

"I'd need to see it." Jack crossed his arms. The find his friend described would bring a tidy sum. "I won't go in blind."

The hotel door swung open. Mrs. Anderson slammed it behind her, rattling the window. She marched toward Jack, hands on her hips and red-faced.

Her schoolmarm look, directed at him instead of her son.

A challenge.

He'd charmed his grammar school teacher. He would charm her too.

Her gumption attracted him. The woman didn't back down. The anger in her face couldn't hide her delicate features. Small but mighty.

Jack stood. He cleared his throat and nudged Sid's chair leg with his boot.

The prospector pushed to his feet.

"Good morning, Mrs. Anderson." Jack kept his tone casual as if he couldn't read the anger in her eyes. He flashed her a grin.

"It is not a good morning, Mr. Taylor." She appeared in control, but her hands trembled where she pressed them against her skirt. "Not a good morning at all."

Part of him wanted to hold her and assure her everything would be all right. The other part wanted to see the full extent of her emotions. He waved a hand toward the window. "Is that so? The sun's shining, and a lovely woman has paid me a visit. Definitely a good morning."

Her eyes opened wide. "Stop playing games, Mr. Taylor. And stop asking around town about me. Stay out of my affairs. And my life."

Before Jack could respond, she spun away and stomped out of the dining room, slamming the door behind her.

His pulse pounded like a drum in step with her retreat as she passed the window outside. He'd stay in Rockledge a little longer.

Sid's gaze moved from him to the window. "I see how it is. A respectable woman like her will never be interested in a prospector." He gave Jack a hard stare. "Not even a wealthy ex-prospector."

True. But he had to try.

A week later Jack took out his frustration on a leather feedbag strapped to the ceiling joist of his carriage house in Denver. The pouch, filled with oats and sawdust, served as his own effigy.

Jab.

How could he get Mrs. Anderson to accept her husband's share of the proceeds from the mine?

Jab. Cross.

He would help her, whether she wanted it or not.

Sweat dripped down his face, stinging his eyes. He wiped at his forehead with his arm.

Jab. Cross. Jab. Cross.

How could he make things right if no one accepted his efforts? He'd been a fool to hold on to Theodore's money for a year.

Left hook. Right hook.

In the old days, Jack needed to be ready for a fight. Now he didn't want to grow soft sitting in meetings about how to spend his money.

He ducked, avoiding an imaginary punch from a fictitious opponent.

One last jab.

After catching his breath, he dunked his head in the horse trough and flipped his wet mane. Water droplets scattered across the wall. The exercise relaxed his mind and soothed his soul.

He'd come home to Denver to take care of business before returning to Rockledge. A summer in the mountains might bring a little adventure and give him time to get acquainted with Mrs.

Anderson. Roy could handle his various investments while he was away. He would leave on the morning train and communicate with his office daily by telegraph.

He returned to his room to pack for an extended trip. His wardrobe held three fine suits. What man needed three suits? He grabbed a pair of trousers and a heavy cotton shirt and placed them in an open trunk.

One Sunday suit. No more.

Would Mrs. Anderson notice the change in his attire? Clothing wouldn't fool her. No. To win her trust, he needed to prove he wasn't anything like she thought. She would never find the old Jack attractive.

He added his mother's log cabin quilt to the trunk. She'd made it when his parents homesteaded. The green and tan pattern with a little bit of red had graced her bed ever since he could remember. He'd huddled beneath it on chilly winter days.

He fingered the fabric, faded and torn at some of the seams. More of a rag than a quilt. He couldn't part with it. His only reminder of his mother.

Jack tucked it in the trunk before closing the lid. It would give him a legitimate reason to see Mrs. Anderson. Although the quilt looked to be beyond hope, he would ask if she could mend it.

He smiled at the thought.

Would she be happy to see him? Not if his last encounter with the feisty widow was any indication.

Chapter 5

Sarah stood next to Rose at the worktable, cutting fabric samples and setting them in a basket. “I hope this works.” She placed the latest copy of *Godey’s Lady’s Book* next to the squares.

“Have faith.” Rose added some lace strands. “The ladies won’t turn me away when they see these pretty fabrics. They’ll all want new dresses.”

“Who do you plan to visit today?” Sarah wished she could make the sales calls herself, but she needed to stay at the shop for her boys.

“Mrs. Clark, the Fitzwater sisters, and the Jackson family. Mrs. Jackson’s three oldest girls need new dresses, whether they know it or not. Especially Emogene.” Rose hooked the basket on one arm and raised the other hand toward the door. “Perhaps Mr. Taylor will come by while I'm out."

Heat filled Sarah's face. "He's long gone. Why do you insist on talking about him?" Sarah wouldn't admit she'd thought of little else since he left.

"Because, dear sister, you need a little adventure." Rose twirled as she checked her reflection in the full-length mirror.

Sarah closed her eyes, took a deep breath, and opened them again. "What I need is stability. And more customers. If I don't take care of my family, no one else will."

The bell above the door clanged.

Mr. Taylor.

His broad frame filled the entry. He stood taller than Sarah remembered. He wore brown trousers with suspenders and a clean white shirt, which failed to hide his muscular build. A bundle peeked from beneath one arm.

Sarah wouldn't let the man unnerve her. She stole a glance at the mirror but remembered she didn't care what he thought of her. No matter that a curl dangled near her eye. She willed her hand not to tuck it in.

"Good afternoon, ladies." He removed his hat and gave an exaggerated bow.

Sarah didn't trust him. No one handed out money without expecting something in return. She sidled next to her sister and kept her voice low. "Get Sheriff Bradford."

Rose gave Sarah a puzzled expression. Where were her actress skills when Sarah needed them?

"The sheriff," Sarah whispered through the side of her mouth. She didn't imagine Mr. Taylor would cause her harm. But a visit from the law would show him she wasn't the lonely, desperate widow he imagined her to be. As a friend of her brothers, the sheriff would be happy to stop by.

Rose answered with a slight nod. Then she gave the man an award-winning smile. "Good to see you, Mr. Taylor." She lifted her basket. "I'm off."

At least she had the good sense to leave the door open.

Sarah steeled herself against her attraction to Mr. Taylor. "I thought you left town." She crossed her arms.

"Temporarily. We have unfinished business." He remained near the entrance and leaned against a wooden pole as if he hadn't a care in the world. "How long until the sheriff arrives?"

"How did—" She wouldn't show him he unnerved her. "Five minutes, if he's in his office."

He nodded. "Fair enough. Have you reconsidered my offer?"

Teddy marched through the open doorway, followed by his little brother. He headed toward the kitchen without a word.

Kenny's singsong voice carried through the shop. "Teddy got a black eye."

"What?" Sarah's head throbbed. "Stop right there, young man."

The boy halted and faced her, revealing a large purple bruise on the side of his face. His shirt hung askew and one of the buttons dangled by a thread.

Mr. Taylor gave a low whistle. "That's a real shiner."

Sarah wanted to scowl at him but instead focused on her son. Couldn't the man stay out of this?

Teddy beamed. "You should see the other boy. I knocked out a tooth. That's what he gets for callin' me a baby."

Sarah's hand flew to her throat. "Oh my. You'll have to apologize to the boy and pay for the dentist."

How much would this cost her?

"I won't apologize. He hit me first." Teddy crossed his arms. "Besides, Marcus says you can stick a tooth back in, and it grows fine."

Mr. Taylor nodded. "It's true. The tooth will heal. Son, I thought we talked about avoiding fights."

Sarah vacillated between correcting the man—Teddy wasn't his son—and allowing him to take Teddy under his wing. They seemed to speak the same language, and he could be a positive influence. Where were her brothers when she needed them?

"Let me show you the fighter's stance." Mr. Taylor set his bundle on the worktable. Then he stepped with his feet apart and held his fists in front of his face.

Sarah jumped between the stranger and her son. "You're not teaching my son how to fight."

"No. The fighter's stance is also good for dodging punches and protection."

Teddy shuffled around her for a better view.

Mr. Taylor shifted his muscled torso from side to side, keeping his hands in front of his face. "Try this."

Teddy's uninjured eye went wide. He moved his feet and arms to imitate the man. "Like this?"

Sarah clenched her jaw. Her boys needed a man, but she didn't know anything about Mr. Taylor. Except that he wore a woodsy cologne and likely left a string of broken hearts in his wake. Where was Sheriff Bradford?

"Bend your knees a little." Mr. Taylor ducked and then jumped sideways. "This sets you up to strike, but you can shift your weight and turn to dodge a punch."

Teddy dodged a couple of imaginary punches.

Kenny imitated his brother, dodging punches too.

"If an opponent sees that you know the fighter stance, most likely he'll walk away without attacking you." Mr. Taylor lowered his arms to his sides. "Maybe later I can show you a few more moves."

Sarah cleared her throat. There wouldn't be a "later."

He tipped his head in her direction. "For defense. If it's all right with your mother."

Her heart longed for him to stay, but she knew his kind. The wrong type of man always attracted her.

She patted Teddy's shoulder. "Go wash up. We'll talk after Mr. Taylor leaves."

"Bye, Mr. Taylor."

Teddy strode to the back door. Kenny trotted after him.

Sarah regained her bearings. He was good with her boys, but that didn't make him the man she needed. "Why are you here?"

He resumed his position against the wooden pole. No doubt, a practiced move to put her at ease. "I still owe you Theodore's share of the profits."

She took a deep breath. "I'll have no part of your ill-gotten gains."

A smile played on his lips. "Profits from a legitimate venture."

She ignored his charm. "With no paperwork?"

"You know how prospecting is." He surveyed her sparse shelves. "I'll find a way to help you, even if you don't take the money."

Sarah's mind raced. What could he mean? "I don't think—"

"I brought some sewing business for you." Mr. Taylor pushed away from the pole and reached for the bundle he set on the worktable earlier. "Can you mend a quilt for me?"

"A quilt?" Sarah struggled to follow his quick change in topic.

He eased the bundle open, revealing a tattered and stained quilt. "It isn't a fancy dress like what you usually make, but I thought—" He fingered the edge of the fabric and dropped the false bravado. A little boy in a grown man's body stood next to her.

She spread the quilt across the table, holding the edges so it didn't drape to the floor. A classic log cabin pattern. Brown droplets splattered one corner, and a dark stain, like grease, covered a couple of blocks.

Although it was well made, most people would have discarded the covering long ago. Sarah would need to replace several squares. She ran her finger along a frayed seam. "Whose was this?"

"Never mind. It's beyond repair." Mr. Taylor snatched the fabric and wadded it into a ball. He tucked it under his arm. "I'll go now."

"Wait." The quilt gave her a glimpse of the man under the suave demeanor. A man she wanted to know better. "I'll see what I can do."

Sheriff Bradford, a heavy, middle-aged man with a shiny star on his vest, clomped into the shop.

"Heard there might be some trouble here."

Mr. Taylor stiffened. Then an easy smile tugged at his lips. "Afternoon, Sheriff."

The man must play a mean game of poker. He tightened his grip on the bundle.

Sarah shook her head. "No trouble. Mr. Taylor brought a quilt for me to mend. Thanks for stopping by."

The following evening, Jack perused a recent copy of *Godey's Lady's Book* in the comfort of a wingback chair in the corner of the hotel lobby. He'd wrapped a newspaper around the outside so passersby wouldn't see the cover. Couldn't have anyone thinking him less of a man.

If he wanted to help Mrs. Anderson, he needed to understand her industry. Good thing the hotel owner's wife left the book on a table for guests to read. Why couldn't Mrs. Anderson own a general store? Or, better yet, a mining supply store?

If she took the money, he could leave. Duty done. Penance paid. He'd return to a confining office in Denver.

But Mrs. Anderson needed him, and her refusal gave him an excuse to stay in Rockledge. Not only could he help with her store, he could teach her boys a few things. He could protect her.

He read the descriptions of dresses from Europe. Like reading a foreign language. Did women understand all these terms? Articles about housekeeping and recipes conjured sweet memories of his mother and of simpler times. As a young man, he'd ached to get away—to see the West. And he had.

At what cost?

Could he have saved her life if he'd been there? He'd returned home a month after her burial. A gang of bandits, they'd said. A woman alone. An easy target. She'd asked him to stay. To run the farm. But he'd made his own plans. Walked away.

He studied the people in the hotel lobby in an attempt to block the memories. A traveling salesman sorted through his case at a dining room table. On the sofa near a window, a young lady sat next to her husband. She stared outside and clenched her husband's hand. The timid woman couldn't compare to Mrs. Anderson in beauty or strength.

The widow had allowed him to stay, even after fetching the

sheriff. He sensed her anxiety, but she held her ground. Had she hoped for an exciting life before she married? Before responsibility took over? He couldn't imagine this woman married to his ex-partner. Theodore lived for the next big opportunity, hadn't even appeared to have a family.

A tall, lanky man strode into the hotel lobby, grinning. He wore clean clothes and sported a fresh haircut. His sunburned face gave him away as a prospector. Must have come in from the fields to get an assay.

He marched to the desk and dropped a small pouch on the counter. "I'll take your best room."

A prospector who'd made a find.

Jack would talk to the man after he settled in. See if his property provided a sound investment. Make use of his time in Rockledge.

He flipped through the pages of the ladies' magazine. Why would women prefer Sarah's product to ready-made goods? He stole a glance at the couple who sat on the sofa. Was the lady's dress ready-made? He didn't think so.

The salesman mumbled to himself as he replaced the goods in his case.

Jack formulated a plan. He would help the handsome widow. And earn her favor in the process.

Chapter 6

Yawning, Sarah carried her tin coffee cup from the kitchen into the dress shop. She'd risen early to send the boys off for a day of fishing with their uncle David. Afterward, when she couldn't fall asleep, she added numbers in her ledgers. How would she get through the rest of the day without a nap?

Rose fed yellow cotton through the sewing machine as she rocked the treadle back and forth with her foot. The worn-out contraption gave a high-pitched screech with each pump, sending a shiver down Sarah's spine. Good thing her new machine would arrive soon.

Singing over the noise, Rose practiced her next opera. How could she focus on the aria with the horrible racket?

Sarah wandered to the sitting area and relaxed in a comfortable chair. She warmed her hands on the tin cup and breathed in the rich coffee aroma. She hummed familiar phrases as she listened to her sister's song. If Rose could ignore the screech, so could she.

Sarah wouldn't think about profit and loss right now. Nor Mr. Taylor. Or Teddy's fights. She let her eyes slip closed.

Rose quieted the machine. "You look relaxed."

"I am." Sarah forced her eyes open, having nearly drifted off.

Her sister resumed singing as she gathered the yellow pile and held it up, revealing a summer day dress.

A booming voice from outside shattered the peace. Sarah jumped to her feet, and her empty cup tumbled to the floor with a thunk. "What in the world?"

Rose shrugged, a twinkle of mischief in her eyes.

Sarah gave her sister a questioning look.

Rose folded the dress in her arms. "It's not my fault. I told him it wasn't a good idea."

"Who?" Sarah pursed her lips as she crossed to the large front window. "What wasn't a good idea?" She peered outside.

Mr. Taylor stood on the boardwalk in front of her shop. Next to him, a gray cotton day dress hung on a dress form.

Her dress form.

One of *her* dresses.

The muscles in her neck tightened, and she clenched her fists. She opened her hands and took a deep breath. She glared at her sister.

Rose bit her bottom lip and made a show of smoothing a seam on the yellow dress.

Sarah would deal with her sister later. Now, she needed to stop the exhibition out front. She marched outside.

Mr. Taylor's Sunday suit accentuated his broad shoulders. Obviously custom made. His top hat gave him an air of importance. He grinned at her and winked.

Heat crept up Sarah's face and neck. She halted. Why did he choose *her* to torment? "What do you think you—"

"Notice the asymmetrically draped overskirt and pleated underskirt." With a gentleman's cane, he pointed to the waist of the dress. "The velvet collar and cuffs complete the ensemble." He waved his free hand in the air.

Hadn't she read that description in the latest *Godey's*? A description that didn't quite fit the dress next to him.

Sarah grimaced. Only snake-oil salesmen sold wares in this manner. The man had turned her into a laughingstock.

Mrs. Winslow neared the shop with her two daughters for their fittings. The petite woman stopped short and gaped at Mr. Taylor's strange behavior. She waved her girls toward the street.

Mr. Taylor pointed to the collar of the dress. "Notice the fine stitching." His gaze met Sarah's, and he beamed.

Was he proud of the spectacle he created?

"And the delicate lace." His hand neared the fabric and hovered over the lace without touching it.

"Mrs. Winslow." Sarah motioned to her shop. "Please, come in."

The trio halted their retreat but didn't move closer. The girls huddled next to their mother, wide-eyed.

As a noisy wagon passed, Sarah stepped between the ladies and Mr. Taylor. Her hands shook, but she held her voice calm, almost singsong. "I'm glad to see you this morning. Won't you come in?"

Mr. Taylor put a hand on Sarah's shoulder. "Yes, come in, madam. Mrs. Anderson will create the finest dresses for you and your lovely daughters."

The woman's lips thinned, and she glanced from Sarah to Mr. Taylor. Her daughters, nearly young women, gaped at Mr. Taylor. One blushed, and the other batted her eyelashes.

Sarah stepped out of reach. She needed him gone.

Now.

She shoved his chest hard and tried to ignore the firm muscles beneath his suit and the warmth of the contact. "Inside, mister. Before you scare all my customers."

He yielded and backed through the still-open door.

Herding Mr. Taylor toward the rear of the shop, Sarah motioned her sister toward the entry. "Rose, help Mrs. Winslow. She and her daughters are here for their fittings. At least they *were* here for fitting."

"Not to worry." Rose lowered her voice. "I know how to handle her." She sashayed across the room, leaned through the doorway, and spoke up. "Mrs. Winslow. How lovely you look today. Have you done something different with your hair? I do believe it makes you look five years younger."

Ah, Rose. Sarah's anchor in the storm that was her life.

Once in the kitchen, Sarah faced Mr. Taylor. "What do you think you're doing?"

"Drumming up business." He removed his top hat and set it on the table. A couple of stray hairs stuck out to the side, giving him a boyish look. Handsome.

Sarah resisted the urge to smooth her skirt.

The man crossed to the potbelly stove. He picked up a tin cup and filled it with coffee from the pot. "Want some?"

Sarah flinched. "No."

He reclined against the countertop and brought the cup to his lips, surveying the room as he drank the coffee. "Do you live here?"

Sarah's mind reeled. "Where I live is none of your concern." What part of this man's boldness should she reprimand first?

He took a slow drink from the mug, making Sarah wish for a cup of her own. "I'll get back to my post when I finish this coffee. Much obliged."

Sarah let her shoulders sag. "Why are you doing this?"

Mr. Taylor set his jaw. "If you won't take Theodore's money, the least I can do is bring in customers." He tilted his head toward the front of the store. "I studied up on women's fashion, crazy as it is. Now I intend to demonstrate the advantages of purchasing from your shop."

"Please, go away. This is a respectable establishment for genteel ladies." Sarah needed coffee, but she wouldn't give Mr. Taylor the satisfaction of sharing a cup with him. "Ladies don't want you shouting at them. It drives them away."

"The Emporium has hired someone to carry a sandwich board in front of their store." He took a long drink. "It's the latest thing."

"Exactly. I'm not selling inferior products to unrefined customers." Weary, she dropped to a chair at the kitchen table.

After setting his cup on the counter, Mr. Taylor rubbed his chin. "Good point. I'll think of something else. I won't leave town until your store is thriving."

With four brothers, Sarah recognized a man's misguided determination. He wanted to fix something he didn't understand. What bizarre idea would he come up with next?

She needed to stop him. "Why don't you come the day after tomorrow? You can help retrieve the new sewing machine when it arrives at the freight office and set it up." If she gave him a chore, maybe he would stay out of trouble.

He stood tall, a sparkle in his eyes. "You can count on me." He picked up his hat and headed toward the main part of the shop.

Sarah jumped from her chair, bumping the table and banging her shin. "No. Go out the back. The ladies don't want a man around during fittings."

"Of course." He replaced his hat as he slipped out into the alley.

After squaring her shoulders and pasting on a smile, Sarah joined Rose and the Winslow ladies.

The youngest Winslow girl stood with her arms out straight as Rose examined the waist of her dress. Mrs. Winslow and the older girl relaxed in the sitting area. They gave no indication of hearing Sarah's conversation with Mr. Taylor.

"Such a handsome man." The older girl blushed. "I'd buy anything he was selling."

"Me too." The younger sister giggled.

Sarah gave her a brief nod. Young girls didn't know enough to stay away from men like Mr. Taylor. But Theodore had taught Sarah to be wary.

Rose stuck a pin in the underside of the sleeve. "He's creative. I didn't know what to think when he asked to take the dress outside."

Sarah didn't need his kind of creativity. How would she convince the man to leave town?

Where was Mr. Taylor?

Two days later, Sarah paced in front of the freight office as she waited for him to help with the sewing machine. After pestering her to the point of distraction, he disappeared when she needed him.

Five steps down the boardwalk. Turn.

Unreliable.

Five steps up the walk. Turn.

Like Theodore.

Five steps down. Turn.

Like most men.

The heavy machine sat in its crate, waiting for him to transport it to her shop. She'd used grocery money to pay for the contraption, but the advertisement promised the machine would sew faster and quieter on any kind of fabric. She needed every advantage. Besides, she didn't know how much more of the old machine's squeaking she could take.

Her boys played on the hitching rails. Kenny flipped upside down and hung from his knees. "Where's Mr. Taylor? Isn't he coming?"

A wagon team rattled down the street, followed by a couple of men on horses.

Still no Mr. Taylor.

A group of ladies waved from the other side of the street as they passed. The afternoon had grown warm, and she pulled at her collar.

"I don't know." Sarah adjusted her hat. She wore her French bonnet in anticipation of seeing the attractive prospector. Foolish. She should've known better. Any of her brothers or her brother-in-law could have helped with the machine. But she'd asked a virtual stranger. An unreliable stranger, at that.

Kenny dropped to his feet and leaned on the hitching rail. "I like Mr. Taylor."

Teddy climbed to stand on the hitching rail and held on to a pole. "I heard he left town. Went with an old prospector."

Of course he left town. Forget his commitment to her.

Sarah sighed.

A few minutes with the handsome stranger, and she lost her senses. She'd wanted to see him again. He made her feel beautiful and special. . .and stupid.

Her shoulders slumped. "Teddy, go fetch Uncle David. Tell him I need help with this crate."

David, the largest of her brothers, could easily carry and set up the machine. If she must depend on a man, at least it would be one who wouldn't leave when she needed him.

Chapter 7

Jack wanted to hurry the old nag he'd rented from the livery as he plodded toward town with the old prospector. Sid's gold tooth caught the sunlight as he rambled on.

Jack wiped the back of his neck with a bandana. Under other circumstances, he would have soaked in the beauty of the surrounding mountain peaks. The mining property his friend showed him would have given him a thrill.

Not today.

He swallowed hard. He reached for his canteen but remembered emptying it earlier.

Already an hour past the time he'd agreed to help Mrs. Anderson. Several miles of rugged terrain stood between him and Rockledge. Another failed attempt at making amends. He practiced an apology in his head. An apology she wouldn't accept.

He'd daydreamed about her on the trip to the claim. Would she enjoy a ride through the mountains with him? Her face might light up when she spied the yellow and purple wildflowers along the trail. Which would be her favorite? She would laugh at the chirp of a mountain pika. The furry little creature would steal a crumb or two of the lunch he would've purchased for them. Would she relax with a few hours away from her responsibilities? And smile. At him.

The ancient prospector next to him droned on about the mining project, talking more to himself than to Jack. "If you invest, we can finish development before winter sets in."

"Why didn't you tell me how far out this claim was?" Jack urged the nag to speed up, to no avail. She held a steady, plodding pace.

Sid spit a wad of tobacco to the side away from Jack. "Relax, son. Time doesn't exist up here."

Jack's stomach tightened. How could he prove himself to Mrs. Anderson if he couldn't make good on the simplest of requests? She had every right to push him away.

The trail crossed a stream, trickling with snowmelt. His mount pulled toward the water, ignoring his direction.

Sid reined in his horse and hopped to the ground. "The horses need a break."

A few minutes wouldn't make a difference. Jack slipped to the ground and let his horse drink. After filling his canteen from the stream, he took a long, cool drink.

"You've got to let up on your mare if you want her to get you home." The old-timer retrieved a pouch from his saddlebag and pulled out a strip of jerky. "Don't think you're ridin' double with me if she gives out on you." He tore off a hunk of jerky with his teeth.

"I'm late for an appointment in town." The declaration sounded weak, even to Jack. "A man is nothing without his word."

Sid swallowed. "Don't you sound like a city boy? 'Late for an appointment.' You're gettin' soft."

Jack stiffened and fixed him with a stare. "I'm not soft."

"You could've headed home anytime if this *appointment* was so all-fired important." The prospector shoved the pouch into his saddlebag. "You know the way to town."

Weary, Jack capped the canteen in his hands. Sid was right. He'd wanted to see the claim. He couldn't give up his old ways. He'd never be the responsible man Mrs. Anderson needed. He wanted to pray, but God wouldn't accept him either. Not until he learned responsibility.

Sid mounted his horse. "Enough lollygaggin'. Let's get goin'."

Because he couldn't change his error in judgment now, Jack set aside thoughts of Theodore's widow for the rest of the ride. Instead, he discussed the merits of the mining claim. Always a prospector—a dealmaker—an explorer. He couldn't change if he wanted to.

As the sun dipped behind the Rocky Mountains, his nag lumbered into town. Jack proceeded straight to Mrs. Anderson's shop and hitched his horse to the rail out front.

When he'd agreed to meet her, he imagined arriving clean. Instead, dirt from the trail clung to his clothes like odor clings to a skunk. That's what he felt like. A skunk.

His chest tightened as he pressed the handle of her front door. It didn't budge. Locked. He'd expected as much. After stepping to the window, he pressed his face to the surface, a hand on each side. His nose pressed to the cool glass, like a kid at a sweet shop.

A couple of lanterns illuminated the room, and Mrs. Anderson huddled with a man over a black contraption on a table. The new sewing machine? Her boys watched from the side, hands behind their backs.

Jack squinted for a better view of her visitor. Did the widow have a suitor? He hadn't considered that possibility. She could do better than an unreliable prospector. Hadn't she already experienced the pain of that kind of relationship with a man just like him?

He let his shoulders slump. He should leave. Seek to redeem himself without interrupting her life.

Teddy pointed in his direction. Recognition lit the boy's face, and he raced toward Jack.

Too late for a quiet escape. Jack waved and replayed the list of excuses he'd practiced all afternoon and evening.

Kenny trailed behind his brother, and Mrs. Anderson lifted her head. She pursed her lips, then said something in the boys' direction.

Jack couldn't make out her words, but he could guess.

The man straightened. Jack exhaled, relief flooding him. One of the widow's brothers. David, if memory served. He'd run across the man a few times in town. A decent fellow. Not overly friendly. Not hostile either.

Mrs. Anderson mouthed something as she tilted her head in Jack's direction, but he couldn't see her face clearly.

One of the lamps shone on David's face so Jack couldn't miss the deepening frown.

Whatever she said, he deserved it. He stepped away from the window.

The door flew open. Teddy and Kenny spilled onto the boardwalk, both talking at once. Something about a fight that wasn't a fight.

Jack nodded at the boys as he tried to catch a glimpse of their mother.

Teddy hopped around in a fighter stance, fists next to his face, his younger brother imitating him like a shadow. "When he saw I was ready for a fight, he ran away like you said he would, Mr. Taylor."

Mrs. Anderson's brother stepped onto the walk, casting a hulking shadow. "Boys, go help your mother."

The younger boy squeezed past the man into the shop.

But Teddy stayed. "This is Mr. Taylor. The man I told you about."

"I know who he is." David gave the boy a hint of a smile. "Go inside now."

Jack tensed, the muscles in his shoulders seizing as if preparing for battle.

Teddy backed into the shop. "See ya, Mr. Taylor."

David pulled the door shut behind him and crossed his arms.

Jack couldn't help but compare his road-weary appearance with the well-groomed man. He held his arms at his sides and relaxed them, which did nothing to ease the tension in his shoulders. He deserved any harsh treatment the man dished out.

Jack swallowed. "I'm here to help Mrs. Anderson with a new sewing machine."

"The matter is under control." The man gave him a cold stare.

"Of course." Jack held his ground. He'd played plenty of bad hands of cards. He would play this hand too. "I'd like to speak to her. To apologize for my tardiness. My meeting ran long. I'm sure you understand."

"A meeting with Sid about a mining claim?" David didn't move.

"How did—"

"Small town."

Jack's mouth went dry. He nodded and cleared his throat. "Mining is my business, at least part of it. If I can speak to Mrs. Anderson."

"I won't let you hurt my sister." Mrs. Anderson's brother, and gatekeeper, reached for the door handle. "Good night."

Jack's mind raced. Could he turn the man before him into an ally instead of a foe? "I came to Rockledge to give her Theodore's share of the profit from the Griffin Mine. Would you convince her to accept?"

"So I've heard." The man drew his eyebrows together. "I would like to see her have it. . .if it is legitimate. I'll look into your offer, but she has her own mind."

The muscles in Jack's shoulders released their iron grip. A glimmer of hope. The chance to make things right. "I'd appreciate it."

"Leave now, and stay away from my sister."

The lock clicked behind him, like the clanging of a prison's iron bars.

Chapter 8

The following week, Sarah ran her hand along the cool metal of the new sewing machine. The word *Singer* in gold block letters gleamed from one side of the shiny black-painted surface. It worked as promised, creating a smooth seam on various fabrics.

With the new machine, Sarah and Rose made quick work of the existing dress orders. But the contraption brought no new business. No one cared how she sewed the dresses, only that she did. A poor investment, indeed.

Only one commissioned project remained unfinished.

Mr. Taylor's.

Sarah closed her eyes, wishing she could forget the quilt. Forget the man. Forget her foolishness in asking for his help. She opened her eyes and blew out a long, slow breath.

He'd proved undependable. Like Theodore in so many ways. His roguish manner and carefree lifestyle attracted her. But she'd walked that road before. She straightened her shoulders, ready to face the quilt and the emotions it carried.

Sarah set her empty coffee cup on the corner of the worktable. She spread the bundle of cloth over the surface. It held a slight smoky aroma, as though it had warmed someone near a hearth. She tried to imagine Mr. Taylor snuggled in the log cabin quilt after a long day of adventure.

Faded colors, once bright, stared dully up at her. Seams along many of the blocks were now loose and the fabric frayed. A couple of unidentified stains marred one corner.

Why would a prosperous man like Mr. Taylor hold on to something so worn? Did his extra helping of confidence hide a sensitive side?

Sarah flipped the quilt over and spread it out to study the other side. A couple of dark lines in the corner showed where initials had been sewn. "R. T." A few pieces of embroidery thread hugged the letters, protecting the fabric under from fading until it too shrugged loose.

Only sentiment for someone dear would cause anybody to hold on to such a rag. A glimpse into the soul of the man. Who gave it to him? What story did it hold?

And what of Mr. Taylor and his offer of money? So odd. No one insisted on giving money without asking for something in return. Particularly no one who would associate with her late husband.

She imagined Theodore with this man, traipsing through the mountains while she tended to her babies at home. Gone for days or weeks, saying only he was prospecting. He gave up cards and saloons only to take on a different kind of gambling. She never knew when—or if—he would come home.

She released a fist from around the corner of the quilt.

Since Theodore's passing, she controlled her own life. Simple and predictable.

Until Mr. Taylor arrived.

Of course she could use money, but at what cost? Even if the money was Theodore's, she didn't want to benefit from his questionable pursuits.

She focused on the quilt, laying out a list of tasks. She couldn't replace the damaged squares with new fabric. It would look out of place. She'd have to find some older fabric to match the color and texture.

Rose burst into the shop, sewing basket hooked on one arm. "Have you heard the news?" Always the actress, Rose made everything sound exciting. Most likely, her news wasn't news at all.

The clattering of wagons and a horse's nickering carried through the doorway. A cloud of dirt billowed past Rose into the shop.

Sarah tapped the quilt with her finger. "Shut the door before we have to dust again today." She didn't ask about the *news*. Her sister would soon spill the story without any prodding.

"I couldn't believe it." Breathless, Rose placed her basket on the worktable. "Needed to check for myself."

Sarah hid a smile. The news didn't matter. She enjoyed her sister's enthusiasm. "Must be true, then."

"Stop teasing." Rose untied her bonnet and hung it on a peg on the wall. She put her hands on her hips. Although given to drama, Rose acted more excited than usual. "You already know, don't you?"

"I've no idea what you're talking about."

Rose reached across the table and took both of Sarah's hands in hers. "Emporium of Fashion is moving. To another town."

Sarah's mouth fell open. "I don't believe it."

"It's true." Rose danced toward her worktable. "I passed the Emporium on my way here. A 'Closed' sign hung in the window, and employees carried boxes to wagons out front."

Sarah dropped into the chair behind her table. She reached for her coffee and put the mug to her lips. Finding it empty, she set it aside. "Why would a successful business pick up and leave town?"

"I asked one of the workers, but he didn't know anything." Rose picked up a pile of purple fabric. "This could be the break we need."

Sarah stepped to the front window and peeked outside, hoping she could make sense of things. "I would welcome the customers. But it doesn't make sense. Thriving businesses don't just move away."

"This one does. Don't question the gift." Rose leaned over the tattered quilt. She fingered a green strip along one of the log cabin blocks. "Where did this come from? Looks like it's ready for the rag bag."

Sarah winced. This quilt carried a lot of meaning. Too much to discard, even if she didn't know its story. "It belongs to Mr. Taylor. He asked me to repair it."

Her sister reached toward the quilt but let her hand drop without touching it. "Not much chance of mending it."

"Forget the quilt." How could Rose dismiss this turn of events? "Did you hear anything to give a clue about what happened with the Emporium?"

Rose stretched her arms wide and twirled in the center of the room. "It's the answer to your prayers. I assume you've been praying too."

Why pray? God had more important things to deal with. "Of course I prayed."

Rose splayed her hands to the sky as though she were on stage. "And God answered your prayer."

Not likely.

Rose swayed as she glided to the sitting area and picked up the latest issue of *Godey's Lady's Book*. She flipped to the fashion plates. "I should brush up on the latest styles."

William strode into the shop, face beaming. He pointed his thumbs to his chest. "Your brother is the best reporter in town. Have I got a story for you."

Finally, Sarah might learn what happened. "I hope this is about Emporium of Fashion's sudden departure."

"Indeed, it is." He stood behind a wingback chair near Rose and draped his arm over the top. "Young Bartholomew, who sweeps their floors, is fond of peppermint sticks. And I happened to have a couple of extra peppermint sticks."

Silence hung in the air as he peeked over Rose's shoulder at the magazine, as though he'd finished his story.

"And?"

Why did he have to drag this out? He was as bad as Rose.

William steepled his fingers in front of his face. "It seems Mr. Jack Taylor purchased the Emporium. Lock, stock, and barrel. And decided the store would serve him better over in Tucker Gulch."

Sarah dropped to the settee across from William and Rose.

"How exciting." Rose closed the magazine.

"Why would he do such a thing?" Sarah pressed her hands into her lap.

"You know why." William gave her a big-brother stare, even though he was younger. "Word is, he feels bad for the state Theodore left you in and wants to make it up to you."

"You're siding with him?" Heat crept up Sarah's neck.

"I've checked around. His story seems legitimate. He staked the Griffin mining claim, and Theodore apparently invested or helped in some way." Her brother sat in the chair closest to her. "I need to check a couple more sources, but he seems genuine."

Sarah didn't want Mr. Taylor's money. Didn't want his help. Didn't want his attentions.

But the absence of the Emporium would increase sales. What kind of person would buy out her competition? She needed to thank him. Thank him and ask him to leave town. Before he broke down the wall she'd worked so hard to build around her heart.

Jack cleared the papers from his table in the Rockledge Hotel dining area to make room for the lunch crowd. As if two old ladies and a couple of groups of single men constituted a crowd. The scent of stew and fresh bread hung in the air.

Mr. Whitfield, the former owner of Emporium of Fashion and now Jack's manager, had given him a progress report that morning. Jack secured a new location for the store in Tucker Gulch, well away from Mrs. Anderson.

Lightness filled his chest. Had she heard about her competition leaving town? Even if she never accepted her late husband's money, he would ensure that her shop earned a profit. Would this last act satisfy his penance? Penance for his part in Theodore's downfall. Penance for his absence when his mother died. Penance for always thinking of himself first.

He'd considered slipping the funds into her bank account. Even set up an appointment with the bank manager. A dishonorable man would sneak around without her permission. The old Jack would have done it.

He stuffed his papers into a satchel when he saw a couple of the older ladies who frequented the establishment. He would disappear into his room before they trapped him in a conversation. Always the same thing. An eligible young man like him should find a nice girl and settle down. He wasn't the kind to settle down.

The sound of a throat being cleared caught his attention.

Mrs. Anderson stood before him with a softer look than he'd seen before. He'd grown accustomed to her fierce protectiveness and even anger. But her gentle uncertainty caught him off guard. His mouth went dry as he studied her face.

If only he deserved a woman like her.

"I heard about what you did. . .with the Emporium." She pressed her hand against her skirt. Nerves? "Thank you for making the gesture."

Jack tried to find suave words, but his tongue betrayed him as though he were a schoolboy afraid to talk to a pretty girl. He simply said, "You're welcome."

"It won't matter." She shrugged. "Another ready-made clothier will take their place."

"I'll buy them out too." He set his jaw and studied her face.

"Go home, Mr. Taylor. Back to where you came from." She turned to leave. "I can manage on my own."

Jack wanted to reach out to her. Make her stay and see reason. "Have dinner with me."

The words escaped before he could stop them. He hadn't planned to woo the strong-willed widow. He held a breath as he waited for her answer.

Pans clattered in the kitchen, and a young man scooted benches around, scraping the floor.

"No." She rubbed her temples as she eased toward the door. "I can't do this again."

"I'm not Theodore." He couldn't stop talking. What kind of desperate sap had he become? "Just dinner. In the hotel dining room. A celebration."

She stilled, facing away from him, like a mannequin in a window.

A well-dressed couple entered the dining room. After a glance in Jack's direction, they selected a table on the opposite side.

Jack waited, heart racing.

He should rescind the offer. He already knew her answer. No sense in making her repeat herself. He opened his mouth to retrieve the invitation.

"I'll have dinner with you."

She shook her head and slipped outside.

His muscles relaxed. He peeked through a gap in the curtain as she retreated down the boardwalk. Why had she agreed? Whatever her reasons, he'd make the most of the evening. He wanted to see her smile or laugh or even provoke her to anger. Anything to see her come alive.

And then?

He wouldn't think about the possibilities. For now, he would revel in the anticipation of spending an hour with her.

Chapter 9

"What was I thinking?" Sarah examined her reflection in the free-standing mirror. She tugged on the bottom of her apricot bodice and smoothed her hands down the matching pleated skirt. Smart and simple.

Mr. Taylor's adventurous nature attracted her. So like Theodore in that respect. A quiet life as a husband and father had never satisfied him. Her husband's wanderlust cost her.

She tucked a stray curl behind her ear. "I can't have dinner with Mr. Taylor."

"Of course you can." Rose leaned her hip against the edge of a nearby worktable. "And you shall."

"I've changed my mind." Sarah edged toward the kitchen. "When he comes, send him away."

Her sister blocked her exit. "No you don't. You can't hide away in a dress shop day after day until you die."

"Until I die? Why must you be so dramatic?" A lump formed in the pit of Sarah's stomach. She couldn't eat if she wanted to. "I don't feel well."

Rose rested her hands on Sarah's shoulders. "You can do this." She twirled her finger in the air, indicating Sarah should model the whole dress. "Let me see."

Sarah spun partway but stopped and resumed her original position. "I'm not a maiden waiting for her suitor." Her face heated. "I'm a business owner and a mother."

"And a woman." Rose took Sarah's hands in hers. "You used to be fun-loving and alive, always up for a new experience."

Those words described the naive young woman Sarah had once been when she fell for Theodore. She set her jaw. "And you see where that got me."

Rose let go of one hand and lifted Sarah's chin. "You're punishing yourself. You've become a haggard old woman."

Sarah flinched, and her stomach clenched tighter. "Haggard?" She put her hands on her hips and stared at her reflection. No wrinkles etched her face, and no gray highlighted her hair. Worn, but not old. Responsible. Determined. Not old. "Why would you say that?"

Rose stood behind Sarah and peeked over her shoulder at the mirror. "Old on the inside. Sweetie, like it or not, you're still alive. And not all men are like the no-good scoundrel you married."

Sarah pushed out a long, slow breath. "You spend too much time on stage."

"Because I'm an actress." Rose struck a pose, chin in the air, one hand on her hip. With the other, she picked up a yardstick from the table. Wielding the stick as though it were a sword, she lunged forward, ready for battle. "En garde."

The bell over the door rang as Mr. Taylor entered. Even in the same Sunday suit he'd worn to hawk her wares, he took her breath away. He removed his top hat and tipped his head in Sarah's direction.

Heat rushed through her body, and she pressed her hands together. If the man weren't so handsome, she could send him away.

Before she greeted him, he spied Rose, lifted his cane, and wielded it like a sword. Jumping into the classic fencing position and holding his hat behind his back, he struck her yardstick. "I'm here to fight for this lady's honor."

The lighthearted exchange relaxed Sarah, and her breathing steadied. She could imagine him as a swashbuckler on the high seas. Her stomach unclenched.

Rose gave him a broad smile and then schooled her features. "No. I'll deliver her to the pirate ship." She thrust the yardstick toward his midsection. "Take that."

He blocked the blow with his cane. "Not if I have anything to say about it."

Theodore never fought for her. Mr. Taylor's broad shoulders and muscular build had caught more than one lady's fancy—she'd heard the talk. His sturdy jaw gave him a strong, confident look—as if he could conquer the world.

He spun in a circle and resumed his fighting position.

Rose twirled around but lost her balance as her feet tangled in her skirt. She toppled toward Mr. Taylor, dropping her stick. He caught her by the elbow and steadied her.

She broke into a fit of giggles.

Sarah laughed too, for the first time in a long time. When had she last done something for fun?

Mr. Taylor propped his cane on the floor and focused on Sarah, his gaze moving from her face to her toes. Not in a lustful way, more like admiration.

Sarah fidgeted under his scrutiny.

A slow smile spread across his face. Hat in hand, he gave a little bow. "If you're ready, Mrs. Anderson, allow me to escort you to a fine dining establishment."

"Fine dining? In Rockledge?" Sarah studied him, curious. Then she took his arm, solid muscle meeting her touch. She breathed in the fresh woodsy scent of his shaving soap. How long since she'd shared a meal with a man who wasn't related to her? No guilt. No fear. She bit her bottom lip and glanced at her sister.

Rose nodded.

Sarah shared easy conversation with Mr. Taylor as he escorted her down the boardwalk and across the street.

He led her into the bustling hotel dining room. Matilda's Friday night pot roast attracted a devoted crowd. Conversations and the savory aroma of beef filled the air. Silverware clattered against tin plates. Miners crowded around a couple of long wooden tables to one side. Smaller tables of diners filled the rest of the space.

Sarah released Mr. Taylor's arm and weaved her way to a small table near the window, the only empty spot. When had she last eaten at the hotel? She served simple fare at home and attended Sunday dinners with the rest of her family.

When she reached for the chair, Mr. Taylor nudged her forward, toward a pair of glass-paneled doors to one side. He opened one, revealing a private dining room. A white linen cloth covered the single table set for two with fine china and crystal glassware.

Matilda's gangly teenaged son stood to one side, sporting an ill-fitting suit. A white flour sack towel hung over one arm, which he held in front of his stomach.

"Good evening, Mr. Taylor. Mrs. Anderson."

He tugged at his collar before he pulled a chair out, tipping his head toward Sarah.

Mr. Taylor shut the door, muffling the sound of the main dining room. "Much better."

Sarah pressed a hand against her chest. "Oh my." She peeked through the glass at the other diners who ate on metal plates and drank from tin cups. She took her seat. "I didn't expect anything so grand."

The young man cleared his throat. "My name is Henry."

Curious. She'd known the boy for years, and Mr. Taylor had obviously made his acquaintance as well.

The young man eyed Mr. Taylor as if seeking approval. "I will be serving you this evening."

Mr. Taylor gave a nod.

Henry stared skyward, as though reading from an invisible menu. "Tonight, we will begin with savory buttermilk biscuits and creamy butter. For the main course, I will bring a plate of slow-cooked beef chuck, seasoned potatoes, and garden-fresh green beans. This will be followed by sweet lemon cake." He returned his attention to Mr. Taylor. "And coffee."

"Savory slow-cooked beef chuck?" Sarah chuckled. "Is that a fancy way to say pot roast?"

Mr. Taylor winked. "Looks like you caught me."

"My ma said she wasn't cookin' a special meal for Mr. Taylor and his friend. Didn't matter how much he paid. She doesn't have time to cater to a city fella during the dinner rush." Henry ran the words together without taking a breath. "Sir."

Sarah put a hand on his arm. A boy in a man's body. "It's fine, Henry. I love your mother's pot roast. Anything else would have disappointed me."

"Thank you, ma'am. I'll fetch the biscuits now."

The bustle of the dining room broke the silence for a few seconds as Henry slipped out.

"This is too much." Sarah fingered the beige linen napkin on her plate. Why had she come? "You didn't need to go to all this trouble. The private dining room. China. Henry. How much are you paying him, anyway?"

"He offered to do it for free, but I'll give him something for his effort." Mr. Taylor's smile faltered, and his voice grew husky. "I wanted to show you I am sorry. I should have been at the freight station on time. I didn't make my commitment to you a priority. I won't make the same mistake again."

Theodore had never apologized. Said he did what he needed to do. None of her concern. She unfolded her napkin and smoothed it across her lap. "It doesn't matter."

"But it does." He set his jaw. "That isn't who I want to be. I'm learning to be responsible. Trying to give you Theodore's share. Why are you refusing the money?"

Did she trust him enough to speak of her difficult marriage? How much should she reveal? "Most of Theodore's 'investments' involved some form of gambling."

"I see." He fingered the crystal goblet and held his face neutral.

No contempt. No pity.

She needed him to understand, so she continued. "When we married, he kept his promise to stay away from the saloons and card tables and attend church on Sundays. But he invested money that we couldn't afford in the mines, waiting for a big win. Spending weeks at a time away from home."

He nodded. "I suppose for some men prospecting is like gambling."

Dishes clattered in the main dining area, but the small room allowed for a quiet conversation away from the local busybodies.

"I don't want anything to do with his gambling. His investments. To take advantage of others for my own gain."

A shadow of regret crossed his face. "Is that what you think I do? Take advantage of people?"

"I don't know."

His jaw clenched and relaxed. "I'll admit to being a selfish cad most of the time. But in this case, the company who purchased the claim did well."

The walls closed in. She shouldn't be this close to the man and the emotions he elicited. Better to see him as the overconfident, fun-loving rogue he appeared to be.

She eased the conversation to safer ground. "How did you go from prospecting to investing?"

He sipped water from the crystal goblet. "Quite by accident, I assure you." His casual grin erased all traces of serious conversation.

"Is that so?"

More at ease now, Sarah studied the man. One lock of hair stuck out. A fresh shave highlighted his strong jawline. No matter how much he cleaned up, he carried the air of an explorer. A rugged, handsome, capable explorer. Sarah's mouth went dry. She sipped her water.

Henry entered, bringing the dining room clamor with him. He placed a small china plate with two biscuits in the middle of the table, then he held out a pewter saucer with a block of butter. "Ma said for you to cut off what you want, but I'm not to leave the plate. She doesn't want to waste butter."

Mr. Taylor gave her a sheepish grin. "We're in Rockledge."

"I don't mind."

Sarah cut off a pat of butter and scraped it onto her plate. Mr. Taylor did the same.

After Henry left and the quiet resumed, she reached for a biscuit. "You became a wealthy investor by accident?"

"It never occurred to me what would happen if I found gold. Struck it rich. I loved the quest." Mr. Taylor transferred a biscuit to his plate but left it untouched. "Exploring. Traveling to places where no one has ever been. Uncovering the mysteries God hid in the earth."

Over dinner, he shared tales about his prospecting. Weathering an early snowstorm. Being lowered by rope thirty feet into an abandoned mine shaft. Fending off claim jumpers.

Sarah leaned into his stories. The way he talked about his work lit a flame in her soul. He brought to life a part of her she thought died with Theodore.

After a time, Mr. Taylor relaxed in his chair. "Enough about me. You probably think I'm no better than a foolish boy running around the mountains looking for treasure."

"When I was a girl, I loved to explore with my brothers. We traipsed through the woods and climbed in abandoned mine workings. If my brothers needed to lower someone by rope, they made me do it. Being a girl, I was lighter weight."

A grin lit his face. "I'm trying to picture little Mrs. Anderson hanging from a rope in a mine. The lure of adventure isn't as foreign as you let on."

"Sarah. Little Sarah. I wasn't Mrs. Anderson then." She wanted him to use her given name. She liked the way he made her feel. She liked him. "Call me Sarah."

His lips parted as if to speak. He paused, then nodded. "Sarah."

A warm tingle ran up her spine. It was as if he'd always known her and called her by her given name.

"You should call me Jack."

She swallowed hard and nodded. "Jack."

Like crossing an invisible line that kept him at a safe distance, calling him Jack pulled him close. Had Sarah set herself up for another fall?

Chapter 10

Sarah strolled down the dark street on Jack's arm to her home behind the shop. For a little while, she let go of her responsibilities. His attention overshadowed her problems.

He stopped outside her door and faced her.

In her window, light shone through the checkered pattern on the curtain and peeked around its sides. Had Rose already put the boys to bed? The evening had gone longer than she'd planned, but still Sarah hated to see it end. Sipping coffee with Jack after the other diners left while Henry cleaned up the main dining room provided a delightful end to the meal.

Long-dormant emotions filled her as she stood before him in the moonlight. Her fingers tingled. Would he try to kiss her?

Did she want him to?

He placed both hands on her shoulders, and the tingling traveled up her arms to meet his touch.

"Thank you for this evening." Sarah itched to tuck in a stray hair poking sideways from under his top hat. "I enjoyed it. I didn't expect to, but I did."

"Should I be offended?" He flashed her a lopsided grin. "I'm not that hard to like."

She gave his chest a little shove, which didn't move him at all. "It's just. . .I didn't want to like you."

"Understood. More than one father has called me a rogue." He slid a hand to her back and eased closer. His touch warmed her.

She took a half step away but didn't break contact. "Are you a rogue?"

His moist breath brushed across her hair. "The best kind of rogue, I assure you. The kind who wants to see you smile again."

He lifted her hand and held it in both of his.

She longed for more—wanted to feel his hand on her back again. "I need responsible."

"I'm trying to mend my ways."

A gentle breeze caused Sarah to shiver. She wanted to believe in his goodness. "We'll see."

An owl hooted, and tinny piano music drifted from the saloons.

Sarah's door burst open, spilling light on Jack, breaking his spell. She jumped away from him, jerking her hand from his and losing his warmth. Teddy and Kenny bounded from the house, both talking at the same time.

Rose shrugged. "I tried to keep them inside, but they heard you and wanted to see Mr. Taylor."

"I was about to come in." Sarah swallowed hard. "Thanks for watching them."

Jack reached for Sarah's hand and brought her fingers to his lips. "I'll take my leave now. May I call on you again?"

The tingling returned. How could such a gentle touch impact her so much? "I haven't been able to stop you so far."

What did she hope to gain by spending time with him?

The following Sunday morning, Jack shuffled into Sarah's church, hoping to see her. The scent of fresh-cut wood filled the modest building, and the pews boasted new cushions.

The day after he shared supper with her, he'd ridden to Tucker Gulch to check on the relocated Emporium of Fashion, so he hadn't seen her since. He should send a telegram to Roy and ask him to find a buyer for the Emporium. Lucrative as it was, he wouldn't stay in the ready-made clothing business.

He hesitated near the back pew. How long since he last attended church? God didn't look kindly on hypocrites.

Sun filtered through stained glass windows, casting splashes of color onto the parishioners. In the front of the sanctuary, a couple of steps led to a platform. Two tall chairs guarded each side. In the center, two candles and a big Bible sat on the altar. A white-haired woman settled in front of a pump organ on a side wall.

Jack's chest tightened, and he glanced skyward. Could his mother see him from heaven? She would be pleased. For an instant, he was a little boy, holding his mother's hand and following her down the aisle to find a seat.

The organ blew out a couple of notes, pulling Jack from his

reverie and silencing conversations. The notes ceased, and the organist flipped the page. Conversations resumed, creating a low buzz.

No sign of Sarah. Should he leave if she didn't show up? He'd come to church for the wrong reason. God frowned upon impure motives.

"Mr. Taylor. Over here." A child yelled over the din of the crowd.

Jack searched for the source of the shout.

Kenny ran pell-mell down the aisle in his direction. Teddy strode behind him, showing more maturity, but the boy beamed. Sarah followed, wearing a fashionable blue dress.

Azure blue? Short bodice? Draped skirt? He shook his head to stop the lady's journal invasion.

Her smile warmed him, like the sunrise on a cool morning.

He breathed a prayer for clarity of thought and speech. Would God hear and answer such a prayer?

Kenny reached him and banged into his knees with force.

The impact jarred him, but he held firm. He ruffled the boy's hair.

"Morning, boys."

Two voices, not quite in unison. "Morning, Mr. Taylor."

"Sarah." Her given name rang foreign on his lips. Should he call her Mrs. Anderson in church?

She tipped her head in his direction. "Jack."

He stepped aside to let her pass with her sons.

The boys shoved each other, and both talked at the same time.

Sarah herded them forward. "We're late. Best get to our seats." She scooted into a pew already filled with relatives, flanked by her sons. "Settle down, boys."

The pipe organ squeaked a few tentative notes, and Jack searched for a seat. He'd hoped to join Sarah. Instead, he slipped in behind her, next to a couple of older ladies. Close enough to see her. He could have smelled her lilac scent if the matron next to him wasn't so generous with the rose water.

On the opening notes of the hymn, the congregation rose, and Jack joined them. Familiar strains of "Amazing Grace" awakened in him a longing from his youth. Didn't church organists know any other songs?

In an instant, he found himself hurled into the past, sandwiched with his sister between his parents. He was always grateful to stand for the singing after holding still while the preacher droned on.

Would anyone notice if he left before the preaching? He didn't need God and the church people to tell him to become a better person. He knew his shortcomings. Could he ever change? How many times had he tried and failed?

The music ended, and everyone sat. Too late for an escape. He didn't need the preacher's words to convict him. He'd already condemned himself.

Jack stared at a warped spot on the floor near his feet. Why hadn't someone repaired it?

Was it like him, not worth fixing?

"Sinners, repent." The preacher pounded the podium with one hand as he lifted a Bible with the other. "Come to the cross."

Jack had repented. Again and again. Then he sinned. Again and again. Always selfish and arrogant. What purpose did repentance serve? He tapped his fingers on his thigh. His attention drifted from the stern preacher to Sarah's soft curls. A couple of strands dangled in wisps like angel's breath. His fingers twitched, aching to touch them, remembering her softness.

"The wages of sin is death." The preacher held the Bible overhead and gave it a shake.

Jack didn't deserve a woman like Sarah, and she certainly didn't need him. She rejected the money he offered and the heartbreak he brought. He would fail her, no matter how honorable his intentions.

He studied people in the pews. David, the gatekeeper from the other night, sat near her, arms crossed. William, the newspaperman, whom Jack met once, whispered to Kenny. Two other men sat between the boys and Rose. And the redheaded man with an arm around Rose must be the brother-in-law.

They would see to her needs and her boys. Good men. They hadn't run him off yet, but they would.

Jack had imagined his church attendance would lead to a lunch invitation. Her family held gatherings every Sunday afternoon, and he hoped—but it didn't matter.

He forced himself to remain in the pew next to the matrons, the nearest one snoring beside him. He studied the windows and architecture, blocking out the sermon.

When the organ bellowed, the matron next to him startled awake. Everyone stood, and Jack made his escape. He wanted to run down the aisle to the exit. Instead, he held his head high and made his way to the door.

He would wrap up his business, return to Denver, and leave Mrs. Anderson in peace. Before he hurt her like he hurt everyone he cared about.

Chapter 11

Two days after his visit to church, Jack stopped at Hanson's General Store to pick up some jerky for his trip to Denver. Each morning this week, he'd determined to return home the following day. To leave Sarah in peace. And every evening, he'd changed his mind. One more day wouldn't hurt.

Something could change.

He could change.

Not likely though.

A handful of customers waited for Mr. Hanson, a man with a bulbous nose and receding hairline. Usually his wife helped him by filling orders, but today, the man handled the counter on his own.

A cowboy at the front of the line tapped his foot, arms crossed.

Jack wandered toward the bin of jerky. Nearby, a modest supply of ready-made clothes caught his attention. A few simple dresses hung on pegs, nothing like the finery Sarah created. When no one watched, he stepped closer to study the frocks.

At the sound of jostling in the next aisle, he jumped away from the dresses.

"I dare you." A lad's voice carried over a tall shelf. "Unless you're chicken."

"I'm not chicken."

Teddy?

Jack leaned to see past the shelf without being spotted.

Red-faced, Teddy stood in the middle of a trio of boys about his age.

One of them put his hands under his armpits and flapped like a bird. "Chicken."

"Keep your voice down." Teddy eyed the counter where Mr. Hanson waited on customers. "Somebody will hear you."

Were these Teddy's friends? And where was Kenny? Jack never saw the brothers apart.

Teddy glanced from side to side. "I'll do it."

Jack slipped behind the shelf before anyone noticed him. He moved to the other end of the aisle to find a new vantage point.

Did Sarah know where her son was and who he kept company with? Jack had traveled with friends like these in his youth.

Trouble.

Teddy put his hands behind his back and sauntered to the candy bins as if on a stroll. The others huddled in a tight group, staring in his direction.

Jack could stop Teddy. Show himself and take the kid home. Instead, he watched. Better to let him think he could get away with something and learn the consequences.

Sarah's son slowed and studied the bins as if making a selection. When Mr. Hanson bent behind the counter, Teddy snatched a handful of peppermint sticks and stuffed them into his pocket.

"Stop, thief!" The proprietor grabbed the boy by his collar and yanked. How had he come around the counter so fast?

Teddy coughed and pulled at the neckline of his shirt. He twisted his body to face the man, nailing the shopkeeper with a self-righteous glare. "What? I didn't steal nothin'."

Jack waited. Teddy would learn more from the harsh man than from his mother's warnings. Where were her brothers? She relied on them to teach her sons character.

The trio of lads shuffled to the door in a lump.

Jack slipped to the exit and lowered the bar into a locked position. Teddy shouldn't be the only one caught.

A hand reached toward the knob, but Jack couldn't tell which boy it belonged to.

"Stop right there," Mr. Hanson shouted over Teddy's head. "You good-for-nothing rabble-rousers."

The hand grabbed the knob and pulled. The door rattled against the bar but held firm. The troublemakers froze like rabbits in a rifle sight.

Other customers watched the show. A matron with a pinched face, who waited in line, shook her head and clucked her tongue.

The ringleader scooted away from the others and grabbed the bar to free himself.

Jack placed a hand on the bar and leaned on it. "What's your hurry, boys?"

Teddy gasped then allowed his shoulders to droop. He stared at the floor, his face turning even redder.

"We didn't do nothin'." The tallest boy, a foot shorter than Jack, held his chin in the air. "You can't keep us here."

Mr. Hanson shoved Teddy into a line with the others. He put his hands on his hips. "Show me your pockets. All of you."

One at a time, the other lads shoved their hands in their pockets and pulled out the insides, revealing the empty linings.

Teddy's bottom lip quivered as he pulled out three peppermint candies and held them up. "I'm sorry."

The man snatched them from Teddy's hand and set them on the counter. "I'll keep these out until the sheriff comes."

"The sheriff?" Teddy squeaked. "I said I was sorry." He sniffed and wiped at his nose with his sleeve.

Jack grimaced. He'd been about Teddy's age when he stole a doughnut from the bakery. The man had called for the sheriff, and Jack learned his lesson. Teddy would learn too.

The proprietor waved his finger at the trio who goaded Teddy. "You three, get out of here. I don't want to see you around here again."

Jack lifted the locking bar and stepped aside. He'd like to take a switch to those boys.

They scrambled out, tripping over each other. None seemed concerned about Teddy. Once outside, they ran across the street and down the boardwalk.

Now alone, Teddy appeared smaller than ever. A child in a sea of adults. Tears trickled down his cheeks, and he whimpered.

The cowboy at the counter cleared his throat, and people waiting to pay shuffled in line. Mr. Hanson glanced at his customers then at Jack. "Will you fetch Sheriff Bradford?"

Jack nodded at the crowd. "I can do you one better. I'll take him there myself. Explain to the sheriff what happened. You tend to your customers."

"Much obliged." The proprietor glared at Teddy. "I don't want to see you around here again without your ma or one of your uncles. You ought to be ashamed."

Teddy stared at the floor as he croaked the words. "Yes, sir. I'm sorry, sir."

Jack put a hand on the boy's shoulder and led him outside. "Come on."

How many times had Jack found trouble when his mother wasn't looking? Papa taught him honor. Sometimes behind the woodshed. Sometimes at his side, by example. Probably still watched from heaven. Jack didn't lie or cheat or steal, but other things got him into trouble.

Teddy trudged next to him down the boardwalk.

Jack remained silent. Best to let him stew. Think about his misdeeds. The boy needed a man to set an example. With all those uncles, one of them should step up.

Teddy's misbehavior would break his mama's heart.

Again, Jack escorted Teddy up the boardwalk, this time toward Sarah's shop. Sheriff Bradford had been kind but firm. He'd lectured the boy about stealing. Then he shut Teddy in a jail cell for a few minutes to teach him about consequences.

Jack entered the dress shop with Teddy close behind. The scent of fresh cotton and the steady chugging of the sewing machine had grown familiar, giving him a sense of home.

If only he didn't have to shatter the peace with Teddy's problem.

Sarah smiled when she spotted him. Moving her foot from the pedal, she quieted the machine. She crossed the room to stand near enough for her lilac scent to reach him. She tilted her head to see around him. "Teddy, what are you doing?"

"Nothin'." Teddy's soft reply didn't seem to alarm her.

Jack's fingers itched to reach for her—to comfort her, but he willed them to stay at his sides.

Sarah's sister dropped a pile of green-and-white fabric onto the table. She pointed toward the kitchen. "I'll get some coffee."

"Stay. You should hear this." Jack pulled Teddy around in front of him.

Sarah rushed to her son. "Teddy. What's wrong? What happened?" She bent to inspect him and took hold of his arms. "Are you hurt?"

"Tell her."

The boy should have considered how his actions would affect his whole family. Jack had learned that lesson the hard way too.

Teddy's face paled. His lips trembled. "I. . .I stole candy from Hanson's store."

Sarah gasped, and her hand went to her chest. "No. No, you didn't." She eyed Jack as if he could change her reality. "Please tell me he didn't."

Jack pressed his lips together and nodded. He couldn't return to Denver and leave her to face this alone. He wanted to protect her. To be someone she could count on.

Teddy lifted his head and met his mother's gaze. "The shopkeeper caught me, and Mr. Taylor took me to Sheriff Bradford."

Sarah's sister stepped toward her nephew. "Oh Teddy. How could you?"

On the way from the sheriff's office, Jack talked to Teddy about the evils of stealing and the importance of choosing honorable friends. Now he would give Sarah time with her son.

"I could use some coffee now," Jack said to Sarah's sister and tilted his head toward the kitchen. "Join me. These two need to talk."

He put a firm hand on Sarah's shoulder as she hovered in front of Teddy and gave her a reassuring nod.

Her eyes glistened.

Jack wanted to be the man Sarah and her boys needed.

Wanted to be strong for her.

Wanted to put others before himself.

Would he ever be that man?

Chapter 12

Sarah cut a green square from one of Kenny's old shirts to cover a stained section of Jack's quilt. All morning she'd dug through a bin of scraps to match the quilt's color and texture. She grew more attached to the man who owned it by the day.

Teddy swaggered in from the kitchen with Kenny trotting behind. Who knew a ten-year-old could swagger? "I've got to check in at the livery about a horse for Mr. Taylor's trip to the mines tomorrow."

Kenny echoed his older brother. "Check in at the livery."

Sarah smiled at the sight of her little boys acting like men. This morning Teddy washed his face without prodding, and Kenny carried his dirty dishes to the washbasin. Jack was the kind of man her boys needed. Unlike Theodore, Jack hadn't let mining take over his life and cloud his judgment.

Teddy jangled coins in his pocket. "And pick up supplies."

"Pick up supplies."

Over the last two weeks, ever since the incident with the peppermint candies, Jack stuck near her boys, giving them odd jobs and showing them how to behave. He talked to them like adults—even little Kenny.

Teddy admired the man a little too much. But in imitating him, the boy's behavior had improved. He stayed out of trouble and did his chores without argument.

"Come straight home after you finish Mr. Taylor's jobs." Sarah pulled a couple of pins from the pincushion. "You need to bring in firewood and dump the ash bucket."

Teddy nodded. "Yes, ma'am." He strode out of the shop.

"Yes, ma'am." Kenny followed his older brother, skipping.

Sarah hadn't even tried to teach the boys to call her ma'am, but Jack said they needed to show respect. She hummed as she pinned the fabric in place. She wouldn't mind if he stayed in Rockledge, if he stayed in her life.

He'd become a regular visitor, eating supper with her family every few days. He showed her sons the best way to sop up gravy with their biscuits. And he wouldn't allow any misbehavior or poor manners.

With school out for the summer, the boys enjoyed an excess of free time. Jack's odd jobs kept them out from underfoot. Lately, Teddy hinted about traveling with Jack to the mines as an assistant. Said he could take care of the horse and run errands.

Although Sarah trusted Jack, she couldn't imagine sending a ten-year-old boy into the wilds with him. Not while she examined her own feelings for the man.

He proved a lively companion and the perfect gentleman. He gave admiring looks, leaving her breathless, but didn't try to kiss her. The more time she spent in his company, the more she wanted to taste his lips on hers.

Her brother David entered the shop as she picked up a needle and thread. The scent of sweat and hard work followed him in. David never came to the shop of his own accord.

Her mind raced, and the thread between her fingers missed the eye of the needle.

"What's wrong?" She secured the needle into the fabric and left it there. "Shouldn't you be at work?"

"Heard your boys are working for Jack Taylor. Trailing him like baby chicks." Her brother towered over where she sat. "Is it true?"

Sarah craned her neck to see his face. "That's not your concern." She fisted her hands and released them, then pressed them against her skirt under the table. "Sit down. You're like a giant."

He spun a chair around to face away from her. Then he dropped into the seat, straddling the back. Still tall, but closer to eye level, he gave her an unwavering stare. "Is it true?"

"Yes, Jack has taken an interest and has given Teddy some odd jobs."

David stiffened. "I don't like it."

Sarah rose and pressed her hands on the table. "Where were you? Where were you when boys picked on Teddy? When he pummeled another child? When he stole candy?" Tears blurred her vision, but she wouldn't let them spill over. "Never mind."

David lifted his hands in surrender, and his tone softened. "Sheriff Bradford told me about the incident at Hanson's store.

Don't know what got into the boy."

"What got into him is that he doesn't have a father. Someone to show him right from wrong. A man to look up to." Sarah struggled to hold her voice steady. "Jack was there. He watched the whole thing. Allowed Teddy to get caught and walked him to Sheriff Bradford's office."

"I can't be everywhere at once." David reached across the table and covered her hand with his. "No one can. But we're watching out for your boys. . .and for you."

His touch disarmed her. David wanted to protect her. All her brothers did. "He's a good man."

Her brother pulled away and cracked his knuckles. "He's an outsider. He'll move on. What will you do then?"

How many times had Sarah asked herself the same question? She nibbled her bottom lip. "I don't know. He's good for the boys." And he reminded her she didn't die with Theodore. "He might stay."

David raised an eyebrow. "He lives at the hotel. Not a permanent arrangement."

Sarah's shoulders slumped. Jack's glimmer of hope, a little branch to keep from drowning, was like a gift. Unexpected. Delightful. But it was slipping from her grasp. Jack would return to Denver, and not only would she have to face her own disappointment but her boys would as well.

David swallowed hard. "I care about you. Keep your eyes open. None of us want to see you get hurt again."

For a long time after David left, Sarah toiled over the quilt, replacing some pieces and repairing others. What did she know of Jack? He carried himself like a rugged explorer but tucked a ragged quilt in his saddlebag. Still, her sons' behavior improved under his influence.

He'd never promised to stay. In fact, he'd told her he would leave. He would return to his life away from Rockledge. It's what men like him did.

Teddy and Kenny arrived home for supper with Jack in tow. The third day in a row. After the meal, she and Jack followed the boys to the creek, where they would chase frogs and climb on rocks.

Jack lifted Sarah onto a tall boulder and hopped up beside her. She wanted to lean into him, to wrap herself in his comforting arms. She would only have to move a little. Already, his woodsy scent tickled her senses and drew her in.

Jack took her hand in his, sending a warm tingle up her arm. "I hear the ladies in town are planning a social, dancing and the like. Would you allow me to escort you?"

"I'd like that." She gave his hand a squeeze. "But Jack?"

"Yes?"

Should she ask about his plans? Her conversation with David played in her mind. How long would he stay in Rockledge?

A cool breeze brushed across her face, and she shivered.

Jack let go of her hand. He took off his jacket and wrapped it around her shoulders. His scent clung to it. The garment not only warmed her but passed his strength to her. The future would come soon enough. No need to borrow trouble.

Teddy dashed from the creek toward Sarah, both hands cupped around something. "Mom, you should see this one."

Kenny raced after him. "He's got a stripe on his back."

Both boys halted in front of Sarah and Jack.

Teddy lifted his hand, revealing a frog. . .or a toad. Sarah couldn't tell the difference.

The creature leaped toward her.

Sarah jumped away.

Jack leaned forward. "A mighty fine specimen."

The frog leaped to the ground and hopped into the bushes. The boys scrambled about for a minute or so then gave up.

Teddy brushed off his pants. "Let's see if we can find another one."

Kenny trailed after his brother to the creek. "Find another frog."

Jack let his hand rest on the boulder near Sarah's, not quite touching her hand.

She stared at her little finger. Should she close the distance?

Jack cleared his throat. "Were you going to ask me something?"

She wouldn't ruin the moment by pressing him about the future. "No." She bumped his little finger with hers, connecting with his strength. "Let's attend the social together."

He brushed his fingers along the back of her neck, sending a pleasant shiver through her before resting his arm across her shoulders.

She pressed into his side, absorbing his warmth and protection. David's warning echoed in her mind, but she pushed it aside.

Jack was here. Now.

Nothing else mattered.

Chapter 13

Jack left Sarah near the dance floor, in search of refreshment for them both. The quartet played, and spectators clapped in time. The hall warmed to an uncomfortable level, even with all the windows open. A layer of sweat dampened Jack's skin under his suit. So much for his earlier bath.

He drank from his glass as he squeezed between clumps of partygoers dressed in their Sunday best. The lemon and sugar mingled on his tongue before slaking his thirst.

"It's not like Sarah to let a handsome stranger turn her head."

Jack identified a wrinkled matron with a pink feathered hat as one of the local gossips. Was she talking about him? He slowed to hear more.

"Those boys need a father. Someone responsible." The tiny,

white-haired grandmother next to the speaker nodded. "Someone like Jacob at the livery or the stagecoach manager, Robert."

Jack bumped into a tall man wearing a top hat. "Pardon me."

The woman in pink frowned. "What does anyone know about him? He claims to be a wealthy investor. Men like him are all charm and flattery until they get what they want."

The other ladies nodded and clucked like hens.

Jack clenched his jaw. Why would the town busybodies discuss him? But he recognized the words.

Ones he'd used to accuse himself a thousand times.

All true.

"Poor Sarah, attracted to the wrong kind of man." The white-haired woman pursed her lips. "No decent man will want her now."

Jack stared at her, and she fanned herself. They could criticize him all they wanted, but he wouldn't ignore these hens as they gossiped about Sarah.

He tipped his head toward the matron with the pink hat. "Ladies."

She cleared her throat and had the decency to blush. "Mr. Taylor."

Instead of creating a scene, Jack hurried toward Sarah. The women gave voice to his doubts. And they were right. Sarah would be better off without him.

As he neared, Sarah gave him a dazzling smile he didn't deserve.

He handed her a tall glass of lemonade. The heat and judgment in the lodge threatened to smother him. "Shall we step outside where it's cooler?"

"Yes. I could use some air." She took his arm with her free hand

and nodded toward the exit. "Shall we?"

Jack tried to ignore the awareness of his own heartbeat as her hand rested on his arm.

A full moon lit the night, and the music faded as he escorted Sarah to a bench on the boardwalk near the general store. The matrons' comments echoed in his mind. He should return to Denver, let her meet a man worthy of her attention.

Sarah sat on one end of the bench and tilted her head toward the space next to her. So inviting. She sipped her lemonade, her delicate lips on the glass mesmerizing him.

Jack leaned against the hitching post, facing her. He wouldn't further muddle his senses by sharing her bench.

"I'm glad we came." She took another sip. A shy gesture? "I haven't had so much fun since—since—not in a long time."

Jack gulped the rest of his lemonade and set his glass on the boardwalk. He cared too much to stay in Rockledge and destroy Sarah's life. But he could appease his conscience. "Have you given any more consideration to accepting Theodore's money? It's your due."

Sarah stiffened and set her glass on the boardwalk near the bench leg. She nodded. "I have. I wondered if you would offer again. Now that I know you, I understand your motivation. I accept."

Jack let out a slow breath. "I'll have it wired to your bank."

"Did you say it was from the Griffin Mine?"

Jack tried not to notice the curve of her lips or the way the moonlight outlined her face. He had achieved his goal. His penance would soon be paid. He swallowed past a lump in his throat. "Yes."

She gave a slow nod. "I remember the name. We fought about it. Theodore invested our grocery money in it. I made do from the pantry. Then Kenny developed a cough."

Jack flinched. Grocery money? Had he grown rich by taking food from the mouths of children?

No. Theodore did that.

"My parents paid for medicine because all our funds went to the mine." She squeezed her hands together in her lap.

Before Jack realized it, he was at her side on the bench. He covered her hands with one of his and draped an arm over her shoulders. "I didn't know."

She gave him half a smile and tilted her head. "You're not responsible for his actions."

"Even if I'd known, I wouldn't have cared." Jack's words spilled out. He needed her to see his true nature. "I didn't have a family. I didn't care about anyone but myself. I needed the money for the project, and your husband provided it. I'm sorry."

She pulled one of her hands out from under his and caressed his fingers. "You're not that man anymore. That man wouldn't come to town and try to return money to a widow."

Her slender fingers traveled slowly across his hand.

He willed the energy passing between them to stop. Thoughts jumbled, he pressed on. "What if I am? What if I never change?"

"Look at me." She waited for him to meet her gaze. Her soft lips inviting. "If that's who you were, you've already changed."

Jack slid his fingers along her shoulder to touch the warm skin on her neck. His pulse raced. "Do you think so?"

"No question." She lifted her face, easing toward him. Her gentle breath brushed across his cheek.

He closed the distance and touched his lips to hers. Soft and sweet as he'd imagined. He closed his eyes to block out all other thoughts.

She wrapped her arms around his neck, holding him in place when he thought to retreat. She responded to his kiss as if hungry for it, her lips seeking more.

At the sound of clomping on the boardwalk, she dropped her arms and straightened, her cheeks pink.

A cowboy ambled past without a glance.

After a couple of deep breaths, Jack cleared his throat. "I—"

"You're the best thing that has ever happened to me and the boys. Thank you, Jack." Sarah rested her head against his shoulder as if she'd been doing it for years.

He pressed his lips into her hair. Her lilac scent caused a wave of calm to ripple through him.

Was she right? Had he changed?

Or would the real Jack resurface at a most inconvenient time?

A few days later, Sarah leaned over her worktable, pinning a green square to Jack's quilt.

He strolled into the shop. "Hello, beautiful."

A pleasant shiver danced up her spine. "Jack. People will talk."

"What people? No one else is here." He crossed the room in a couple of quick strides to stand next to her. "We're completely alone."

She pushed the last pin through the fabric and straightened into his arms.

He closed them around her and dropped a quick kiss on her

mouth before scooting in to see her work. "Is this mine? I barely recognize it."

"Yes. I'm about halfway done." She lifted the unfinished half that hung off the side of the table to show him the difference and then let it down again.

He gave a low whistle and ran a finger along a new green block. "I didn't think this could be repaired. Thought about throwing it out more than once, but. . ."

"I stretched new blocks over a few of the more damaged ones." She studied the piece, remembering the process of restoring each block. Some required a few stitches. Others, cleaning. Still others, a complete rework.

He slid his fingers along the restored section. "I can't even tell which parts you replaced."

"I dug through old scraps to find perfect matches. I kept as much of the old fabric as possible and scrubbed each piece clean. I didn't want to lose the character of the quilt."

"You kept the good parts and replaced the bad." He pulled his hand from the fabric and straightened. "Too bad it isn't so simple with people."

Sarah raised her eyebrows. "What?"

"Nothing." He ran his hand down her arm and stood near enough to kiss her again.

The door to the kitchen banged. Teddy and Kenny bounded in. When Teddy caught sight of Jack, he stood tall and walked like a little man. The marshy scent from the creek bank entered with them.

Sarah wrinkled her nose. "What have you been into?"

Kenny beamed beneath the streaks of dirt on his face. "We

found the best place to dig for worms."

"Moist soil full of decaying leaves. William said it's where worms like to live." Teddy pointed a thumb toward the kitchen. "Got us a big pail of 'em."

Sarah grimaced. "I hope you left them outside."

"We know better than to bring a smelly pail of worms into the kitchen." Teddy eyed Jack. Seeking approval?

Jack chuckled. "Bring 'em in, and they could end up on your plate for supper."

Sarah waved the boys toward the kitchen. "Take your smelly selves outside and wash off that stench. It'll drive my customers away."

Teddy put a hand on his hip and raised his voice to imitate a lady. "Oh my. I couldn't buy a fancy dress in a place that smells like a swamp."

Behind him, Kenny put a hand on his hip too. "Smells like a swamp."

The boys ambled outside, leaving Sarah alone with Jack once again.

He returned his hand to her shoulder in an intimate gesture. "Where were we?"

"Enough." Sarah swatted his arm. She wouldn't be caught in a compromising position in broad daylight in the front of her shop.

"For now." Jack stole another kiss, leaving a lightness in Sarah's chest.

"We'll see." She led the way to the kitchen. "Do you want some coffee?"

Pewter mug in hand, Jack leaned against the counter, reminding her of the day he stood on the boardwalk hawking her dresses like snake oil. So much had changed.

"Sarah, with your permission, I'd like to take Teddy with me to the Culver Creek workings in a couple of days."

Her stomach tightened. She'd learned to trust Jack with her heart, but did she trust him with her boys? She bit her bottom lip. "I don't know."

"I'll keep an eye on him and won't let him near anything dangerous. I can give him some jobs." He drank his coffee and waited.

Her baby. She smoothed her skirt with her palm. Such a little boy. He needed her. But Teddy matured with Jack's influence. He admired Jack. She pressed her eyes closed and opened them again to face him. "I don't know."

"Hard to learn to be a man growing up in a store full of women's frippery." He poured himself a second cup and let the silence hang. "Makes a man soft."

"My brothers see to him." Why had they failed as father figures for her boys?

He nodded. "I'd be happy to take one of them along if it makes you feel better."

She'd relied on herself for too long. Even before Theodore passed. She let out a slow breath. And then another. A good man stood before her, offering to help.

God hadn't called her to take charge of everything. He put people in community. In relationships. Could she trust Jack? Trust God to watch over Jack and Teddy?

She swallowed hard and nodded. "I'll let him go with you."

"You won't regret it." He set the coffee cup on the table and stepped toward her, arms open.

She entered his comforting embrace and pressed against him. His woodsy scent soothed her. "I hope not."

Chapter 14

Two days later, Sarah pulled hot buttermilk biscuits from the oven and set them on the counter to cool. She checked the clock for the fifth time in the last three minutes. Jack and Teddy should have been home from Culver Creek by now. He said suppertime—six o'clock.

She forced her mind to the task at hand. After eating hardtack and jerky on the trail, they would appreciate a home-cooked meal. Beef stew simmered on the stove, filling the room with a savory aroma.

Kenny sat at the kitchen table, stacking a set of wooden dominoes to form a tower. "When will they be home?" Without a big brother to trail after, he was out of sorts. "I miss Teddy."

"So do I." Sarah tickled Kenny's ribs, and he bumped the table, sending the dominoes toppling with a clatter.

"Awww." He scooted them around with his index finger.

She gathered the dirty dishes from preparing the meal and baking biscuits. "They'll be here in time for supper."

"When's supper?" He lined up the little blocks like soldiers. "I'm hungry."

Sarah glanced at the clock again. "Soon." She pulled in a deep breath. Couldn't be soon enough for her. She'd slept fitfully the night before, waking up every few hours. A couple of times, she'd even checked on Teddy asleep in his bed. Was he old enough to spend a day in the mountains with Jack?

Kenny straightened the procession of dominoes. "When will I be old enough to go with Mr. Taylor?"

"I don't know. Let's see how it goes with your brother." Jack might take her boys on many such adventures.

Pouring boiling water from the cast-iron kettle into the dishpan, Sarah let her gaze wander to the clock.

Four minutes past six.

She settled a mixing bowl into the dishwater and pushed it under to fill. When the heat reached her finger, she flinched. She forgot how hot the water was.

Her attention had wandered all day. She'd poked herself with a needle twice and had to rip out the entire side seam on Mrs. Shannon's dress.

She needed to shake the clouds from her head before she incurred a serious injury. But how could she when her little boy explored the mountains with Jack? How well did she know the man, anyway?

The clacking of dominoes drew her attention. Kenny grinned at the parade of fallen soldiers, all piled in a line. "Do you think Mr. Taylor will play with me when he gets here?"

"He'll be tired after his trip."

Jack would make a fine example for her boys. A fine father. A fine husband. She blushed, remembering his kisses. But where was he? Did he think she served supper at seven o'clock?

Rose stepped in from the shop. "The dresses for the Winters girls are finished. I locked up."

The words hung in the air before Sarah realized she hadn't responded. "Thank you." She poured cool water into the steaming washbasin.

Kenny jumped from his chair and tugged at his aunt's arm. "Aunt Rose, do you want to play dominoes?"

She ruffled his hair. "Another time. Uncle Patrick gets grumpy when I don't feed him."

The boy made a pouty face and shuffled to the table. He scooted the dominoes around in a new pattern.

Rose rested a hand on Sarah's shoulder. "Are you all right? I know it's tough, but Teddy's fine. Jack's a good man."

After a hard swallow, Sarah forced a smile. "I know, but I'll feel better once they return."

Rose leaned in and whispered, "So he can kiss you again?" She waggled her eyebrows.

"Stop." Heat crept into Sarah's face. She gave her sister a playful swat and tipped her head toward Kenny. He paid no notice.

"I'll see you tomorrow." Rose slipped outside, leaving Sarah to her thoughts.

"I'm hungry." Kenny pushed out his bottom lip.

She ladled some stew into a bowl and handed him a biscuit.

"Blow on it. It's hot."

She watched the time as her son ate. Then she sat across from him and flipped through the pages of the latest *Godey's Lady's Book*.

After finishing his stew, he carried his dishes to the washbasin. Then he sat at the table, where his chattering stopped and his eyes drooped.

The stew continued to simmer on the stove, and the biscuits cooled on the counter. The *clack, clack* of dominoes and *tick-tock* of the clock created a cacophony in the otherwise silent room.

Darkness closed in.

No Jack.

No Teddy.

Images of the day Theodore died flooded her mind. He'd been late, and dinner awaited. Just like now. She'd waited and wondered. Finally, a rider had brought the horrifying news.

Sarah's hands trembled as she flipped the pages, not concerned with their contents. Where could they be?

Kenny traded his dominoes for a blue top, which he spun on the table. It bumped into dishes and silverware that awaited Teddy and Jack, grating on Sarah's nerves.

Her stomach clenched, and frightening images played through her mind. Teddy alone somewhere in the mountains. Teddy lying on the ground bleeding. Teddy lost and shivering in a stranger's barn.

Stop being silly. Jack was with her son. He would bring her precious boy home. Nothing to worry about.

She breathed a prayer for Teddy's safety. . .and Jack's.

She washed Kenny's dishes. His bedtime came and went, but

she let him stay up. She didn't want to sit alone with her terrifying thoughts.

Still no Jack.

No Teddy.

No word.

Finally, at ten o'clock, she marched Kenny the few blocks to the cabin her brothers William and David shared.

Kenny badgered her with questions. "Where are Teddy and Mr. Taylor? Why aren't they home yet?"

"I don't know." She held back tears as she made her way down the boardwalk. "I'm sure they're fine. Just running late."

When William answered the door, she fell into his arms. She could count on him. Not on Jack. What had she been thinking?

She filled her brothers in on the details while Kenny dozed on the couch. She longed for a warm cup of coffee, but the stove had cooled. "I don't know what to do."

David tied a bundle of blankets with a rope. "Where were they headed?"

"Culver Creek. He was going to check on a small mining operation." Sarah took a long, steadying breath. "Do you know of it?"

He clenched his jaw. "They should have been home hours ago. It's not that far from here." He hefted a saddlebag over his shoulder. "I'll get the horses." He gave William a nod. "You fetch Matthew, Timothy, and Patrick and meet me out front."

"I'll bring Rose too." William lit a lantern. "She can wait with you at your shop."

All her brothers and her brother-in-law. They would find her little boy.

William gave Sarah's shoulder a squeeze. "I'm sure they're fine."

She shuddered and pushed aside the images of the night Theodore died. She tried not to think about the time Jack agreed to help her with the sewing machine and didn't show up.

If—when—Teddy came home, she would never let him out of her sight again.

Sarah opened her eyes to sunlight peeking through the window. Her sister snored next to her on the bed. She sat up and winced at the ache in her neck and shoulders.

Had her brothers found Teddy?

The house remained still, except for the ticking of the clock. A reminder of the passage of time. Time her son hadn't returned.

Who could she rely on to keep him safe?

Not Jack.

Not God.

Not anyone.

She would be everything her boys needed.

No help.

No interference.

She tiptoed into the room her boys shared, where Teddy's bed sat empty. Kenny lay in a peaceful, innocent sleep. Sarah brushed his hair off his face, and he wiggled into a new position.

She wandered into the kitchen and stoked the coals in the stove. Her head pounded and cotton filled her mouth. After grabbing a wooden pail, she headed toward the door.

Teddy burst in, talking so fast she couldn't comprehend his words.

She dropped the pail. With trembling hands, she held his

shoulders and stooped to his height.

Dirt covered the boy from head to foot, and his hair stuck out in every direction. No visible injuries.

"Teddy." She hugged him tight. "Teddy."

Patrick stepped in behind him, but she paid little notice. She kissed the top of her son's head. She would have thanked God, but God hadn't gone after him.

Her brothers and Rose's husband did.

"Mom, let go." Teddy's muffled voice sounded from within her embrace. "You're squishing me."

She loosened her grip. "What happened?"

Her son puffed his chest. "There was a cave-in."

Her eyes widened. She held Teddy at arm's length and checked again for injuries. "What were you doing in a mine?"

He shook his head. "I wasn't *in* the mine, but I helped."

Jack entered the room and stepped next to Teddy. "You should be proud of your son. He—"

"You!" At the sight of Jack, all the terrible memories and images from the night filled Sarah's mind. Her gut clenched and her vision blurred. She stomped up to Jack and poked his chest with her finger. "What were you thinking? I trusted you. And you put him in danger."

"It wasn't like that." Teddy tried to step around her.

She blocked his path. She wouldn't let Jack near him again.

"He carried water from the well to the rescue workers." Jack smiled in the boy's direction. "He was never in danger."

Rose came from the bedroom, rubbing her eyes. She put her arms around Patrick and stood in his embrace. "They're here. I told you they'd be fine."

But nothing was fine. Sarah had to send her brothers out after Teddy. She couldn't trust Jack. What did she know about him? That he aligned himself with Theodore? A fact that didn't set her mind at ease.

"Go away, Jack." She shoved his chest, but he didn't budge. "Not in danger? Go back to Denver. . .or wherever it is you came from."

"I can explain." Jack reached toward her shoulder. "Give me a chance."

She backed away, bumping into Teddy.

Patrick cleared his throat. "I'll take Rose home now. It's been a long night." He nodded to Sarah and Teddy.

Rose took her husband's arm.

"You two can sort this out." Patrick gave Sarah a sideways glance and shook Jack's hand before ushering Rose out.

Jack remained in the kitchen with Sarah and Teddy. He lifted a hand in her direction, and she pulled away, keeping her son safely behind her.

"We were about to head home when the signal rang out for help." Jack lowered his brow. "We couldn't leave without lending aid. What kind of man would I be?" He spoke in soothing tones, but the trauma from the previous night overpowered anything he said.

She couldn't—wouldn't go through that again.

Not for anyone.

"Go now." She thrust her hand toward the door and pointed. "I never want to see you again." Her head grew light, dizzy.

"You can't do that." Teddy darted from behind her and wrapped his arms around Jack's waist.

"I'm sorry." Jack ran a hand through his hair. "We never meant to frighten you."

Her vision blurred. "And keep your money. I don't need it."

"But—" Jack lifted a hand in her direction but let it drop.

She spun away from him.

Teddy stomped past her, mumbling something under his breath.

The door opened and clicked shut, removing Jack from her life.

Forever.

Sarah would return to her quiet, ordered existence. She would run her shop and raise her boys. Nothing else mattered.

Chapter 15

In Denver, Jack stood next to the open window on the fourth floor of the mining exchange building. An early snow left white patches on the distant peaks as they called to him. A welcome breeze drifted in. It cooled the meeting room and carried his mind away from this stuffy place. To Rockledge.

To Sarah.

If she would give him another chance, he'd make better choices. Consider her perspective. Not remain in Culver Creek. Or send Teddy home with someone else while he aided the miners. But lives had been at stake.

After arriving in Denver, he made one final effort to aid Sarah. It may not bring her back to him, but her shop thriving would be enough. One unselfish act. He didn't deserve her anyway.

A banging on the massive mahogany table startled him from his musings.

"Mr. Taylor." The stout, balding man at the head of the table frowned at him and tapped a finger on a stack of papers—papers he hadn't read. "What is your opinion?"

Around the table, six suit-clad men stared. Waiting.

Jack glanced toward Roy, hoping to garner information about the discussion. His accountant and associate thrived on tedious meetings. But the man's gaze dropped to his own stack of papers.

Jack cleared his throat. "I agree. It's a good idea."

"Poisoning a city is a good idea?" The leader raised his eyebrows. "Mr. Taylor, we called this meeting at *your* convenience to discuss *your* business needs. The least you could do is give your full attention."

Jack's neck heated, and he resisted the urge to tug at his collar. No amount of money could turn him respectable. He'd never be more than an unreliable cad.

Sarah knew it, which is why she sent him away.

The men around the table knew it. They watched, waiting for him to fail.

God knew it.

He would never measure up.

Jack shoved his chair backward with a loud scrape and stood. He tipped his head in Roy's direction. "My associate will handle the meeting from here."

Someone near him harrumphed.

Roy nodded. "Gentlemen, please turn to page three of my report."

Jack held his chin high as he strode to the door and pushed it open. He loosened the stifling collar and loped down the stairs to the ground floor. His boots clomped on the marble as he passed through the opulent lobby. He didn't belong here. Didn't need a group of fancy bankers.

From now on, Roy could handle these men. Jack would spend his time on. . .on what? He skidded to a halt. He couldn't return to Rockledge. Not while Sarah loathed him. He could stake a new claim in another valley. Wouldn't even have to beg for investors. The life of a vagabond prospector had suited him before.

Before Sarah and her boys climbed into his heart.

Sarah bent over her ledger, wishing she could change the numbers. She didn't need Jack's money. . .or his interference. But the ledger said she did. Sales had improved since Emporium of Fashion left town, but not enough. If only a new seamstress didn't offer cheap inferior services. "She's picking up where the Emporium left off."

Nearby, Rose handstitched lace onto the bodice of an evening dress. "I've heard she plans to open a storefront."

Sarah let out a slow breath. "There's not enough work for both of us. Why doesn't she stay on the farm with her husband? She doesn't need the money."

"You know how she loves people. She wouldn't be happy." Rose tied a knot in the thread and snipped the end. "You could create some simpler designs to appeal to the masses. Use less expensive fabric."

Sarah cringed. "I'd lose my existing customer base. Mrs. Winslow comes for my exclusive designs."

"Have someone peddle your wares on the street like Jack did."

Rose laughed. "Made us the talk of the town for weeks."

Sarah squeezed her eyes closed. Would she ever be able to hear his name without longing for his touch? "Always full of ideas. I'll give him that."

Jack's quilt sat folded on a nearby shelf. She'd completed the restoration shortly after he left but couldn't bring herself to send it to him. She couldn't let go of this little piece of him.

Had he already been gone three weeks?

"I know you miss him." Rose threaded a needle. "You could ask him to come. I know he would."

"At what cost? I can't rely on him." Sarah's chest ached, and her throat went dry. "I need to focus on my shop. My boys."

"I hate to say it, but sales are down, and Teddy's more difficult than ever. You need to rely on someone." Rose stilled her hands and flattened her lips. "If not Jack, then someone else. Patrick and I—"

"I'm not a charity case." Sarah missed Jack. Not only because of her business and her boys. She missed the man. The strong, handsome, fun-loving man. She missed his companionship and passion.

Rose averted her eyes. "I didn't mean—"

"I'm sorry. I know you want to help." Sarah shut the ledger. Staring at the numbers wouldn't change them.

"Jack was nice to have around." Rose focused on her stitches.

"Yes." Sarah swallowed hard. "But it isn't enough. Not this time."

Sheriff Bradford clomped into the shop, dragging Teddy by an arm while Kenny trailed behind.

Sarah tensed. "What's he done now?"

"Ladies." The sheriff pulled Teddy closer when he tugged against the man's hold.

Rose set her sewing aside and stood.

The sheriff removed his hat.

Sarah's cheeks burned. Third time this week someone had dragged Teddy home. Until now, they'd left the sheriff out of it. She crossed her arms and eyed her wayward son.

"He helped a bunch of boys tear up Old Man Denton's chicken coop." The sheriff shook his head. "Destruction of property. He'll have to see the judge and pay a fine."

She couldn't afford a fine. What could she say? Her son's behavior worsened after Jack left.

Teddy wriggled in the sheriff's grip. "Weren't no chickens in it. The thing was just sitting there, half-falling down. We didn't hurt nobody."

"You know better." Sarah spoke more for the sheriff's benefit than for Teddy's. He would ignore her words. "You'll pay the fine too. Work it off."

The sheriff let go of Teddy, who stepped out of reach and crossed his arms. "I'll let you know when he needs to see the judge."

Sarah pointed toward their living quarters. "Go to your room. I'll talk to you in a minute."

He huffed and stormed out.

Instead of following, Kenny huddled next to Rose.

Sheriff Bradford gripped his hat with both hands. "If there's anything I can do—"

"There's not, but thanks." Sarah rubbed her hands together. Jack would know what to do.

"William or David could talk to him. Put him to work or something. Might keep him out of trouble." The sheriff replaced his hat on his head. "If he keeps up like this, he'll end up in jail. I'd hate to see that."

"Jail." The word squeaked from Sarah's lips before she could stop it.

"I'm here if you need me." He left the shop, the dreaded word echoing in his wake.

Sarah dropped to the nearest chair and rubbed her pulsing temples. Teddy wanted Jack to return. He said as much every evening at supper. She'd come to dread the nightly confrontations, but giving in to the boy's misbehavior wouldn't teach him any lessons.

She couldn't reach out to Jack now, even if she wanted to. Teddy might need Jack, but she didn't.

Kenny shuffled to the kitchen, leaving Sarah alone with her sister.

Rose pulled a chair next to her. She sat close and draped one arm around Sarah's shoulders. "Let me pray with you."

The warmth of Rose's touch comforted Sarah. She wasn't alone. Not really. Unable to force words past the lump in her throat, she nodded.

Rose shut her eyes and squeezed Sarah's hand. She talked to God like a friend in the room, explaining the troubles and asking Him to bring comfort.

A peace washed over Sarah for the first time since Theodore's death, maybe longer. God hadn't turned His back on her. He'd sent Rose and her brothers and Sheriff Bradford. She'd pushed them all away, including God.

After a time, Rose loosened her grip but didn't let go.

"Do you think God sent Jack?"

"I don't know." Rose let her arm drop. "He uses people. People like Jack. Like our brothers. Even me and Patrick."

Sarah sniffed and wiped at her damp cheeks. "I don't know what to do."

"Keep praying, and let the people around you help."

"What about Jack? I treated him horribly."

"It's in God's hands now."

Jack pounded nails into the roof of the little church the morning after the ill-fated meeting. Hard work in the blazing sun would ease his conscience. If he couldn't make amends to those he wronged, he would put his effort into the house of God.

Parson Baker, a tall, skinny man with a beak nose, worked near him. Sweat dripped off his forehead. Jack didn't expect a man of the cloth to work so hard, imagining the whole lot of them to be soft.

The parson stood and stretched. He waved an open canteen in Jack's direction.

Jack wiped his forehead with his sleeve and accepted the offering. He took a swig. Although warm, the water quenched his thirst. With any luck, the sun would disappear behind a cloud.

The parson perched himself near the peak of the finished section of the roof. He nodded to a spot next to him. "Take a break. We've got a long way to go."

Jack's mouth went dry. He didn't want to speak to the parson. He hoped to serve the church and God without speaking to anyone. Slip in. Work. Slip out. Pay penance.

The man pulled an apple from a bucket and a knife from the sheath on his belt. He sliced off a hunk and held it out to Jack. "Mrs. Baker keeps me well fed."

"Thanks." Jack bit into the fruit. He wouldn't have to talk with his mouth full.

"You've made yourself a fixture at the church." The parson cut a slice for himself. "I've seen you every day for the last two weeks."

How had Jack found himself trapped on the roof with a preacher? Not trapped exactly, but he couldn't make a quick exit. He chewed in silence for a while, as did the parson.

The parson tossed the apple core over the side of the roof and into a bush. He wiped his knife on his pants and sheathed it. After stretching overhead and rubbing his shoulder, he leveled his gaze at Jack.

Jack knew how to sweet-talk all kinds of men, but not a man of the cloth. "I thought I'd help out. . .while I'm at home. I travel a fair bit. For work."

"In my experience, men don't show up at the church and work as hard as you without a reason." The parson flexed his fingers and checked each one as if wondering if they still worked after a morning of hammering.

Jack's chest tightened. "Don't have to have a reason."

"I never complain about laborers the good Lord sends my way." The man stood and picked up his hammer. "Prefer to count my blessings."

Had God sent Jack to the church? To this parson who worked as hard as any man in the goldfields? "I've got some things to make up for. Seemed like as good a place as any."

The preacher arched his brows. "Doesn't work that way. Can't earn your way to heaven and all that."

Jack stared at his hands, dirty and calloused from hard labor. How could he make amends, if not to God? "Can't hurt."

"True enough." The parson reached in his shirt pocket and pulled out a small volume. "But God's forgiveness is a free gift. You don't have to earn it. Why don't you read up on what Jesus has to say about it, and we'll talk?"

"I have a Bible." Jack waved for him to keep the book. "It was my mother's. I haven't been able to look at it since. . ."

"She'd want you to read it." The parson pocketed the volume and returned to where he'd been working and positioned a nail. "I'm here when you're ready."

Jack stood, grabbed a shingle, and set it in place. "Thanks."

Could God forgive him?

And what of Sarah?

Chapter 16

When her brother William entered the shop, Sarah stopped feeding blue taffeta through the sewing machine.

What had Teddy done this time? He likely hid behind his uncle. The now quiet room pressed on her, stealing her breath.

William answered her unspoken question. "I left him sorting block letters for the printing press. Should take him most of the afternoon."

Tension drained from Sarah's shoulders. "Thank you."

Her brother dropped two brown paper–wrapped bundles on the worktable. "These packages came for you. I said I'd bring them over."

"Curious." Sarah pushed her chair back and crossed the room to meet him. "I didn't order anything." She eyed Rose. "Did you place an order? I can't afford—"

"Not me." Rose stepped toward the table. "Whatever could it be? I love surprises."

Sarah ran her fingers across her name in neat printing on the outside of the packages. "Who could have sent it?"

William picked up her good fabric shears and held them out to her. "One way to find out."

Sarah shook her head. He had no idea the damage twine could do to her shears. They would be useless for fine silks. She worked the twine with her fingers until the knot came loose. Then she peeled the paper away. The scent of cedar wafted into the room.

A folded piece of paper and two thin cedar blocks sat atop a worn nine-patch quilt. Sarah fingered the ripped seams and frayed edges. "Why would someone send me this?"

Rose picked up the paper and unfolded it. She read,

Dear Mrs. Anderson,

I have it on good authority you are an expert seamstress, particularly in the area of restoration. My grandmother made this quilt as a girl. It graced her bed until the end of her life. As you can see, it has been well used.

I will pay whatever you require if you can restore this family treasure for me.

Sincerely,
Mrs. Emily Martin

William studied the fabric on the table. "Can you do it? Fix the quilt?"

Sarah pushed a strand of hair off her face while her mind

outlined the tasks and materials needed. The last restoration was Jack's. She eyed it on the shelf. After completing the work, she had left it there, not wanting to give up the remaining piece of the man who had stolen her heart.

"Our sister can do it." Rose put an arm around Sarah's shoulder. "She can do anything."

"Yes." Sarah unfolded a corner of the bundle to inspect it further. "But why would someone from—"

William scanned the paper. "Denver."

Sarah knew only one person who lived in Denver, and she tried not to think about him. "Why would someone from Denver send me a quilt to restore?"

"It's a mystery." Rose clapped her hands. "Open the other one."

William retrieved the scissors from the table and cut the twine in one swift motion. Sarah cringed. She could have untied it.

She opened the wrapping. This one smelled of rose water.

A pinwheel quilt.

It also included a folded paper and a scrap of newsprint.

William lifted the clipping. "It's an advertisement for your quilt restoration services. From the Denver newspaper."

"I didn't place an ad."

Rose quirked an eyebrow. "Then who?"

"Jack." Sarah's voice came out a whisper.

The man who filled her every waking thought and often drifted into her dreams. From the day she met him, he'd tried to help her. And her boys. She'd never met anyone more creative or devoted.

"He would take out an ad like this." Rose gave a solemn nod. "Always trying to find a way to build your business. Now he's doing it from afar."

Sarah took long, slow breaths. The kindest, most giving man she'd ever known.

And she'd sent him away.

William set the advertisement on the quilt. "You were pretty hard on him when he brought Teddy home from Culver Creek. The man is a hero. Pulled a couple of guys out before more rock fell. And Teddy was never in harm's way."

Sarah had judged Jack unfairly. Her gaze wandered to his quilt. Time to return it. She needed to make things right.

Would he accept her apology? Would he give her another chance?

She didn't deserve either.

Jack stepped into the post office. He could have paid someone to pick up his mail. But what else did he have to occupy his time? The church roof was done.

"A package came for you." The skinny widow who managed the post office pushed a brown paper–wrapped bundle across the desk. "From Rockledge. You have family there?"

His heart pounded, and he couldn't contain his smile. Sarah? Ignoring her question, he thanked her and left with his package. He squeezed its sides. Soft, like clothing. Had Sarah returned his quilt? He'd hoped it would give him one last chance to see her.

With the bundle under one arm, he hurried the three blocks home, dodging a buggy along the way. He carried the package straight to his study and slit the twine with a knife. Then he peeled the paper away to reveal his old quilt. But it looked as good as it did all those years ago with its clean fabric and tidy stitches.

As he rubbed the material between his fingers, a flood of memories choked his thoughts. His chest ached at the image of his mother and her gentle ways. As a little boy afraid of nightmares, he'd snuggled under its warmth. Later, after she died, he'd gripped it as he held back tears.

And new memories. Sarah. She cut new blocks as replacements and cleaned others. The faint scent of her lilac soap lingered. Holding the quilt to his face, he inhaled and closed his eyes.

Why had she sent it? To rid herself of him? Move on with her life? Jack heaved a sigh. When he shook the quilt to spread it across a chair, a piece of paper fluttered to the hardwood floor beneath his feet. Did he want to know?

He picked up the note and unfolded it.

Dear Jack,

Here is your quilt. I finally finished it, good as new.

Please forgive me for lashing out and sending you away. I overreacted. I miss you and long to see you again.

Teddy and Kenny miss you too.

But I'm sure you have found a new adventure by now.

All my love,
Sarah

The last part looked erased and written over several times.

The tension in his shoulders slipped away. She wanted to see him again. Like dawn peeking over the mountains after a long, cold night, her letter delivered hope for the future.

But a wave of inadequacy washed over him. He didn't deserve her.

Then, a phrase in her letter replayed in his head. *Good as new.*

He studied the quilt before him.

Good as new. He ran his fingers along the tight stitching on the seams.

Good as new. He studied a corner that used to be stained.

Good as new.

He dropped into his chair and pulled his mother's Bible from the drawer. After his first talk with the parson, he'd read it every night.

Good as new. The Bible said something about being made new. He searched the bookmarked pages until he found Second Corinthians, chapter 5. He ran his finger down the page to verse 17. Yes, "a new creature." Like the quilt, he had been made new. The old had passed away.

He rubbed a finger along the quilt again. God never intended for him to spend his life punishing himself and serving penance. His mother wouldn't want him to either. Sarah and her boys needed him. He needed them more. If her note was any indication, she already forgave him.

He remained in his study until long after suppertime, examining each piece of the restored quilt and thanking God for his restored life.

Now to win Sarah's heart.

Chapter 17

Sarah found herself in yet another shouting match with a ten-year-old boy. Why couldn't Teddy behave? She'd visited the judge with him and made him pay the fine. Still, he courted trouble.

"No." He shouted loud enough for the neighboring shops to hear. "I will not bring in firewood. I don't care if we have a fire. Why should I have to do all the work?"

Sarah shook a finger at him. "You like to eat, don't you? We need a fire to cook food so we can eat. I'll add washing breakfast dishes to your chore list."

Thankfully, her brother William had taken Kenny for the evening. He was starting to pick up some of his brother's bad behavior. She didn't need him to witness another argument.

Teddy stomped a foot and crossed his arms. "I won't do it."

"We'll see how you feel after missing supper tonight."

Teddy opened his mouth to argue, but instead, his eyes widened, and he dropped his arms to his sides.

Had someone come in behind her?

Sarah turned to see who it was. "Jack." Warmth radiated through her cheeks.

The man flashed Sarah a lopsided grin, melting her insides. "In the flesh."

Teddy ran toward Jack, arms open for a hug. He skidded to a stop, stood tall, and swaggered the rest of the way and extended his hand.

Jack shook it and pulled him in for a hug. He messed up Teddy's hair before releasing him. "Have you been obeying your ma?"

Teddy puffed his chest out. "Yes, sir."

Before she could correct him, Jack spoke up. "Is that so? I could hear you from down the block."

Teddy's head dropped. "No, sir."

"You need to apologize." Jack eyed Sarah over her son's head. "A real man knows how to apologize."

"Yes, sir." Teddy didn't meet her gaze. "I'm sorry. It won't happen again."

"Now, run along and do the chores, like your mother asked."

"Yes, sir." Teddy dashed to the kitchen. "Right after I find Kenny and tell him you're here."

Could this be the same boy she'd held the shouting match with moments ago?

Jack gave a shy smile. "I had similar outbursts with my mother. It doesn't mean he doesn't love you more than anyone in the world."

"Thank you for the reminder."

Now that she was alone with Jack, his presence filled her with longing. Her mouth went dry, and she licked her lips.

Jack opened his arms, encouraging her to come to him.

She let out a breath and closed the distance to embrace him. A safe, warm, comforting embrace. "I've missed you."

"I've missed you too."

He released her and eased away to see her face. "And I'm sorry. Sorry for being selfish and untrustworthy. Sorry for keeping Teddy out."

"I'm sorry too. I should've trusted you."

He put a finger to her lips as if to silence her. "Aren't we a fine mess?"

When he caressed her hair, pleasant shivers rippled up her spine. With one finger, he tipped her chin upward.

Her lips parted of their own accord, waiting for the sweetness to come.

He didn't disappoint. He dropped his lips to hers in a delicate kiss. "Thank you for giving me another chance." The warm breath of his words brushed against her cheek.

Her fingers grazed his jaw, brushing against a bit of stubble. All man. "Thank you for coming back after the way I spoke to you."

"We both needed to do some soul-searching." He pulled her close and rested his chin on her head.

The steadiness of his heartbeat comforted her. . .and awakened a passion. She drew back enough to wrap her arms around his neck and pull him into a hungry kiss.

When she took a breath, he stepped away. "Let me do this right."

Sarah caressed his arm, not wanting to lose contact.

Reaching into his trouser pocket, Jack pulled out a handkerchief. He unfolded it to reveal a gold band. "This was my mother's wedding ring."

Sarah held her breath.

"I'd be honored if you would wear it, as my wife."

"Yes." Sarah threw her arms around his neck, pressing his hands and the ring between them. "I'll marry you."

Teddy and Kenny leaped in from outside, shouting and dancing. "Jack's going to be our father."

"You rascals were eavesdropping." Sarah tried to scold but couldn't hide her joy. They needed a father.

"Course we were." Teddy hugged Jack and Sarah.

Kenny joined in. "Be a family."

"I'll hold on to this until we find a preacher." Jack folded the ring into the handkerchief and tucked it in his pocket. "Don't you boys have chores to do?"

Sarah nestled in the comfort of Jack's arms as her boys trotted outside.

He dropped a kiss on the top of her head. "I don't plan to hold on to this ring for too long, you know."

"I should hope not." She rested her head on his shoulder. "I need you here with me."

Three months later, Sarah sat with Rose, sewing a gown for Mrs. Winslow. She pinned the lace to the neck.

Teddy ambled into the shop with Kenny close at his heels. "I'm so hungry I could eat a whole cow."

The scent of manure and hay wafted through the shop, assaulting Sarah's senses.

Rose scrunched her face. "You boys stink."

"Jack's got us mucking out stalls." Kenny stuck out his chest and tucked his thumbs into his pockets. "Cuz we're men now."

Sarah shook her head. "I told you to come in through our living quarters."

"Sorry, Ma," both boys said in unison.

"Go wash up for dinner." Sarah tipped her head in the direction of the kitchen. "Is Jack coming?"

"Yes. He sent us ahead. Said we needed more washing than him." Teddy disappeared through the door with Kenny behind.

Rose stood and put a hand on her back. "I can't believe Jack bought the livery, of all things."

"Said boys need hard work. They shouldn't spend their days in a shop with women's frippery."

Sarah's heart warmed as she remembered the day he told her about the livery.

"I don't think I've ever seen you so happy."

Sarah fingered the wedding band she'd worn for two months now. Every day Jack found new ways to surprise her. "I am happy."

"Me too." Rose ran a hand down her stomach. "Soon I'll have to let this dress out to make more room for this little one."

Jack stepped into the shop and crossed to Sarah. He dropped a kiss on her lips. "How's my beautiful wife today?"

"I'm good." Sarah sniffed at his shirt. "You don't smell anything like the boys."

Jack gave her a saucy grin. "I leave the dirty work to the younger men. I make arrangements with customers. Wouldn't want to smell like a barn."

Sarah nodded. "And you get to spend the day jawing with all the old prospectors who come through."

"That too, my love." Jack gave her another kiss. "Best of both worlds."

Sarah breathed a prayer of thanks. God had met her needs. And He'd given her Jack.

Suzanne Norquist serves as the treasurer to her local ACFW chapter and coleads the chapter's critique group. She completed the Christian Writers' Guild's Apprentice Class and has attended and helped organize numerous writers' conferences. She holds a doctorate in economics and a bachelor's degree in chemistry. As a result, she has worked at many jobs that sound interesting. Her work frequently involves technical writing, where the attorneys insist on two spaces after every period. Her husband and adult children make sure she doesn't take herself too seriously. In her free time (what little there is), she participates in kickboxing fitness and mountain climbing in Colorado.

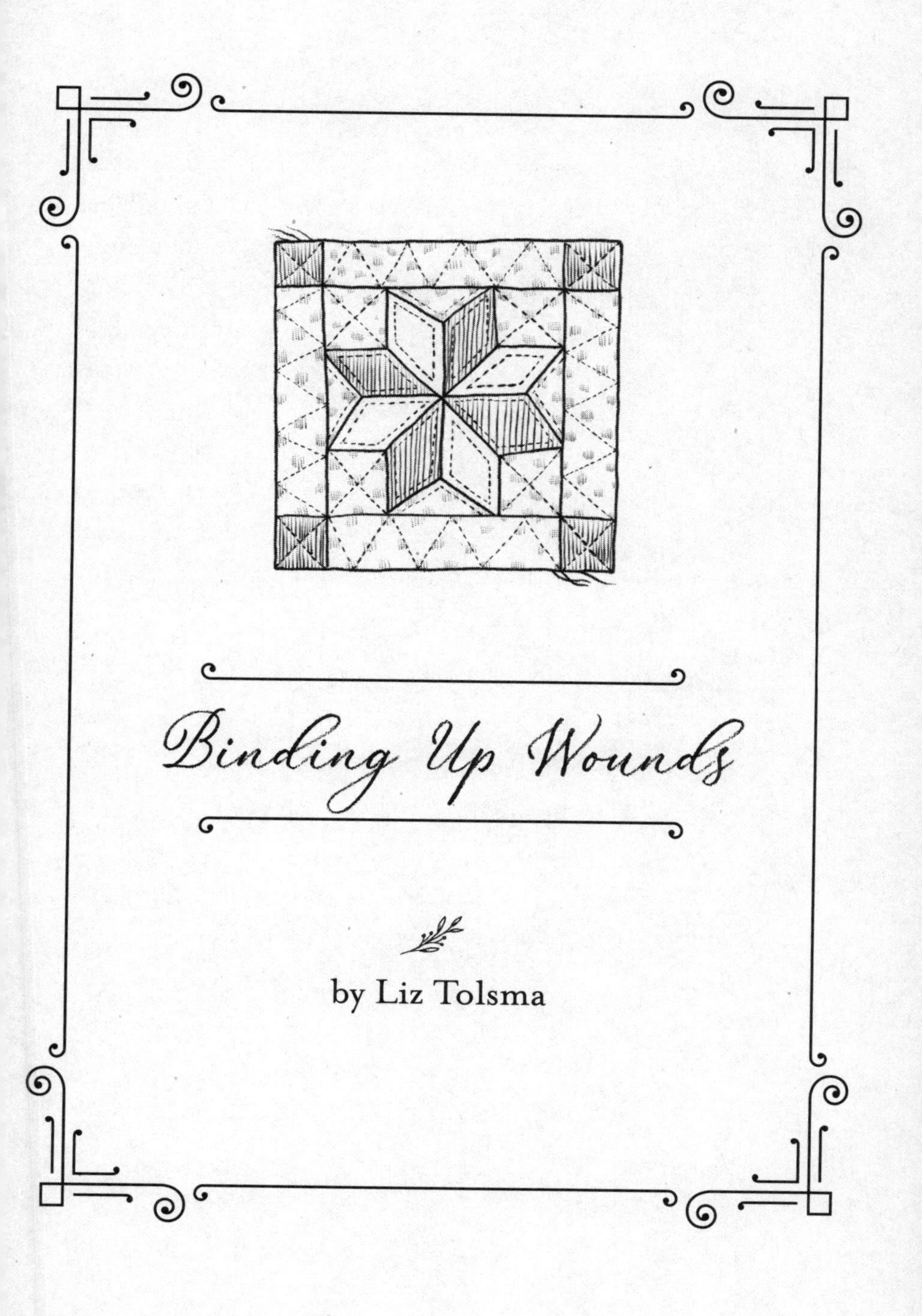

Binding Up Wounds

by Liz Tolsma

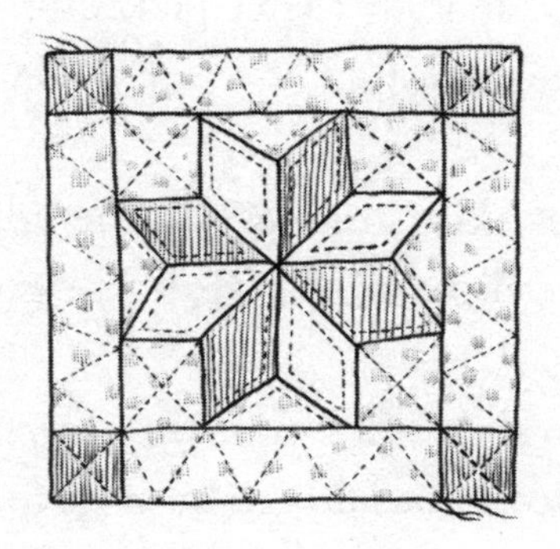

Chapter 1

May 1865

The train's whistle broke the stillness of the Wisconsin woods as Lance Witherspoon pressed against the window's glass. Outside, a deer bounded over a downed log. For a time, a little stream raced alongside them.

He shifted on the bench. From the seat beside him, he picked up the box containing a multihued patchwork quilt and held the reason he was traveling all the way from Virginia to the edge of the wilderness.

During a brief stop in Madison, a middle-aged woman with a wide hoopskirt boarded and chose to sit next to him. He slumped farther into the red velvet seat. The entire journey he'd sought solitude. He shouldn't have picked up the quilt. If he'd left it lying beside him, she would have sat somewhere else. Anywhere else.

She settled her skirt around her, the voluminous folds taking up a full two-thirds of the seat. He huddled closer to the window.

"I apologize for disturbing you. The car is rather full today."

He nodded. Mother would tan his hide for his rudeness, but he couldn't speak to the woman.

"I'm Margaret Simpson. Traveling to see my grandchildren in Prairie du Chien. And you are. . . ?"

Heavens to Betsy, he would have to answer. "Lance," he mumbled.

"Nice to meet you. Are you on your way home from the war?"

He nodded. In a way, he was.

"Where is home for you?"

This Mrs. Simpson sure was a chatterbox. He couldn't tell her Richmond, unless there was a Richmond, Wisconsin. But he had no idea. "Regent."

"That's not far from my stop. I've never been there myself, but I hear it's a beautiful little town."

"Yes, ma'am." As soon as the words crossed his lips, he covered his mouth. He couldn't have sounded more Virginian in that moment.

Mrs. Simpson widened her robin's-egg-blue eyes. "Are you a Southerner?"

Time froze for a second. He bent over and rubbed the top of the box.

Mrs. Simpson rose. "You ought to be ashamed of yourself." She proceeded down the aisle and out the car's door.

This had been a mistake. Coming to find the woman who had pieced the quilt and had written the funny little verse on it was the worst decision of his life. But with Richmond in ruins and Mr. Clark seeking his hide, he had nothing holding him in Virginia.

And Melissa Bainbridge, the woman who had sewn this blanket, had saved his life. He owed her a great debt of gratitude. Too many of his own company had died in a sudden winter storm. Because of this seamstress, he was alive.

Would the town of Regent welcome him with open arms? Not likely. In reality, he would probably get a reception more like the one he'd gotten from Mrs. Simpson.

If only he had the money in his pocket to turn around and head south again. Where he belonged. To do that though, he had to work for a while. Earn a little bit. He had no other choice. He had to go to Regent, come what may.

After again setting the box on the seat beside him to discourage any more talkative women from joining him, he stared out the window. While Virginia would be in full bloom, the summer's heat almost upon them, Wisconsin was just waking from its winter slumber. In between the dense stands of trees, farmers plowed their fields to ready them for planting. A few patches of winter wheat added depth to the pale-green scene.

In between stations, the train swayed, lulling Lance. Preparing him for whatever lay ahead.

"Regent, next stop." The conductor ambled down the aisle, calling out the announcement.

The only time Lance's heart had ever beat faster was in battle.

Now his imagination was running away with him. Mrs. Simpson was just one person. He was no longer the enemy. With the war over, they were all Americans again. Weren't they?

A few minutes later, the train chugged into the station and, with a last belch of soot and steam, came to a stop. A small platform held a handful of people. He was the only one in his car who exited.

A cool breeze struck him as he made his way down the steps. One man tipped his bowler hat in Lance's direction. Lance shot him a small smile, then collected his bag and headed toward the town.

A clutch of false-front buildings huddled along the dirt road that ran through the village. A couple of taverns. A livery. A general store. A school. A church. A hotel. Several homes. That was about it. So different from the hustle and bustle of prewar Richmond.

But maybe quiet was what he needed most right now.

He arrived at the hotel, the pine boards still yellow, the scent of sap in the air. A rotund older man stood behind the front desk. "Welcome. Did you just come in with the train?"

Lance nodded.

"What can I do for you?"

"I need a room." He spoke with his best Northern accent.

The clerk lifted one gray eyebrow and pursed his lips. "I'm sorry, we don't have any vacancies."

"Is there somewhere I can get a place to sleep? Maybe a warm meal? I've been traveling for a mighty long time."

The clerk shook his head. "I'm sorry. You won't find anything around here. My best advice is to get back on that train and return to wherever you came from."

Lance stuck his hat back on his head, picked up his carpetbag and the quilt box, and went out to the street. Just what he'd been afraid of. Regent wasn't about to welcome him with open arms. But now what?

He stood staring into the blue sky. "Lord, just work this out." A hawk sailed overhead.

Lance sighed. Maybe there was a boardinghouse around. He spun to look and bumped into the most beautiful woman he'd ever beheld.

Melissa Bainbridge ran into something hard. Correction. Someone. In the collision, she dropped the packages in her hands, the paper splitting open, fabric and yarn spilling into the dirt.

"Pardon me, ma'am."

The Southern drawl brought her up short. She gazed at the man with the greenest eyes she'd ever seen. "Oh, it's no problem." Why had she said that? With her heart skittering, she broke eye contact with him and bent to retrieve her spilled items.

"Let me help. It's my fault, after all."

"I wasn't watching where I was going. People tell me all the time I'm too busy thinking about other things."

"I'm the one who wasn't paying attention." He scooped up the material and pressed it close to his chest. Melissa winced. His shirt was rather rumpled and, well, had smudges all over it.

Not to mention they were gathering quite a crowd. "Thank you. I'll take that now."

"And who is this young man?"

Grandfather's voice behind her sent her jumping and almost made her drop her belongings again.

"Just someone I ran into. Literally. Let's go home. I'm sure Grandmother has lunch waiting." She spun around to leave, her straight skirt swishing around her ankles.

"You seem to be a little lost, son." Grandfather approached the man.

He shook his head and stepped backward.

"If you're looking for a place for some refreshment, the hotel is the one and only in town. I take it you're new to the area?"

The stranger nodded.

"I can introduce you to the proprietor, and he can get you set up."

"They don't have any rooms available."

Grandfather crossed his still-muscular arms and eyed the newcomer up and down. Oh no, that was not good. Melissa had seen it too many times in her life. Grandfather would never leave a stranger on his own without offering hospitality. He always said it was his Christian duty.

Melissa glanced away and spied a group of young women in bright dresses gathered on the wooden walkway. They tittered and pointed. She hissed in her grandfather's ear. "You can't. Please, don't."

He flashed her a glare that would have withered the most robust cornstalk. "Where are you from, son?" Despite the look on his face, Grandfather's words were gentle.

"Down south."

"And what brings you to our little town?"

The man scuffed the toe of his worn boot in the soft earth, his attention affixed to what he was doing.

"I'm not judging you. We don't get many strangers around here, that's all."

"I'm searching for someone." The man bit the inside of his cheek.

"Well there, I can help you with that. I've lived here my entire life and know everyone within at least a nine-mile radius."

And that was the truth. Grandfather never met a person he couldn't befriend. Unfortunately, he hadn't passed that trait on to his granddaughter. Melissa tapped her foot. She itched to get away from the crowd's stares and begin sewing a new batch of dolls.

"She made a quilt for the Sanitary Commission."

At that, Melissa's ears pricked. She'd sewn one to send to the men fighting for the Union. The Union. Not the Rebels. No, it couldn't be her. Nor anyone else around here.

"Her name is Melissa Bainbridge."

Melissa's world went silent, as if she'd just plunged her head in a full watering trough. "No."

Then like a wave, voices rushed over her. "She was aiding the enemy? How could she do such a thing? Traitor. Traitor. Traitor."

"I sent it to the Sanitary Commission in Washington, DC. I have no idea how this man got it."

The man gazed down at her, his eyes hooded and unreadable, part hardness, part softness hiding in their depths.

She broke his gaze.

Grandfather motioned for the bystanders to be silent. Then he turned to the newcomer. "I'm Hiram Bainbridge, and this is my granddaughter, Melissa. So it seems you've found who you've been looking for. We'd be happy to welcome you to stay in our home. Betsy is sure to have something warm on the stove to fill up your insides."

The man glanced around, his neck reddening. "I couldn't impose."

"No imposition. Some have entertained angels unawares."

Melissa shook her head. Bad enough the townspeople already thought her to be a traitor. Worse still if the Southerner stayed under their roof and benefited from their hospitality.

"I assure you, I'm no angel. I just wanted to thank your granddaughter for saving my life."

If she didn't have her hands full with her packages, she would have covered her face. As it was, heat rose from her chest, up her neck, and into her cheeks. She had saved the life of a Johnny Reb?

"You're a man with a need, one that we can meet. My wagon is parked by the mercantile. We're headed back there now. I won't take no for an answer."

"Grandfather." The word burst from Melissa's lips.

"I've made up my mind. This man has come a long way to thank you. The least we can do is provide him with a roof for a few nights."

And there was no more arguing with Grandfather.

"I'm much obliged, sir. Ma'am." The man tipped his slouch hat.

Melissa followed them toward the wagon, her focus on the tips of her black shoes that peeped from beneath her skirt as she walked. The onlookers didn't even try to quiet their voices. "Can you believe the nerve of that man?"

"Which one? The Reb or Mr. Bainbridge?"

"Both of them. Imagine harboring the enemy right in your own home."

More laughs floated on the morning air.

Each one stabbed Melissa.

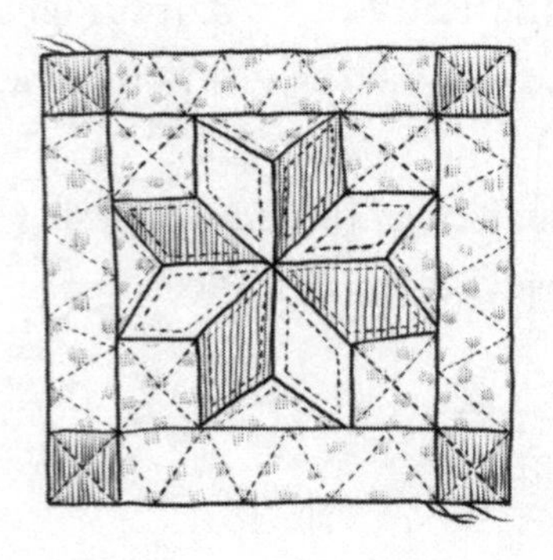

Chapter 2

Lance pushed away from the Bainbridges' farmhouse table. "I'm obliged, ma'am. That was a mighty delicious meal. Best one I've had in many years. Not since my mama cooked for me before she died." He swallowed the lump in his throat.

Mrs. Bainbridge and Melissa set about clearing the plates from the table. The older woman nodded in his direction. "Thank you. But I hope you're not too full. I have a plate of oatmeal cookies for dessert."

"Well, I couldn't pass that up." He glanced at Melissa, receiving a glare in return. With his napkin, he dabbed at his mouth.

"Why don't you go into the parlor? I'll bring the coffee and cookies in there. Much more comfortable than a hard kitchen chair." Mrs. Bainbridge shooed everyone from the room, including Melissa.

But she didn't take a seat in the parlor. Instead, she continued out the front door, slamming it behind her. He followed her outside, closing the door with less force. "Miss Bainbridge. Melissa."

She trotted down the steps and across the yard in the direction of the barn. He hustled after her. "Please, can I just speak to you? A few minutes of your time is all I ask."

She huffed but didn't turn to face him. "Say what you came to say and have done with it. Then you can be on your way."

"I only wanted to thank you for the quilt. Last winter, a fierce storm blew up, all unexpected-like, and the temperature plummeted. There we were in the middle of the blizzard, our uniforms threadbare. Some in my company had no shoes, just rags wrapped around their feet."

Her shoulders relaxed.

"And then I found this quilt. It saved my life. You saved my life. From the bottom of my heart, thank you."

She tensed again, and this time spun around. "A note dropped into the mail would have sufficed." Much to his surprise, her words were soft.

"It wouldn't have. Not for all you did for me."

She twisted a loose tendril of hair and bit her lip. Her pretty blue eyes softened, hardened, then softened again. "I'm sorry. I-I haven't been very kind to you. I'm sure my grandparents are going to scold me for my behavior. I don't know what came over me."

"Well, I'm sure I'm not the one you expected your quilt to help."

"No."

"If it gives you any comfort, I'm sure there was a Union soldier who also benefited from it. By the time I found it, the quilt was already well worn."

"Can I see it?"

He liked this gentler side of her much better. And what he said was true. His appearance in her town must have shocked her. And everyone else. His reception wasn't the warmest. He'd overheard what the townspeople had said, not only about him but also about Melissa and her family. "I'll get it. Shall I meet you on the porch?"

"That would be nice. I'll get a plate of cookies."

He ran up the stairs to the small bedroom the Bainbridges were allowing him to use. Nothing more than a wrought-iron bed and a washbasin and stand, but a sight better than the battlefield.

He grabbed the quilt, the silence of men dying of hypothermia surrounding him. He shook his head. No, that was over.

When he returned to the porch, Melissa was sitting on the swing, rocking back and forth, light spilling from the parlor window, illuminating her, setting her red hair on fire.

My, she was beautiful.

His mouth dry, he joined Melissa on the swing. "Here it is. I cleaned it up the best I could."

She took it from him, running over the stitching. "The Sanitary Commission put out a call for quilts to keep our boys warm during the winter."

"You enjoy sewing?"

"I make rag dolls that I sell to various stores around the country."

"Then I take it that you do."

"Grandmother taught me. Said it was a useful skill for a young woman to learn. And yes, I do love to sew. I can focus my full concentration on the work in front of me and not worry about life out there." She gestured toward the barnyard.

What an odd comment. Lance clamped his teeth to keep

himself from asking her about it. Something held him back. "What I loved the most about it was the verse you penned on the back."

A slight smile crossed her lips. "I'm glad. I was worried whoever it went to would find it odd and laugh it off."

"Not at all." He cleared his throat. "'Icicles in your beard, frost on your nose, snow on your lashes, cold in your toes, may this quilt warm you, wherever you goes.' The first time I read it, I laughed out loud. You don't do much of that on the battlefield."

"You didn't think it was strange? After all, it isn't even proper grammar."

"And I knew you did that on purpose. That little touch made it even more charming."

"I'm glad. And honored you would come all this way to thank me in person. I truly am."

Stillness settled over them, broken only by the chirping of crickets. For a long while, they sat there together. Then the clanging of a horse's bridle and the squeak of wagon wheels interrupted the peace.

Melissa came to her feet. "Who on earth would be visiting this late?"

"Ho there." A man's voice called to his team. With a *thump*, he jumped from the wagon and strode to the porch. As he stroked his scruffy beard, he examined Lance from head to toe. Lance squirmed.

"So it is true. You are aiding and abetting the enemy right in your own home. Why, I ought to. . ." The man clenched his fists.

Lance steeled himself for the blow.

At the sight of Mr. O'Connor winding up to slug Lance, Melissa jumped to her feet and placed herself between the two men. "Mr. O'Connor, please. This is my home. We will not tolerate violence here."

"And this is my town. We will not tolerate Rebs here." The brute of a man spit a stream of tobacco onto the porch.

"The war is over. There is nothing left to fight about. We're one country again. Somehow, we need to find a way to get along with each other. To put the division of the past four years behind us and heal our nation. This man came all this way to thank me for the quilt I made that ended up in his hands. That is the best beginning to putting this land aright I can think of." Her speech left her breathless. Never had she spoken so many words in a row to someone other than family.

The front door creaked open, and Grandfather stepped into the cool evening. "Mr. O'Connor. To what do I owe the pleasure?"

"How long do you plan to let this man remain under your roof?"

"As long as he needs my hospitality." Grandfather fingered his gray mustache. "And I fail to see how long I entertain a guest in my own home is any of your business."

"You know what happened to my son. To too many of our sons in the Iron Brigade. Do the names Antietam and Gettysburg ring a bell with you?"

Melissa shuddered. Between those two battles, this little town lost ten young men. Had Lance fought in them? Had he perhaps killed James O'Connor?

"The war was devastating for everyone." Grandfather managed to keep his voice steady and even. "We sympathize with your loss. Regent suffered a great blow in those fights."

"Listen, I don't want to cause any trouble." Lance stepped backward, toward the door. "I'll just be on my way. Thank you again, Melissa." He turned.

She grabbed him by the forearm. "Stop. Don't leave. Don't let Mr. O'Connor run you off like this. I'd, well, I'd like you to stay. For a few days, anyway. I mean, the strawberry festival is coming up, and it's quite the gathering, so much fun. You don't want to miss it." Her mouth ran on like an uncontrolled locomotive. Her heart pounded in her throat.

"Thank you. I'm much obliged, but I've caused you too much trouble."

"It's no trouble at all. Really."

"I'm in full agreement with my granddaughter."

Mr. O'Connor blustered. "This will not be the end of the matter. I'm not the only one in town who feels this way. You just wait and see. One way or another, we'll be rid of you." He marched to his wagon and disappeared into the gathering darkness.

Grandfather slapped Lance on the back. "How do you feel about a game of checkers?"

"I'm all for it." The two men entered the house, leaving Melissa alone on the porch.

She picked up the quilt from the swing and sat with it on her lap. How many nights she had pored over it, crafting each stitch with as much love and care as possible, dreaming of the man beside the campfire who would wrap it around his broad shoulders.

Not a Rebel.

Imagine Lance being the one to find her quilt. Imagine that it saved his life. Imagine that he even enjoyed her little verse on the back. After she'd sent it off, she'd lain awake for hours, staring at her ceiling. Why had she written something so trite and childish? The man who received it would laugh at her. Would show his friends, who would join in his mirth.

But Lance had liked it.

Why on earth had she urged him to stay? He'd come and offered his thanks. With Mr. O'Connor and surely others in town threatening Lance, perhaps it would have been best for him to leave. Who knows what the townspeople would do?

The spring air held a chill, so she wrapped the quilt around her shoulders. She had never expected to see it again.

For the longest time, she stared at the stars. Then she closed her eyes and listened to the chorus of bullfrogs in the nearby pond.

The swing shifted as someone sat down. She opened her eyes. Grandfather.

"You've been out here alone for a while. Lance already turned in for the night."

"I know."

"I'm proud of you, Sissy."

She smiled at his nickname for her, even though she had no siblings.

"You did the right thing by defending Lance. I can tell he's an honorable man."

"You think that of everyone."

"Not true. I wouldn't put Mr. O'Connor in that category. What you said to him tonight took courage."

"Maybe Lance should go though. Mr. O'Connor might not leave so peaceably next time."

"We'll keep doing the right thing and let the Lord take care of the rest. The townspeople will come around in time."

Would they? Melissa didn't share Grandfather's confidence. Every little taunt and jeer she'd heard on the street today still stung.

And as long as Lance stayed under Grandfather's roof, there would be many more of them.

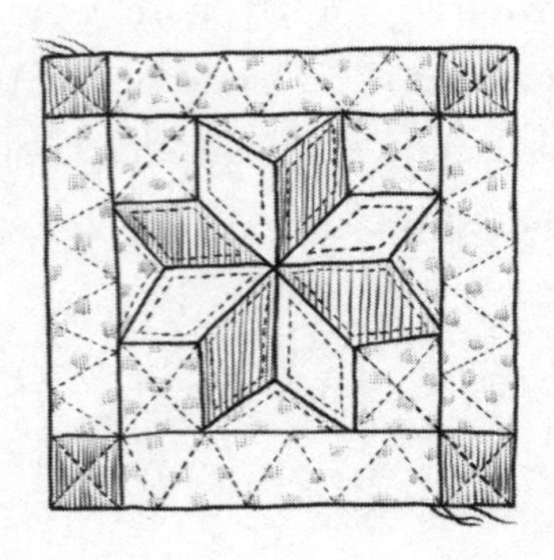

Chapter 3

The early morning sun streamed through the gleaming kitchen window as Melissa sat at the kitchen table with a pen, an inkpot, and a sheet of paper. She licked her lips. For this to be effective, she had to word the letter just the right way. Already a couple of rejected drafts sat crumpled on the chair beside her.

Dear Editor,

At least she had that part perfected.

She also had to make sure no one in town would realize she was the one composing the letter. How to accomplish that?

Lately, a newcomer has graced Regent with his presence.

She scratched out the word *graced.* Not the one she wanted. Not the sentence she wanted. With a blot of ink, she crossed out the entire line. *Lately, a newcomer has arrived in our fair town.*

Much better. Now for the next sentence.

"What are you doing?"

Lance's voice in her ear sent her jumping from her seat.

"I'm sorry. I thought you heard me coming, but you must have been too engrossed in your work." He pulled out a chair and sat across from her at the table. "What are you writing?"

She flipped the paper over. "Nothing."

"Another verse?"

"No." Time to change the subject. "Can I get you a cup of coffee?"

"Yes, please."

She rose to pour a steaming mug from the pot on the stove. "What are your plans for the day?"

"Find a job."

The hot liquid sloshed out of the cup and over her hand. "You plan on staying in the area?"

"There's nothing left for me in Virginia. My home state is in ruins. I have a little money in my pocket, enough for a couple of nights at the hotel and a meal or two, but that would maybe get me as far as Chicago."

"Oh." The word came out as a squeak. "I didn't realize you wanted to settle here." Was it a good idea he was even considering staying? Perhaps Kentucky or Tennessee or somewhere that wasn't here would be a better choice.

"I don't know about staying. But if I want to leave, I need some cash in my pocket."

"Well, good luck." He would need it.

Grandmother bustled into the room. "You two are up bright and early this morning. And you have the coffee brewing. Thank you." She kissed the top of Melissa's head, much the way she had every morning since Melissa had come to live here when she was five.

Melissa set aside the ink and paper and helped Grandmother get breakfast on the table. Throughout the meal, they chatted about life in Regent and life in Richmond. What different worlds they were.

"That was another delicious meal, ma'am. I'm obliged."

"No need to keep thanking me like that. You're not obliged at all. It's nothing more than Christian hospitality."

"Still, my mama, God rest her soul, would skin me alive if I didn't use good manners. And now, I'm off to search for work." He turned to Grandfather. "Can you give me any suggestions where I might look? I'm educated but never made it to study at the university. I'm also strong and don't mind physical labor."

"I heard that Mr. Wendt at the feed mill was searching for some help. You might go talk to him. On the edge of town, opposite where you came in on the train."

"Thank you. I'm ob—" He laughed and stuck his slouch hat on his head. "Thank you."

As soon as the dishes were done, Melissa gathered her writing and headed upstairs. If this was to be kept anonymous, she didn't want anyone knowing what she was penning. Not even her grandparents. She had an order of dolls for Wilson's Toy Emporium in Madison she needed to get to work on, but something drove her to compose this letter first.

This gentleman—yes, that was an accurate description of him—*traveled from a fair distance to meet one of our burg's own denizens.*

Was her speech too flowery?

It has come to my attention that this visitor was not welcomed with our usual Christian charity and hospitality. We know that the recent conflict that drove our nation apart has concluded. It is time to heal our country and to act with civility toward each other regardless of the color of our uniforms. No longer are we blue and gray, but we are now all red, white, and blue. Let us treat our community's latest arrival with the dignity and respect all God's people are due.

Melissa chewed on the end of her pen and reread her words. She'd worked hard to sound like the newspaper's editor and not like herself. All in all, the result was good.

Once the ink dried, she folded the paper and slipped it into an envelope. In block printing, she addressed it to the editor of the *Regent Reader*, their local newspaper.

And no time like the present to mail it. Before she lost her nerve. A short time later, she was hustling down the walk toward the mercantile.

A tall, well-dressed man in a bowler hat and round glasses went by. The editor. Would he make the connection between her being in town and the arrival of the letter? If only she could slink away and hide behind someone or something.

But the street was quiet. No one else was around. He tipped his hat. "Good morning, Miss Bainbridge."

"Good day, sir."

They each went their separate ways. But it set her hands to shaking. What if someone put the pieces together and figured out she wrote the editorial? Her humiliation would be complete.

Lance emerged from the feed mill, staring at his feet. Lucy Miller kept a wide berth as she went by him.

Melissa straightened her spine and continued on her way. She purchased the required postage and slipped the letter in a stack of other correspondence for Mr. Alden to mail. That way he wouldn't know the letter in the paper came from her.

For better or worse, what was done was done.

Lance shuffled from the feed mill, keeping his concentration on the dirt road in front of him. Even so, from the corner of his eye, he caught a glimpse of a young woman in a bright yellow day dress cutting a wide path around him.

The mill owner would only say they weren't hiring. Wouldn't give him tips on any other job prospects. So Lance moved on.

Up ahead, a building with a false front proclaimed it to be the livery. Perfect. He'd ridden with the cavalry until a Yank shot his horse from under him. He knew his way around the animals. Perhaps this owner would be kinder.

He stepped inside the dim building, a sweet odor of hay mingling with the sweaty smell of horseflesh. He took a long drag of the air. Mama had always said if you drank in that fragrance, you would live to be a hundred.

What a strange saying.

"Morning." A husky, bearded man stepped from an office to Lance's right. "You're new in town, aren't you? In need of a horse?"

"I'm Lance Witherspoon." Even though he did his best imitation of a Northern accent, a drawl still marked his words.

"Oh. I heard all about you. The Reb."

"That's me. And before you judge me on the color of my uniform, I want you to know I was a simple farmer before the war. No slaves. Didn't believe in it. Only fought for the South because it was my home. I was in the cavalry. Know horses. Was wondering if you're hiring. I'm a hard worker."

"Nope. Good day to you." The man turned his back on Lance and returned to his office.

The sun rose higher in the sky. He passed over the hotel, knowing the owner wouldn't give him a second look. If he wouldn't rent him a room, he would never offer him a job.

He entered the mercantile, crowded with barrels of flour and sugar, bolts of material, and various farm implements. Melissa stood at the counter, speaking with the thin clerk who snapped his suspenders every now and again.

Good. A friendly face. He made his way over to them, dodging displays of knitting needles and skeins of yarn until he stood beside her. "You didn't mention coming into town today."

She peered at him, her eyes as blue as the James River, and smoothed down the fabric on her rather old-fashioned pale-pink dress. "I-I just needed to run a quick, um, errand. Yes, that's right, an errand. One I wasn't—well, it wasn't worth mentioning. So here I am. And now I'm done, so I'll head home."

"Do you have any packages I can help you with?"

"No, no packages. I mean, it's something I'll get later. I know you're busy. Have you had any success so far?"

"No. But perhaps you can introduce me to this gentleman and give me a good reference?" He flashed her a grin.

"I don't know you well enough for that. But Mr. Alden, this is Mr. Witherspoon. Mr. Witherspoon, Mr. Alden. Mr. Alden, I think this man would be an asset to the store, if you have a position for him. And now, I really need to get home. I have dolls to sew."

Before Lance could catch his breath, she ducked away and left a trail of flowery perfume in her wake. He stared after her as she exited, the little bell above the door jangling a merry tune.

She'd behaved in such a strange manner. Almost nervous around him. Yet last night she'd been kind. He'd thought they were getting along. Even this morning, she was more than polite.

Did she not want to be seen with him?

Whatever the case, he had a job to secure. He turned to speak to Mr. Alden, but the man had disappeared. Lance peered around the store, the handful of men and women inside staring at him.

He wouldn't gain employment here.

Nor did he find work at the railroad depot. And he wasn't about to step foot inside any of the taverns. He stood at the end of the street and gazed across the town. Those were his options, and he'd exhausted them.

There was nothing left to do but return to the Bainbridge farm. He would have to take the train as far south as he could and then perhaps he could find some work.

He kicked at the stones on the road as he made his way out of town. A row of trees along the way provided shade from the weak spring sunshine. Off in one of the fields, a farmer worked the plow, urging his team onward to break the soil for planting.

Perhaps he could use some help. Even if the man paid him for picking stones out of the dirt, it would be something.

Lance left the road and hiked over the furrows to approach the farmer. He stopped a distance away. Perhaps from this far, the man wouldn't hear his accent. "Good morning." He waved.

The man returned his wave. At least he didn't order him off the property right away. Lance waited until the plow approached. "Wondering if you had any work for me around the place? Helping with the planting at all?"

The farmer grew closer.

A man with a scruffy beard. Mr. O'Connor. "You!" He bellowed and blustered. "How dare you trespass on my property. Get off my land. Now. Before I get my shotgun. And don't ever show your face around here again."

Heart thumping and hands sweating, Lance raced from the property. Didn't stop running until the Bainbridge home came into view.

This morning made one thing perfectly clear. He had to get out of this town.

Now.

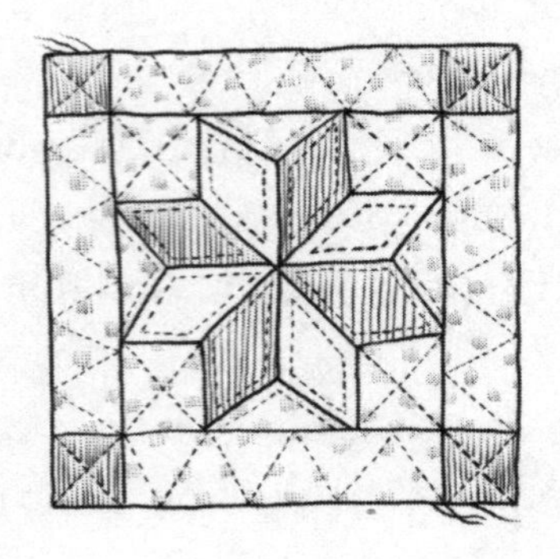

Chapter 4

Lance thumped into the Bainbridge home, not caring that the door slammed shut behind him. He pounded up the stairs to the small room the kind people had offered him.

The only kind people in the entire town of Regent.

What a fool he'd been. Coming here so soon after the war had been a mistake. Wounds needed time to heal. A chance to scab over.

He yanked his carpetbag from underneath the bed and flung in the two pairs of pants and two extra shirts he'd brought along. He turned to grab his comb from the washstand to find Mr. Bainbridge standing in the doorway.

"You going somewhere, son?"

"No one is hiring. Time for me to move on. I've got a little bit. Maybe enough to get south of Chicago, enough to where someone will take me on. I should never have come."

"Nonsense. Why don't we go downstairs and have a cup of coffee and talk about this? Betsy has gone to town and so has Melissa, so we have the place to ourselves. The train doesn't come through until tomorrow anyway, so you're not going to be able to leave today."

With a sigh, Lance followed the older man into the kitchen. Mr. Bainbridge retrieved two cups from the shelf and filled them from the pot on the back of the stove. Then he sat across the table from Lance and stared him dead in the eyes. "Now, tell me what's really going on. You're running from something."

Lance turned the cup around several times, studying the way the dark liquid swirled. "I don't know what you mean."

"You came here to thank my granddaughter for the quilt. Fine gesture, very noble of you, but considering you don't have much money, a letter would have been sufficient. So why bother? What were you leaving behind?"

The man was much too perceptive for his own good. "I'm not running."

"I can understand you wanting to leave. You haven't been welcomed, and nothing is holding you here. But why did you show up in the first place?"

"I told you. When someone saves your life, the right thing to do is to thank them in person."

Silence filled the room, more oppressive than a Virginia summer's humidity. Mr. Bainbridge didn't so much as clear his throat. Didn't even sip his coffee.

And Lance couldn't look him in the eye. Because the man was right. Lance was running from something. Someone. "I came here to flee my past."

Mr. Bainbridge still didn't move. But when Lance glanced up, the man's face wasn't hard or his eyes narrowed. Instead, his features were soft. Fatherlike. Filled with a compassion he hadn't seen since his own father died years ago.

He swallowed hard. "I was supposed to be on guard duty one night back in '63. Times were tense. The war's tide was turning. My mama had died the year before of scarlet fever. I was a mess. And I drank too much."

His head pounded even now. What a stupid way to deal with his troubles. Mama would have been so disappointed in him. "I fell asleep. That night, there was a full moon. The Union attacked. Killed many of our soldiers."

The shots, the screams, remained with him. The smell of gunpowder and death. The sight of bodies torn apart. Scenes he would never forget. Not ever.

"One of the men who died that night, while I was supposed to be on watch, was a friend of mine. But our fathers weren't on the best of terms. And that's putting it mildly. Some old land dispute."

Mr. Bainbridge nodded. Oh, how much he reminded Lance of Papa. Otherwise, he wouldn't be able to share this story with a stranger. Or maybe it was because he was a stranger that he was able to pour out his soul.

Lance inhaled. "When he learned of his son's death and the circumstances behind it, he went crazy with grief. Blamed me, which he should have. It was my fault. But promised that he would hunt me down and get his revenge for all the Witherspoons had done to him.

"I believed him capable of doing just that. But where would I go? The quilt gave me the perfect answer. That's why I'm here."

By the time he finished, he shook from head to toe. Mr. Bainbridge patted his hand. "You don't need to worry, son. If you can stay sober and can stand staying in this town, I'll give you a job for as long as you need."

Melissa picked that moment to step into the kitchen, her mouth set in a firm line. "So the death of your friend was because of your inebriation?"

She'd heard his entire story. She must move like an Indian, on silent feet. He stood. "Yes. I take full responsibility. But I've changed my ways. Haven't touched a drop of liquor since then and don't ever plan to."

"You're a changed man?"

"I am. But one not welcomed many places. I hope this doesn't change your opinion of me. That you'll allow me to accept your grandfather's job offer. At least for a little while. If you object, I'll move on. I understand."

As she bit her lip, he held his breath. "If I ever find you anywhere near alcohol, I will sic Mr. O'Connor on you."

Lance couldn't help the smile that spread across his face. "I wouldn't expect anything less."

A soft, early summer sun caressed Melissa's shoulders as she waited in the wagon for Grandfather and Lance to finish their business in the feed mill. At least with Grandfather around, no one bothered Lance too much. Instead of outright hatred, for the last several weeks the townspeople had treated him with cold silence.

While she waited in the mid-June sunshine, she reached for one of the dolls she was working on and proceeded to attach two black buttons to the face. Good thing she had thought ahead to bring work with her. Since she didn't have much to get and didn't stay to chat with the other young women, she always finished her business well before Grandfather.

She glanced through the mercantile's window where Lucy, Susan, and Ginny shopped. Susan peered up, and Melissa brought her attention back to her work. But within a couple of minutes, the door opened, and the tittering of the women's giggles reached Melissa.

She pretended to be busy fishing more buttons out of the bag at her feet on the wagon's floor. To no avail.

"Still playing with dolls, I see." Lucy's nasal voice sent goose-flesh skittering down Melissa's arms.

"I have an order for them from a store in Madison."

"Isn't that sweet?" Ginny leaned over to peek inside the wagon, the scent of her toilet water strong enough to make Melissa's eyes water.

Melissa stabbed her needle in the middle of the doll's chest. "Can I help you with something?" If only they would go away and just leave her alone like they usually did.

Susan reached into her reticule and pulled out a newspaper.

Melissa sucked in her breath and pressed on her stomach just under the empire waistline on her outdated but so comfortable Georgian-style dress. She braced herself for what was to come.

"There was this very interesting article in the *Regent Reader*." Susan thrust the paper under Melissa's nose. "'This gentleman traveled from a fair distance to meet one of our burg's own denizens.' My, what big words you use."

"I didn't write this." The lie rolled off Melissa's tongue before she had a chance to check it.

"Come, come, Miss Bainbridge, who else would use words like 'burg' and 'denizens'? Not even an educated man like Pastor Blake puts on such affectations. Oh goodness, now I sound like you."

Melissa straightened her spine but couldn't stem the tide of heat rising up her neck and into her cheeks, which must be blooming red about now.

Ginny joined in. "'No longer are we blue and gray, but we are now all red, white, and blue.' My, my, it's almost poetic. So rousing and stirring and patriotic. Perhaps you should run for mayor." The three girls burst into a fresh round of laughter.

Now would be the perfect time for the Second Coming. Anything to deliver Melissa from this misery.

But no trumpets sounded from heaven. She twisted a bunch of material from her skirt in her hands.

"Don't have anything to say?"

Why couldn't she think of a smart, glib retort?

"Good afternoon, ladies."

Just when this day couldn't get any worse, Lance had to show up. Melissa dared to peer through her lashes as he strode in her direction, his chin set.

"If it isn't Johnny Reb himself." Ginny spoke the words with a honeyed tongue, but they dripped with arsenic. "Seems you have a champion in Miss Bainbridge. Perhaps even an admirer."

He furrowed his forehead.

"Haven't you seen this week's paper?" Susan yanked it from Melissa's lap and handed it to Lance. "All about you, right there on page three."

He studied it for a moment, his expression never changing. "I don't see that Miss Bainbridge wrote this. It's not signed. Perhaps it was one of you fine young women."

Susan's fair face paled even further.

Melissa bit the inside of her cheek to keep from smiling.

"I find the letter to be well written, thoughtful, and very kind. At least there is one person in this town who possesses some Christian charity. And now, if you'll excuse us, I'm going to escort Miss Bainbridge to the hotel's dining room for a cup of tea while we wait for her grandfather to finish his business. Good day."

No, no, having the town witness him squiring her around would do her reputation no good. But he held out his hand to help her from the wagon. What other option did she have?

She clasped his warm, calloused hand and stepped from the wagon. With her fingers looped around his elbow, they made their way down the walk and entered the hotel.

He held out a chair for her at one of the tables to the left of the entrance, and she settled herself across from him.

"It was you, wasn't it?"

Straightening her cotton skirt, she squirmed under his intense gaze. "Yes."

"Thank you."

"I didn't do anything wonderful."

"You did. No one else, save for your grandparents, has stood up for me. And you did so in such a thoughtful, kind, and eloquent manner. Now I can say that I'm much obliged."

"But those girls." All she'd done by writing that letter was open herself up for increased ridicule. How much more could she take?

"You shouldn't pay any attention to them. You're a much finer lady."

"That's funny. You haven't caught me wandering through the woods or wading in the stream or up a tree yet."

He couldn't stop from grinning. "It's a sight I can't wait to see. Or join in."

"No." She shot to her feet. "Don't you see? I'm not much of a woman. That's why I don't fit in. And now I've only made everything worse. Much, much worse for all of us." A well of tears sprung to her eyes, and before she could allow him to see them, she rushed from the hotel.

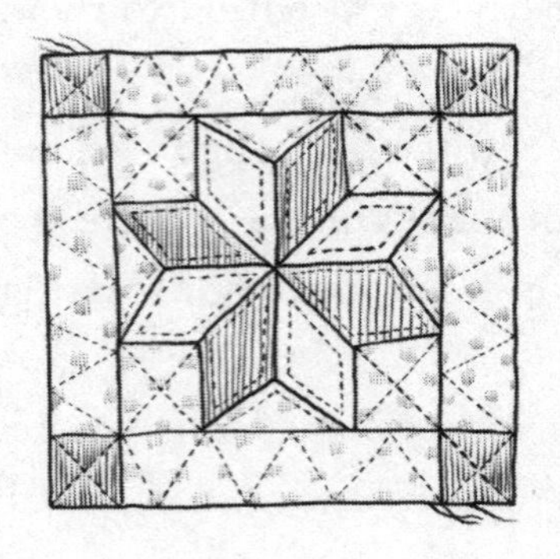

Chapter 5

Lance discovered Melissa huddled in the back of the wagon clutching one of her half-finished rag dolls to her chest. Tears streamed down her pink cheeks. What had he done to cause this?

He stepped to her. "Melissa?"

She drew her attention to him and wiped the tears from her face. "Please, I don't want to talk about it."

"Was it something I said?"

She shook her head.

"Then what?"

"You wouldn't understand."

He gave her a sideways glance. "Those girls don't know what they're talking about."

"But they do. They're right." She squeezed the doll harder and then flung it to the side. "Look at me. I don't dress right. I can't stand all those crinolines and full skirts. They get in my way. And I think this style is so much prettier. But then, what was the first thing I did when I got upset? Picked up a doll. At my age."

"We all have something that makes us feel better. That quilt you sewed gave me such comfort."

"A quilt is a lot different than a doll."

"I don't see how."

"Thank you for being so kind. And thank you for coming to my defense. But I shouldn't be whining to you about my problems. Here comes Grandfather. We should be on our way home."

All the way to the farm, Lance glanced beside him from time to time to check on Melissa. How could anyone treat a person with such a tender heart in such a cruel manner? True, she wasn't your usual female, but that was what made her intriguing. Unique. A peacock among geese.

As soon as they arrived at the farm, she jumped from the wagon and disappeared into the house. Mr. Bainbridge unharnessed the team and led the horses into the barn. Lance followed.

"Have those girls always treated Melissa so badly?"

Mr. Bainbridge fed Stormy a handful of grain. "Since the day she arrived after her parents' deaths. She's shy and awkward, not a bit like the other young women, and doesn't care to imitate them. And I'm glad of that. But they've shunned her. Hurt her terribly over the years. Made her retreat further and further. Getting her to go to town is a struggle."

"If I could, I'd have them drawn and quar—"

"Remember, the Good Book says we are to turn the other cheek."

Like his neighbor in Virginia turned the other cheek and showed Lance Christian charity after his son's death? Turning the other cheek had its limits. Lance had just about reached his. Melissa hadn't done anything to deserve being shunned. Being shy and dressing in old-fashioned clothes was no reason for such treatment.

And the letter she'd written to the newspaper touched his heart. To have a few friends in this town meant everything.

For the rest of the afternoon, he worked with Mr. Bainbridge, plowing the ground and planting wheat. Mrs. Bainbridge served dinner, but Melissa picked at the venison, pushing the meat and asparagus around her plate.

After devotions, Melissa left the house. Lance followed her to the porch. He found her just where he thought he would, sitting on the swing, staring into the darkness.

"Mind if I share this seat?"

She scooted over. "Fine. Though I don't know what you want to speak to me about."

"We don't have to talk. We can sit here together and enjoy the evening." Which they did for quite a while. Her soft breathing blended with the songs of the crickets and the bullfrogs. Every now and then, a set of green glowing eyes appeared at the edge of the woods. A deer perhaps.

"They've always teased me."

Her quiet words startled him. He touched her hand. "That must have been so hard growing up. You've lived here most of your life?"

"My parents died when I was five. I don't remember them very much. I was always shy. I realize I have quirks. If I dressed as they do, maybe they would accept me. If I didn't sew dolls all day long, maybe they wouldn't laugh at me."

"But those are the things that make you who you are. If you changed them, you wouldn't be Melissa anymore. You'd blend in with the crowd and get lost."

"Maybe that's what I want. Not to be the strange girl, the one who always sticks out, the one who is the center of unwanted attention. Grandmother and Grandfather told me to not worry about being part of the crowd. I've listened to them, but maybe it's time for me to try something different. I can't live here the rest of my life and be picked on all the time. Either I have to leave, or I have to try to fit in.

"Perhaps I should go shopping. Have the girls help me pick out a pattern for a couple new dresses. I have a large order for Wilson's Toy Emporium in Madison, so I can splurge a little." She didn't make eye contact with him the entire time she spoke.

"Is that what you truly want?" He'd hate for her to change. Yes, he'd only been here a handful of weeks, but something about her drew him in. Her unique style, her sweet personality, her quirkiness. Underneath it all, she was a gentle soul.

Someone he wanted to get to know better.

She licked her lips and gave a single nod.

He squeezed her hand. "Just don't go changing too much."

"Are you sure you want to do this?" Grandmother squeezed Melissa's shoulder as she drove the wagon into town. Tied inside a handkerchief in her reticule was a good chunk of her savings.

And the beginning of a new life.

Did she want to go ahead with her plan? How could she ever talk to the girls who had teased her with so little mercy for so many years? But if she wanted to fit in, if she wanted to be part of their group, she had to put aside her shyness and let the words flow.

Still, a gaggle of butterflies, or more like a colony of bees, took up residence in her stomach. What if they rejected her and laughed at her? Well, it wouldn't be any different than any other day.

"Melissa?"

Melissa inhaled, long and slow. "If I ever want to belong here, truly be a part of this community, then I have to." So why was her stomach bunched in knots? How could she ever say the words?

"Your grandfather and I love you just the way you are. Nothing can replace your loving disposition. I hope that doesn't change."

"Of course it won't."

"And I know a certain young man who might have an interest in you."

Melissa shot Grandmother a glance and raised her eyebrows. "Who?"

"Do you not see it? Lance is quite smitten with you."

"Lance?" Sure, he was nice enough. Nicer than any boy had ever been to her. And there was no denying he was handsome. With his slicked-back, wavy brown hair, his oval face, and his piercing green eyes, he was a good catch. But interested in her?

Even smitten? No man had ever paid the least bit of attention to her.

"And why not?"

"Talk about misfits."

"And that makes you the perfect match. You understand each other."

The way Grandmother said it put to rest any other argument Melissa might have mounted. But she didn't want to encourage any kind of romantic relationship with him. It would only fluster her. And change things between them. For the first time since she was seven, she had a friend.

One she didn't want to lose.

Before Melissa could finish her thoughts, Grandmother pulled up to the mercantile and set the wagon's brake. Melissa ran around to help her down.

"Thank you, dear. My old bones don't want to move as fast as they used to."

"Tish tosh. Your old bones are just fine." They moved into the store. No surprise that Susan, Ginny, and Lucy gathered in a huddle in the back of the store near the dry goods.

Melissa wandered in their direction, glancing at the flour barrel and examining a pair of gloves on her way toward the threesome. Putting off the inevitable for as long as possible.

Ginny sniffed. "Come to get more supplies for your baby dolls?"

Melissa willed her lunch to stay in her stomach. "No." She stared at her shoes, her hands shaking like leaves in the wind. "As a matter of fact, I was hoping to run into you today. I'd like to, well, update my, um, wardrobe. And I was wondering if you could help me pick out some more, um, fashionable patterns."

Susan widened her brown eyes. "Really? Well then, girls, we have our work cut out for us. What do you think of this pink gingham for her?"

Ginny shook her head. "With her pale complexion, it might wash her out. She needs a brighter color. Maybe this medium blue would work well."

"And you'll need some hoops."

Melissa shook her head. "No hoops. That's where I draw the line. I want to be comfortable."

"All right." Ginny sighed. "We can bring you up to date without the hoops. And I can show you how to do your hair nicer."

"My hair?" Melissa touched the bun at the base of her neck. "What's wrong with it?" This was spiraling out of control. Maybe asking the girls for advice wasn't her smartest decision.

"It's too severe, especially for a young lady. Wear it in soft waves over your ears. That would be much more becoming on you."

"Oh look, girls, Mr. Alden just got in this mint-green windowpane material. Isn't it lovely? It would look so nice on you, Melissa."

She had to admit the fabric was lovely. How beautiful it would be underneath her fingers as she sewed the dress. "I do like it."

"It's so much more modern than the usual fabrics you pick. Let your grandmother wear them. They were popular when she was your age. And this way, you'll attract attention from lots of other young men, and you can be rid of that awful Southerner. We're so glad you came to your senses. Now he can go back to where he belongs."

Melissa opened her mouth to reply to Susan's comment but

then shut it. By doing so, she would only alienate the girls and ruin whatever chance she had at being friends with them. So far, they were being nice to her. Much more than at school. Maybe she should have done this years ago.

Before she had a chance to catch her breath, Melissa had enough fabric for two new dresses and a couple of ideas for different hairstyles. She counted out the money for Mr. Alden, who wrapped her purchases in brown paper and tied the bundles with string.

"Thank you so much, ladies, for the assistance. I appreciate it." Melissa waved to the girls.

"Wait a minute." Ginny scurried to catch up to her. "The strawberry festival is next Saturday. Maybe you would like to meet us there and sit with us for the meal. And join us for a game of croquet?"

They wanted her to be part of their group? Not since her childhood friend Frances had moved back East years ago had any other girl invited her to do anything at all.

What was this all about? Were they genuine in their sudden positive interest in her? Or did they have ulterior motives? Was a simple change in dress all it took to make them like her?

Her head swirled. For a long moment, she stood in the doorway, her hand on the knob, mute. Unable to utter a single syllable.

Then Grandmother pulled the door open. "There you are. Just about ready to go?"

"I'll be right there." Melissa turned to the trio of girls. "That would be nice. I'll see you Saturday."

Lance wiped his sweaty brow, surely leaving a streak of dirt across his forehead. Age hadn't slowed Mr. Bainbridge one bit. Not even Lance's long marches during the war with all of his supplies had prepared him for the work he did today. Bed tonight would feel wonderful.

As he turned for the house, Melissa and Mrs. Bainbridge pulled the wagon into the yard. A sudden surge of energy rushed through him. He rushed to the horses and grabbed one by the bridle. "Hello, ladies. I hope you had a successful shopping trip."

Melissa tipped her head and flashed him a coy smile, one he was more used to from the Southern belles he'd known. He furrowed his brow, and her grin faltered.

After he helped her grandmother from the wagon, he turned to take care of the horses. Melissa usually hopped down on her own. But not today. Today she motioned for him to help her too. He shrugged and lent her a hand.

"Thank you, Mr. Witherspoon." She blinked fast.

"Do you have something in your eye?"

The winking or whatever it was ceased. "No. I'm fine." She marched toward the house, then spun around. "Please bring in the packages."

He obliged her and carried in the bundles.

"Just place them in the parlor, and make sure you wash your hands before supper."

"Yes, ma'am." Again, he followed her wishes.

An hour later, the family sat at the kitchen table, a bowl of steaming venison stew in the middle.

Melissa spooned a small amount of stew onto her plate. "Ginny said a woman needs to watch her figure, so I have to be careful how much I eat. Lucy told me I need to brush my hair one hundred strokes every night. Oh, and use some onion juice on it. Do you have any onions, Grandmother?"

Both of Melissa's grandparents gave her the same sideways glance. The one Lance worked to keep from his face. What was going on with Melissa? He had cautioned her not to change too much.

She wasn't heeding him.

After supper, he caught her between the kitchen and the parlor. "Are you feeling well?"

A too-bright smile crossed her face. "Never better."

"Good. I'm glad to hear that. Do you know what I found when I was exploring the woods beyond the wheat field the other day?" This would be a true test if she was the same Melissa he had bumped into and who had stuck up for him against the town.

"I have no idea." There she went trying to bat her eyelashes again. Once more, without success.

"An old swing hanging from a tree. I know you love the one on the porch. I thought we could have a contest and see who could go the highest."

She raised one auburn eyebrow. "I can't believe you would invite a grown woman to a swinging contest. I haven't touched that thing since, since. . ." Color rose in her cheeks.

Lance suppressed his laughter. If he had to guess, he would say she had been on that swing last week.

"I find nothing funny, Mr. Witherspoon." With that, she stomped up the stairs.

Mr. Bainbridge slapped Lance on the shoulder. "Women. There's no figuring them out."

But Lance knew just what had gotten into Melissa. And he had to say, he liked the Melissa he met weeks ago a whole lot better than this one.

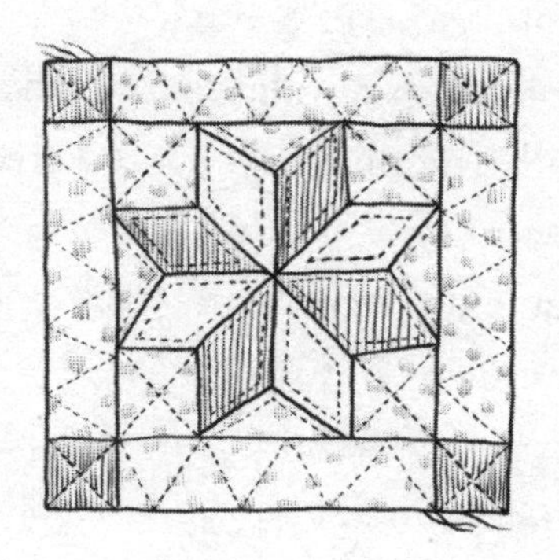

Chapter 6

Saturday morning dawned bright and clear. For the first time in a long time—maybe forever—Melissa hopped from bed and hummed a tune as she splashed her face with cold water from the pitcher and basin. While she helped Grandmother get breakfast and do the dishes, she wore her old gray work dress.

As soon as she hung the dish towel over the wooden rod in the kitchen, she dashed upstairs. On a hook beside her bed hung the sunrise-yellow dress she'd spent every free moment this week sewing. She'd closed her eyes in the wee hours of this morning after tying off the final thread.

A row of white buttons ran down the bodice, and Grandmother had crocheted a white lace collar for the creation. White piping edged the long sleeves. Though simple, it was by far the most fashionable dress she had ever owned.

After pulling on layers and layers of crinolines, she slipped the dress over her head. The hem just graced the floor. She spun in a circle, the wide skirt almost knocking over the washstand. How would she ever maneuver down the stairs and into the wagon, let alone through the crowds in town?

She combed her hair as the girls had instructed, leaving soft waves over her ears. Peering at herself in the hand mirror, she had to admit she didn't look all of her twenty-four years. She gave herself a smile.

As she made her way down the stairs, however, holding up the skirt so she wouldn't trip, her stomach flopped around. Would people stare at her? Laugh even harder?

Lance stood at the bottom of the steps. As she approached, he whistled. "Why, Melissa, if I didn't know you lived here, I wouldn't have thought it was you."

What did he mean by that? "Should I be flattered, sir?"

She came to the bottom, and he took her by the hand. "You, Miss Bainbridge, are a vision of loveliness no matter what you wear or how you style your hair."

"And you, Mr. Witherspoon, are nothing more than a silver-tongued flatterer."

"My mama taught me to never lie."

Grandmother peeked in from the kitchen, a strawberry pie in her hands. "You do look lovely, Melissa, though I have to agree with Lance. Beauty does not come from outward adornment but from within. Now, if you two are ready, Grandfather is waiting for us with the wagon."

Melissa tied her bonnet strings underneath her chin and nodded to Lance. "Grandfather's been the horseshoe champion for the past five years and is anxious to defend his title."

"Then let's not keep him waiting." Lance had to hold the door open for a good while to allow Melissa and her large skirt to make a complete exit. What a bother. But when the girls saw her today, it would be worth all the trouble.

Climbing the wagon wheel proved to be another challenge. Grandfather held the horses steady as Lance assisted her in making the precarious ascent. Well, perhaps she would get better at it in time.

The butterflies in her stomach grew in number the closer they got to town. Many wagons and a few buggies joined them on what was usually a quiet road. Families waved to each other as friends reconnected.

Grandfather pulled as close as he could to the white clapboard church. Lance gave Melissa a hand down and escorted her to the festival. Behind the place of worship, tables had been set up, and women surrounded them like bees on a hive, busy setting out platters of ham, loaves of bread, jars of pickles, and everything strawberry as far as the eye could see.

Ginny, Lucy, and Susan were decked out in their finest, the lace, ruffles, and frippery almost disguising them. "Oh Melissa, if you aren't a vision. Look at you. We knew there was a fashionable woman underneath there. And your hair. It's divine. So stylish." Ginny pulled Melissa from Lance's grasp. "You don't mind if we borrow her for a while, do you?"

The girls led her away from Lance. She glanced over her shoulder, and he stood, openmouthed.

Susan hissed in Melissa's ear. "The last thing you want to do is be seen with the likes of him. If you're trying to gain a position in this town, you want to steer clear of him. Why, he'll ruin you in a second."

The jeers the first day Lance arrived still rang in Melissa's head. She allowed the girls to spirit her well away from Lance.

She filled her plate with food and followed the young ladies to a blanket under a nearby oak tree. But while they chatted with each other, she pushed the food around her plate. She'd had Grandmother lace her corset so tight this morning, she couldn't breathe, much less force anything into her stomach.

She couldn't help but search out Lance. There he sat, against another oak, slouch hat over his eyes, very much alone. The horseshoe game occupied Grandfather, and Grandmother was most likely helping with the food.

She picked up her plate and stood to join Lance.

Lucy reached out and grabbed her. "Where are you going?" She must have spied who Melissa was gazing at. "Why don't we play croquet instead? Remember what we said?"

She did remember, but the sight of Lance by himself twisted her heart. After she had defended him, she turned her back on him. But she went with the girls.

Though she had never played before, she discovered she was rather good at the game and caught herself smiling a time or two. Then she hit her ball far out of bounds, right to the feet of a gentleman.

None other than Lance. "Shall I show you how it's done?" His green eyes glimmered.

"Come on, Melissa." Susan tugged on her arm. "We're finished here. I believe it's time for pie."

Once again she followed the girls. But the way Lance's shoulders slumped and the way he bowed his head soured her for anything sweet.

What was she doing?

Laughter and happy voices swirled around Lance as Melissa glanced over her shoulder, then walked away from him again. With those girls.

That same group of girls who had taunted her, derided her, and made her existence miserable for most of her life. How could she want to be part of their group? After he had heard some of her story, it was impossible to believe that she longed to be friends with these women. They were not friends of hers.

She was too nice to be part of their group. Hadn't she written that letter to defend him?

She disappeared around the corner of the church, out of his sight, without another backward look.

Leaving him standing in the middle of the festival hubbub by himself. Snubbed, shamed, scorned. Because, through no fault of his own, he fought for the country he lived in. Protected his home.

Someone slapped him on the shoulder. "Did you see that dead ringer I made? Horseshoe champion yet again."

Lance plastered on a smile for Mr. Bainbridge. "Congratulations. Well done. How was the competition this year?"

"Pretty tough. Frank Erwin has been practicing, but in the end, I managed to squeak by him. I'd better keep up my game if I hope to beat him again next year. Have you had something to eat? You can't go wrong with Betsy's strawberry pie."

"I haven't had the pleasure yet."

"Then you're missing out, son. Let's get some, before it's all gone."

As they approached the table, the crowd around it parted. Several of the men and women crossed their arms or glared at him. Only Mrs. Bainbridge kept a smile on her face. "Come to get some of my pie, men? Two pieces left just for you."

"What're you doing serving him? He's killed Yankees. Maybe even my own son." Mr. O'Connor. One among many people it would have been good not to run into today.

"Leave him be, O'Connor." Mr. Bainbridge tightened his jaw.

No, the old man couldn't, shouldn't fight Lance's battles. He stepped in front of him. "Leave Mr. Bainbridge out of this. It's me you have the problem with, not him."

"Truer words were never spoken. How would you like to be knocked to next Sunday? You and your kind killed my boy. My only son."

"And I'm mighty sorry about that, sir. Many good young men on both sides died." And the fact was that Lance probably had killed a Yankee. Maybe more than one. He closed his mind to the images of torn, bloody bodies.

"The only good Reb is a dead Reb. And that goes for you."

By this time, a crowd had gathered around the two men. "Get him, Charles. Do away with him, like those Rebs did away with James."

O'Connor took a step in Lance's direction.

At the edge of the crowd stood a young woman in a yellow gown. Her eyes were round, large, her mouth open. But she didn't move forward. Didn't speak up.

"I've had enough fighting. Too much American blood has already been shed. I don't aim to spill any more of it. The war is over. Let's act like it." Lance turned to walk away.

"Lily-livered coward. That's all you are. You and your kind. Nothing but a bunch of bullies. Go back where you came from. We don't need you around here."

Lance held back his laugh. Southerners were bullies? He'd never met such a bunch of hypocrites in all his life.

Too bad the Bainbridges weren't ready to head for home. He couldn't stick around any longer. Had to get out of here. Before he did strike someone. Hard.

He meandered away from the crowd and into the woods that bordered the large clearing. A swarm of mosquitoes attacked him when he entered, but they didn't bite him. Mama always told him it was because he was too sour. But she'd said it with a gentle chuckle. If only she were still alive to give him advice.

Part of him dreamed of Virginia. A plate of collard greens and okra. The song of the cicadas in the summer's heat. A cool swim in the river.

He scrubbed his face. Perhaps it was time for him to move on. While Mr. Bainbridge's offer was selfless and generous, the truth was that next time, Mr. O'Connor might make good on his threat. Might not allow Lance to walk away.

And he couldn't hide on the farm forever. That was no kind of life.

The remnants of last fall's leaves crunched under his boots as he ducked under low branches and skirted blackberry brambles. The gurgle of water led him to the edge of a stream. He couldn't resist slipping off his shoes and socks and wading into the cold water.

Wow, that was bracing.

Worse than Mr. O'Connor's threats was Melissa's behavior. He scratched his head but could come up with no logical explanation for it. What had turned her into one of them?

A soft rustling sounded behind him, and he spun to catch a flash of yellow in the trees. "Stupid skirt."

"Melissa?"

She stepped from the woods to the creek bank, her dress torn and her hair disheveled. "You are not an easy person to find."

"What are you doing here?"

"I could ask you the same question."

"But I posed mine first. You've ruined your dress. What is it you want with me? Why don't you leave me alone like you did before?"

"Let me explain."

All of a sudden, his head pounded. He changed his mind. He didn't really want to hear this.

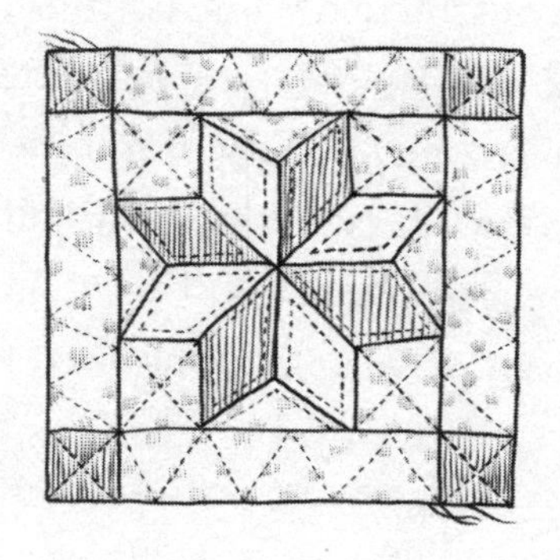

Chapter 7

Before Melissa could utter a word in defense of her actions—though truthfully, there was no defense—Lance raced from the brook, forgetting his socks and shoes. Even barefoot, he was swifter than she. She hiked up her skirt as far as she dared and took off after him.

But her billowing skirt with its layers of crinoline hampered her. The material caught on every branch and twig and prevented her from spotting the vines and rocks and tree roots in her path.

Her foot caught on something, and she tumbled forward, hitting the ground. The overabundance of material cushioned her fall. If she'd been wearing her usual straight skirts, this would never have happened. She would have had a fighting chance of catching him.

By this time, however, she had no idea where he had gone. She sat in an avalanche of stiffened white cotton. Tears burned the back of her throat. With no witnesses, she permitted them to flow.

What had she become? A fake, a phony. No, worse than that. Someone who tossed aside everything she believed in and held dear for a fleeting moment of pleasure.

"Oh Lord, You must be so disappointed in me. I'm a traitor to all You've commanded, all my grandparents have taught me. Forgive me, Lord, forgive me."

After a good wallow, she wiped away her tears with the back of her hands. Only then did she notice they were dirty. Now her face must be streaked black. She must be a sight. And not a good one. But she had no other choice. Grandmother and Grandfather would be worried about her, searching for her. She had to return to the festival to ease their minds and to catch her ride home.

Home. As soon as she got there, she was going to go straight to bed and pull the quilt over her face and never come out.

She followed her own trail of torn bits of yellow fabric hanging on branches to find her way out of the thicket. She emerged to discover cleanup underway. Women collected empty plates from the tables, and men broke down the sawhorses and wood planks.

And in the middle of it all stood Ginny, Lucy, and Susan, huddled together.

Lucy peered up.

Oh no. Straight at Melissa.

If only she could melt into the trees. But it was too late. Here they came.

Ginny puckered her face. "My goodness, Melissa, where on earth have you been? You're a positive wreck. Like you've been gadding about in the woods."

"I have been."

Susan sucked in her breath.

"All in search of Lance. Have you seen him?"

"Why would we want to?" Lucy shook her head.

"Because I'm afraid we've behaved badly toward him. Me most of all. I turned my back on him when he was only trying to be my friend."

"You don't need friends like that."

A thousand words danced on the end of Melissa's tongue. None of them good. She bit them back. Across the yard, Grandfather was leading Grandmother toward the wagon. "I have to go." Decorum be hanged. She hurried in their direction.

Grandmother's gray eyes widened, magnified by her round glasses. "My dear, whatever happened to you?"

"I'm fine. It's not important. Can we go home? Now? Please?"

Grandfather caressed her arm. "Of course." He helped her into the back of the wagon and clucked to the team.

Melissa sat with her hands over her face the entire way home. Even when one of her grandparents asked her a question, she answered with nothing more than a grunt.

Mercifully, they arrived at home. She jumped out the back with as much grace as possible and headed for the door.

"Sissy, wait." Grandfather's voice stopped her.

"I don't feel like talking."

"That's fine. You can listen. Come with me to the barn while I comb the horses and get them fed."

Like a dutiful grandchild, she followed him inside, the sweet odor of hay tickling her nose. She sneezed.

Grandfather grabbed the curry brush and got to work. "I

couldn't help but notice some of what went on today."

Melissa moaned.

"No, you hear me out. I know how difficult life has been for you. Never fitting in. Always doing your own thing. I thought you didn't mind. You kept it hidden well for so many years. I was proud of you for being your own person and not bowing to the pressure of the crowd.

"But something has changed in you in the past few weeks, ever since Lance arrived."

"I can explain."

"I wasn't finished."

She leaned against the stall's doorway.

"At first, you did what I expected of you. You stood up for him. Treated him like a human being and not like the enemy. Showed him God's love and compassion.

"But then you bought all this material and sewed yourself a fancy new dress. And then you behaved the way you did today."

"I just couldn't take it anymore." She choked on her words.

"I understand it's not easy to always be the object of people's ridicule. I've endured enough of it in my life. A scrawny kid who didn't get into trouble at school. Yes, I was picked on plenty by the bigger kids."

Melissa drew in a breath. "Didn't you ever want to do something about it?"

"Sure. So one day, when Daniel Folkner teased me one time too many, I swung back."

"Did it feel good?"

"Can't say that it did. I bruised my hand, and he broke my nose."

"So that's why you have a crooked nose. I always wondered."

"The fight didn't do me any good, because then I got known as the kid who ran home crying to Mama."

"I know I treated Lance poorly. He's been the one person who has understood me and been a friend to me. Not since Frances moved away have I had that. And now I've gone and messed it up. And it might be too late to fix it."

Darkness had fallen by the time Lance slipped into the farmhouse's back door. No lamps lit the space. All remained quiet other than a soft snore from the dog curled up on a rug in a corner of the kitchen.

He slid off his shoes so as not to wake anyone, but the floorboards creaked under his weight. Moonlight streamed in through the glass-paned window, illuminating red hair.

Melissa sat at the kitchen table. "You've been out a long time."

"I didn't mean to worry anyone. In fact, I don't want to be a worry or a burden to your family anymore."

"Please, listen to me. I need to talk to you."

He couldn't put himself through that kind of grief again. "No. We've said all we need to say. You made your choice today very clear."

"But that wasn't my choice."

"It wasn't your idea to dress up like the other young women?"

"Well."

"And it wasn't your choice to turn your back on me?"

"You're twisting around what I said."

"If those girls make you happy, if being like them gives you a warm feeling inside, then I'm happy for you. But I don't have to sit around here and pretend I like it. The time has come for me to leave. If you'll excuse me, I have to go pack."

"Lance, wait."

At her loud whisper, he came to a halt. But only for a split second. The longer he stayed around, the longer he enjoyed her presence, the harder the leaving would become. The more his heart would hurt when he walked out the door. No, better to just make a clean break. To get this pain over with and get on with the rest of his life.

He bounded up the stairs two at a time. But a set of delicate footfalls followed. He scurried to his room and shut the door. A few seconds later, a knock sounded. "Please, Lance, listen to me."

If he didn't talk to her, she would wake her grandparents, and he would never be able to make his escape. He cracked the door.

"Go ahead."

"Can't we speak in the kitchen so we can sit across the table from each other?"

He sighed and followed her downstairs.

She sat and fiddled with the cup she had been holding when he walked through the door. The coffee in it had to be long cold. "While I waited for you, I practiced what I would say. Now I can't remember a word of my prepared speech. So maybe I should just speak from my heart."

He gripped the edge of the chair. He didn't need her to become emotional and make leaving even more difficult. He needed to be out of this town as soon as possible. There were no trains on Sunday, but he'd walk until he found one.

However long that took.

She touched his hand, and it sent his breath racing. "Can't you look at me?"

He gazed into her thin, heart-shaped face, her auburn brows arched high.

"I behaved abominably today. I don't know what got into me. The way I treated you was very, very wrong. Can you ever accept my apology and forgive me?"

He cracked his knuckles. "What I don't understand is why. I thought we were friends. That's the worst part of it. If you had treated me that way since the day I arrived in town, it would have been a different story. But you had been nice to me. You wrote that article about me. And then suddenly, you're a different person. I don't understand."

With her hair loose about her shoulders, Melissa twisted a curl around her fingers. "I know you don't. I'm not sure I understand myself."

He scooted his chair back. "Then I should be going."

"When I was five, I came to live here after my parents died in a wagon accident. I barely remember them."

Lance remained in his seat but didn't push back to the table.

"Though I loved my grandparents, and still do, I didn't know them well at the time. We didn't see them much when my parents were alive. I was a frightened, lonely little girl."

Lance could only imagine. It was hard enough to lose everything you loved when you were an adult. How much tougher when you were just a child. He clamped his lips shut.

"Ginny, Lucy, and Susan have always made fun of me. I was happier with my dolls, sewing little clothes, than I was playing with other children. I had a weak constitution, so I would spend recess time at school inside with my needle and thread rather than jumping rope or rolling hoops with the other girls."

"I don't see what this has to do with today. In fact, it only deepens the mystery. If they've been picking on you for so many years, why would you suddenly want to be part of their group?"

"I did have one friend in those days. Frances. She loved dolls and dressing them up almost as much as I did. We played together for hours. She invited me to the tea party she had when she turned seven. Grandmother and I made a new dress for me. I felt pretty. And for that one afternoon, I belonged.

"The next day, she told me her family was moving away. Come spring, they packed their wagon and headed west. I never saw her again."

Lance rubbed his temples. "I'm sorry about that."

"Don't you see?"

He didn't. "It must have been hard for you to lose a friend. That makes it even more puzzling why you would work so hard to alienate me."

"No, that wasn't the case at all. I just wanted to belong with the girls again, for one afternoon."

"Well, you got your wish. I hope you're happy." This time, Lance stomped from the room and didn't pause, not even when Melissa's cries pierced his heart.

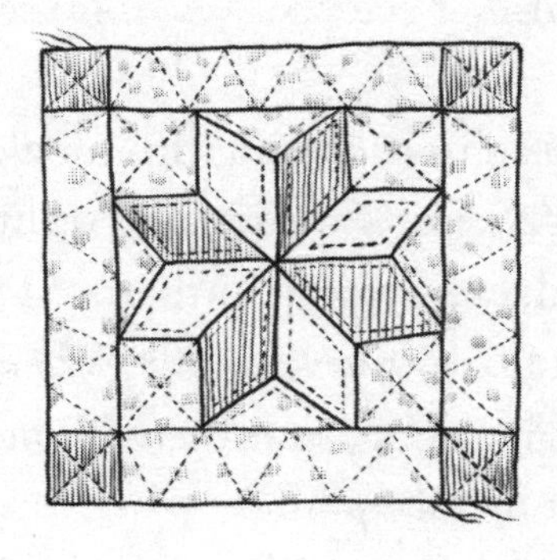

Chapter 8

As a pale dawn peeked through the dark clouds and into Lance's east-facing bedroom window, he threw his two pairs of pants, his clean Sunday shirt, and his work boots into his blue-and-gold carpetbag. Just a short time ago, the stairs had creaked, and Melissa's bedroom door had opened and shut. Now, all slumbered in peace.

All but Lance. He glanced around the spartan, utilitarian bedroom. Funny how in the few weeks he'd been here, it had become home. As much as any place had been such a thing in the past four years.

Who knew where this next leg of his journey would take him? He would miss the Bainbridges' hospitality most of all. They had been kind when not many others were.

A crack of lightning startled him and sent his heart to racing. That was close.

He should be glad to be leaving this place, a place where hatred continued to live. Where Christians persecuted each other in the name of blending in. Belonging. Fitting.

One thing had become very clear to Lance in the past twenty-four hours. He did not fit or belong here. Time to head south, where his accent wouldn't handicap him.

He picked up the patchwork quilt, the one Melissa had sewn for the Sanitary Commission in the hope that it would aid a Union soldier. "Icicles in your beard, frost on your nose, snow on your lashes, cold in your toes. May this quilt warm you, wherever you goes."

Such a sweet, funny sentiment. At first, it had matched the woman who had penned it. But in the last week or so, she had become a different person. Then again, he hadn't known her very long. Perhaps he hadn't known her at all.

With a charcoal pencil, he scribbled a hasty note to Mr. and Mrs. Bainbridge to thank them for their hospitality. He even used the word *obliged*, though they didn't like it. He did owe them a great debt. They had taken in a hated stranger and had made him welcome.

Along with the paper, he left a handful of coins. While not near enough to repay them for all they had done for him, they deserved at least that much. He had precious little left for a train ticket. Perhaps enough to get him to central Illinois.

Making as little noise as possible, he turned the doorknob and eased himself into the hall. If not for the weak daylight seeping up the stairs, he might not have been able to see his way out. As he trod on one step, it groaned. He stopped, holding his breath. It would be no good if anyone in the family woke up and tried to stop him from leaving.

No one did. He continued down the steps, out the front door, and across the wide porch. Even though summer was in full swing, the early Wisconsin morning held a chill, and dew clung to the spiderwebs strung across the rosebush branches lining the path to the road. Good to get his journey started before the day's heat kicked in.

Was that a beam of light coming from the shed? No, not a steady beacon but a flickering light. A strange, glowing orange light.

His heart pounded in his ears. Fire. The shed was on fire. The shed where Melissa stored her dolls.

Lance dropped his carpetbag and raced toward the door, his mouth dry, his hands sweating. He flung the wood bar up and swung open the doors.

Flames shot out, searing his face, burning his hands. Smoke filled his lungs. He coughed. Choked.

The roar of the fire filled Lance's head. He shot into the barn and picked up a gunnysack. Once he had plunged it in the watering trough, he scurried to the shed and worked to beat out the flames.

But the fire licked up the shed walls and consumed the dolls, smiles sewn on their faces. This was a losing battle.

He dropped the burlap bag and darted to the house. He raced up the stairs and knocked on both bedroom doors. "Fire! Hurry! The dolls are burning!"

Melissa tumbled from her room, wrapping a dressing gown around her shoulders, her hair in a long red braid down her back.

"Not the dolls. No, no!" She tripped down the stairs and outside. He followed close on her heels.

In a moment, she disappeared into the smoke.

"Melissa, get out of there!"

She didn't answer.

She didn't emerge.

Thick, dark smoke surrounded Melissa, blacker than the blackest moonless night. Flames crawled up the far wall and leaped from the shelves of dolls she stored in there.

Wilson's Toy Emporium was depending on this order, on having it delivered to them next week. The shipment was supposed to go out on tomorrow's train.

She had to save the merchandise.

Taking a deep breath, covering her mouth while coughing, she plunged forward. The heat of the fire pushed her back. But she wouldn't allow her business to be destroyed. Keeping her head down, she fought against the heat that seared her lungs.

The cotton fabric that composed the dolls caught in no time. Every second, more disappeared into the flames.

She stepped forward and reached out. At the pain, she yanked her hand back. Gritting her teeth, she tried again. Almost there.

Her head swam.

The world spun.

And then there was pressure on her shoulder.

Someone dragged her backward.

She fought against him.

Kicked. Squirmed. Wriggled.

To no avail. "Let me go." Her words were weak.

In a moment, she emerged into fresh air. She gulped, clearing her lungs of the smoke, coughing until blackness edged her vision.

"What were you thinking? You could have died!"

"But my dolls. My business is ruined."

"Your life is worth more than dolls. More than a business. More than anything."

"No." Tears burned the back of her raw throat. "My dolls are all I have. No friends. No. . ." She almost said *you.* But she didn't deserve Lance. Not after yesterday's behavior. "Just my grandparents."

He held her up by her forearms. Gazed into her eyes, his look so intense, she turned over her shoulder to stare at the blaze.

She swallowed hard. "We have to do something."

"Your hands."

She followed his gaze. Angry red blisters covered both hands. In that moment, the pain struck her. Awful. Intense. Breath-robbing. She screamed.

Grandmother and Grandfather rushed from the house. Grandfather took charge. "I'll get some buckets from the barn. Lance, start drawing water from the well. Betsy, take Melissa to the house. She doesn't need to see this."

Grandmother touched her shoulder. Soft. Gentle.

"But I have to help. These are my dolls."

"The men will do all they can. I need to bandage your hands. Then we can make some coffee for them. Breakfast for when they have the fire out."

"No. Grandmother, you have to understand." The tears that had threatened now spilled over her warm cheeks.

"I do, my darling, I do. Come now. Come with me." Her words were a brook over rocks. Calming and soothing. With one last gaze at the fierce fire consuming her livelihood, Melissa followed Grandmother into the house.

"Sit at the table there while I get the salve and bandages."

But the pain in her hands was the least of Melissa's troubles. Not only had she lost her one means of income, she'd lost Lance.

And her heart cried out for him.

"There, there, my dear." As Grandmother gathered her into an embrace, the scent of vanilla and roses enveloped Melissa. The delicious odors of home. Of love. The place she belonged.

"How could I have made such a mess of things?"

"You don't need to worry about anything. God has a way of working things out. Right now, life may appear very dark. But when we walk through the valley with Him, on the other side, we step into the light."

"I don't see how. One hundred dolls due to the shop in Madison by the end of the week. That order alone took me more than a month. How will I ever get the material I need and remake the dolls in time? I'll lose the order. And my reputation." The pain in her heart over Lance was more than she could speak about now.

She laid her head on the table and closed her watery eyes. How could life get any worse?

The sounds of Grandmother opening and closing cupboards, mixing, rattling on the stove, lulled Melissa. She blocked out the shouts of Grandfather and Lance, hollering directions to each other.

Her heart beat out the minutes. After many, many of them passed, the door squeaked open. Two sets of footsteps crossed the floor. Kitchen chairs scraped back. The strong, acrid odor of smoke surrounded her.

She lifted her head and glanced between Grandfather and Lance. Soot streaked their faces, sweat cutting rivers through the dirt. No light gleamed in either set of eyes.

Grandfather shook his gray head. "I'm so sorry, Melissa. We couldn't save anything. The shed is a complete loss. All of the dolls are gone."

She nodded. "That's what I was afraid of. I will have to telegraph the Madison shop and tell them I won't be able to fulfill the order. I used all the advance money they allotted me to purchase the materials. Then I spent my savings on the material for those new dresses. I don't have any money. Even if I did, I would never get the dolls done in time."

Lance frowned. "I wish there was something I could do."

"You don't have a fortune to become an investor. And even if you did, you don't have the manpower to sew dolls faster than anyone ever has before."

"You're right. I learned a little bit of mending in the military. Just trying to keep our uniforms in one piece. Keep the elements out. But not enough to sew dolls."

"And two people sewing day and night would never be enough to make it on time. Let's face it. I'm ruined."

"Please, don't talk like that. God has a way of—"

"Grandmother already gave me that speech." Melissa tightened her jaw and spoke through clenched teeth. "I used to believe God was my one friend. I was wrong."

With that, she stomped from the room.

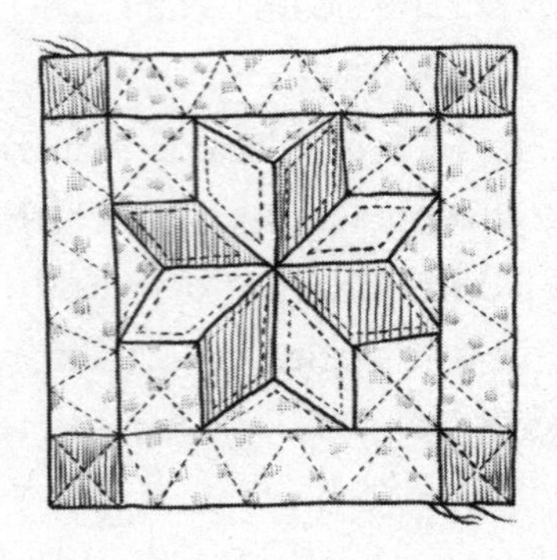

Chapter 9

After the tragedy of the fire, Lance couldn't bring himself to leave. Instead, he washed and went to worship with the family. Though the music of the hymns, especially the newer hymn "O Day of Rest and Gladness," brought a measure of relief from the misery, it didn't solve the problem.

Melissa had lost her business. What was most precious to her in the world. Somehow, someway, he had to find a path to help her. One last gesture of gratitude before he walked out of her life forever.

As soon as the sun crested the horizon on Monday morning, he reached into the brown wool sock that he had stuffed into his carpetbag and pulled out the small wad of dollar bills. The little he had left. Would it be enough? He had to count it with great care.

Maybe do some wheeling and dealing once he reached Madison. Because he also needed money to return to Regent.

He grabbed a cup of coffee from Mrs. Bainbridge, gulped it down, and set his slouch cap on his head. "I have a few errands to run today, so I won't be around. If all goes well, I'll be home by supper. If not, please go ahead without me."

"What is this all about?" The old woman wrinkled her already-lined forehead.

"I don't want to say. It may not work out. But don't tell Melissa. Just let her know that I'm out for the day."

"So it has something to do with her?" The furrows on Mrs. Bainbridge's brow eased.

"I'm not going to say. Now, I really must go."

"I'll pray that God will bless whatever it is you are trying to accomplish."

"Thank you. I appreciate that." Before Melissa came down to help with breakfast, he slipped outside and set a jaunty pace down the dirt road.

The train's horn whistled over the fields and through the woods as Lance approached town. The shopkeeper was opening his store for the day, sweeping the walkway in front of the door, but he didn't greet Lance. Neither did the livery owner in the entrance to the stable, who was currying a horse. Only a scruffy man stumbling from the saloon waved to him.

Lance came to the station and purchased a round-trip ticket to Madison. Before he knew it, he was on the train chugging toward the small city. He arrived and hustled down the train's steps. He presented the porter with a slip of paper with the store's address. No use in getting shut down here because of his accent.

The dark-skinned man pointed right, left, then right again. Lance concentrated so he would remember the directions. Then he scooted off. If he hoped to have time to catch the train to Regent yet that evening, he had to hurry.

He followed the porter's instructions, wending his way through the midmorning crowd, and soon found himself standing in front of Wilson's Toy Emporium. He entered the store filled with china dolls, dollhouses, wooden guns, little soldiers, and many other games he had only dreamed of as a child.

He stepped to the counter. A bald man with a mustache and round spectacles approached. "May I help you?"

"Are you Mr. Wilson, the proprietor?"

"I am."

"You are expecting a shipment of rag dolls from Miss Melissa Bainbridge by the end of the week?"

"I am. She does such fine work. Her creations are much in demand with the little girls of the area. I sell out so fast that I placed a rather large order this time."

"That's what I'm here to speak to you about. I've traveled all the way from Regent this morning. Early yesterday morning, there was a fire in the shed where Miss Bainbridge stores her dolls. Though we fought it with everything we had, I'm afraid the entire inventory was a total loss."

Mr. Wilson sighed and stroked his dark mustache. "I'm sorry to hear that, but business is business. I need those dolls. If I don't have them, I may be forced to cancel the order."

"And she wants to prevent that."

"You are here on her behalf?"

"You could say that. Is there any way we could work out an

arrangement so she could repurchase the materials needed for the dolls? Perhaps some kind of advance on the profits?"

"I don't know."

"Not a minute ago, you said her work is much in demand. You don't want to lose that business. It's in your best interest to help Miss Bainbridge fulfill this order."

Mr. Wilson removed his spectacles and rubbed his nose. Then he replaced them. "You do have a point. You aren't from around here, are you?"

"No. I'm here to rebuild my life. To make amends after the war. To make right what was made wrong. I believe we are no longer blue and gray, but all are red, white, and blue." He stole Melissa's beautiful words, but perhaps they would be enough to sway the man.

"Perfectly said. And the fire wasn't her fault."

"No. We have no idea how it started. But the entire family was sleeping when it broke out."

"That is a shame. What if we split the cost of the goods? But I can't give her an extension. I'll lose business if I don't have the dolls on time. My customers will go elsewhere. The end of the week. That's the best I can do."

How long would it take to finish the order? Was four days enough? Whether or not it was, it was a deal. A chance for Melissa to redeem herself. "That sounds agreeable."

The two men shook on it. Mr. Wilson handed him a good stack of cash. Perhaps if Lance could swing a deal with the owner of the dry goods store, Melissa stood a chance.

Now all he had to do was tell Melissa she had four days to sew one hundred dolls.

Even as the sun marched toward the western horizon on the day after the fire, all Melissa could do was stand and stare at the shed's remains. Everything gone. Everything consumed.

And she was alone. With no one to blame for that but herself.

Lance had been gone all day on some mysterious errand. Grandmother either didn't know anything else or wasn't saying. Would Lance even return? Perhaps he'd had enough of the quiet and not-so-quiet remarks about him that he'd decided to leave.

Who could blame him?

Then from behind her came a whistle. Not a singular whistle, but a tune. Jaunty. Happy. Melissa spun around. Ambling down the lane came Lance.

How could he be so happy on such a dreadful day?

As he approached her, the smile gracing his features faltered. "Melissa."

She turned from him and faced the ruins. "I can't believe they burned up just like that. Grandfather says a spark of lightning likely caused it, followed by no rain to put it out."

"I'm sorry."

She wanted to say a thousand things. Like how she was sorry for the way she treated him. Like how she was grateful he had saved her life when she ran into the fire. But all the words stuck in her swelled-shut throat.

"But I have good news."

Was there any left?

"Come away from there." Taking her by the elbow, he led her to the porch swing. The swing where they had spent many happy hours. "Aren't you curious about where I went?"

"I try not to pry into other people's business." In truth, if he went to earn money for a train ticket home, what little that was left of her heart might break into a thousand pieces.

"I'm asking you to ask me."

She peered into his eyes, so soft, warm, and sincere. When he gazed at her that way, it spread a warmth throughout her body. She could deny him nothing. "All right. Where did you go today?"

"Madison."

She raised both eyebrows. "How did you even get the money? I thought you were broke."

"I had a little bit remaining in my pocket, and I've been working for your grandfather. It was just enough to get to the city and back."

"But why would you go there?" That's where the order was supposed to ship. Did his trip have something to do with that? She held her breath.

"I spoke to Mr. Wilson."

The air rushed from her lungs. "You did? About the fire?"

"Yes, about the fire. You were going to send a telegram, but I thought it would be better to speak to the man in person. To get him to understand the woman behind the dolls and the tragedy that befell her."

She clung to the edge of the swing so tight that her fingers went numb. "What did he say?" Her question came out as a whisper.

"Let go of your death grip on the seat."

"That's what he said?" She couldn't resist ribbing him, even as she relaxed her hold.

"He is a very reasonable man."

Her heart beat a little faster. She warned it to slow down, but it refused to listen. "And?"

"The fire wasn't your fault. He's a shrewd businessman. Your dolls are very popular among the young ladies of Madison. He doesn't want to cancel the order, because they sell well in his emporium."

"They do?"

"Why do you doubt yourself?"

"Because it's a silly hobby I thought I could make some money from."

"Who told you it was a silly hobby?"

She shrugged. They both knew.

"Well, it's the last thing from silly and the furthest thing from a hobby. You have a successful business. In fact, Mr. Wilson has agreed to give you the cash for half the goods."

Like flowers in a summer's drought, she wilted. "Then you wasted your money on the trip. I don't have cash for the other half of the material, and there is no way four days will be enough for me to complete the order. Thank you for trying. I do appreciate the effort. It was a kind gesture to someone who hasn't been kind to you."

"The material is at the train station. I have to borrow your grandfather's wagon to haul it here. There was no way I could carry it all."

"What do you mean?"

"I worked a little magic with the woman who runs a dry goods store there. Apparently, her mother was a Virginian. For once, my accent was a good thing. She gave me quite a discount on everything she said you will need and agreed you can pay her the remaining money a little at a time from your profits. She even helped me pick out the material and the notions."

"Really?" Melissa couldn't help squealing like a little girl.

"Really."

"But they're due at the end of the week. That's all the time I have to do the sewing?" Not to mention that her hands were blistered.

"Leave that up to me."

She chuckled. "You're going to help me stitch, I suppose. Or did you hire someone to do that too?"

"No. But you'll have all the help you need and then some. I promise."

How on earth did he propose to keep that vow?

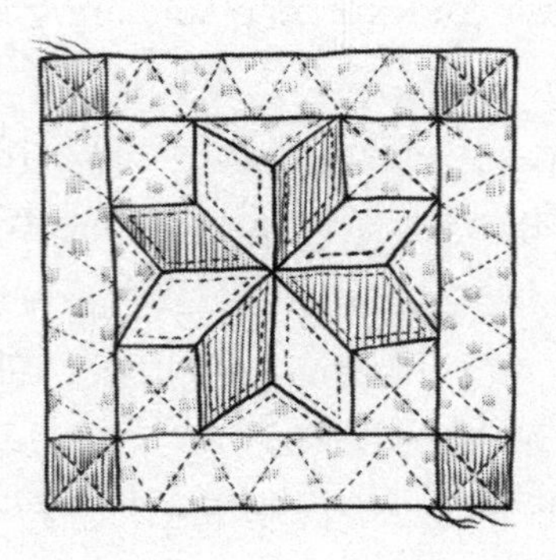

Chapter 10

Thank goodness it was just past the summer solstice. The sun set so late, it gave Lance plenty of time to explain his need for the wagon, get the team hitched, and make his way into town. The evening was so lovely and soft, many of Regent's residents were out enjoying the beautiful weather.

That would make what he had to do all the easier. Monday night was choir practice at the church. The perfect opportunity. He parked the team in front of the now-familiar white building and made his way through the door.

Ginny, Lucy, and Susan sat together in the front row of chairs at the head of the sanctuary, all facing the door. As soon as he entered, their eyes widened, and they stopped singing. They leaned together and whispered. The message was passed throughout the choir until only the director, Pastor Blake's wife, Nancy, made any music.

Ginny rose from her seat and marched right to him. "Just what do you think you're doing interrupting our rehearsal?"

He ignored her and continued up the aisle until he stood beside Mrs. Blake. Even though Lance's knees shook, he cleared his throat. "I know y'all don't have very kind feelings toward me. And that's fine. I'm an outsider, and all the wounds from the war have yet to be healed. But your behavior toward Miss Bainbridge is another matter entirely."

The choir gasped. No matter, he'd come this far. He might as well say what was on his mind and have done with it. "You are no better than the Southern slave owners who call themselves Christians but beat other human beings just because they are different from them."

Mr. O'Connor wound his way from the third row toward Lance. "Now see here."

Mrs. Blake glared at the man. "Sit down, Charles. Mr. Witherspoon is right." Though a moment before her voice was all vinegar, when she turned to Lance, it was all sugar. "Please, continue."

"Thank you, ma'am. Miss Bainbridge is someone very special, only you folks, in all the years she's lived among you, have never taken the time to get to know her. She is sweet and kind and caring and only wants to be accepted.

"You laugh at her for playing with dolls, but did you know she is a very gifted seamstress? The dolls she creates are in high demand in places like Madison."

A few people shook their heads.

"Little girls all over the city want to play with her creations. But most of you wouldn't know that, because instead of speaking to Miss Bainbridge and getting to know her, you ridicule her for the way she dresses and how she chooses to spend her time.

"And how many of you know she has an order for one hundred of these dolls to be delivered to a toy store in the state capital by this Friday?"

No one answered. Not even Mrs. Blake.

"She does. And how many of you know that the shed where she stores her dolls burned to the ground Saturday night, along with the almost-completed order?"

A murmur rose from the group.

"I took a trip to Madison today to speak with the shopkeeper. I procured enough material and notions for Miss Bainbridge to complete her order. But she has only till Friday to sew one hundred dolls. Even if she and her grandmother sew night and day, they will never get it completed."

"And how's that our problem?" Mr. O'Connor stood with his arms crossed against his barrel-size chest.

"I thought I told you to be quiet, Charles." Mrs. Blake turned to Lance. "You're right. I'm so ashamed of my behavior toward Melissa. Henry and I have been pastoring here for over a year now, and I never once went to have tea with her or stopped her to converse after service. You can count on my support. I'll sew as many dolls as I'm able."

The young woman turned to the rest of the choir. "It took an outsider, a former enemy, to make us see what fools we've been. I intend to reform my ways and help a Christian woman in her time of need. I suggest we all do the same."

Mr. O'Connor lumbered down the aisle and out of the church. But Ginny rushed to Lance's side. "The girls and I have been wrong to be so hard on Melissa. She really is a nice person, and I feel badly about her business. I'll help too."

Susan and Lucy added their voices to the chorus of volunteers.

Nancy nodded at him, a lone tear dripping down her cheek. "Thank you for helping us see the light, Mr. Witherspoon."

"Just have your crew at the Bainbridge home by eight o'clock tomorrow morning. We have much work to accomplish."

Wait until Melissa saw this army he'd recruited to help.

By the time Lance had returned last night, the sun had almost set. Grandfather's wagon was filled with all kinds of material. In the dim light, Melissa had perused the contents of the packages. Such wonderful patterns and colors. Perfect for the dolls. He had done a great job.

Thanks to him, she had everything she needed to fulfill the order. Everything except time.

But Lance promised her a surprise this morning.

She rose with the sun and didn't take much time to dress, slipping into a yellow-and-green high-waisted dress and pulling her hair back as she always did. If she ran out of material, she could use what she'd bought for the other dress she had planned to make. Never again would she wear something so cumbersome and constricting.

Even though she hadn't taken much time dressing, Lance still beat her to the kitchen. He had a pot of coffee warming on the stove. "You're up early."

Her cheeks warmed, and it had nothing to do with the temperature of the kitchen on this summer day.

"A little bit excited?" A hint of teasing colored his words.

"Yes. I love surprises. Grandmother always has one for me on my birthday and plenty around Christmas. This is a good surprise, right?"

"A very good one."

Was there some hesitation on his part? "Are you sure?"

His countenance brightened. "Of course it is. In my world, there are no such things as bad surprises. Those are called tragedies. And we won't have any of those today."

"That's a deal." She started breakfast and, once they had eaten, helped Grandmother wash the dishes.

The door opened and closed, and she startled, almost dropping the dish she was wiping. At the sight of Lance, his green eyes sparkling, her heart raced as fast as a team spooked by a mouse.

To think that he had used the last of his money to go to Madison on her behalf. To think he had been persuasive enough with Mr. Wilson to give her money for more material to make the dolls. To think he worked a deal for the supplies she needed.

There could only be one explanation for his actions. And her heart responded with the same feelings. "Is my surprise ready?"

"Your surprise is coming to you. Be patient. Very soon."

In the meantime, she spread a red-and-white-checked gingham across the kitchen table and proceeded to cut out a few of the dolls from patterns she pinned to the material. With the blisters on her hands, she had a difficult time making clean cuts.

From outside came the jingling of a harness. No, not a harness, but several harnesses. She turned to Grandmother, who was peering out the window. "What is it?"

"You have to come here and see for yourself."

Into the yard drove two wagons with several women in each. From the middle of the crowd, she picked out Ginny, Lucy, and Susan. "What is going on?" Melissa scurried outside to greet the guests.

Nancy Blake was one of the first people to climb from the wagon. She hustled to Melissa and hugged her. "Oh my dear, we are so sorry about the loss of your dolls. What an awful thing to have happen. Lance told us all about it and what he did to get you running again. We're here to help in any way we can. I brought all my sewing supplies."

Ginny came up behind Nancy. "We all did. With so many of us working, perhaps we can get the order completed in just a few days."

Grandmother would tell her to stop gaping like a fish, but Melissa couldn't help it. A lump in her throat choked off her airway. She couldn't breathe. Couldn't talk.

Lance appeared at her side. "What do you think of your surprise?"

"This is it? You did this for me?" The words came out in a squeak.

He leaned over and kissed her temple. "All for you."

Her eyes watered, blurring the scene in front of her. "Thank you. No one has ever done such a wonderful thing. Not in my entire life."

"You deserve it and so much more."

She giggled, then chuckled, then laughed heartily. "This is fabulous, but there's not room in the kitchen for everyone."

"Problem solved." Lance motioned toward the barn. "I set up some plywood and sawhorses in there. You'll have plenty of room for everyone to work."

Her impulse was to kiss him, but with eight or so women staring at them, she resisted the temptation. "You've thought of everything."

The pastor's wife broke the moment. "Show us what we need to do, and we'll get to work."

They all made their way into the barn. With the cows out to pasture, the stalls mucked, and fresh hay down, it smelled sweet. With her, Melissa brought what she had started that morning and gave directions for what everyone should do.

Throughout the morning, the ladies chatted about cooking and baking, how the farms were doing, and plans for the annual Fourth of July box lunch social. Lucy elbowed Melissa in the ribs. "You should bring Lance. I think he's sweet on you. And so handsome too. And he must truly love you if he went to all this trouble to make sure you fulfilled your order."

"I-I don't even know what to say to that."

"Well, he does. You're very pretty. Even your dresses are nice. They highlight your slim figure. And they must be more comfortable than all these crinolines."

"Thank you. They are. But Lance plans to leave here as soon as he has money to go south."

"That's too bad."

It was, because when he was gone, Melissa's life would never be the same.

Chapter 11

Within three days, the women had managed to complete all the dolls. Lance helped Melissa pack them, and they were ready to head out on the train the following day.

Much as it would break his heart, he would be going with the shipment and not returning. Mama taught him to never overstay his welcome. Mr. Bainbridge had paid him yesterday, so he had a little money. Enough to get to Madison. Perhaps Mr. Wilson would pay him for helping with the unloading. Then he could move on.

After supper, he found Melissa in her favorite spot, on the porch swing, staring at the stars. He sat beside her.

She touched his hand and rubbed the top of his thumb. "How can I ever thank you for all you did?"

"There's no need."

"As you would say, I'm much obliged."

He chuckled. "No obligations, remember. No debts to be paid. I was happy to do it for a friend." If only it could be more than that. But though the town may have embraced her, it would never welcome him. Some circumstances were impossible to overcome.

"Then thank you, friend. My best friend."

That didn't leave room for anything more. She made it clear where their relationship stood. He loved her. He couldn't be just her friend.

"I told your grandfather earlier, but I waited until now to tell you because I knew you were busy."

"Tell me what?"

"I'm leaving in the morning. For good."

She sucked in a breath. "Leaving?"

"Yes. You have helped me heal. To see the good in people again. It's time I make a place for myself in the world. And I don't think Regent is going to be it."

"Why not?"

"They may accept you now, but they never will take me in. I'm too much of an outsider. I always will be."

"But you can't go."

His arms ached for her. To draw her close, breathe in the scent of fresh air that clung to her, touch her soft cheek. "I wish it could be different."

"It can be. If they came around with me, they'll welcome you sooner or later. Give them time. The ladies got to know you well the past few days. They'll tell their husbands. Whatever you said in the church the other night brought about a change in them."

"Only God could do that. With His strength, I spoke those

words to them, but He was the one who changed their hearts. I had nothing to do with it. Maybe in time they would come to view me as a member of the community, but I don't have time to wait."

For the longest stretch, they sat in silence. What might she be thinking? Would she tell him how she felt? Should he tell her? No, it would make walking away even more difficult. Already his stomach tightened when he thought about tomorrow. How lonely his life would be.

"Will you write to me? At least let me know you're safe?"

"I will, of course. And you'll write back?"

"Certainly."

Silence settled over them. Lightning flashed across the sky, and a chilly wind blew across the open fields. Melissa snuggled closer to him, her body trembling.

He smoothed her hair from her face and held her close. A memory he would always cherish. One that would keep him warm on the long, cold nights ahead when he had nothing more than the quilt she had sewn.

"Lance?"

He gazed at her, her eyes shimmering in the pale light from the kitchen window. He leaned in, cupped her face, and kissed her. Gentle at first, then harder, his lips against hers conveying the love he had for this woman.

She reached around him and pulled him even closer, kissing him back.

The barn door slammed shut. Lance broke away and jumped to his feet. His pulse pounded in his neck. "Melissa, I—" Why couldn't he come out and say the words?

"What?"

"Good night." Without another word, he whirled and strode into the house.

Melissa wrapped herself in a blanket and sat on the rocking chair in the parlor, a perfect view to the front door. By the time she had made it into the house, Lance had locked himself in his room and had refused to answer when she knocked.

Her only alternative was to catch him first thing in the morning when he left for the train station. She couldn't let him leave without knowing how she felt. Even if he didn't return those sentiments, at least she would have shared her soul with him. Left no doubt in his mind.

About three o'clock, when deepest darkness descended, she allowed herself to doze. When anyone tiptoed across the floor, there was one board that always protested. That would be enough to wake her.

What must have been only a little while later, she rubbed her eyes, the bright sun waking her. She stretched, the star quilt falling from her shoulders.

She bolted upright. Sunbeams streamed through the window, rousing her. How had she managed to sleep so long?

Lance. She raced from the room and into the kitchen. Grandmother stood at the stove, pancakes bubbling on the griddle. "Has Lance left?"

"A while ago. I'm surprised you didn't hear us chatting. You must have been very tired. I told him I would wake you, but he didn't want me to disturb you. Said you needed your rest."

Melissa glanced at her pale blue-and-white-striped dress.

Though sleeping in it had wrinkled it, at least she hadn't slept in her nightclothes. No time now to worry about the state of her hair.

"I'll be back." She rushed to the barn and pulled Stormy from his stall, mounting him and riding him bareback. His hoofbeats thundered down the road as hard and as fast as her heart raced. If Lance boarded that train and steamed out of her life without knowing the truth, she would always wonder what might have been. She couldn't miss him. She just couldn't.

Never had it taken her so long to get to town. On Sunday morning, when she dreaded facing the girls at church, they always arrived so soon. Now, the miles moved along at a snail's pace. She urged Stormy into a canter, praying she wouldn't miss the train.

Even this early in the morning, the humidity pressed on her. Her breaths came in uneven gasps. At long last, the small cluster of buildings appeared on the horizon. She rode Stormy as fast as she could push him.

Through the trees came the train's whistle. It must be nearing the station. The stop in Regent wasn't long. Just time enough for a few to climb off and for a few to board. She had to hurry. "Please, Stormy, a little faster."

She could see nothing but the road in front of her, hear nothing but the throbbing of her pulse in her ears, feel nothing but the pressing urgency in her chest.

At last she entered the town. Already, a few wagons and several pedestrians milled about. She had no choice but to slow the horse.

Mrs. Blake waved to her from the parsonage. Melissa waved back but didn't cease her trek to the station. Just a little farther and she would be there.

The whistle blew again.

One more block to go.

A steady *chug, chug, chug*. A familiar belch of steam.

The train was leaving.

She halted Stormy, slid from his back, and dashed toward the tracks.

Just in time to see the black behemoth snake its way out of Regent.

Carrying Lance away from her forever.

She slumped her shoulders. Of all mornings to oversleep, this wasn't the one. And why hadn't he allowed Grandmother to wake her? Perhaps the feelings she believed he harbored were part of her wild imagination. Maybe he was nothing more than a friend. Would never be more than that.

There was no use staring at the empty track. She could stand here all day, but it wouldn't bring him back. She turned on her heel to leave.

"Melissa?"

Oh, that deep, rich, melodic voice. She had to be dreaming. Just in case she wasn't, she glanced to her side, to the platform. There, on the edge of the tracks, stood Lance. Tall. Regal. So very, very handsome.

She clutched her middle. "You're here."

"Yes, of course I am. Why are you?"

"I couldn't let you leave. Couldn't let you walk out of my life that way."

"I tried to go so I wouldn't drag you down. So I wouldn't stand in your way of being welcomed here."

"But don't you see? Even if everyone in the town accepts me, without you, it means nothing. Besides God and my grandparents, you're the only one I need acceptance from."

"I couldn't leave you. When it came down to it, I couldn't get on that train. I saw you in the distance, riding that horse, galloping toward me. And in that moment, all my dreams came true. No matter what, I'm not going anywhere."

Lance gathered her close. Yes, this was where she belonged. Where she fit just the way she was.

"My darling." He kissed her temple, then released his hold.

Before she knew what was happening, he dropped to one knee. "Melissa, you are my home. The one and only place on this earth I want to be is with you. I love you so very, very much. Allow me the pleasure of spending the rest of my life showing you just how much. Will you marry me?"

Melissa gasped, then giggled. "Oh Lance, I didn't know what I was going to do without you in my life. I love you too. As long as you are with me, I know I'll always be cherished and accepted. Yes, yes, I'll marry you."

He picked her up and swung her in a wide circle.

"Wait, wait. We have to change the rhyme on the quilt."

He put her down and pulled it from his carpetbag. "What do you suggest?"

"Smiles in your eyes, a twitch in your nose, love in your heart, a dance on your toes, may this quilt cover us, wherever we goes."

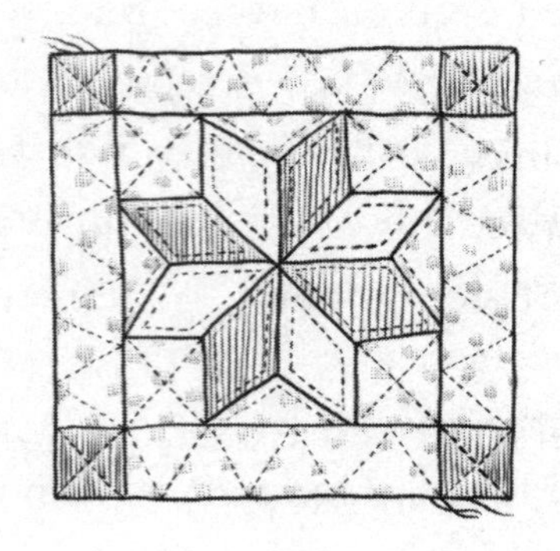

Epilogue

The crisp fall breeze caught the corner of Melissa's high-waisted, long-trained lace gown as she stepped from the parsonage.

"Hang on a minute." Nancy Blake, her matron of honor, stopped to adjust the dress.

"I don't know how much longer I can wait. Seems like it's taken me my entire life to get to this point, and I just want to marry Lance as soon as possible."

Nancy chuckled. "It has taken you your entire life to find him."

Heat rushed into Melissa's cheeks. "Of course. What I meant was—"

"No need to explain. I understand perfectly." Nancy turned behind her. "Are you ladies coming?"

Lucy, Ginny, and Susan emerged from the little stone house,

each in a different pastel shade Georgian-style dress. Ginny patted a stray hair into place. "I can see why you prefer these gowns, Melissa. They are simply so light and easy to wear. I wonder why we ever gave up this style."

Melissa couldn't stop grinning. "And may I say that you look lovely."

Lucy kissed her cheek. "Not as beautiful as you. You are a stunning bride. Lance is a very lucky man. He's going to keel over when he sees you."

Melissa patted her chest to still the thunderous beating of her heart. The flowers in her other hand quaked.

Nancy led the way. "Let's get Melissa married. She's waited long enough." The others followed.

Grandfather waited for her at the church's front door. "My, oh my, Sissy, don't you look exquisite? I can't believe you're all grown up and about to become a wife. I couldn't be prouder of the young woman you are."

She kissed the tip of his chin. "Thank you. Without your guidance, I wouldn't have become the person I am today. You taught me to love everyone, no matter what other people thought or believed. Without that kind of upbringing, I might have turned out like every other girl in this town. Or the way they were before. I would never have given Lance a second look."

He nodded. "You are not only beautiful on the outside, but also on the inside, where it counts the most. Are you ready to meet your groom?"

"Yes, please."

On Grandfather's arm, she marched down the aisle. Lance stood at the end, his dark hair slicked back, a smile lighting his entire face. At last, she reached him.

She gave her bouquet to Nancy, and Lance took her by the hands, giving them a squeeze. "I can't believe you're mine."

"Forever and ever."

Pastor Blake probably said some very nice words and probably prayed a very nice prayer. But all of that was a blur to Melissa. She could only stare at Lance, at the cleft in his chin and the dimple in his cheek.

"And now, Lance and Melissa would like to do something a little different than you've seen at most weddings." From a chair behind him, the pastor pulled the quilt Lance had found on the battlefield. The one that had saved his life and led him to Melissa.

Grandfather and Grandmother wrapped the quilt around Melissa and Lance's shoulders.

Pastor Blake prayed. "Oh Lord, as this quilt binds Lance and Melissa together, may You bind them together. As it warms them, may You warm them with the light of Your Holy Spirit. As it guided them to each other, may You guide them in the way they should go all the days of their lives. Amen."

Melissa opened her eyes and gazed at Lance.

"I now pronounce you husband and wife. What God has joined together, let no man put asunder. You may kiss your bride."

"I love you, Melissa."

"I love you too, Lance." Could a woman's heart burst open?

As Lance bent down and kissed her, she trembled. The entire congregation applauded.

This is where Mr. and Mrs. Lance Witherspoon belonged.

Liz Tolsma is a popular speaker and an editor and the owner of the Write Direction Editing. An almost-native Wisconsinite, she resides in a quiet corner of the state with her husband and their two daughters. Her son proudly serves as a US Marine. They adopted all their children internationally, and one has special needs. When she gets a few spare minutes, she enjoys reading, relaxing on the front porch, walking, working in her large perennial garden, and camping with her family.

More of Barbour's Romance Collections!

Cameo Courtships

4 Stories of Women Whose Lives Are Touched by a Legendary Gift

Follow along as the "Victoria Cameo" is passed through a family with the promise to inspire romance in every life it touches. Clara, a journalist; Petra, a frontierswoman; Lizzie, a Pinkerton agent; and Bertie, a librarian, each receive the cameo at a time when romance is the last thing on their minds. But is God's timing the perfect timing?

Stories from Susanne Dietze, Jennifer Uhlarik, Kathleen Y'Barbo, and Debra E. Marvin

Paperback / 978-1-64352-048-3 / $14.99

Mail-Order Mishaps

4 Brides Adapt When Marriage Plans Go Awry

Journey along in the Old West as four women travel to meet their husbands-to-be and discover that nothing is as it was planned. Eve's fiancé is in jail. Amelia's fiancé has never heard of her. Zola's newlywed husband is dead. Maeve's travel is misdirected. Can these brides find a true love match?

Stories from Susan Page Davis, Linda Ford, Vickie McDonough, and Erica Vetsch

Paperback / 978-1-64352-000-1 / $14.99